ENCHANTED WATERS

A MAGICAL COLLECTION OF SHORT STORIES

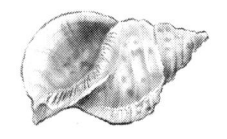

ENCHANTED WATERS

A Magical Collection of Short Stories

All rights reserved. No part of this work may be reproduced, uploaded or transmitted in any form without the author's written consent. This is a work of fiction. Similarities to real people, places, or events are entirely coincidental.

Published July 2021

Second edition 1st August 2021

Copyright © 2021 Alice Ivinya, Astrid V.J, N.D.T. Casale, Jennifer Kropf, Lyndsey Hall, Ben Lang, Sky Sommers, Elena Shelest, Helena Satterthwaite

Illustrations by Helena Satterthwaite and Elena Shelest

Edited by Dr Edith A. Kostka, Carolyn Gent, Shreeya Nanda, Astrid V.J, Alice Ivinya

Cover design by Dark Wish Designs

Formatting by Alice Ivinya

❧ Created with Vellum

Dedicated in honor of Boyan Slat who founded Ocean Cleanup at the age of eighteen. Thank you for being an inspiration to us all.

"The sea, once it casts its spell, holds one in its net of wonder forever."
- Jacques Cousteau

1

DAUGHTER OF THE SELKIE KING
LYNDSEY HALL

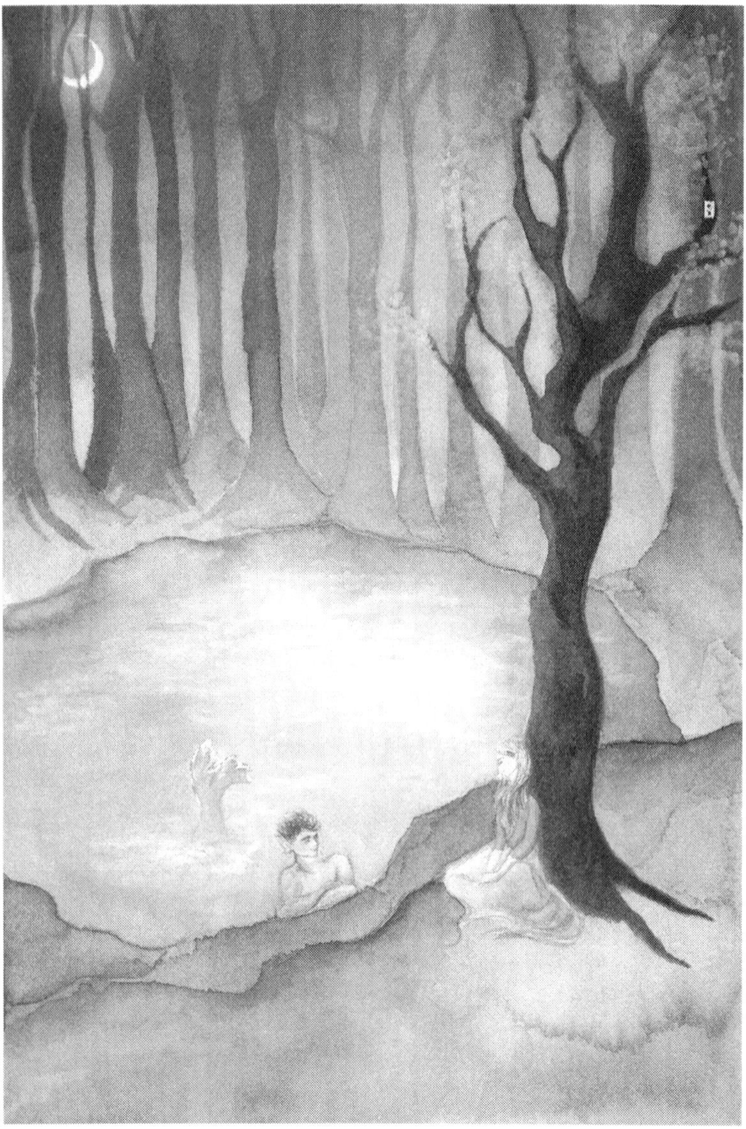

WATER OFF A DRAC'S BACK

"Where are you taking me?" Delta asked, following Lorelei through the trees. Her friend's bright red hair shone like a beacon in the dying light, guiding her. The leaves above their heads were gilded by the dusky pink and orange sky—another glorious June evening in the Ondine Kingdom.

They headed deeper into the forest that bordered Aberness, separating the Ondine Kingdom from the Celeste Kingdom in the north and following the curves of the River Aspid to the west. Delta knew that deeper still in these woods, the Ondine Palace stood, hidden from view by a great waterfall and protected from intruders by an ancient Solitary creature.

Rumour had it the beast was an Aspidochelone—the creature the river had been named for—but no one had dared venture too close to the palace in years. The Ondine Queens were private, cautious women. They rarely left the palace now, although Delta's mother had spoken of a great celebration for the royal wedding twenty years earlier, before Delta had been born.

Delta wondered absently which sea creature had been so corrupted by the First Fair Queen's aether magic at the creation of the Fair Realm all those centuries ago that it had become the monstrous Apidochelone. A whale? A giant sea turtle? She shuddered.

Solitary creatures were terrifying, and the waters surrounding Aberness were filled to the brim with them. Selkies, dracs, ashrays. Delta had never seen one up close herself, but her mother, Dorit, had told her many tales. Bedtime stories of men lost at sea in sudden swells that stopped as quickly as they'd started. Women seduced by a lone Solitary creature in the skin of a Fair male. Children snatched from the water's edge by scaly, grey hands.

It was the reason she had never so much as dipped a toe in the water.

Lorelei had been vague about what they were doing tonight. The only thing Delta did know was that they'd be drinking the wine she'd pilfered from her mother's inn—the bottles clinked merrily in her rucksack with every step.

"Just wait and see," Lorelei said in her husky voice, squeezing Delta's fingers and picking up the pace. Something was glowing up ahead—a faint, warm light leaked out between the tree trunks, making the rapidly falling darkness around them seem even denser.

They stepped into a large clearing that had been studded with lanterns, candle flames flickering in the evening breeze. Noelani and Rafferty were already there, sitting on either side of an inky-dark pool, their feet dangling into the water and sending ripples across the surface.

Delta's blood chilled and goosebumps rose across the exposed skin on her arms and legs. *What was this?*

"It's a natural spring," Lorelei said, excitedly. "Hardly anyone knows it's here, I overheard a customer telling my mother about it in the shop last week. It took me a few tries to find, it isn't on any maps." She looked pleased with herself, which only angered Delta further. "It's supposed to have healing properties."

Lorelei must have noticed Delta's unease, because she added in a low voice, "I know you've never swum before, but you can just stay at the side. And we're all here if you need any help." Lorelei gave her friend an encouraging smile, but it did little to quell Delta's nerves.

Delta knew how rare it was for an Ondine—a water-magic wielding member of the Fair—to be unable to swim. But that didn't change the heavy sense of trepidation in the pit of her stomach.

They stepped closer to the pool and Delta stared into the water, the darkening sky reflected on the surface, making it look fathomless, infinite. She felt as though she was looking into the abyss, and it sent a shiver through her.

Lorelei gently took the rucksack from Delta's shoulder and passed a bottle of honey wine to Rafferty, taking the other bottle and going to sit beside Noelani, who nodded by way of a greeting and continued to twiddle the string of opals in her hands.

Delta took a few steps towards Raff, dropping down next to him with her legs crossed and accepting the now open bottle he proffered.

"You OK? You look a bit...shell shocked."

Delta nodded, swallowing a mouthful of the sweet white wine. "Fine, thanks." It was a lie. She felt...betrayed, somehow. No doubt Lorelei believed she was helping, giving Delta the chance to face her fear, to swim for the first time in a secluded, safe setting. If open water could ever be called *safe*. But she supposed this pool was infinitely less terrifying than the River Aspid with its powerful current and murky depths, where all manner of piscine Solitary creatures lay in wait.

Lorelei passed her wine bottle to Noelani, talking animatedly about a customer that had come into her mother's apothecary shop earlier that day, looking for a way to curse her boyfriend after discovering his cheating. Lorelei's mother was an older but equally beautiful version of her daughter, with matching red hair and a talent for natural remedies.

Since the war between the Five Kingdoms, Celeste healers were rarely found outside of their own kingdom, so the other four kingdoms relied on those with knowledge of natural medicines and treatments, but these tended to be few and far between.

According to Lorelei, her mother had told the woman she didn't sell anything like that, but she could try grinding up some castor beans and adding them to his morning coffee if she really wanted to punish him.

A small but wicked smile curved Noelani's full lips as she raised the bottle to them, and Lorelei, noticing, beamed.

Delta might have been warmed by the sweet moment if her stomach hadn't been roiling with anxiety.

"Planning on sharing that?"

She snapped her eyes to Raff, who gestured at the bottle she'd been hogging with a raised brow and a quirk of his mouth. She passed it to him and rubbed her hands over her face, taking a deep breath in and letting it out slowly.

He watched her, but didn't say anything. She knew she could count on Rafferty for that at least—he didn't pry. Lorelei was the one who insisted on sharing their feelings, sitting with them, and letting them go. Occasionally by screaming into the wind until they were hoarse.

The sky had darkened to midnight blue and they'd almost finished the bottles of wine when Lorelei suddenly stood, kicking her shoes to one side, and started to peel off her black, handkerchief dress. "Come on, let's get in."

Raff gave Delta a quick look and stood up too, pulling his t-shirt up over his head and exposing his smooth, tanned chest. He discarded his sneakers and jeans, and sat on the edge of the pool in just his boxer shorts. "You coming in?"

Delta chewed her lip, gazing into the water, the reflections of the lanterns rippling softly across the surface. The wine had warmed her skin and soothed her frayed nerves, and no creature had appeared in the hour they had been sitting around the pool, the others with their feet dangling in the water. How bad could it be?

Lorelei was already in, shoulder deep in the inky blackness, red hair piled on top of her head with a black velvet scrunchie. She was resting her elbows on the side, still chatting to Noelani who apparently wasn't in the mood for a swim either. Lani didn't like to get her textured, black hair wet if she could help it.

"I don't think so," Delta said, hugging her knees to her chest.

"You could just dip your toes in?" Lorelei suggested, leaning back now and floating on the surface.

Raff slid in and completely submerged for one heart-stopping moment. Then he broke the surface and tossed his head, spraying water droplets all over Delta. She gasped and ducked her head behind her knees.

"Sorry," Raff said, colour rising to his cheeks. The water clinging to his hair and olive skin glistened in the lantern-light, shimmering like the glints in his clear-blue eyes.

Delta shook her head and gave a small, shaky laugh. A few drops of water weren't going to hurt her. She was being silly.

"The water's gorgeous," Lorelei murmured, closing her eyes and leaning back on the pool's edge. Lani began plucking small wildflowers from the grassy bank and tucking them into Lorelei's vibrant hair, fashioning a sort of floral crown.

Rafferty said in a low voice, quiet enough that Delta knew the others across the pool wouldn't hear, "You could just dip a toe tonight, and then both your feet another night. And eventually, maybe you'll be ready to try swimming. But you don't have to do anything tonight if you don't want to. Ignore Lorelei, she means well but she doesn't know what it's like when you're not..." He struggled for the words. "Like her," he said finally.

Delta assumed he meant confident. Brave. Completely self-assured, even in the face of all the whispers and comments. The name calling and innuendos.

Lorelei's mother had been the subject of much gossip when she'd arrived in Aberness twenty years earlier—widowed and pregnant—and had opened up her apothecary shop. Dorit had told Delta once that the villagers hadn't taken to Lorelei's mother, particularly the older women, calling her a *siren* and avoiding her shop, and the young, new mother had struggled to feed her child and keep a roof over their heads. Dorit had always made a point of popping in and purchasing some balm or ointment on her errands, deliberately overpaying on occasion, only for the flame-haired shopkeeper to chase her down and hand her change back.

Proud. That was how Dorit described Lorelei's mother, and she'd passed that trait on to her daughter. As Lorelei had grown into a young woman with beauty to rival her mother's, the whispers and small-minded gossip had transferred to her, but they didn't seem to have any effect on her.

The friends had bonded over their status as social pariahs, and daughters of spirited single mothers, becoming inseparable by the time they reached their teenage years, and gradually they had added Rafferty and Noelani to their number. It had been that way ever since, the four of them fitting together like puzzle pieces.

Delta often wondered how Lorelei let it all go, like water off a drac's back, when Delta herself wallowed in self-pity at every cruel joke or snub aimed her way. She couldn't remember which had come first, her fear of the water or the jibes of *seal girl* and *freak of nature*. The whispers that her skin would turn slippery and grey the moment it came into contact with the water, prompting cruel children to flick their drinks at her during lunch.

It was ridiculous, childish nonsense. She'd bathed every day for eighteen years and never seen so much as a scale or webbed-toe.

Her friend seemed to possess endless self-esteem, and Delta couldn't help but feel the sting of jealousy as she watched Lorelei drifting on the surface of the pool, black underwear clinging to her alabaster skin, completely at ease with herself and her surroundings.

Delta bit her lip, steeling herself. She kicked off her boots and socks. Rafferty gave her a surprised look, his eyebrows disappearing into his floppy, brown hair. She felt a rush of pride at having been underestimated. It spurred her on. She didn't stop at her socks—she unbuttoned her dress and pulled it up over her head. Cool night air kissed her bare skin and she shivered, but the wine and the burning desire to be brave like her friend warmed her from the inside.

She dropped down on the bank and shuffled forward until her feet were just inches from the water. Silence filled the clearing, her friends seemed to be holding their breath as she lowered herself closer to the pool's surface. She hesitated for just a second, then with a sharp inhale, she touched her toes to the water.

BENEATH THE SURFACE

Nothing happened.

Delta could see her toes, pinkish and separate, turquoise nail polish intact, just beneath the surface.

"There! That wasn't so hard, was it?" Lorelei said, upright now, watching Delta with a gleeful look in her shimmering brown eyes. No doubt proud of her own part in Delta's progress.

The water was cool but not freezing, it felt quite nice between her toes. Delta shuffled forward a little and dangled her legs in a bit further.

This wasn't so bad, what had she been so scared of? She'd let the ridiculous rumours get to her, burrow their way into her heart and mind, and keep her from experiencing something so normal and natural. Pleasant, even.

She felt a tiny stab of anger at herself for waiting so long to experience this, she couldn't imagine everything she'd missed out on over the years. The beach days and sea swims, the boat rides and rock-pooling trips she'd turned down out of fear and embarrassment.

She tied her hair up in a messy bun using the hairband

around her wrist and moved to submerge herself in the pool. Raff put out a hand as though to steady her and opened his mouth to speak, but before he could get a word out, water erupted from the centre of the pool, spraying them all and making Delta yelp and scurry backwards onto the bank.

As the waves settled, a new figure bobbed in the pool between them. A boy with silvery translucent skin above the water, darkening to black under the surface where his selkie form remained. He had eyes of the most piercing, unsettling green. Which he focused on Delta.

"Evening," the selkie boy said, a smile dancing at the corners of his mouth.

Lorelei had also clambered out of the water and now sat gripping Noelani's arm, soaking her friend's t-shirt. "Who the hell are you?" She sounded braver than she looked.

The selkie turned his head slightly but his eyes never left Delta. "My name is Vance. What's yours?"

Nobody answered for a moment.

"I'm Lorelei. And this is Noelani."

Rafferty didn't speak, but the selkie didn't seem to care. "And you?" He said, arsenite eyes boring into Delta.

She swallowed, mouth suddenly drier than a creek bed in summer. "Delta." It came out as a croak.

"Delta," the boy—Vance—repeated. "That's a beautiful name. It means *mouth of a river*, did you know that?" She didn't reply. "Did your father give it to you?"

She opened and closed her mouth, unsure how to answer. She didn't exactly feel like telling this strange creature that she didn't know who her father was.

"What do you want?" The suddenly brave voice was Rafferty's.

The selkie looked surprised and tore his gaze away from Delta for the first time. "Me? Nothing at all. I was simply hunting nearby and sensed your presence, so I thought I'd introduce myself." His eyes were back on Delta, who tried to ignore the fact he'd said *hunting*. "I've never met anyone like you before."

"Anyone like me?" Delta said, her voice barely above a whisper. A sick, shivery feeling crept over her. She had a terrible sense that she knew what he was going to say.

The boy's smile was vulpine. "A half-selkie."

BRITTLE AS ICE

Delta's stomach plummeted. Silence settled over the clearing but the rushing in her ears was deafening.

A half-selkie. The rumours had been true then, she was a seal girl. An abomination.

She took in the shocked and horrified faces of her friends, Lorelei's hands were over her mouth and Rafferty's eyes were wide, his mouth open in surprise. Noelani was shaking her head and frantically twirling the opals on her string.

Delta couldn't stand to see them looking at her like that. Like she was a monster. Unnatural.

She scrambled to her feet, snatching up her discarded dress and shoes, and sprinted through the trees as fast as her legs could carry her.

She thought she heard them calling after her, but she didn't slow down or turn back. She kept running all the way to the inn.

Throwing open her mother's bedroom door, she stood on the threshold, chest heaving, blonde hair wild.

Dorit sat bolt upright at the sight of her daughter so dishevelled and upset. "What happened? What's wrong?"

When Delta didn't start speaking immediately, her mother climbed out of bed and crossed the room in an instant, taking her daughter's hands and scanning her face. "Delta, tell me—"

"You lied to me." Her voice was thick, her tone blunt.

Dorit dropped Delta's hands and took a step backwards. "What? I don't know—what do you mean?" But her expression told another story.

"Who is my father?"

Dorit's face paled in the moonlight filtering in through the thin curtains. "He was just...why are you asking this now?"

"I know the truth, mother. I know he's a selkie." Delta's voice broke on the last word. Dorit's mouth fell open, but she didn't speak. "Why didn't you tell me? All these years, you told me the rumours weren't true, that the kids at school were just bullies and their parents were narrow-minded, small-town folk with nothing better to do than judge and gossip. But they were right, weren't they? I am a freak." A sob escaped her chest.

Dorit's expression turned hard and she snatched Delta's hands back, forcing her to look into her eyes. "*No*. You are not a freak. You're *my* daughter. It doesn't matter who your father is. He's nothing to you. Nothing." She shook her head vehemently and her blonde hair came free of her braid, silver strands glinting where the light caught them.

"But I'm not even human!" Delta cried out, tears welling in her eyes again.

Her mother gripped her shoulders and gave her a small shake. "You are more human than anyone else in this godforsaken town, Delta Irving. You are the kindest, most gentle soul I've ever known. If that isn't human, I don't know what is."

Her expression changed from stern to suspicious in the blink of an eye. "Who told you this, who told you about your father?"

Delta froze. "A selkie boy."

Dorit's fingers dug into Delta's skin a little harder. "Where were you? Delta, where did you see this selkie?"

Reluctantly, she told her mother about the hidden spring Lorelei had discovered.

Voice as cold and brittle as ice, Dorit asked, "You didn't swim, did you? You didn't go in the water?" She shook Delta a little harder this time. *"Delta, tell me you didn't."*

Delta shook her head, confused and frightened by her mother's reaction. "No, I didn't. I didn't go in. The selkie appeared before I could."

Dorit narrowed her eyes. "What do you mean?"

"He said he sensed my presence and wanted to introduce himself. He said he'd never met a half-selkie before."

The blood drained from Dorit's face in the pale moonlight. "He *sensed* you?"

Delta nodded slowly. "Yes. I dipped my feet in and—"

Dorit dropped her daughter's hands and backed away, shaking her head, tears lining her grey eyes.

"Oh, Delta." Her voice was a rattling breath. *"How could you?* You don't know what you've done. I warned you, I told you never to go in the water. Why didn't you listen to me? Eighteen years, and now..." She dropped down onto the edge of the bed, face in her hands.

Delta was taken aback by her mother's reaction. She'd always been told to stay away from open water, to never swim or paddle or go on a boat, to respect and fear the sea. She had assumed her mother had known someone who drowned or was lost at sea, Dorit never spoke of her reason for being so fearful of the water. Now, Delta felt something else under the surface of her mother's warnings.

She crouched on the floor in front of her mother and gently took her shaking hands, pulling them away from Dorit's tear-stained face. "Mum, what is it? What are you afraid of?"

Dorit looked at her with her large, grey eyes, flanked by

long lashes. Her mother had been a real beauty in her youth, Delta had seen pictures, and she could still see the fine features that had lured a selkie man straight out of the sea.

Her voice was a broken whisper. "He'll come for you now. Your father. He'll come to take you for himself."

DIRTY SECRET

Delta's blood turned cold. "What do you mean?"

Dorit had paled to an eerie white. She rubbed her hands over her face and sighed, resignation settling over her expression. "Why do you think I always told you to stay away from the river? If you so much as dipped a toe in the water he will know of your existence. He knows everything that goes on in his underwater kingdom."

She didn't understand. What was her mother trying to tell her?

"His name is Malik. King of the Selkies." A small, strangled sound escaped Delta and she took a step back. Her mother hurriedly continued. "But I didn't know that when I first met him, I had no idea who he was." She sighed, but Delta got the impression she was relieved to finally get the truth off her chest.

"I had gone for an early morning swim in a secluded pool—probably the same one you went to tonight—and he just appeared beside me, all flowing black hair and a jaw as sharp as cut glass." Dorit stared over Delta's shoulder as she spoke, her eyes glazing as her mind took her back almost twenty years.

"He was so handsome, Delta—and charming. I was just nineteen, I hadn't really dated much and I couldn't believe someone so...so mature and charismatic, would be interested in me." She looked down, shaking her head gently. "I know that's no excuse, but if you'd met him you'd understand."

Delta let out a sharp laugh. "If I'd had the chance, you mean! What did happen then? He seduced you and was long gone before you knew you were expecting me? That old chestnut?" She knew she was being cruel, but Elements above, she deserved an explanation. Her mother had made her fear the water her entire life, and all Dorit had truly wanted was to keep her from her father. To keep Delta from discovering the truth of her creation, her heritage. To keep her dirty secret hidden, forever.

Dorit shook her head sadly. "No, it wasn't quite like that. We were in love." She looked into Delta's eyes then, and Delta could see the truth of it in her mother's sad smile. "He tried to stay, for a while. We told people he was a travelling salesman, like I told you all those years. And it was wonderful, for a time. Until the waterlust set in."

"Waterlust?" Delta felt a cool dread begin to flood her veins.

Dorit reached out and cupped her daughter's face, pressing her lips together as tears slipped down her cheeks. When she spoke her voice was quiet and strained. "The irresistible craving for the water. All selkies feel it when they're ashore. It drove him mad, the desperate need to be back under the waves. I tried to ignore it for as long as possible, but he was drowning in the air. It became too hard to watch him battle against his true nature. So finally I told him to leave."

Delta frowned. "You told him to go? And he did? Just like that?"

"I told him I didn't love him. I was convincing. And a little cruel. But I knew in my heart I was doing what was best for all of us."

Realisation dawned on Delta. "You knew. You knew you were carrying me, and you sent him away without telling him. He didn't even know I existed, did he?"

Dorit shook her head, a fresh wave of tears streaming down her face. "Until now."

WATERLUST

Delta tossed and turned, kicking the covers off as a hot flash burned her skin, before wrapping them back around her when the shivers took hold. After a few hours of this—stealing snatches of sleep, during which she dreamed she was drowning, choking on salt water, clawing at her throat as the need to draw breath became too great and she drew in a lungful of water instead—she gave up and crossed to her small window, throwing it wide and inhaling gulps of cool, night air.

Her mother's bedroom overlooked the River Aspid, but Delta's room was in the back of the little inn, and from her window she could just see the tips of the tall pine trees that encircled the hidden lagoon.

Thinking about it now, she wasn't sure if her mother had chosen the front room to prevent Delta from looking out at the water, or because she herself wanted to gaze into the depths and dream of her selkie lover. Whatever the reason, her decision had backfired, because Delta could feel something dark and prickly deep down inside as she looked out at the forest, something pulling her towards that inky-black pool and the truth about who she was.

Waterlust, her mother had called it. Could the desperate craving for the water afflict half-selkies too? Or was it simple curiosity that tugged at her limbs and consumed her mind?

Half-selkie. She recoiled internally at the term. How could she not have known? How could her mother have kept this from her for eighteen years? Her mother had known exactly where her father was this entire time, it had been her choice to keep them apart.

Delta gripped the window ledge, knuckles white as bone. She wanted to scream until her throat was raw, to kick and lash out or fall to the ground, wracked by sobs. She hated her mother for what she'd done.

Before she could think better of it, Delta had pulled on her jacket and boots and shimmied down the drainpipe to the street below. She walked quickly between the quiet houses that crouched on either side of the cobblestones, ducking into a shadowed doorway when a candle flickered to life in an upstairs window.

Once her heart rate had slowed from a hummingbird to a mere jackrabbit inside her chest, she slipped from the darkness and continued on her way.

A perfect stillness had settled over the clearing since the commotion hours earlier. The lanterns were gone, but the moon cast a silvery glow on the calm, dark water, bathing the whole area in a soft light.

Delta walked around the edge of the pool, arms wrapped tightly around her body, watching the reflection of the moon move over the glassy surface. Her breathing had slowed, but an anxious feeling had settled in her stomach and she wondered if she'd made a terrible mistake. She was risking everything by being here, her mother would kill her if she knew. And if Dorit was right and her father would try to take her, this would be the perfect opportunity.

Delta wondered what her father would be like—strong and authoritative? Apologetic and emotional? Would he command her to come with him? Or ask her to meet him in secret so they could get to know each other?

From the way her mother said it, she was inclined to believe the former.

Gazing into the fathomless blackness of the pool, Delta felt that sickly pull again, the weight in the pit of her stomach, the crawl over her skin, the need to submerge herself and breathe in the cool water...

She stumbled back, realising how close she'd come to the edge. Her breathing quickened and she hugged herself tighter, still staring at the water with wariness.

She'd been foolish, she should return home and get back in bed before her mother realised she was gone. She mentally shook herself and turned to leave. A movement between the trees caught her eye as she did.

"I hoped you'd be back." The voice was warm and low. And it came from behind her.

DAUGHTER OF THE SELKIE KING

Delta swung around to find the selkie boy from earlier that evening bobbing gently in the middle of the pool, a smirk on his mouth.

"You—"

"Vance," the selkie reminded her. "And you're Delta." He inched closer as he said it, eyes glistening as they roved over her. There was a hungry curiosity in those green eyes that gave Delta a thrill, and at the same time frightened her.

"I should go." She started to back away, boots slipping slightly on the dewy grass.

"I wish you wouldn't. I wish you'd stay, just for a while." He was at the water's edge now, and he leant his elbows on the side, his chin resting on top of his hands. Water ran in rivulets over the pale skin of his arms and formed droplets in the dips created by his collarbone. That smirk returned as he watched her noticing. "Sit down, talk to me."

Delta hesitated, she'd come here to be alone with her thoughts, not to see the selkie boy.

Liar, a voice whispered inside her head. *You came here for answers.*

Vance patted the grass, head tilted to one side. Delta finally gave in with a roll of her eyes, and sat down cross-legged, well out of the selkie's reach.

"There you go, that wasn't so bad, was it?"

She flared her nostrils. "Go on then, say whatever you came here to say." She knew she was coming across a little hostile, she just hoped he couldn't see the real reason—fear.

She was face to face with a Solitary creature, alone in the middle of the night. All it would take was for the selkie to leap out of the water and he'd be on her in seconds, tearing her throat out with impossibly sharp teeth, or dragging her down to the bottom of the pool, drowning her.

And that was before she considered what he might say, or whether her father would appear.

Humour danced in the boy's eyes and he suppressed a smile. "I don't know what you mean. I only wanted to get to know you."

"You don't have a message from my father?"

His dark eyebrows pulled together. "Why would I have a message from your father?"

It was Delta's turn to frown. "You mean he doesn't know I'm here? That I—" She'd been about to say *exist*, but the word stuck in her throat.

"The only way he'd know you were here is if I had told him, and I haven't said a word to anyone. Why would I?"

"Oh I don't know, loyalty to your king, perhaps?"

Vance's eyebrows shot up towards his hairline and his mouth fell open. "King Malik is your father?" He let out a low whistle, clearly impressed. "Then, forgive me, your Highness." He affected an elaborate bow, flourishing his hand several times, eyes cast downward in mock respect.

When he looked up again his face split into a wide grin and laughter as bright and clear as cool water rang out around the clearing.

Delta scowled, she hated being laughed at.

"I'm just teasing, don't look at me like that," he said. She rolled her eyes and pulled a blade of glass out of the ground, twirling it around a finger like a ring.

"So you're the daughter of the Selkie King, huh? What's that like?"

Delta snorted. "I wouldn't know, would I? I've never met him. I didn't even know I was—" she couldn't bring herself to say it, "what I am, until you appeared."

Vance raised one eyebrow, mouth quirking to the side in an awkward expression. "Sorry about that, I just assumed you knew. Perhaps I need to work on my delivery. I was just so excited to meet you—like I said, I've never met a half-selkie before."

Delta threw her arms out dramatically. "Well, now you have! You can die happy." Her tone was bitter, but there was no strength to it. In fact, she felt deflated. The adrenaline that had pushed her out of her bedroom window and through the winding streets of Aberness all the way to this clearing had burned away. Now all she felt was cold and humiliated.

And the creeping sensation under her skin that tugged her towards the water. She shook her head, forcing it away. She couldn't even swim, there was no way she was throwing herself into the lagoon.

"Would you want to meet him? Your father. If you could?"

Delta twiddled the blade of grass, considering. Would she? She was certainly curious, but she didn't want to break her mother's heart, or put either of them in any danger. If her mother had chosen to keep Delta's existence a secret from him, she must have had her reasons.

But then, she had been young and in love. She'd believed she was doing the best thing for all of them. What if she'd gotten it wrong? Maybe if Malik knew about Delta he'd come back, maybe he and Dorit would rekindle their romance. Her mother hadn't had a serious relationship since Delta had been born, perhaps she was holding out for her first love?

"I don't know," Delta said. She ran her hands through her long blonde hair, closing her eyes. Until she remembered that she was alone in a dark wood with a Solitary creature, and she opened them.

Vance hadn't moved, except to lean his head on one hand, the other plucked a flower from the grassy bank. He held it to his nose and sniffed, but it must have smelled different to the underwater plants he was used to, because he wrinkled his nose in disgust and tossed the flower away, shuddering.

"Devil's weed," he muttered. He splashed his face with water and shook his head, spraying droplets in every direction. A few hit Delta and she stared at the places they'd landed on her bare legs, feeling the tingling sensation they created, resisting the urge to wipe them away. A coolness had begun to form in the pit of her stomach—something like dread.

"I could take you to him, you know? If you wanted to meet him. You only have to say the word."

She opened her mouth to respond without really considering her words, but a crashing sound in the woods behind her made her turn instead, mouth hanging open.

"Don't go with him, Delta!" Rafferty stood in the clearing, chest heaving, eyes burning bright in the low light.

INTO THE DRINK

"Please don't do it, Delta, you can't trust him."

"Raff? What are you doing here?" Delta leapt to her feet, heat rushing to her cheeks. She felt something swell inside her, burning away the cold dread and replacing it with a hot, uncomfortable feeling.

It was shame she felt. And that made her angry. "Did you follow me?" Her voice came out harsh and too loud. She didn't sound like herself.

Rafferty tugged at the cuffs of his hooded sweatshirt. "I saw you—out of my window. I didn't know where you were going. I just wanted to make sure you were okay. You know, after...earlier." He shifted his weight from one leg to the other, unable to meet her eyes.

"Go home, Raff. You shouldn't be here, you'll get into trouble."

He shook his head. "I don't care, I can't leave you alone here with that thing."

Delta started to reply, but something stopped her, the words dying on her tongue.

That thing?

If Vance was a *thing*, what did that make her? Half-thing?

"What's that supposed to mean, Raff? I'm just as much like him as I am like you. Half-selkie, half-human. Does that make me a *thing*, too?"

Rafferty's eyes went wide and he fumbled for words. "No, I didn't. I don't...I mean, you're you, and it's..." Delta waited while he struggled, like a fish flip-flopping on the shore. She wasn't quite ready to take pity on him and throw him back into the drink.

"*It's* what? A monster? A dark creature with no morals or soul?"

Vance had stayed quiet this whole time, watching them argue with a smug look on his face, but now as Delta gestured towards him she saw his smirk slip.

"Hey!" He clearly took exception to the suggestion he was a soulless beast.

Delta flapped a hand in his direction. "I was just making a point."

His voice took on a note of childish petulance. "You didn't have to make it quite so pointedly. That was just hurtful."

Delta groaned, exasperated. "Both of you, just shut up. Vance—I'm sure you have a soul, I bet it's a very nice one with lots of ethics and principles and stuff. Rafferty—I don't appreciate you following me here, trying to be some knight in shining armour, like I can't look after myself. I'm a big girl, Raff, I don't need a hero."

"You were about to go with him until I got here!"

"I was not!"

Vance coughed suggestively. "You were considering it."

Delta shot the selkie a look that had him dipping back below the surface, before popping up just enough to peer over the grassy embankment at them.

"Rafferty," she said with what she hoped was a note of finality. "I don't need your help. Please. Just go home, Raff."

A muscle flickered in his clenched jaw and he crossed his arms over his chest. "I'm not leaving without you." His voice was strong, but his eyes gave away his uncertainty and desperation as he stared Delta down, waiting for her response.

There was something else in his expression that she didn't want to examine right now. She had enough to worry about without considering her friend's feelings—no, she couldn't even think about that now.

"Yes, you are. This doesn't concern you, Raff."

"You're wrong, Delta, it does concern me. I can't let you fall for its tricks, I won't watch you drown because—"

Vance raised his hand. "Um, sorry to interrupt, but half-selkies can't drown. It's a physical impossibility. But, no, you carry on." He gestured to Rafferty to continue before resting his head on his hand again with a condescendingly patient expression.

"Shut up! Don't listen to it, Delta. They lie, this is what they do, they tell you what you want to hear, but it's not true. You're not a half-selkie, Delta, don't fall for it."

"YES, I AM!" A fragile silence fell over the clearing and all Delta could hear was her own heavy breathing. She was sick of everyone telling her who she was or wasn't, what she should or shouldn't do. Had anyone thought to ask her who she wanted to be?

She smoothed her jacket down over her nightdress and brushed her hair back from her shoulders, standing up straighter. "Yes, I am. I am a half-selkie. Tonight, my mother finally told me who my father is. I'm the daughter of the Selkie King." When her friend's expression remained sceptical, she added, "It's true, Raff. She told me the truth this time, I know it."

He shook his head. "That doesn't matter. I don't care who your father is, I care about you."

Delta told him, "It matters to me." Her smile was tinged

with sadness. "And I think if you really thought about it, it would matter to you too. What you're asking me to do is be human—wholly human—and forget my selkie side." The rushing in her ears had been rising in volume ever since Vance splashed water on her bare skin. The feeling as though some magnetic force pulled at her blood. Her words, although barely above a whisper, rang out clear in the quiet clearing. "And I don't think I can do that."

EXILED

Rafferty moved towards her then, closing the distance between them in two strides of his long legs, a panicked look on his beautiful face.

He *was* beautiful, Delta had always known that, in some distant part of her brain. But he was Raff, just Raff. So when he took both of her hands in his and brought his face close to hers, she felt nothing but a vague sense of warmth. Her friend looked worried, she should reassure him.

But that need, that craving for the water had grown into a pulsing thing, clouding her vision and shrinking her consciousness down to one tiny point. To the pool just a few feet from where she stood.

"Delta, I don't want you to forsake who you are, I just don't want you to fall for the tricks that these creatures are famous for playing." When she opened her mouth to respond, Rafferty shook his head and quickly added, "I know, you say you're half selkie too, but the difference is you're half human. You have a human heart, Delta." He covered her hand with his and placed them both on her chest, over her heart. "You're a good person, the best person I know. You're nothing like them," he gestured behind her to where she assumed Vance was still watching them. "And you don't need a father who abandoned you without a single thought—"

Delta shook her head, clearing the fog that had begun to settle over her mind. "He didn't abandon me," she pulled her hand from his grip and took a step back, out of his reach. "He didn't even know I existed."

"Still doesn't," Vance chimed. They ignored him.

"My mother hid me from him. She lied to me my entire life about who he is—how is that right? How is that *good*? Being human doesn't mean we're any better than anyone else. It just means we *think* we are."

She could see the desperation in Rafferty's eyes as he tried to find the words to convince her, to make her stay. She realised that that's what was going on here. He had been trying to give her a reason not to go with Vance, not to leave him and Aberness for her father's underwater kingdom. She'd never truly intended to go, but now she couldn't see how she could stay.

She gave Rafferty a sad smile. "They'll hate me when they find out the truth, I won't be able to stay. You know just as well as I do what will happen when the rest of the village discovers the rumours are true. That I am a seal-girl. I'll be cast out. Exiled."

Raff tried to take a step towards her, but Delta moved backwards, and looking down at her feet, he hesitated. She felt the slope of the ground beneath her boots, she was close to the water's edge.

Silver lined Rafferty's eyes as he reached towards her, shaking his head. "I'll protect you. Delta, I won't let anything happen to you." She could see the words he couldn't say out loud clearly in his glittering blue eyes.

She'd only hurt him more if she stayed.

She swallowed, taking in every freckle on his face, every strand of brown, wavy hair that fell into his eyes, every curve of his mouth as his lip quivered and he shook his head, refusing to accept her decision.

"Tell my mother I love her."

Delta hesitated before taking the selkie's outstretched hand, and with one last look over her shoulder at her friend, she dove into the pool. The last thing she heard before her body hit the water was Rafferty's yell as he leapt to grab her, to stop her, but he hadn't moved quickly enough.

Now, Vance pulled her down, down into the inky darkness, deeper and deeper, until she could no longer see the light of the moon on the water's surface or hear her friend's cries.

They seemed to sink forever, the selkie pulling Delta with him. The cold seeped into her bones and all she could hear was the rushing water as Vance dragged her endlessly down.

Delta's chest grew tighter and more painful as she fought to hold her breath. All around her was blackness, the only solid thing she was aware of was the selkie's slippery, grey body as she clung on tightly.

Consciousness began to slip from her grasp, and just as she opened her mouth to inhale a lungful of icy water, unable to hold her breath any longer, Vance pressed his wide mouth to hers, filling her lungs with his breath.

In the distance, Delta saw the faint lights of the selkie kingdom beneath them, twinkling softly. She closed her eyes, letting euphoria overcome her.

AUTHOR'S NOTE

Daughter of the Selkie King is set in the same world as Lyndsey Hall's full length novel, The Fair Queen. Available here https://mybook.to/TheFairQueen

2
MERRILY MERRILY
JENNIFER KROPF

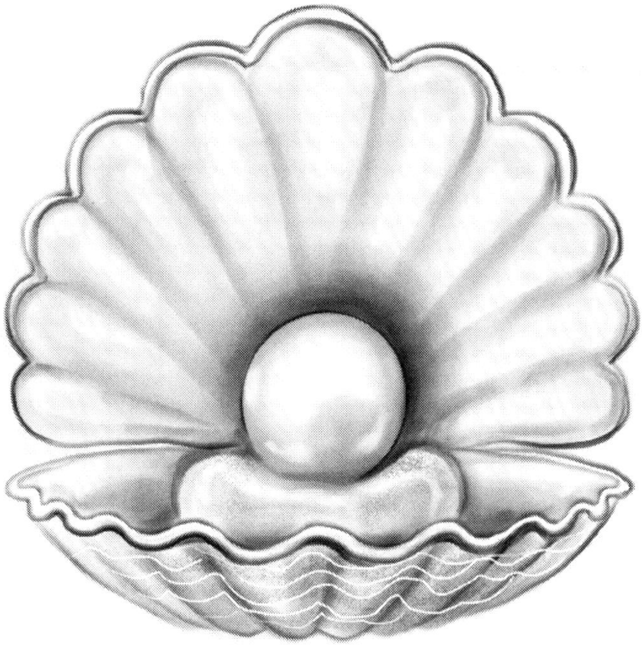

MERRILY MERRILY

FIRSTLY,

There was not enough snow in all of Winter to wedge between Zane-Cohen-Margus Bowswither and Tigrus Oran-Mathsideon to create sufficient distance between the two. Born rivals, they were—even at a dozen seasons old.

Before a sky bleeding scarlet and succulent orange, Zane stared across the deck at Tigris's twinkling smirk and the iron in his narrowed eyes. The boy's obsidian hair was soggy with perspiration, but he seemed otherwise well; fit for a race. Healthy enough to bury Zane's glory at the bottom of the snowseas.

Unfortunately for Tigris, Zane very much hated to lose. And he was rather good at races.

With folded arms and a sweet wink at his foe across the deck, Zane went over the rules of the race in his mind—rules that had been changed at the last minute by his mother who stood by to watch.

It was a true season's-end miracle that she was present at all. His mother—the prophetess, vision seer, and *steerer of the ship*—had become the interim ruler during this freezing quarter until a new captain was selected; a title which should have been Zane's birthright, but his mother was too mystical and scheming to simply hand such a position over. Reasons ranged from, *"It's not yet time,"* to *"You're still too young,"* plus, *"I cannot bloody see what you're hiding from me!"*

The prophetess had come to watch the race, but she had not spoken a word to Zane since she ascended from belowdecks where she had spent nearly a full quarter summoning her energies and scribbling visions on parchment. She had not sent for him in all that time, either.

Tigris, however, had been summoned a fair measure of times.

How fitting, that the prophetess might rise to the fresh air only to witness Zane beat her beloved Tigris, who had long since taken Zane's place at his mother's side after Zane had refused to let her glimpse into his heart to steal his secrets a time or three.

Zane folded his arms and did not hide his scowl at her long black dress-train gliding over the sunny deck, or the windswept waves of her glossy nut-coloured hair. Though the woman was his blood, he did not trust the future-seeing, fortune-sputtering ashworm with anything.

But in a short measure, his mother would see how foolish she had been to parade Tigris around before the crew. The Captain she "foresaw" to inherit the ship in his future, as was spoken to her through a vision. A future not put in stone—but one she would surely craft the way she wanted it to be.

The waves raged in hunger, spurting through gaps of broken ice the Kelidestone had shattered to make space for the duo of pirates to swim. All for this game of theirs. All for this race that Tigris Oran-Mathsideon would lose.

"Are you yet ready, sputtlepuns?" Sembleton scratched his burly throat. The one-eyed crewman held an ice-shredded scrap of flag in his fist that had once boasted a bone skull with a frostlilly as its mouth but was now too mangled to make out.

The cries and groans of the ice below filled the air as the last of the ice was snapped and dragged away by chains and hooks to make a large hole for entry into the dark snowseas. The Kelidestone was a beautiful and mighty ship with blood red sails—meant for gliding over open seas, chopping through ice-topped lakes, and plunging across the snow dunes by the windmill-wheels hugging the bottom that could be rowed from inside.

Sembleton raised the tattered flag to the wind, giving brief life to its tendrils, and Zane crouched to dig the heel of his boot against the deck. It was time to show Tigris what a saltworm he was.

"Wait." The prophetess raised a hand, halting the theatrics, and the game.

Zane slid his frosty gaze to the woman, eyeing the dark serpentine tattoo spreading up her neck into that wavy pecan hair of hers—the same shade of brown as his.

With convincing grace, the prophetess rose from her seat and glided over the deck to where Zane stood. Tigris eyed them carefully from his spot, feeling left out, no doubt.

Zane adjusted himself from his readied stance to stand tall again, wishing only to remind his mother how much he had grown these last seasons. He was taller than her now. Some might consider him a young man and no longer a boy.

"Steelheart." A smile cracked at the furthest edge of her red-painted lips. Her hand came against his forearm, patching over his permanent ink symbol that informed all those he crossed that he belonged to this crew.

Zane's eyes darted down to that hand.

"Good luck," was all she said.

Her wild eyes had grown paler this last quarter and Zane fought a shudder at the sight of them. "I don't need your luck," he promised. He had done just fine without it in his seasons. "But I wonder what will happen to poor Tigris when I beat him? Do you think the crew will still want him as their captain after I scrub the seaweed floors with him?"

Those pale eyes flickered. "Careful, Steelheart." The whisper was sweet, but a warning. A threat.

Zane released a laugh. "I bloody better be. I have no doubt you're counting down the sunsets until you can turn this crew on me and carve a bone dagger into my back," he snorted. "Leave me to my race, Mother. Watch me beat your champion."

Silence. Zane could almost taste the fury leaking from the woman.

"As you wish." A tease. A gloat.

Zane eyed her as she sauntered back to her seat across the deck, listening to the necklace of bones at her throat as they clapped together.

Frostbitten cursed woman.

"*Go!*"

At Sembleton's roar, Zane spun back to find Tigris already bolting across the main deck.

Snarling, Zane sprinted after his rival and hopped the rail, falling far and fast towards the needles of ice stabbing from where the frozen blanket of the snowseas had been shattered.

Zane twisted his body to avoid the needles and straightened into a dive as he hit the water, gliding beneath the bitter waves like a bird arching through a rippling sky.

Numbness bit at his nose and extremities upon entry—a feeling that might render most to panic, but Zane had swum these waters before in races such as this one, all to hold his spot at his mother's side when he once cared to do so. Now, winning was not about reclaiming his title as the future Captain, or appeasing his mother. It was about wiping the haughty smirk off Tigris's face and proving to his mother that she did not get to adjust his future with a mere flick of her fingers whenever she liked.

A low groan rumbled through the water and Zane grinned —a brush of icy current leaking against his teeth. Through the snowsea weeds, he spotted Tigris diving deeper into the frosty marsh in search of a pure black pearl. It was a gamble to test these weeds, as sirens often came out to play when the plants were disturbed. They guarded their pearls with passion and rage—Zane had heard many dreadful stories.

But he knew his own way around the marsh, knew where to best look for a pearl of his own.

Paddling around the weeds, Zane scanned the dark sea floor for signs of a gem that might have spilled away from the sirens' troves. Even as the seconds slipped by, Zane kept his calm, paced his energy so he might hold his breath longer. He had been under water so many times as a boy that it was second nature now—he might transform into a handsome merman soon.

Another grin at that thought.

A shuffle in the marsh halted Zane's search. He wondered if Tigris was in trouble, if the sirens had found him after all. As he peered into the slimy grasses and sponge, he did in fact see Tigris. But he was not in trouble.

The young sputtlepun was reaching into his pocket and drawing out—

A pure black pearl.

The bloody ashworm was cheating.

Zane abandoned his search and headed into the weeds, certain this race had just turned into something else. If Tigris intended to swindle a win, Zane would steal the pearl right from the boy's hands and deliver it to his mother with a smile. He had left his cutlass on deck, but his bare hands were more useful than most, even under water.

Tigris's silver eyes rose as Zane slashed away the weeds

between them. The boy's grip tightened around the gem and he certainly sensed what Zane intended to do. But to Zane's surprise, Tigris drew a dagger and raised it, stopping Zane's pursuit.

No weapons during a race—rule number four.

They floated there like that for a heartbeat until Tigris's hoary gaze dropped to Zane's arm, to his tattoo. And then back up. A slow sneer followed.

Odd.

Zane's own eyes drifted down to his forearm where the skull and crossbones had been inked with such precision by the prophetess herself when he was only nine seasons old.

Zane barely had a chance to sort out his curiosity when a sea-shuddering current barrelled into him and tipped him off balance. Tigris too went spinning, falling into the blackest pit of the marsh. Zane stared after the boy with wide-eyes until the current came again—a punch of a wave against his flesh that sent his skull colliding with the jagged underside of the Kelidestone.

"Bloody frostbite!" His underwater curse let in a mouthful of water and he batted his arms to collect himself.

Tigris swam like a panicked gull to the surface, the pearl still clutched in his grip. Zane blinked against the bubbles, peering through the black sponges muddying the water and through the tendril of red—*red*.

Zane's eyes fired back to his tattoo, to that spot on his forearm where his mother had touched. And he saw it—the pin-point prick into his flesh where his blood leaked. He hadn't felt it beneath his mother's hand, due to some numbing concoction on her fingertips, he guessed.

His growl was drowned by the third current that plunged against his body and pushed his back against the daggered wood of the ship. He thrashed as the water fought against his pinched mouth, against his nostrils, trying to make its way in and drown him.

In a pocket between currents, Zane kicked off the ship and paddled for the hole in the ice where Tigris had disappeared. There was no game to play anymore. Something was down here in these weeds, something dreadful. Something that perhaps his mother had known was waiting.

Above, the ice was a solid wall, and Zane bit his teeth as he saw how well the trap had been laid. His mother's careful touch, Tigris's planted pearl, even Tigris having a dagger on him when he should have been searched by Lother before the race.

His own crew. His own mother.

They would all frostbitten suffer for it.

Zane slapped a hand over the needle-point cut in the eye of his tattoo and kicked for the hole above that now seemed much too small and far to reach. His mind burned through every spell he knew—ones he had been taught by his mother and ones he'd learned on his own—and every curse he could spit towards whatever creature was hunting him below.

But he already had an idea of what sort of creature had awakened in the bowels of the snowseas. One that would smell his blood. And one that would never forget it once it did.

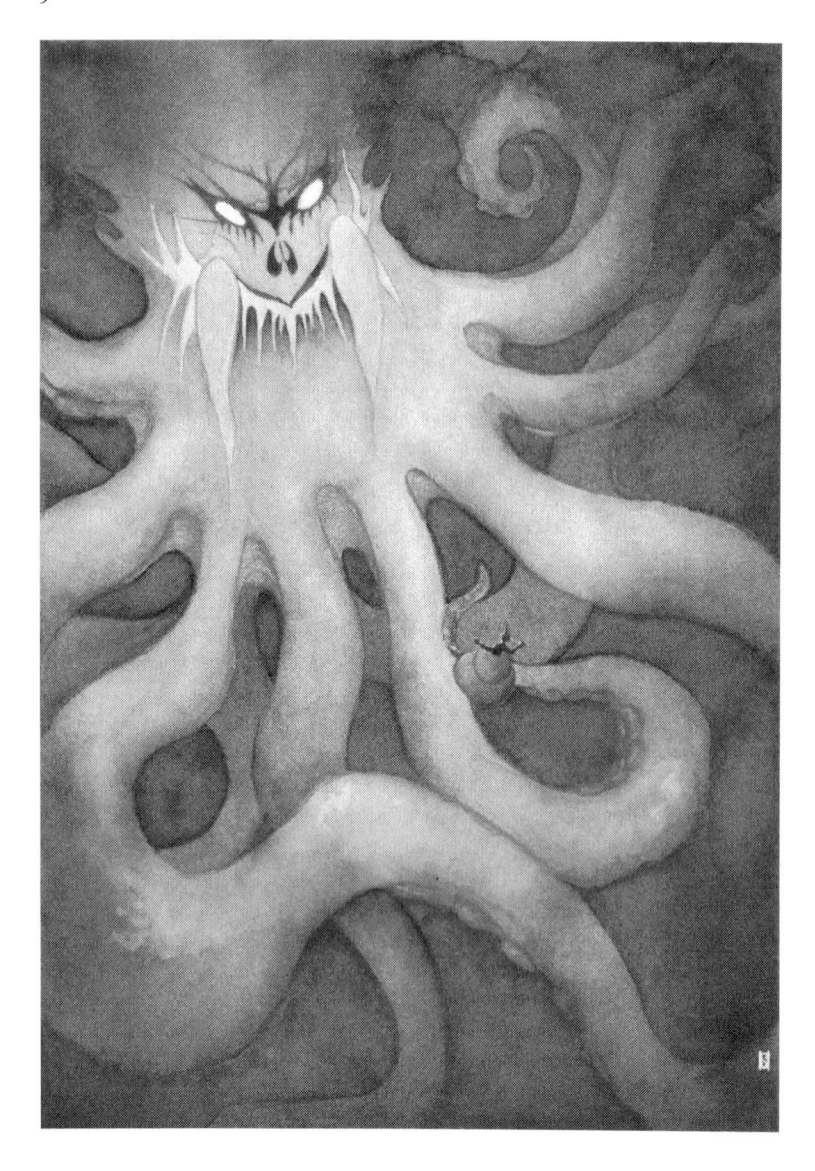

SECONDLY,

The octosiren was half the size of the Kelidestone; its fangs longer than Zane's own legs. He had no cutlass, not even a bone dagger to defend himself when the creature slid from the blackest cave below, bronze and brass treasures spilling out over the sea floor. The creature rushed to circle him like a nightmare, its scales tipping out like knives to pierce Zane's flesh as it closed in.

I smell you...

The octosiren's cold whisper drove into his chest and turned the dull colours there to ash and cinders.

I smell you, too. Zane jested back, though he wasn't sure the creature could hear him, if he had the same sort of speech as this *thing* in the water.

But a low, cruel chuckle told Zane the monster had heard him just fine.

Zane's eyes slid closed. He would die here like this—in the pit of the snowseas. Perhaps it was where he was always meant to meet his fate—a fair payment for the villages he had pillaged and the cruel things he had helped his mother do in his seasons as a child. Things that had killed his spirit at first, made him ill and sent him into the corner of his cabin to tremble night after night as visions of the bloodshed haunted his dreams and daydreams alike. He had learned to sing himself to sleep, and he had taught himself to read to pass the worst of times.

Under the water, his supply of air had vanished. The pale colours began to swim in his chest, his heart writhing for life he did not have left to give. And so, a prayer of forgiveness was what slipped into his mind, to an old Truth of legends he did not believe in, one that might spare him a pinch of forgiveness in the afterlife for his crisped soul. A thing he had read about in a book or three he had stolen from one of those coastal villages he had destroyed to please his mother.

But the idea struck him right as he was nearly encompassed by the octosiren's long, serpentine body and slimy black tentacles.

Might we make a deal? Zane's gaze slid over to seek out the octosiren's dreadful face.

His mind and body were failing; he would die in this watery ice coffin if he did not surface soon. If an ancient miracle awakened and allowed him to escape this fate, he would kill Tigris for this cruel joke. Their pranks of rivalry had settled on the side of dangerous and unforgivable over the seasons, but this… this was a new level of backstabbing.

Interesting, the thing said back. *But now that I've smelled you, I'm sure I'll want your blood incessantly.* A pause as the creature quivered, perhaps in pleasure, or thirst. *Your blood smells of mint and the forests above. And…anger. Pure, lovely, undiluted anger.*

Fine. Zane swallowed, his chest burning like open flames. *Hunt me for the remainder of my timestring if you must. But even so, I'd like to make a deal.*

And what are you willing to bargain for? the thing asked.

Well. I'd rather like to live today.

The red and orange sky had melted to gray and purple when Zane climbed the ladder and tumbled to the deck. Cries of surprise lifted from nearby crewmen at the sight of his saturated, shivering body.

"Frostbite!" Sembleton leaned to see Zane for himself. "We saw the octosiren's fins brushing the underside of the ice! How did you escape?"

But Zane's cold blue stare slid across the ship to Tigris. To his mother, who stood tall at the cheating boy's side. "I have my secrets, too," he said. Tigris snarled and looked away to study his nails, no shame on his face for what he had done.

But the prophetess stared with those unwavering, pale eyes. She looked upon her son who had survived, despite her meddling. And in her own dark, subtle way, she looked pleased that he had found a way out.

"Well done," her voice was barely a whisper.

Zane rolled to his feet, fighting the shivers driving against his bones through his dripping wet clothes. He stared back at his mother, bottling the fury that tempted him to shout at the woman and toss Tigris back into the snowseas to face the octosiren himself. But, instead of exploding with the anger that had gained him a pebble of respect and fear from his crew in recent seasons, Zane marched across the deck and stood eye-to-eye with the prophetess.

"I don't know what you're up to. I don't know what game this is. But leave me bloody out of it."

If the woman was insulted, she didn't show it. That same curve of a smile tugged the edge of her red mouth. It was infuriating, and so Zane left for his cabin, craving dry clothes and a warm blanket.

"You lost the race, Steelheart." Her voice trailed after him. "The crew will not be forgiving of that."

THIRDLY,

Tigris Oran-Mathsideon was a bad apple. Zane was quite certain of it. A time or three Tigris had left little critters in Zane's bed to keep him awake at night. Zane had growled in annoyance on the mornings when he would wake with red bites peppering his torso. But he always retaliated, and he always did it well. Zane's clever mischiefs forever left Tigris more enraged and swearing revenge with each new idea that sprang into Zane's mind.

It had been a contest of pride in their childish seasons. Now, it was a contest for the hearts of the crew. And he was growing exhausted fighting for their attention when most days he wasn't certain he still wanted it.

After Zane had shivered for hours and tossed back and forth in his hammock in a fitful sleep, he rolled to his feet to face the night. The soreness lingered in his cold bones, reminding him of that octosiren's sharp scales and pointed teeth. He dragged on his warmest coat to storm through the ship and find something to drink that might numb the pains in his muscles, quiet the voices in his head, and ease the loathing in his heart.

But the question would loom over him, no matter how much he drank. He knew it.

Had his mother tried to kill him? Or was this a test to see if he was worthy of her blessing to be Captain of the Kelidestone? He had after all outwitted the octosiren—for now.

Fear's cold touch dragged up his spine as he imagined what might happen to him the next time he dared to poke a toe into the snowseas. He shuddered at what was waiting for him down there, what now craved his blood and would follow this ship wherever it went, ready for the moment it might feast upon that blood it claimed smelled of cheap pirate-mint and *anger*.

Zane shook his head. He wasn't old enough to be captain, but neither was Tigris. So, what was his mother's play? He was tired of always trying to figure her out.

The deck was nearly empty when Zane stomped up the narrow stairs, but even Brox and Mollbane went silent as the son of the prophetess clattered his way over the deck boards, kicking aside bottles and baskets of fruit until he reached the full bottles of fermented ice-berry juice.

They would consider it a sputtlepun temper tantrum, but Zane didn't care.

"A bit early for that, don't you think, Steelheart?" Mollbane muttered from across the deck and Zane flinched. He turned to the older man, taking in the sight of the aged pirate's bristly beard and half-sagged eyes. A man bitten with the curse of age.

"Do you want to quarrel, Mollbane?" Zane tested, uncorking the bottle against Mollbane's warning.

But Mollbane grunted, sizing up Zane's young, energetic frame. "Your lassie is on board. Flew in off the cliffs last night. Might want to stay clear headed for when you face her."

Zane's hand froze on the bottle's mouth.

"Sentra..." he spit her name, wary of saying it loud enough to stir the Winter winds, "is here?"

"Consider yourself warned," Mollbane snorted and strutted to the opposite side of the deck.

For a breath or three, Zane stood under the Winter stars, staring out at the hazy horizon black with night and sleepless curses. "Bloody ashworm," he muttered, shoving the cork back into the bottle and turning to hurl the entire thing into the snowseas. "Bloody conniving, spellcasting *ashworm*."

He would bury his mother in the dunes by the end of this quarter if she didn't let up.

Zane stormed into his mother's cabin. And lo' and behold, she was there—Sentra. The girl's ink-black hair and even blacker eyes tightened the skin on his shoulders as he tried to avoid meeting the beady gaze of the rival pirate crew's prized gift to his mother. To him, apparently.

"What is *she* doing here?"

His mother lounged over her cushioned bed with her feet up.

Sentra growled in response—a feline sound that fitted her. She wasn't quite normal, not a colour-blooded Rime Folk. Something dug up from the pits of the snowseas and given legs and a beautiful body and face. But those pure black eyes...

"I invited her." His mother's voice was sugar and spice.

Only now did Zane realize he was bare chested beneath his

coat which hung open wide. With a snarled lip, he yanked his coat shut and folded his arms to conceal himself from the two devils before him.

You will marry Sentra Donspellis, his mother had informed him two quarters ago—when their feud had truly begun.

I certainly will not. Zane had not been joking then, just as he was not joking now as he glared down at the two conspirators who seemed so determined to decide his fate for him.

His mother had thrown a fit of rage, claiming Zane did not care for his crew and that he would not be captain if he could not take care of his own men. But Zane refused to be married during the season next when he would be merely ten plus three seasons old—and to the demon-eyed daughter of a rival crew at that.

She was ten plus seven seasons old and certainly planned to control him after the treaty was sealed by their dreadful union. Zane would not do it.

It was why his mother had not spoken to him in almost a full quarter—until now. Until she had wished him luck before the race and pressed a pin into his wrist so the octosiren would smell his sweet blood and become infatuated with it.

The prophetess's façade dropped as she looked up at her son in the doorway. Sentra stared at him, too, glare equally as piercing. Even her leathery wings seemed arched in disdain.

And so, Zane smiled.

"I'll leave you lassies to your ugly scheming." He bowed, like a servant. "But as always...Find a way to leave me out of it," he said the last part to his mother, ice-blue eyes sharp.

She snarled at his back like a polar bear when he turned.

"*Steelheart*," the name rolled off her poisonous tongue. "Stop."

The air in the room seemed to change, and Zane was met with the sound of his mother lifting from her cot. He found himself smiling again.

So, they would finally speak, then. Finally sort this out. But when he turned back, he saw that his mother was not bracing for a quarrel.

"I don't answer to you," Zane reminded her, leaning in to emphasise it. "When I'm captain, you will answer to *me*. And after you tried to feed me to the octosiren this sunset past, I vow I'll come up with all sorts of dreadful little ways to make you hate your life on my ship." *The same as what you did to chase off my father*, was what he did not add.

His mother shut her mouth. And so, Zane made his exit.

But he did not storm down the hall as he might normally have done. He slid against the wall around the corner to listen. And he hated himself for it—that he was so desperate to learn what his mother was doing, to learn what the moves she had been making these quarters were leading up to.

She had begged him to let her see the secrets of his heart when he was a younger lad, and each time, he had refused. So, she had tried anyway, working her visions and spells to dive into his heart against his will. She had been furious when she realized she couldn't get in—something Zane himself did not understand either but had been all too pleased to discover. The woman claimed a wall of steel existed around his heart.

"That boy is not going to wed me," Sentra's gurgling fish-voice slipped out from the cabin.

"He will. I will bloody make him," his mother cooed. "I need this treaty to work. My supplies won't last another season and we've already pillaged most of the coastal villages we can reach. I need more cutlass wielders. I need a new crew with a hunger for blood." There was a pause and Zane shook his head in disgust. He already knew he was a pawn in her game, but all this over a few more weapon-hands? He had discovered at a young age that she would do anything to get what she—

"You can kill him after the wedding."

Zane blinked. He stared at the chipping boards across the hall, not truly seeing them at all.

"You're certain? I don't want a prophetess's retaliation for it if you decide you regret it." Sentra's voice held no conviction, and Zane's jaw solidified. His fingers tapped his bone dagger as he considered marching back into that cabin and ending their conversation for good. But he did not think he could take them both on—he was strong for his age, but his mother could wield a cutlass too, and he knew she kept one by her cot.

"My son will not be Captain of Kelidestone," his mother whispered. "My Steelheart has no interest in fulfilling the role I made him for, and I won't spend the next twenty bloody seasons putting up with his insubordination."

Whether it was anger or sorrow that touched his stomach with heat, Zane didn't know. But he pulled himself off the wall and walked on light toes to his cabin in silence.

All night he lay awake, ignoring the pile of books stashed on his night table which he would read at times like these to keep his mind from caving in on itself. But he only stared out the oval window at the Winter stars now, singing along to a song he had learned as a boy.

"Row, row, row your boat..." his hum took over for a verse when he couldn't remember the words, "Merrily, merrily, merrily, merrily," His sweet, high voice was coveted by a member or three of the crew who often pushed him to sing for them when he did not want to. "...Life is like a dream."

He ended the song as it settled in him what he was: unwanted. Someone not worth fighting for. Only an animal to be forced into submission. He was a creature of the seas, abandoned by his father, and hated by his mother.

And one day; perhaps, he would make them all pay for it.

FOURTHLY,

Zane marched through the snowy village with heavy boots the next morning, trampling an already footprint-congested road. Most of the coastal villagers surrendered, but a few fought back as their homes were torn apart while the Kelidestone crew searched for anything of value. The villagers who rebelled had to watch their wood houses go up in golden flames.

The prophetess stood on the shoreline in her long, silken cloak, the fur of her hood brushing her chin. Her pale eyes took it all in as she was no doubt already counting the worth of her new treasure. A trident rested in her grip—a gold trophy she had once stolen from a siren in the early seasons of her timestring, or so she claimed. It was for show though; Zane had never seen his mother use the thing.

Tigris led a band through the alleys to hunt those trying to flee, to steal the necklaces off their throats and the rings from their fingers.

Zane rolled a long necklace of black snowsea pearls over his fingers, staring at them. The string of black round stones glimmered in the direct sunlight; a gift likely given to a wife, or a daughter, or as a proposal. Easily fetched—unlike the underwater pearls Zane had not managed to find during the race.

A girl with bouncing orange curls had sprinted into her front room and *thrown* them at him, as if the surrender of their most valuable treasure might somehow keep the young pirate demon at bay. Then the girl had fled out the back door after her family.

The leaking kohl on his lids stung his eyes, adding to the irritation from his terrible sleep the eve before.

A shuffle of white feathers brushed Zane's cheek and he swatted at it before realizing what it was. Silver twinkled upon a bird's wings. It arched and landed in the street before him.

Zane blinked. The bird was *very* white.

His mind danced over the value of meat it might provide if he could capture it—not that he felt like selling the meat or even sharing it. Hunger rolled into his stomach and he took a slow step forwards, but as if sensing his dark motives, the creature flapped and lifted back into the air. Zane watched as it joined with a host of others—just high enough above the village to stay out of reach.

When he turned back, his gaze found a trio standing at the end of the street, side-by-side, and his brows furrowed.

The three statue-still bodies wore black clothing, curled-toe boots, and tall hooked staffs balanced in their grips that reminded him of large, wood fishing lures. Two were in their early twentieth seasons if he had to guess, and one was middle-aged like Mollbane.

All three were striking. Not in the typical way; there were no bells or garlands to be seen. But it was the way they stood together—shoulder-to-shoulder—that struck Zane the most. As though they were different parts of a single body.

Challenge ignited the eyes of the middle-aged one with creamy-toned hair and a beard to match. Zane found himself drawing forwards, stalking them like an ashworm slithering through the grass.

As villagers rushed by in every direction, Zane kept his gaze on the trio, certain they were about to do something, though he could not guess what. But when the middle-aged man's warm sunflower eyes dropped to lock onto Zane's ice-cold ones, Zane halted. The man smiled, and Zane felt a touch of fury warm his blood.

Was that a *taunt*?

Zane barely realized he was standing before them now, just an arm's reach away. "Here to defend the village?" he guessed, eyeing the staffs they carried. A twinkle found the silver eyes of the boy on the man's right, and a slit of striking white teeth showed when he smiled.

"Ragnashuck, Pirate. I'd think you'd know a takeover when

you saw one," the boy said, daring Zane to do something about it.

But the middle-aged man cast the boy a look. "Manners, Nicholas. We're not here to make enemies." The man's voice was calm; like a quiet brook Zane had once heard in the woods.

Zane shook the thought from his mind as the boy on the right flashed his devilish grin again. "Aren't we?" he taunted, silvery eyes glimmering at Zane.

Zane looked at them one by one until his stare fell back on the aged one in the middle. "Move your merry scotchers," he said with demeaning articulation. "Or you'll be tangled up in those wood hooks and pretty black clothes when I'm done with you."

All three blinked.

Suddenly, the silver-eyed boy threw his head back and barked a laugh. Zane tilted his head like a crow, deciding he would tackle *that* one first.

The middle-aged man sighed and looked to the sky where the birds circled overhead. The winged creatures wove in and out of each other's paths in perfect circles—not a feather brushing each other.

"No need to get hissy, Pirate. We're only here to play," the silver eyed boy wiped a bead of moisture from his lash.

"Alright," the middle-aged man said, "Nicholas. Posineon. Clear the street's edges. I'll sweep the middle."

All at once, the black-cloaked trio moved. Zane's eyes darted between them as he drew his cutlass, trying to decide which to take as they all brushed past, sketching their staffs over the snow and gliding like melting butter on a fire-roasted fish.

Frustration boiled Zane's blood as the three snuck up on bellowing Kelidestone crew members who snatched what they could. The silver-eyed boy and his companion blocked blades with skill and tossed the pirates into the snow like flimsy branches needing to be cleared away.

A growl lifted in Zane's throat and he tore after them, reaching the middle-aged man first. His trained cutlass swished by the man's ear, but the man whirled and locked his staff against the cutlass before Zane could strike again.

Then, Zane's smile returned. "You're making a mistake, old man," he said.

To that, the man arched a light brow. "Am I?"

Zane's grin widened. He slashed, chopping a notch into the old man's cane. "Only half my crew has made land. The other half is marching up the beach as we speak," he laughed. "I might be young in seasons, but you could learn a thing or three from me."

Zane expected the man's face to fall, and for the old brute to holler to his allies to retreat, but he did no such thing. He stared at Zane for a measure, looking him up and down as if surprised. His golden eyes roamed until Zane shifted on his feet.

"Like I said," Zane cooed. "Move your merry scotchers." His fingers buzzed against his blade, ready for another fight.

The man's eyes lifted to the shore where, sure enough, the rest of the Kelidestone crew marched in from the row boats.

"Mikal!" one of the boys in black shouted from the street as he noticed them, too. In the same moment, Lother sprang from the shadows like a demon with wings and brought his cutlass across the boy-in-black's shoulder.

From across the street, the silver-eyed boy's gaze shot up at his ally's cry.

But still, the middle-aged man did not move, did not unlock his weapon from Zane's where they were knotted together—curved staff against arched cutlass. Even as Lother took off to chase down a villager. Even as the silver-eyed boy fired across the street and rammed Tigris into the siding of a house as the young pirate came to finish what Lother had started.

As if they were speaking on a silent thread, the silver-eyed boy looked up to the older man in question as he took the arm of his injured ally and slung it over his own shoulders to carry him away.

The middle-aged man looked back at Zane though, instead of retreating. "Take Posineon home," he called over the street as it flooded with new pirates.

The silver-eyed boy darted between two houses—sliding over the snow on his toes—and disappeared.

Zane glanced to where their weapons interlocked. The sleepless night put fire in his veins, and he shoved with all his might, forcing the man back a step. From there, Zane raised his cutlass to the man's throat and ten plus three pirates filed in to surround him, along with the prophetess who drifted around to watch.

The man dropped his staff to the snow in surrender.

"Welcome to the snowseas, old man. Let's see if I let you survive until sunrise." Zane's mouth tipped upwards in victory.

But there was no dismay on the man's face, even as he finally replied, "I am *not* old."

The ship rocked the crew to sleep, the easy sway soothing Zane's weary body as he stared through the cage at the prisoner the crew had dragged belowdecks. His mother had declared the prisoner to be worth a ransom, should his two allies return. So, they hadn't killed him. Yet.

It was very much like his mother to decide the prisoner belonged to her.

After an hour or three of mocking the middle-aged man, the rest of the crew had drifted away to their cabins, or to the main deck to set sail with his mother behind the wheel, until only Zane and Tigris remained.

"You cheated," Zane finally said it. Even with everything that had happened since the race, he wanted Tigris to know he had seen it.

Tigris's lip curled into a snarl. "You *survived*." The words were so wicked, Zane looked at the boy.

Once, Zane was praised for his childishness, his pranks, his way to draw a laugh or three. Now, he had been handed a platter of frustration in place of it. Tigris was always the first to toss a cutting word in Zane's direction, or fling a fish at the back of Zane's head to make the men laugh. Zane's temper had become a thing so easily triggered, he was sure the crew placed bets on it.

Tigris's eyes slid over, too, a gloat stealing his face. "I win, Cohen. Your ship. Your life. It's mine."

Zane grunted and looked back to the man in the cage who said nothing. It didn't seem as though the old man was listening as he stared through the small window at the snowseas, but Zane had a feeling the old bat had heard every word.

I win, Cohen.
Your ship.
Your life.

How many seasons had they been at war this way? How long had Tigris looked upon the destiny before Zane and coveted it with such outrageous passion? How much further was Tigris willing to go to get it?

Apparently far enough to conspire about feeding Zane to the octosiren.

But Zane could hold on. Had to hold on. Or he would have nothing. Being a pirate, son of the prophetess, was the only thing he was—as much as he hated it most days.

"We'll see," was all he said before Tigris's quiet chuckle

Enchanted Waters

filled the ship's belly. The boy strutted off to command the sails alongside the prophetess where he believed he belonged.

Zane was glaring when the old man glanced at him. To Zane's ever-growing frustration, the man did not even look afraid. Nor did he appear bothered by the ring of purple around his left eye, or the swelling bruise along his jaw.

The prophetess would consider all her options before she decided what to do with the prisoner. She would settle on whichever one filled her pockets with the most gold rings.

As he stared into the older man's honey irises, Zane found his mind back in that snowy street of the village with the trio in black. He considered how the trio had moved in unison, so quick and without complaint at the brief command of their captain. How obedient they all were. How loyal.

Zane folded his arms as he played it over and over and over, especially how the silver-eyed boy had rushed in to save his friend from Lother's and Tigris's cutlasses.

It was all rather unusual, and Zane's stomach tightened as he wondered if Tigris would ever perform such a rescue for him if he took a cutlass to the shoulder. The bloody pirate would probably stoop down to dig the blade in deeper.

"Who are you?" Zane finally asked when the silence had gone on too long.

"My name is Mikal Migraithe." Simple.

With that shallow answer, the man stood and limped across his cell on limbs still stiff from whatever beating he had taken from the crew on the way down. Zane watched, bored.

He was growing tired after his dreadful night and wondered if the crew would leave him alone for a measure to gain a few hours of sleep before he was wakened to serve his shift as lookout.

Zane turned to leave when the man's voice stopped him, "You're very angry, boy."

His back tightened like he could feel the man's eyes upon it.

And he didn't know why he admitted it, or why he cared to even respond in the first place. But Zane heard himself say, "Yes."

He left the belowdecks after that.

FIFTHLY,

The morning sun was blinding. Zane lay out over the crates, shielding his eyes with an arm until a shadow blocked the light. He peeled his lazy eyes open, bothered by the interruption, and a piece of half-rotted fruit hit his stomach.

He gawked and flew to sit up, growling a curse at Tigris, but did not find his rival when he dragged himself to his feet.

Sentra stared at him with her sleek black eyes, unblinking. The deck was mostly empty behind her, and Zane flexed his fingers as he considered how easy it would be to toss her overboard to face the octosiren lingering below the ship. Zane imagined the creature might grow impatient and bite out the ship's belly to sink it soon.

Sentra dared a glance at the snowseas, too. Zane prepared himself in case she struck. He would not go over the edge easy, and Sentra was no bigger than he was. But her glassy eyes shifted back to him—he suppressed the shiver crawling up his spine.

It was bloody impossible to tell what she was thinking behind those horrid black eyes.

"I'm here to warn you," she gargled.

Zane blinked, slow and doubtful. But the tightness in his limbs trickled away as he studied the enemy pirate. "Of what?" He was sure she was about to lie—all part of his mother's game.

"Your mother wants you dead. She's trying to kill you."

At that, Zane slackened, hardly believing her willingness to admit it. "I know," he said, cringing at that awful conversation he had overheard. He angled his head. "But why are you telling me? We're not friends."

But a dangerous smirk found her mouth. "No, Steelheart. You don't have any friends." Zane flinched as her finger came up to trace the buttons of his coat. "Tigris found your weakness, you know. It's how he was able to get your mother and crew to turn over your birthright."

Zane clenched his jaw and pretended not to care. "So?"

"So, you and I are the same. I'm horrid and mean and vengeful," she said. "And my spirit repels people. Perhaps you'd like to feed this crew to me and my father. Perhaps you'd like to donate this magnificent ship to our fleet and help me rule another crew at my father's side." She pursed her large lips. "Your mother is a cunning ashworm with her deals. But I know you can make deals, too."

Sentra's unusual eyes kept her from being truly beautiful, but she was confident, and for the first time, Zane saw it as something to be admired. Something he might use to hurt those who had wronged him—starting with his mother. And then Tigris.

"It is a sad day on the Winter snowseas when a mother turns on her own child," Sentra dropped her hand and levelled her onyx eyes on him again. "My father says we cannot trust someone willing to turn on their own offspring. It means they will turn on anyone if the price is right. And I'm inclined to agree."

"I could kill the octosiren," Zane considered. "I could win back the favour of my crew. Take them out from under my mother's rule."

But Sentra let out an unfeminine grunt. "Your mother fed you to that octosiren in the first place. If you can't admit that to yourself, Steelheart, maybe you deserve to die in that beautiful monster's jaws."

With that, the enemy pirate turned and sauntered over the sunlit deck, her layers of skirts fanning out with the sea wind. Zane rolled his eyes.

Only Sentra would consider the grotesque octosiren to be a *beautiful* thing.

"I'll be back in ten days plus one to hear your answer." She glanced back—a warning. "Don't go anywhere, Steelheart."

Zane's face changed. Was that a threat?

But she paused to stare up at the skies. "And those birds…" she grimaced. Zane glanced up, only now noticing how many white creatures circled above their ship. Some had landed on the rails—he hadn't noticed while he had been napping. Sentra's black eyes dropped back down to him curiously. "They're watching you," she stated.

Zane stared after Sentra until she moved to the edge of the boat and hopped off, her wide, dreadful wings ripping out from her back to take her over the snowseas, scaring some of those white birds away. He envied how easily the girl could come and go. And he imagined what a battle between his crew and hers would look like—with her crew able to fly and land on their deck at will.

He shook the thought from his mind and eyed the birds wreathing the pink skies as he stormed across the deck, deciding he did not care for sunshine anymore.

Bloody frostbitten Sentra. It seemed even she wanted to use him for something.

No marriage, then. It seemed he would not be forced to wed the enemy after all—but her price was his ship and crew. He was not sure he could stomach the idea, even after how they had turned on him. And he did not trust Sentra. She would probably kill him anyway.

"I can show you how to handle that," a voice like a river filled Zane's head and he snapped his eyes over to the middle-aged man—Mikal Migraithe.

The man rested on the bench in his cage. Zane looked around in surprise and tried to remember why he had come down here. "Your anger," Mikal clarified.

The man pinched a tiny white flower with a gold centre between his fingers—a fragile thing in comparison to his muscular frame. There were no flowers at sea apart from frostlillies. Zane might have asked how the man had come by it but assumed the old man was hiding garden pieces in one of the many pockets on his black jacket.

"I used to be angry, too," Mikal said, plucking the last few petals from the flower and dropping them into the pile already scattered over the floor.

Zane eyed him and allowed another step towards the cage doors. "How did you deal with it? How did you make your anger go away?" He could not help but notice that this old man radiated a sort of peace that was foreign to Zane—in the way the man spoke, and stared, and observed. It was all rather...*quiet*.

Finally, the man raised the petal-less flower, and pitched it to the floor where Zane's eyes followed it. "Verses." He brushed his hands clean of the flower's remains. "Wisdom," he then added.

Zane cocked a brow. "Wisdom?"

"I can teach you some, if you'd be willing to listen." Mikal's gaze flickered up.

But Zane only folded his arms. If the kohl lining his eyes was not evidence enough, he was sure the snarl upon his lips would be. "I have better things to do than listen to an old man ramble on about a thing or three."

At the *old man* comment, Mikal seemed to stifle a grunt, but he repositioned himself on the bench and leaned back against the bars of the cage. He appeared comfortable, even though nothing about the ship's cages were comfortable. Zane had been shoved in them plenty of times during the early seasons of his timestring when he disobeyed his mother, or broke a rule of the ship, or angered one of the bigger crewmates. He could never sleep on those damp, hard floors, especially with an empty stomach.

"What would you do if you could master your anger, pirate?" Mikal asked, folding his arms and displaying trained muscles.

Zane shifted his jaw back and forth, wondering why this man bothered to ask. No one ever asked him his reasons. No one bothered to ask him much about anything. "I would take back my ship," he decided. "I would win the affection of my crew."

"Do you *want* their affection?" The man drummed his fingers against his biceps.

Zane shrugged. "I suppose. I don't want to wind up dead or..."

Alone. That was the word he did not finish with.

Zane slammed his mouth shut, his eyes narrowing in on the prisoner that had already gone too far with his questions. Mikal raised his palms in his own defense. "I didn't ask you for your secrets, boy. I won't pry them from you. I wish to offer a solution to your anger. To see what you might do with the solution if I give it to you."

Zane did approach the cage now, hands curling around the bars as he stared down at the arrogant fool before him. He imagined how he could make this man suffer if he continued his little manipulative game of questioning. Zane could practically *hear* the man knocking against the steel coating his heart, trying to get in to destroy him.

"Secrets. Everyone wants my secrets," he muttered. "Even you, it seems."

At that, Mikal stood, but Zane did not cower or back away even though the old man could reach through the bars and grab him. "I don't want your secrets," he said again. "I will offer you verses at no cost to help you with your anger if you want them. That is all."

"That is all?" Zane mused, not believing it for a second. "You don't wish to make a deal for your freedom? You don't wish to trick me into letting you out?"

And the man sighed, much like he had done in the street when the silver-eyed boy had run his mouth. "In the early seasons of my timestring, I had a temper. I let it flare until I had driven away all my beloveds," he said. "So, I learned verses. I still recite them in my mind, even now. The wisdom keeps my heart steady."

For some bloody reason, Zane didn't think the old man was lying.

"I have my own ways to do that," he said, thinking of the books on his night table. Books he had kept hidden for all the seasons he had been collecting them, since Tigris would howl with laughter if he ever discovered Zane liked to read. "I suppose I study verses, too," he realized.

The man's interest piqued at that. "Is that so? Do you like books, then?" A funny smile tugged at the corner of his mouth even though he tried to suppress it—as though it stirred a hidden joke in his mind.

But Zane dropped his hands from the cage and took a step back.

A secret. The books were a *secret*. And this man had just dug it out of him—no magic or spells or visions of the future were even used.

"You're dangerous," Zane realized.

Mikal shrugged. "Some might say that. But not for the reasons you think."

"Who are you? And don't just tell me your name this time," Zane's hand padded along his hip for the grip of his cutlass.

"I'm the Commander of the Patrols," Mikal answered, and Zane felt the colour drain from his face.

He had heard of the Patrols—a legion raised by powers Zane knew little of. He had never met one, wasn't even sure they existed, until this moment. But confirming stories of the land folk was difficult when the Kelidestone spent most of its seasons on the dunes or far into the snowseas.

Mikal's face glimmered with a smile, his butter-gold beard glowing in the sunlight from the window. "Yes, boy. You can bet your scotcher we're as real as the ship below your boots. And I can show you how to become someone with honour. Unless you think you're better off with the bloodthirsty ashworms on this boat that want you dead."

Zane could not move now. He stared at the man with the golden hair and serene eyes, replaying again that moment in the street when the two others in black moved as a single unit in perfect agreement.

"You want to learn how to control your anger? You want to see what a real family looks like?" the man went on, and Zane found himself moving away until his back hit the wall. "Then come with me." Mikal's eyes sparkled—a light of their own— and Zane was sure he was dreaming it.

"Are you mad?" His own voice was high and wrong and... "You're my prisoner. You're not going anywhere, and neither am I. I'm going to be the bloody captain of this ship and you're going to shut your..." His voice trailed off as the man reached for the hooked staff that was leaning against the wall below the window.

"I told you I'm the Commander of the Patrols," Mikal said, studying his weapon for just a moment. "And you now know I'm dangerous." His topaz gaze flickered back up. "So, do you really believe I would have been taken by that flimsy crew if I didn't want to be?"

Zane's blood turned cold as the man tapped the heel of his staff against the cage door and it swung open, as though the lock had been picked hours ago.

The man—Mikal—walked out and came to tower over where Zane found himself shaking against the wall. His hands fumbled for his cutlass, and he drew it, holding it up towards the great man on his wobbling fish legs. "You're my..." Zane choked.

"Prisoner?" Mikal guessed. "Yes, yes." He waved a tired hand through the air and turned towards the stairs. "Time to go, boy."

Zane watched in dismay as the man climbed the stairs at his leisure until his black clothes disappeared through the door at the top.

Zane was frozen—a pillar of flesh and pumping blood in the ship's belly—until he snapped back into himself and raced up the stairs.

He could *not* let the prisoner get away. He whirled the cutlass in his grip, shaking out of his trance and reminding himself how to slash and destroy. He was a pirate. A bone-snapping, weed-eating pirate.

His mother's pale eyes would spill with disapproval if he lost her prized trading piece—and Tigris's cutting words would eat at him for days. The crew would abandon Zane if this man escaped; it did not matter that Zane was the one to capture him in the first place.

His colours burned red and angry in his chest as he realized he had been duped.

The sun blinded him when he plunged out onto the deck, but he skidded to a halt at the sight of his *entire* crew standing in defense, cutlasses drawn, staring at this one man with golden hair who looked back at them with a lethal gaze.

Zane eyed the man's back—right between his shoulder blades. He could sneak up behind him. He could—

"I wish to make a deal with the prophetess of this ship," Mikal's voice was a clean current; a symphony of wild nature. "And I'm in a bit of a hurry, if you all don't mind."

Zane's gaze fired over to where his mother swept down the stairs to the main deck, long black skirts gliding behind. Her cherry-red lips curled up as she looked Mikal over, likely deciding what she was going to do with him for his outrageous demand that she *hurry*.

"And what sort of deal would you like to make, Commander?" she purred.

Zane blinked. So, she knew then. She had seen what Mikal was when he was captured—somehow.

"I wish to fight your best pirate," Mikal said. "You choose who. And if I lose, I will bring you ten plus two troves of gold rings and fine pearls, which is everything I have to my name. A fair price, I imagine."

Zane cringed at the glistening in his mother's eyes. "And if you win?" it was a hungry whisper. She wanted to play his game, to prove her crew would crush him if she wished, and Zane knew then that this Mikal Migraithe was truly mad. Most knew better than to challenge a prophetess in the first place, let alone one as renowned across the snowseas as his mother.

"If I win," Mikal rolled the hooked staff back and forth against his palms like this was a dip of merry fun. He limped a step to keep his balance, agony etching between his brows even as he tried to stand tall.

Yes, certainly mad, then.

"If I win," Mikal said again, "I would like to leave this ship unharmed, firstly. And I would like Zane Cohen-Margus-Bowswither to leave with me if he wishes."

Zane's face paled. "What—"

But the prophetess's mocking laugh cut off Zane's question. "You have a deal," she snapped, and Zane staggered a step back, blood thickening to fire and ice.

The arrogance. The *confidence* in what she thought Zane would decide...that he would bow a knee before her if given the choice. The shock hit him in the gut—the same way it had when he realized his arm had been pricked to leak the smell of his blood into the water for the octosiren.

Not only was she willing to give him up for a chance at treasure, willing to bet away her own offspring, she had done it *easily*. Even after all this time, the fortune teller thought she had Zane pinned under her spell.

But she hadn't called him Steelheart all these seasons for nothing.

Mikal cast Zane a look of understanding, and perhaps sorrow. By his angle, the man's face was unseen by the rest of the crew. "Only if you want to, Son," he added, leaving the choice in Zane's hands.

But Zane stared.

Son?

A strange mixture rose in Zane's lungs and he could have sworn he felt cool violet creeping over the bleak shades of gray and fiery reds. His hand drifted to his chest and he rubbed it, testing the sensation he did not recognize.

It was *agonizing*. Truthful. Interesting...

When he glanced up, Mikal, along with the rest of the Kelidestone crew, waited with bated breath. His mother's pale eyes were sharp as fangs as she realized his hesitation. He wondered if she wished she could take back how quickly she had responded.

Steelheart, indeed.

For the first time in his timestring, Zane realized he could forget this crew he had tried so hard to keep, this mother who had tossed him away, and the soiled memories that came with them.

The two boys from the trio in the village filled his mind. Their faces had not been wicked or malicious or filled with bloodlust. They had been laughing because maybe...maybe they were happy.

"*Steelheart?*" The prophetess's tone was cold. Threatening. Demanding that he answer.

Zane glanced at the snowseas, the blazing sun above, the

crates of fish and rotting fruit and the spilling burlap bags of peppermint. Could he leave this?

Yes, he bloody well could.

"Do it," he breathed, eyes flickering to Mikal Migraithe. The man's staff stopped its spinning the moment the words were spoken.

Mikal cast him a small smile of agreement.

The prophetess was silent, for the first time in Zane's timestring. Poison filled her stare, pale eyes narrowing. "I choose Lother," she spat, the act of the sultry sea witch vanishing.

Lother. Because Lother was the most fearsome of the crew. Lother was the one who had taught Zane to seek, kill, and destroy, and Zane felt that new violet in his chest wither away to gray again. Zane had been trained right into the dirt and sea and sand, which was how he knew Lother was a pillar, not easily tipped over.

Zane pulled his shaking hands off his cutlass and clasped them together to watch. To witness his luck or lack thereof.

Lother sneered, dragging his hands to the barrel of spare cutlasses, not even testing them to select the best one.

Bloody overconfident ashworm.

Mikal waited as the prophetess slithered over the deck to extend her hand to seal the deal, the promise of rings and pearls dancing across her unlit eyes, and a spark of worry lingering in the corners that she could not quite hide. Mikal shook her hand, wincing at the stiffness in his arm as he raised it to do so, and Zane watched his fate be passed, just like that, into someone else's hands.

If Mikal won, Zane would leave. He was sure of it now as his mother's eyes settled on him from where she fidgeted across the deck after the impulsive deal she had made. She was a woman who was meant to see the future, who perhaps had not checked the future of *this* deal.

Lother was a giant in comparison to Mikal's aching, hunched frame as the two readied themselves. One of them would be dead soon and Zane felt a stone of regret sink through his stomach that he might witness this old man's death at the hands of his ruthless former teacher.

But everyone had always fought against Zane. No one had ever fought *for* him.

Until now. Until Mikal Migraithe.

SIXTHLY,

Lother prowled like a sea demon, sniffing the fear in the air as he rounded to the main deck's centre. Mikal waited until the pirate was ready—a respectable act considering no pirate would have granted him the same respect.

The scars along Lother's shoulders gleamed in the late morning sun as he slid off his coat and tossed it in a heap. He kept his violent yellow gaze on Mikal, certainly deciding how he might snap the middle-aged man's bones and wet the deck with his blood.

Zane found himself holding his breath. If Mikal lost to Lother, Zane would have a dreadful price to pay for the risk he had taken. Lashings at the very least. He might be thrown to the octosiren after all.

Finally, Mikal took a deep breath and marched to the centre of the deck to meet his foe, and Zane faltered at Mikal's walk. For, gone was the limp. Gone was the slow moving and stiffness, the weak muscles the old man had convinced everyone he had developed from the beating he'd taken as he was dragged onto the ship.

"Bloody ashworm," Zane whispered, and grinned.

Lother stopped his cutlass twirling, sizing up the man who appeared before him, who held out his staff at the ready and cast a polite smile as a cracking sound filled the air.

Frost and ice spiralled out the end of Mikal's tall cane, like a dozen silver blades.

And Zane found himself laughing, to his mother's disdain.

Lother snapped his cutlass across the space, attempting to get a slice in before Mikal was ready, but Mikal didn't seem the sort to be taken by surprise. He ducked like a youth, moved like a sputtlepun, and unleashed strikes like an ashworm taking its bite. Perhaps Mikal was not wrong when he claimed he was *not* old.

The dreadful dance was fast and cold and startling—pirate metal against ice and wood—until Lother's cutlass was slashed from his hand. The pirate's yellow eyes trailed his weapon and he gawked as the foot of Mikal's staff landed in his gut, sending him tipping flat onto the deck. Lother didn't scramble back in panic, though his eyes assured he wanted to; he remained steady for the killing blow Mikal would give.

But a dozen points of ice hovered at the pirate's throat, and Mikal's warm golden gaze flickered up to the prophetess who was a porcelain statue by the rail. She glared down at Lother, at her failed crewman.

"I think I win," Mikal's cool river's voice blanketed the tension on the deck.

Zane unclasped his hands and found his fingers grazing over his cutlass again; he didn't know why. Didn't know what he would do with it if he was compelled to draw it.

But his mother's dim gaze fired up to the middle-aged man —the man who was meant to be her prisoner.

"You don't win until he's dead," her voice cracked. "Finish it."

Crew members grumbled amongst themselves, unnerved by the command. But, Lother had failed her, so even if Mikal didn't finish the pirate, the prophetess would cast him to the sirens soon enough anyway. Zane wondered why the old man didn't just kill Lother and be done with it.

But Mikal stood tall and stared at the woman whose pecan hair fluttered in the sea breeze. He looked past her to where the shore was in view, close enough now to reach by rowboat. "I'll take my leave," he said, clear and certain.

But the prophetess smirked, those cruel red lips doing nothing to waver Mikal's attention. "My son does not belong to you unless you win, Commander."

Mikal bowed slightly and Zane's heart sank as he wondered if Mikal would agree. But the old man raised himself and a flit of fire burned in his golden eyes. "Your son does not *belong* to anyone. Not even you. The spells you've wound around his heart and soul have loosened, milady." The prophetess's face fell. "And don't try to spit those spells to keep me here, either. They won't work."

A crumpling sound filled the air and Zane's eyes flashed to the snowseas where a path of ice was forming from the coast. It raced over the rippling water like a white banner, reaching for the Kelidestone.

Zane's heart began to thunder with a sound he did not know his body could make. When he glanced at the old man, he realized Mikal was still. The path of ice over the snowseas was not being made by him.

"It's your decision, Son." Mikal's voice carried over the deck to Zane as the pirates began to stir. The crew looked to the prophetess to see what she would do, to discover their orders.

That pounding in Zane's chest grew to war drums as he looked to the beach and saw them—the army in black. There were dozens; their crow-black jackets sharp against the white snow on the shore. They had made the ice path. Mikal's allies.

Without another thought, Zane bolted. His breathing hitched as he stumbled down the stairs belowdecks, so riled he nearly missed the door to his own cabin. But he sprang back and tried to think, tried to sort through what he would need.

His belongings were few; his books, his bone dagger, his cutlass.

Zane's hands shook as he scraped what he could off the surfaces of his room into a burlap sack.

When he was finished, he turned for his door. He took one last deep, shuddering breath and looked around: the creaking walls, the tipping floor, the dirty window…The bad memories.

Perhaps he was not running away from it all.

Perhaps he was only running towards something else.

The sky seemed a heavier blue when he came back. Every crewmate on the Kelidestone had their weapons drawn. The air was tense and thick, and Zane looked from one crew mate to the next, then to his mother, who steamed like a burning ship in battle when she saw his satchel of belongings.

"Let's go," Zane heard himself say, dragging his gaze back to Mikal.

Though the ship was filled with enemies, the old man did not look afraid. A knowing smile warmed his face and he nodded, extending a hand. "To land, then."

Zane took the man's hand, not caring if those watching thought it unusual or weak. Mikal hopped onto the rail and Zane followed, and only then did he realize why he would need the old man's grip: for balance.

A long icy slide lay before them, down to the snowseas. Zane's chest tightened at the thought of that ice snapping, of finding himself in the water and being snatched up by the octosiren still waiting in the depths.

But Mikal didn't give him a measure more to debate. The old man pulled him onto the rink and Zane's stomach leapt as they slid down the slope. He nearly screamed at how fast they moved—certain he would never slide over ice and snow like this again if given the choice.

A few in black had come to meet them; they were halfway across the bridge when Zane overheard his mother's growling voice from the Kelidestone, "Do it! Kill him!"

"But the *deal*—" It was Tigris, of all mates, who protested.

"I agreed not to kill the Commander. I said nothing of *Steelheart!*"

Zane's blood ran cold as her furious growl roared over the snowseas. He did not have time to spin before the golden trident she hurled into a deadly spiral reached him.

But the trident did not spear through his chest. Zane turned to find three wooden hooks before his face, all snatching that trident from the air and holding it in place before it met its mark.

He blinked at the staffs; Mikal's was not even one of them.

"Ragnashuck, she has good aim," one of them muttered, and Zane looked to find the silver-eyed boy at his side, gripping one of those staffs holding his mother's heartless blow. "Maybe *she'd* like to join us," he added with a grin to the others, all of whom chuckled—a sound that hit the colours in Zane's chest with a burst.

They dropped the trident onto the bridge and Mikal used his heel to nudge the gilded weapon into the snowseas where Zane watched it sink and sink and sink.

A shuffle of white and silver appeared in his peripheral vision. The birds—those same ones that had been circling above his ship—spiralled towards the Kelidestone. They landed on the rail, building a wall of white feathers between the boys in black and the crew of the ship, staring at those on board with narrowed, beady eyes.

It was the most absurd thing Zane had ever bloody seen.

The silver-eyed boy snorted. "Those pesky critters seem to

like *you*," he said to Zane on his way by as he headed down the bridge.

"If you were nicer to them, Nicholas, they'd like you to," another boy spoke up as he followed—Posineon. The other boy from the street; his shoulder was wrapped in bandages now.

And the last boy was not a boy at all, but a girl, Zane realized. Uneven stems of choppy, light hair stuck out from the hat wrapping her head. Her eyes were large and fishlike, and when her gaze slid to Zane, she smiled to reveal a set of crooked teeth. Zane glanced away.

"Wanda, at least *try* not to scare the pirate-boy," Posineon called back at her, and she grunted.

"What's your name anyway?" the silver-eyed boy yelled from where he twirled his hooked staff with long, slender fingers. His grin was a pinch wild, and those white teeth glimmered as much as the snowy shores behind him.

Zane opened his mouth, but paused. There was a river of blood on his name, and so much of that name belonged to the woman who had just wanted to see him die, and a man he had barely known who had left him with that woman.

"Steelheart," he decided.

At that, the boy, Nicholas, stopped walking and cocked a doubtful brow. Then he rolled his eyes. "Don't be so *dramatic*, Pirate," he said, turning back to the shore. "Giving yourself a nickname like a circus clown," he shook his head. "Who does that?"

But it did not sound like a true mockery, perhaps an invitation to share his real name whenever he decided the time was right.

Zane glanced once more at the Kelidestone where the birds held their barrier of beaks aimed the other way. For the first time since Mikal had struck the deal, Zane did not feel afraid to turn his back on the ship. To that woman who called herself his mother. To those titles and labels he had carried for all his seasons.

He swivelled on the ice and trotted after the boys in black, Mikal following close behind. The old man *slid* over the ice on his heels, his staff gliding along behind him as though it were the force moving him forward.

Fresh snow sparkled the shore, blanketing the land in white where the rest of Patrol waited. Two of them didn't carry a staff like the others, and in place of the pure black garments, they wore white coats lined with silver threads.

Though the boys in black began hiking up the snowy hill, using their staffs to force the snow to part before them, one of the boys in white remained.

He was young. Messy light-blond hair swept over his head, not quite as tidy as the impressive coat he wore. The boy was no older than Zane by the looks of it; not as old as any of the others in the group. He had a funny smile that blended warmth and cunning—like Mikal's.

The odd boy extended a gloved hand towards Zane, who stopped at the very line where the sea met the snow. All the others, including Mikal, journeyed up the beach, but it seemed this boy was in no rush to catch up.

"I'm Thomas," he said.

Zane studied the hand, looking for a threat. Waiting for the boy to spew a harsh word or three to claim his territory among this group.

But the boy's smile only widened, reaching his bronze eyes. "Ragnashuck, you're going to be trouble, aren't you?" He studied Zane's worn clothes, the torn sleeves, the skull and frostlilly tattoo, the kohl ringing his eyes. "What's your name, Pirate?"

Zane wasn't sure why this boy had a different spirit than the others, why the twinkle of mischief in his bronze eyes told tales and held promises of devilish fun in the future.

Zane found himself raising his hand to shake the boy's —Thomas.

His name was Thomas.

"I'm Zane Cohen-Margus-Bowswither," he heard himself say.

The boy scowled. "Well, ragnashuck, I'll never remember all that. Can I just call you Zane Cohen? Half a name is easier than a whole one like *that*."

A true smile came out, and Zane folded his arms. "Alright," he agreed. "And to answer your question, yes. I imagine I'm going to be all sorts of bloody trouble for your merry scotchers."

Thomas bellowed a laugh, a *real* laugh that made the colours in Zane's chest glow.

SECOND-TO-LASTLY,

The snowseas had never felt so cold and empty. The octosiren paced the waters, abandoning its lair from sunset to sunrise, searching for him: for the boy with blood as sweet as mint and sap, and as vibrant as the magic of the ancient Winter woods.

He was not like the others—that boy who had bartered and bantered, and had reeked of desire to be playful and young. The others always smelled of salt and sea and sails and greed. Of dirty metal swords and violence.

The orange and bloodred surface of the snowseas shattered when something plunged into the waters, disrupting its near silence.

But it was not the boy who returned. It was not the mint blood it smelled, but an icy will and the dark, sticky blood of sin.

Pecan-brown hair drifted around the woman as she descended like a hunting siren, lovely and pale-eyed. She hovered in the seas before the octosiren, who let its grin slide open so she might witness the sheer length and atrocity of its teeth.

You are not as afraid of me as you should be, Prophetess, the octosiren warned.

The woman tilted her head—a predator herself in a way.

I've come to strike a deal, her mind's voice carried on the current.

But the octosiren's smile only grew. *I see.*

The creature began to slide, moving around in idle circles where the prophetess floated in grace. *But I've already made a deal. With the boy you sent me: your son.*

That boy is not my son. Not anymore.

Shame. I rather liked him. He smelled of dreams and promise. The octosiren paused, then added, *And he smelled of an animal locked in a cage for too long.*

The prophetess's lip curled into a snarl. *You will bring him to me when you catch him*, she said. *That is the deal I wish to make. He will return here in the future, during a time when the stakes will be quite high for him. Once you catch him, I want him delivered to me.*

The octosiren considered this. *How interesting*, it said. *I suppose I can barter another deal, in addition to the one the boy made with me. I rather liked his deal.* Another long smile, and the prophetess's face changed.

What did he offer you? Worry slipped into her silent tone.

Your riches. The octosiren's slit eyes travelled up to the surface where the Kelidestone's belly coasted through the patch of iceless waters. *He showed me the precise spot where I must bite through your ship to have them. He negotiated my patience —that I would have to wait until you came down here to barter. And now that you have arrived, my lust for gold shall be satisfied.*

He...what...? The prophetess whirled back to her boat, to her home, to her rings...*Why would he tell you to bloody wait for me to come to you?!*

So that you might watch. The octosiren's roaring laugh rippled through the waters as it spiralled once to gain speed, and punched through the bottom of the ship, spilling away timber and supplies, jewellery and rubies.

The prophetess screeched a mouthful of cold water as the ship groaned and teetered, her life's work leaking from the Kelidestone's broken guts in a river of gold rings and black pearls.

Though the sight of the monster gobbling down her riches was more than she could behold without a shudder of rage and an underwater scream, the prophetess felt a tug of admiration in the corner of her spirit for the boy who had sold out her troves of treasure for his own survival. Who had discovered a way to harden his heart from her for all his seasons, and who had abandoned her in the end.

He was a bloody clever boy.

AUTHOR'S NOTE

Follow Zane's story in *A Soul as Cold as Frost* (Book #1 of *The Winter Souls Series*)
By Jennifer Kropf

3
THE KELPIE OF LOCH LINNHE
ALICE IVINYA

Enchanted Waters

THE KELPIE OF LOCH LINNHE

The mist crept out of the shivering waters of the loch. It coated the rocky shore and hugged the ankles of the barren hills, swirling back in on itself. Above, the clouds heaved their wet underbellies over the summits and drained the world to grey.

The knight sighed. He'd been hoping to catch some food before dusk, but now the mist hid the tracks in the soggy ground and the chill would be driving any prey to hide away. It was going to be a hungry, cold night. The day had been full of bad luck.

He stopped and cocked his head, listening. A few high notes, weak as spider thread, sounded on the breeze. Transfixed, he followed the sound towards the shore until a woman's clear voice echoed words through the hills. The song was sad and spoke of heartbreak and heather and the sea tide.

Perched above the fog, the knight made out a figure. She was sitting on a rock facing the loch and hadn't heard his approach. Her clothes were dry but her dark hair was wet and long and tangled. She must have been swimming in the loch alone. She was combing her hair with pale fingers.

He stopped on the edge of the shore, stones crunching

beneath his boots. "Hullo there, lass," he called, not meaning to startle her.

She jumped and turned. When she saw the man alone, she stood and took a few steps back, stumbling on the pebbles. He saw her eyes were red from tears, but her face was still very lovely.

He held up his palms to calm her. "There, there, lass. Ah mean ye no harm. Ah'm the Laird of Appin's man. He sent me here to aid folk." The girl cocked her head slightly but still looked nervous. Her fingers gripped a string of green sea urchin shells around her neck. The knight took a crunching step towards her, arms outstretched in peace. "Whit dae they cry ye?"

"Ailie," the girl murmured. Then louder, "Ma name's Ailie." She looked so delicate, she could fade away with the mist.

"Tis a bonnie name." The knight smiled. "Ah wondered if ye could aid me? Ah've been sent to look into why folk been disappearin' hereaboot. Four in one month, the Laird was told. Ye ken any folk?"

The girl shook her head and lake water speckled the mist around her feet. "If ye from the Laird of Appin, where's ye horse?" she called, bolder now.

"The wee brute scarpered back there. Something spooked him. Ah'm fair scunnered." He gestured to the top of the darkening valley behind him. "Have ye seen him?"

The girl took a step forward and her eyes widened. "Naw but ma horse did the same. Ah only went for a wee swim and something scared her off. Maw is going to get fair het up, and now the weather is bad, and it's a far way home through the mist."

The knight walked up to the girl and put a hand on her shoulder. She looked up at him with big dark eyes. "Now, lass. Don't ye go cryin'. We'll find ye horse and get ye home. Where ye fae?"

"Onich, yonder. Thank ye, sir." She smiled up at him with relief and he noticed her lips were tinged blue from cold. "Do ye think there be wolves about?"

"Come now, lass, don't fret. Let's get ye going. Ah'll keep ye safe." He gestured for her to lead the way and she set off across the pebbles of the shoreline. Her hair, still wet and matted, swung as she nimbly crossed over rocks slippery with red seaweed, that lurked in the mist. The knight found himself admiring her grace and lithe figure. "What's ye horse look like?" he called after her.

"She's a dapple grey. Bonnie she is. She belongs to the Laird. Ma paw borrows her for his field. Ah dinnae ken her well, but she ne'er did bolt before."

"Ah'll keep an eye out as ah'll keep an eye out for mine." He gazed around the silent shore, and saw no movement and heard no whinny. He scratched his head. "I dinnae ken what made them act so."

They continued in silence as the mist thickened, dancing around their ankles, then waists. He wished the girl would sing again to lift his mood, but didn't want to ask. The clouds darkened until the knight was sure the shrouded sun had sunk far below the hills. He gathered his plaid tighter around himself as a chill shivered up his bare legs. He'd never minded the wet, but cold was another matter. The girl turned and looked at him, the mist hugging her skirts, and gave him such a smile. He grinned back and hoped the horse would appear before it got any darker. His gaze turned to the still waters of the loch, almost hidden by fog. The girl was mad to swim alone, though it had been bright enough this morning.

"What folk have gone missing?" asked the girl over her shoulder. She didn't seem to feel the chill.

"Three lads and a lass. All young and healthy. Naw reason for them to have got into trouble. Ye shouldn't be wanderin' around abee. Tis dangerous."

The girl shrugged. "Ah felt safe enough on ma horse. And ah got ye now. The road to Onich is just further along the shore. Ye welcome to stay with ma maw and paw tonight for will be dark by the time we get there. Tis very good of ye t' walk me home. They won't mind."

The knight nodded in thanks then stopped as he noticed movement further inland. A copse of hawthorn and rowan, heavy with violent red berries, splashed colour through the mist. Behind them a tail swished and a foot stamped the ground.

"Lass, lass!" he called. "Look! A horse!"

The girl looked up and scrambled towards the beast, calling a name. The horse gave a sharp whinny in reply and glided from the bushes. She was tall, elegant and pale grey as if she had solidified from the mist. Her mane and bridle were wet and tangled with dark red seaweed. Her eyes were wild, but she came eagerly enough.

"Looks like she went for a wee swim an aw, lass," called the knight, relieved the horse had appeared. They were running out of time.

The girl pulled the mare beside a boulder and clambered on her back. The mare kept still, her head lowered and her wild mane hiding her face. The girl happily arranged her skirts and slipped her feet into the dripping stirrups. "She ain't normally so good. She scant ken me, so she'd be fine with ye an aw. Come up and ride." She held out her hand.

The knight shook his head. "Naw lass, ah'll lead her so she cannae bolt agen. She's too fine a beast for the likes o' me."

He flicked the sodden reins over the horse's head, pulling some dark orange seaweed free, and led her to where the pebbles turned to boulder strewn grass. The fog was thick now and it was hard to see the girl perched high on the mare's back behind him. A burst of unseen birds leapt from the rocks nearby and scattered noisy shadows around them. The mare threw her beautiful head up and her forefeet left the ground for a stride. He kept his grip and mumbled to the beast to be patient. They would be home eating supper before too long.

The girl leaned forward until her fingertips grazed his shoulder. "Do come up behind me, sir. We'll go quicker, and it cannae be easy walking athort these rocks in the mist."

"Aye lass, but if she bolts agen — would be treacherous. And anyway, it ain't proper for me t' ride behind an unwed lass like yerself."

The girl sat back and the knight led her steed faster. The horse chomped at her bridle, foaming around the bit. Her ears flicked back and forth and her tail swished with agitation. When the knight looked he could see there was something unusual about her teeth.

"There's a river soon, sir," said the girl. Her high pitched voice was almost disembodied behind him. "Tis not deep but flows fair fast. If ye wade ye will be drookit and cold if ye don't ride with me. Ah dinnae mind, and she's strong enough for both o' us."

"Aye lass, ah can hear it ahead. Don't ye worry 'bout me. Ah don't mind a wee bit of wet. Ah'd rather keep ye safe. Tis ma job."

The girl leaned forward over the mare's neck and her face was pleading. Her wet hair hung to the mare's sternum. "Ah'll feel more safe riding with ye behind me."

The knight merely gave her a confident smile to rest her

fears. The sound of running water bubbled ahead, and the shore sloped downwards so their feet sent pebbles tumbling into the whiteness. The horse became more agitated and the knight tightened his grip on the reins. "Easy lass," he whispered. "Aamaist home."

The river emerged as a dark channel cutting through the fog. The knight unlaced his shoes with one hand while still holding the reins of the impatient mare.

"Sir," said the girl in a strange tone of voice. "Something ain't right. Ah... ah don't think this is ma horse."

"What d'ye mean, lass?"

"Tis hard t' see in the mist but... ma horse had strands of black in her mane. This mane's aa white."

"Ah, don't ye worry. The light and the mist plays tricks as ye say. And her mane is aa tangled with weeds."

"Ah dinnae ken, sir. Ah think she's paler an aw." Her voice was soft with fear.

"Come now, lass. Don't let fancies take ye."

He took a step into the water and felt the insistent tug of the current. The horse became wilder as her hooves struck water, foam flying from her lips. She took a few dancing steps into the river and started to prance and buck. Her beautiful long limbs flew through the mist. The knight stood still and silent to calm her. The tugging of the current became stronger, willing for him to give in.

"There, there, lass," he spoke to the horse. "Just let me sort out ye bridle." He raised his voice. "Are ye aaricht up there, lass?"

The girl's voice was small. "Ah'm holding on, but ah'd be much less scared if ye sat behind me. Please, sir. Something ain't right. She don't feel right."

"She's just spooked and spirited, 'tis all."

He reached up to the buckle behind the horse's eye and quickly unfastened it. With one fluid motion he pulled the bridle from the horse's head and freed the bit from her long, curved canines. "Off ye go home, lass," he grinned at her.

The horse reared and leapt, shooting spray up around her. The girl screamed, clinging to her mane. The kelpie sped down the river with impossible speed, the mist fleeing from her path, until she thundered into the vast expanse of the loch. The depths swallowed them both.

The waters eddied and swirled, then were mirror-still. The mist crept back over as if it had never been disturbed.

The knight smiled and stretched his back. The hunt was over. Maybe tonight he wouldn't be so hungry after all.

He unwound his plaid and tugged off his tunic, folding them neatly on a high rock, and placed his boots on top. He splashed back into the river. The current tugged and tugged, stronger and stronger. He gave in, letting his true form burst free and rearing his hooves to the sky with a cry of triumph. The kelpie galloped through the water to join his companion in the loch for their dinner.

AUTHOR'S NOTE

For more YA fantasy and fairytale inspired stories by Alice Ivinya, why not check out Feathers of Snow? Available on amazon.

4
THE BRIDGE
BEN LANG

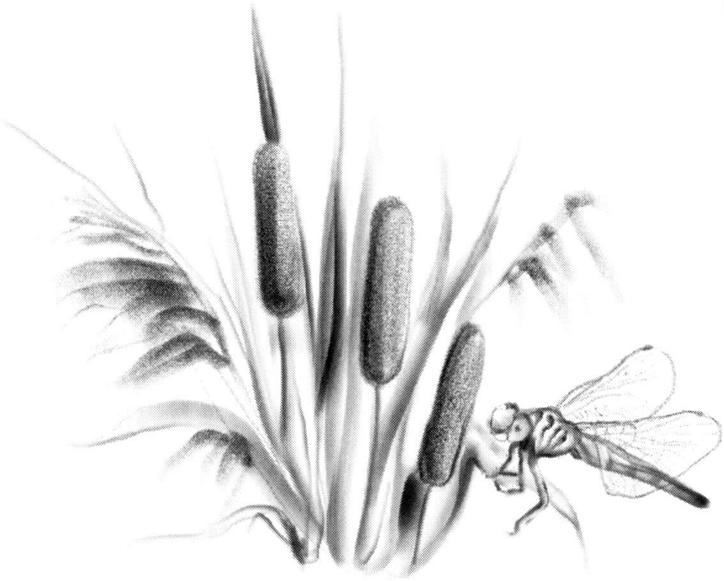

THE BRIDGE

They met at the edge of the river.

The monsoons had come and gone, so the river no longer overran its banks but flowed fat between the trees.

The young woman had walked from home to wash her clothes. The warrior-pilgrim had stopped to water his elephant and fill his canteen.

She was knelt on the bank, rubbing at her prized, pink dress. She made such a splash that the first she saw of the other was his elephant passing around her to drink. The proximity of the beast startled her such that the dress escaped and ran into the river's current.

With warrior's reflexes the stranger saved the dress with the handle end of his weapon-rake.

"I am sorry to startle you, good lady," he apologised, returning her dress.

The woman stared hard at the stranger. She saw his great elephant mount, pale almost to white. She saw his weapons; a battle-rake in his hands and several other polearms in the elephant's harness. She saw his yellow sash, the sign of a preacher. Her vision was sharp, and, despite its subtle character, she saw the eyelid in the centre of his forehead where he hid his third eye. The unmistakable sign of enlightenment.

"It is no worry at all, pilgrim," she replied with a polite bob of the head. She asked where he was travelling.

He patted the flank of his drinking elephant absent-mindedly while pondering the question. The elephant, apparently oblivious, slurped from the river through its trunk.

"I am just passing through" he eventually answered, evading the question. "Once my elephant is watered, my canteen filled, and my mahout repaired I will be on my way. That will be before an hour is gone."

"My name is Senieta. It is my sister's wedding this evening," said the woman, "If you could stay just the one night to bless her marriage it would be a great honour. There is food to be had; a wedding feast. It must be far better than your travel provisions."

The stranger thought long in silence. Then he asked, "If it is her wedding this evening, why do you wash your dress now? It will still be wet."

"Because the river people always carry out weddings sodden from head downwards and standing in water. This is such a wedding." Senieta herself was obviously not a river person: her eyes were hazel, not blue and despite being wet from washing, her hands had not become green or webbed. By way of explanation she added, "It is my step-sister's wedding." She felt a flush of shame as the words escaped; that river people were related to Senieta by marriage still mortified her.

The stranger mused only a moment longer before agreeing to the invitation. She led him and his mount into the jungle, along the path to the village of the river people. They passed under the familiar trees, but at the familiar, old bridge the strange warrior drew to a stop.

Senieta turned back to see what was the matter.

"This bridge should be cleansed" the stranger said, gesturing. "A Shido has taken it. Do you know what that means?"

She shook her head.

"A Shido is a lesser spirit, a malevolent creature. They take control of a bridge, or sometimes a doorway or step of a stair. Then they take a toll in lifespan from each person or creature to pass. Every crossing of this bridge costs a few weeks of youth."

Senieta was aghast. "But I must have crossed this bridge several dozen times! Am I going to age prematurely?"

"A little, and much more if you continue to use the bridge without cleansing it" he replied with a nod. He then led them around the bridge, gesturing for her to mount the elephant to ford the river nearby. As he helped her to mount the beast she was shocked to find a clay statue lying on top of it. Human shaped, and almost life sized.

"Just sit here" he indicated a part of the elephant's shoulder.

"What is this?" Senieta asked of the clay statue.

"It is my mahout, usually it drives the elephant." he answered, pulling himself up onto his mount. "It was damaged by the hot sun of the last days; it has dried out too much to move without cracking. I can repair it with water and mud, I will do so in the morning. The important thing is that bridge. You must cleanse it as soon as you can; tomorrow."

"How?" she replied.

As the elephant carried them over the water, he told her how to cleanse the bridge.

"First, a new broom should be made from dried branches - any wood will do. Second, a rope should be laid across the river, downstream from the bridge. Third, the broom should be used to sweep the bridge. It does not matter if there is actually any dust to sweep or how effective the clean is. All that matters is that every part of the walking surface is swept over with the broom and that the broom has never previously been used.

"Once the bridge has been swept entirely the rope should be collected and burned to ash."

As they dismounted on the other bank, Senieta reflected that it was fortunate the Shido had possessed *this* bridge. It was true and stone, presumably of importance in some ancient time. But now it served only a niche purpose; it was the way from Senieta's family farm and their neighbours to the village of the river people.

It was widely said the river people were frog-like monsters in human guise, that their touch corrupted the water and made the crops fail. Even that they kidnapped children for their stews. Senieta herself, not one to forego gossip or grim speculation, had sometimes been the one to say it. *Real* people rarely visited river people nor vice versa. Hence this barely-used remnant in a land criss-crossed with bridges, all others carrying more traffic.

At length they reached the place of the wedding. On the banks of the tributary stood tables, food, drinks and cookfires. In the shallow stream itself was the altar for the ceremony.

The pilgrim's arrival was cause for great excitement. Children dared one another to touch his elephant, while adults practically queued to seek the preacher's blessing. The only one disappointed to see him was the priest of the river people. He had just finished painting an eye on his forehead for the ceremony. He washed it off and sulked on seeing the true three-eye arrive.

Icy stares and unstated disapproval - this surely, was how Senieta would have been received. But by bringing the holy preacher she had dulled the sharp reception. The welcome she received was neither hostile, nor friendly.

Glares and silence were now familiar staples to poor Senieta. It had started a year earlier, when her father had been seduced, or maybe bewitched, by a river lady. From the moment they were a couple Senieta's social life had died. Her friends all still lived, but behind a wall of stigma. They would not talk kindly, eye contact they avoided. The barrier was social in nature, but as impervious as thick stone. Recently, in lonely desperation, Senieta had sought contact with the river people instead, but here she found a similar obstacle. To her own people she was a consort to frog-monsters, to the river people she was an outsider.

Even her relationship with father had soured. How many times had she shouted at him that his new romance would ruin them? How many times had she screamed that he was endangering her own engagement? But he had not cared, the foolish, selfish man. And now her beloved fiancé had broken off their engagement while her friends ignored her.

Her father was content with his new wife. He barely seemed to care that his neighbours would not speak to him. But Senieta had no one amongst the river people she could speak to, even if she had fully wanted it. Even her adoptive step-mother seemed disinterested.

By bringing the pilgrim here she had hoped to make her way into their circles and finally end her year of loneliness.

She was shocked from her musings by a frightful sight. A man, ordinary enough looking, had lifted a bucket to dowse himself, and had been replaced with an amphibian creature. Green, with webbed fingers and toes. Froglike, hideous. Senieta's breath caught, her hairs stood on end, and her every instinct was to run and hide.

She stayed, but he was only the first. Soon all the guests stood sodden and ankle-deep. Senieta, her father and the pilgrim alone were human. All others reverted to their true forms for the wedding. Skin: green, fingers: webbed, eyes: bulbous. Their faces twisted and monstrous.

Senieta had seen her step-mother's hands turn green and webbed occasionally when they washed dishes together, but she had never before seen a person turn entirely into a monster. With the local priest sulking, the pilgrim blessed the couple and conducted the ceremony, before a standing crowd of frogmen. Senieta stood with crossed arms and darted her fearful, suspicious eyes about whenever one of the monsters that stood about her moved. Through the whole ceremony she stood alert and on edge.

Later, on the banks, was food and drink aplenty.

Resuming their human shapes the guests danced to joyous music or sat at long tables to eat. The preacher watched carefully as his elephant lifted laughing children with its trunk. But while others revelled, Senieta sat quiet at the edge. She was traumatised, or something like it. Frozen still in her chair while inside she lurched between terror, revulsion and hate.

She had hoped to build bridges by bringing the preacher. It was unfortunate that this plan had succeeded on the same day she saw their true forms. She had seen *them* for the first time. Surrounded by monsters, she realised they could never be her friends. They should not even have been allowed to live near *real* people.

While the evening's merriment and feasting buzzed around her, Senieta sat alone in the company of her dark thoughts.

The next day the pilgrim repaired his clay mahout at the river's bank, then rode west on his secretive quest. Before he was fully lost to the forest, Senieta set out to make a new broom.

It took only the morning to make a broom, but when it was completed Senieta set it aside. She would not visit the bridge until night when she could be sure of not being seen.

Under cover of darkness, with a rope under one arm and the broom under the other, she set out to the bridge of the Shido. Her plan was simple and possibly desperate. But she reassured herself that it was, fundamentally, risk-free. If she had made any false assumptions she could resort to simply following the preacher's exact instructions.

"Shido! Shido!" she called, standing on the bridge. "Shido! Shido! I know you have taken this bridge. The pilgrim with three eyes saw you and pointed you out! You are undone, I am here with a new broom and a rope for you!"

"But I can spare you," she said into the night. "What can you offer in exchange for being left alive? Being spared?"

"LIFE," came a whisper from the darkness. "I can offer life. I can give a share of my takings."

"What share?" called out Senieta. "If you offer less than half I shall destroy you now."

"Half then," whispered the surrounding night.

"An excellent place to begin the haggling," replied Senieta with a manic smile.

Once a deal was made, and the Shido had promised to give two-thirds of all its tolls to Senieta, she moved on to the second part of her plan.

"Shido, the village downriver is populated with monsters: river people. They are frog-newts, terrible and clearly evil. In the centre of their village is a bridge, which they cross back and forth many times each day. If I sweep this bridge clean, but leave no rope to catch you downstream, will you wash downriver and take control of this bridge in their village?"

"Yes," replied the dark. "Yes. But I do not wish it. I have no need of more than a day of life per day to sustain myself, and, despite your bargaining, you have no need for more than that either. This bridge is crossed most weeks, and each dry season a caravan passes. That is sufficient for sustenance."

"Sustenance is not vengeance," shrugged Senieta as she began to sweep the helpless Shido downriver.

The next year was a thrill for Senieta. She had never before chosen a course of action that could have real consequences before. Her whole life prior, she had followed the flow of things. The thrill of action soon gave way to the dizzying thrill of power, as some of the river people (those who commonly crossed the bridge) began to age, sicken and die. When the first funeral procession was held, Senieta laughed so hard her ribs ached. The entire village crossed the bridge *twice*, the first procession to the shrine where the corpse was embalmed, then a second procession to the sacred place where the mummified body was released to the river.

As time passed it became obvious to the river people that some evil had befallen them. They burned offerings in their temple, they cursed the memory of the travelling pilgrim who seemed to have brought the curse. They begged for help as they rapidly grew old and died.

Senieta was not the only one enjoying herself. While they still shunned Senieta herself, her people, the real humans, watched the demise of their neighbours, the river people, with a mixture of feelings. As they themselves were unhurt by the blight, most of them decided that it was some kind of punishment and therefore deserved. A few were more sympathetic, but never in public.

Senieta's father soon perished. She decided she did not much care, since he had ruined so much for her by marrying into the frogs. Her eyes briefly betrayed her one night, but she suppressed it and she was genuinely pleased when her step-mother expired.

What was left of the river people fled only a few months after.

The year that followed was dull and sad by comparison. Senieta still had no friends, no one to talk to, and her ex-fiancé was now married to someone who had once been a close friend. She maintained her farm, and people were willing to reluctantly trade with her for her needs. She no longer felt the thrill of secret power, as it was no longer in use.

She had hoped that killing or driving away the river people might have made her own people forgive her. Instead, they had just as much hate to channel as ever and she was the only associate of the river people remaining to direct it against.

The pilgrim was over two years gone when she was attacked. She was in the village to sell some of her produce and procure goods. As she bartered for salt she was struck by a stone, thrown by a child. The smirking gang of children fled at her gaze, laughing and shouting at having hit the frog-witch. She gave chase, which immediately proved to be the wrong move as the agile children evaded her, laughing with delight at the sport.

No one intervened. Most just pretended to have not noticed. Some seemed to find it amusing and smiled small smiles.

That evening she went upriver to the bridge in the abandoned village of the river people. She carried a new broom under one arm, but did not even bring a rope this time.

By a great stroke of fortune, the bridge through her hometown was the very next downriver.

As she worked, the surrounding dark spoke to her. "It is far too soon! Wait a century at least, please! We have all we need for now and much longer. There are only so many bridges before the sea. It is wiser to play the long game, perhaps a family will make home near these ruins. There is no need to keep moving so soon. Moving too fast could bring attention."

She had nothing to say in reply, so simply did her sweeping.

This second act of vengeance was as sweet as the first. She watched the old friend who stole her husband grow old and ugly. She watched some of the children who'd thrown stones wither like old men. They grew strange indeed, child-sized with elderly complexions, wrinkled skin and weak limbs.

She was unable to watch as closely as she would have liked,

as rumours of witchcraft were enough to place her in some danger. It was odd, but Senieta, fearing accusations of witchcraft, took pains to keep herself unnoticed and far from town. Other women, with nothing to hide, continued to act as normal and thus drew the undeserved attention of panicking men. Much to Senieta's amusement two other women were blamed for the curse of ageing and burned as witches.

This village too was abandoned, and so ended Senieta's second game.

More years passed. Living alone proved very difficult. Senieta had to make long journeys to trade for necessities like tools. When Senieta's neighbours had fled the mysterious curse, they had carried with them rumours of her, so that even in these distant villages people were fearful and distrustful. They seemed to think *she* was a river person. It occurred to her at this time, that she could have simply travelled to one of these places long ago. If she had not destroyed her home, its inhabitants would not have fled with their poisoned rumours about her. She could have maybe found a husband and had children. She was still in the prime of her youth after all and probably would be for a great many years.

But she had not. So instead she was forced to work hard alone at her farm. Forced to travel long distances to replace damaged tools or sell surpluses.

She met him on the road, while her mule carried her cart to market. He was taking the path west, riding a black warhorse with mad red eyes. This man had no third eye or preacher's yellow. He wore sturdy armour and carried a sword and lance. He was young, handsome, and his eyes gleamed with barely-tamed violence.

She too was passing west, and as he drew level to overtake

he spoke first. "Is this land truly so safe that husbands allow such beautiful wives to travel unaccompanied?"

Excited by the compliment and possible flirtation she responded to make clear she had no husband.

He slowed to match the pace of her mule. He asked about the reasons for her journey.

"My farm is far from the closest village, so I must travel to sell and buy," she replied.

"I know very little of farming." The stranger scratched his nose. "Why is it I do not see more people travelling for this purpose?"

She cautiously answered that most farmers lived close to a village.

They spoke for the rest of the day, although little of substance was said. They were attracted to one another but both were cagey and gave little information to the other. He did tell her his name was Khajar.

Come evening they arrived at the village that Senieta had set out for. Her plan had been to sleep beneath her cart, then attend the market day the next morning before heading home. However Khajar insisted on rooms for them both from the man who let his spare rooms, this being the closest thing to an inn in the village. The kindness of the offering caught her off guard, but she was still disappointed that it was two separate rooms.

The evening was warm, and the night before market day was often a night where people would drink, eat and dance under the stars in the village square. The strange man passing through, clearly a warrior, drew many stares and much attention, but Senieta's presence with him caused some apprehension. She noticed one person whisper to him, no doubt warning him of her supposed frog-hood or witch-ness.

She bit her finger and worried that these rumours might drive him away from her.

There were players to make music for the dance. The musicians played a short burst of chords to summon any stragglers, and one stood to make some welcoming address to those gathered.

But, before he could speak Khajar stood up on the stage and waved at the crowd.

"A moment of your time, good people, before we dance. Just a short moment of your time, if you will indulge me. I am seeking a warrior who passed through this land about ten years ago."

"Ten years ago?" shouted someone incredulously.

"You would remember him had you seen him," Khajar assured. "He rode an elephant, wore the yellow of a preacher, and had the third eye of enlightenment. His mahout was shaped of living clay. He might have been travelling in a hurry, so possibly didn't stop for provisions or seek out contact with people."

The crowd were greatly surprised to hear that the strangest man they had ever seen was searching for a man even stranger than himself. None of them had seen this elephant-riding preacher. It seemed that, after attending the wedding of the river people, the mysterious traveler had ridden on west without stopping or revealing himself to any of these people. So only the river people (now scattered, fled or dead) had seen him, and so, of course, had Senieta.

She chose not to rise and say so in front of the crowd. Khajar came back from the podium, clearly disappointed to have heard nothing from anyone after his announcement. He sat heavily next to her as almost everyone else began to dance.

Senieta tapped Khajar on the shoulder for his attention. "Sorry, I am not in the mood for dancing." he replied with some bitterness.

"No," she whispered. "I met the man you describe. He was travelling west like you, he stopped for my step-sister's wedding."

"What? Please tell me everything." He sat up straighter.

"After a dance," replied Senieta with a smile. Khajar smiled back and danced with her gladly through all of many songs until the music stopped playing.

That night, when the villagers were all asleep, the two of them sat in the living room of their host, whose two spare rooms Khajar was renting.

She recounted her encounter with the preacher although she of course left out the Shido.

Khajar thought about her story hard before speaking. "I understand now why these people treat you with such cruelty and suspicion. It is deeply unfair, you could hardly have helped it if your father married into the river people. So what happened to that village? I asked for directions to all settlements around here and neither your village nor the river people were mentioned."

Here Senieta was forced to tell the tale of what was common knowledge. How a strange curse of wasting had hit both settlements. He accepted this with a nod.

"There are things that can do that," he nodded, "and they are becoming strangely more common."

She asked him who this man he pursued was and why he pursued him.

"His name is Weito." Khajar began, and he recounted the substance of Weito's quest.

It started with the coronation of the young queen. She was just over ten on the day of her coronation, her father and mother having been struck down young by a blaze in the palace. She had survived the fire, although was badly marked by the flames.

The child had the wisdom to see that she was not wise in statecraft, so she placed trust in her advisers, and no adviser did she trust more than Weito who had saved her from the fire.

Weito was concerned that a darkness had fallen on the

land. He warned the queen and her court that dark things were more common than they had once been and growing more common still.

He proposed that a warrior be sent to the west, to journey through the endless jungle, to then take the broken path through the hostile wastelands, finally to climb the great staircase, Genjiha, with eleven thousand steps and eleven more.

Then, at the mountain's peak where the stairs ended, to catch the perfect light of the dawn into a glass trap. To bring this light to the great pagoda at the heart of the kingdom and from the top of this pagoda use the light to drive the evil from the land.

The queen's uncle warned the assembled warriors of the great dangers, of the terrible demons of the stair and the hungry wolves of the wasteland. In the end none volunteered except Khajar.

"But at the time I was barely ten years old myself and still a squire. I wanted so to fight demons and brave wolves for my kingdom and my queen."

With no volunteer but an overeager child, the queen decided to send Weito himself.

"Weito was shocked at her command. He had thought to try and persuade other warriors as he did not wish to leave her side. But his loyalty and obedience were above reproach. On the honour of his house he swore to do as his queen commanded."

And so Weito disappeared into the west. A year passed, the queen's health deteriorated, and she succumbed to a sudden illness.

"It was very sad. She was such gentle child."

Her uncle became the new king.

Although very young Khajar held himself to adult standards, and high ones as well, those befitting a knight. He felt snubbed, dishonoured by the queen turning down his sword for the quest. He had been older than *her* after all.

So Khajar trained hard to be as strong a warrior as he could be. As strong as Weito he would make himself. So strong that his sword would never again be denied for a great quest. He ran obstacles every day and sparred until his arms felt heavy as elephants, sparred until he was black and blue with bruises, then sparred more until he was never again marked or bruised.

Not so long ago, he was granted his first quest by the king.

First the king asked him to swear on his honour and his family that he would undertake the quest he was given, no matter how dangerous or how much it might pain him. Of course Khajar eagerly swore this.

The king ordered him to travel to the west, through the endless jungle, along the broken path and up the stair, Genjiha. There he was to find Weito and to deliver to him a royal command, stamped three times with the royal seal, witnessed by the council of five-and-a-half and signed twice by the king himself, ordering Weito to abandon his foolish quest and return home.

"I warned the king that Weito had sworn to his quest on his love for the queen, and upon his honour. I said that he might not accept an order from any hand but hers. The king saw my worry. He had indeed anticipated it." here Khajar fell quiet.

Khajar continued in a quiet, bitter voice. "So he told me to keep my sword as sharp as a razor, because should the preacher ignore the thrice-stamped royal command I am ordered to stab him through the heart."

Here Khajar slammed his cup down with some frustration. He was proud to have been chosen and proud to serve his country on a mighty quest. Senieta saw that he could not even entertain the thought of breaking his vow and wondered if it was honour or foolishness. She saw that it would sadden him to kill his hero: his inspiration. She saw also that he had no doubt that he could succeed, should the need arise.

The next morning Khajar proceeded on his quest and travelled onwards to the west. After waving him farewell and making her trades Senieta began her slow, dull way home.

When she returned to her shack she saw her fields in need of scraping and her chores in need of doing and she could not bear it. In a moment of wildness, she decided she would chase after Khajar. She would see this thing to the end.

She gathered a rope and the broom she kept unused and went to the empty town, where once her people had lived. She placed her rope downstream and brushed the reluctant Shido into it. Of course she did not burn it. Instead she loaded her Shido-holding-rope and as many provisions as she could find onto her cart.

He rode a pedigree warhorse, she had only a cart and carthorse. He had a day's head start and was used to travel. She had a day's head start in the wrong direction and would soon be further from home than ever before.

But she chased with determination.

Across the endless jungle she chased him. There were many rivers in this land and so many bridges she crossed that at least one must have hosted another Shido that took some negligible portion of her huge reserves of youth.

Past the land-of-many-rivers the jungle did not end, and a great swampy country followed. Here the people did not know her and were not afraid, and she found some hospitality despite her poverty. They gave her directions and told her Khajar had passed through.

Beyond the swamp, the jungle did not end, but there came strange kingdoms ruled by men who wore white chalk on their faces and whose dead were painted with ochre and stood like scarecrows in the sun to mummify. In this land none spoke any familiar language, and the people were as scared of Senieta as she was of them. Here she found no hospitality, but robbed the hanging ochre corpses for material to sustain her or bartered with gestures for what she needed.

Finally the endless jungle ended, and a vast plain of shale and flint opened before Senieta. Every rock looked as if it had once been a stone knife. They covered the ground and extended into the horizon.

There had once been a highway of cobbles across the plain. But the imported cobbles for the road were too round and forgiving for this land. The land had shattered them to sharp fragments and though they were not yet as bad as the native rock, in a few decades or maybe a century they would be.

The sun was hot with no canopy to filter it. The road cut through Senieta's battered shoes. Her horse had long died, her cart was long abandoned. There was little water, and what water there was was sprung from puddles only reachable by digging a number of the razorlike stone daggers out of the way. Even with the knives parted, the water was cruel, cold and bitter.

Senieta lost much blood to her cuts, and the chill nights hurt her terribly. If she had worn her true age these hardships might well have killed her. In fact, she suspected that without the life fortune she carried she might have been slain by them anyway.

After days and days on the broken path, she saw the mountain in the distance.

Each day she thought she must be close to the mountain. It dominated the horizon so completely. Surely it must be close? But it was not. Each day she faced the double disappointment of not yet reaching the peak and its size and height becoming larger in her mind and eye.

On the road were, here and there, signs of the previous travellers. Old horse dung and very old elephant dung. Discarded whetstones and a large, dried out lump of clay.

Wolves patrolled the wastelands around the broken path. They were grey enough to disappear into the shale and they were harsh and fierce enough that the cruel land allowed them to live, and chose not to hurt them with its blades. Thus, the wolves ran across the landscape of daggers without suffering harm.

One day a pack of them attacked Senieta. She was no fool, so when she saw them approach she lifted a shard of cobblestone to defend herself. If the native rock refused to cut them she would not waste her time with it and instead would fight with the foreign cobble-shard, even if it was a less potent weapon.

The wolves had every advantage, but had not met one as cunning as Senieta before. Seeing her armed with rock they did not take care to encircle her or to attack as a pack, instead they trusted to the land's love of them and attacked without any thought of avoiding her blows.

This was a great misjudgement. She stabbed with her cobble-shard with all the strength of one who is cornered and outnumbered.

She slew a wolf with repeated blows, and the others were panicked and fled.

After this the land of the broken path respected Senieta. The flint no longer cut her whenever she stepped on the loose stones. She found water more easily and she covered ground faster. It was as if before her strides had been cut short, but they were now as long as her legs allowed.

The mountain grew on the horizon. After only a few days more she stood at the foot of the great stair, Genjiha.

It was said the stair had eleven thousand and eleven steps. Senieta could believe that; seen from its base the staircase disappeared into the clouds high above. The steps were in pristine condition and were wide enough that ten people could walk them abreast. A few skeletal trees clung to the bottom of the mountain where it touched the broken path.

They had been cut to pieces. Most in Senieta's sight had been felled and those still standing had many branches missing.

Senieta then saw what had become of the wood taken from the trees. On the first step of the stair sat a discarded broom. Then on the second step another broom, the third step too and every step thereafter as far as Senieta's healthy, young eyes could see.

Weito had been forced to sweep every single step with a new broom. She saw the first of the piles of ash, the remains of what had once been a large fire. There must have been a Shido on every single one of these steps, and he had burned them all. She sensed a shudder of fear and awe in the rope she herself carried.

She climbed the hard stairs for a day and still every step bore a once-used broom to mark that it was dealt with. Periodically there were piles of ash where many ropes had been burned together. For the lower steps these ash piles had the fibres of normal rope, but here the fibres were grass and hair. Perhaps human hair from Weito's head and what few hairs he could find on his elephant.

She climbed for another day. Still every step had a broom left on it. The preacher and his elephant together could not have possibly carried this many between them. He must have been forced to go all the way down the stairs again to make and gather new brooms, many times.

At night Senieta burned some of the brooms for warmth. She learned to spot the changes in the wood, there would be a great number in a row with a slight greenish hue to the wood, then a number without it. Then the green would return. She recognised this as the seasons at which Weito took the wood from the trees. He had been working at this for years, hence her having a chance of catching up.

The mountain around the stair was steep and treacherous, but did at times form flat shoulders on which grew fruit trees and berry bushes. It was these that sustained Senieta through the long days of stair climbing.

After a time she reached the first landing, a paved area with huge, brass gongs hung under stone arches. The ropes lifting the gongs were new. Senieta surmised that Weito had taken the old ropes and used them to burn Shidos, and so these new ropes had to be from Khajar. But why had the warrior used ropes of his own to re-suspend the gongs?

These new ropes had been woven from the scraggly grass that bordered the stair in places. Weaving rope from grass was a difficult skill, one rarely used given the poor quality of rope it produced. Khajar had likely been heavily delayed making new ropes for these gongs.

That meant it was important. One should not pass here without ringing the gongs, and one could not ring the gongs if they were not hung. She looked at each in turn. They all bore the marks of time. Indeed, the strange characters that marked them had been battered to near illegibility by repeated use.

After some consideration Senieta tried to ring one.

The rock with which she struck the gong turned to dust, and her striking arm became shrivelled, old and decrepit instantly.

She camped that night in the circle of gongs, considering her options. They presented a puzzle. They were clearly required to progress but also guarded with deadly magic to harm those who failed.

By morning her arm was its young self again, repaired no doubt by the reservoirs of youth she carried. She thought again of the children who had thrown stones at her, of how they'd grown elderly at a child's size. Her glee was gone and now she felt only pity for them. The life she stole from them could be put to good use, it was the least she could do. Indeed, by climbing this stair she sensed she was putting her time to good use, but was not yet fully sure which warrior she would aid or hinder if she reached the top in time to make a difference.

Thinking of those children brought the idea of throwing stones to her mind.

Standing at the circle's centre, she threw stones at the gongs. Throwing the stones did her no harm, but more often than not the stones would shatter to dust as they struck without even sounding a note.

She destroyed many stones, but eventually she discovered the correct order. By trial and error she found the tune and she knew she was finished when all nine had been rung because she recognised the tune as a prayer-song.

Satisfied that, by sounding each gong her task here must be complete, Senieta continued on her way.

Other landings came soon after. On one were many prayer wheels in need of turning, on another disks were impaled on poles and in need of re-arrangement and on yet another were enormous, strange abaci with runes that demanded a particular pattern.

Past all these landings the stairs continued, each still with a once-used broom.

Finally the stair ended. It terminated in a final platform, perched on a shoulder of the mountain. Ahead, a sealed stone doorway stood carved in the mountainside. Before the door were the remains of two offerings: a dead elephant and a dead horse. Both corpses were relatively fresh, the elephant still had flesh while the horse still dripped blood.

Senieta had counted only eleven-thousand steps. The final eleven were beyond this door.

The door demanded a meaningful offering, she could sense it. The elephant and horse had been offered by the two before.

She looked at the rope she carried that held her bound Shido. She thought about why she had brought it: as a weapon to be unleashed upon her enemies. The thought seemed unworthy now. To prepare for future acts of cruelty was surely terrible.

She grabbed a nearby broom with which to make a fire. As she prepared to burn the rope the Shido spoke: "No, you must not! Our bargain still holds! You could set me onto another bridge simply by letting this rope pass under it on the water. I could give you more life, you need never die! You have wanted revenge twice before, what if others wrong you? I can help you again if need be!"

The voice faded as the rope burned away.

The stone door rumbled open. The mountain's tip was still a mile or more above the landing on which Senieta stood, but behind the door was a blessed tunnel that covered the full distance to the peak with only eleven gentle steps.

She emerged from the stair-tunnel into a garden of light and warmth. A place of heavy fruit trees and bright flowers under a golden shimmer of sun-rays.

Pressing through the trees Senieta found those she followed. There stood Weito in his yellow sash, older by far than Senieta remembered. At his feet lay the twice-signed royal command, which he had just thrown to the ground in disgust.

Two paces from him stood Khajar, his hand on the hilt of his sword.

"You were always kind Weito, it shall sadden me to kill you. But I have sworn my oath just as you swore yours. I must pierce your heart if you do not take heed of the royal order."

Weito readied his weapon rake. "A terrible thing is done if you stop my quest, but I hold no ill will towards you for following your king. Only ill will towards that king."

Senieta shouted. She did not know what she shouted or why, but the two warriors were too intent on one another to notice her in that moment. Their weapons were drawn and their worlds had narrowed to these weapons and one another.

Under the strength of two arms the rake lashed out in a downward arc.

Rake was sidestepped. Khajar's foot stamped to drive its teeth into the ground while his blade swung for Weito's neck.

Shaft of rake deflected blade. The stamp briefly caught the rake but imbalanced Khajar: both sides slowed equally. Without pause both of them fell into a new attack.

Slash of sword met the swing of rake. The blade trapped between the rake's teeth with a scream of metal.

A trap works both ways. With both shoulders and hard-won speed Khajar twisted his sword, throwing the rake from Weito's hands.

Before it even landed, Khajar stuck again, thrusting his sword through Weito's heart.

Senieta ran forward to help the stabbed preacher as he fell to the ground.

Khajar exclaimed in surprise on seeing her. She pressed her hands feebly against the river of blood that burst from Weito's chest. The old, wounded preacher fell across her lap. He blinked upwards, and on seeing her he was so surprised he did not trust his mortal senses so his third eye opened wide for confirmation.

"You burn brighter than anyone should," he gasped through his dying breaths.

"We should make him comfortable, so that his passing is as painless as it can be," said Khajar putting his hand sadly on Senieta's shoulder. "I have a poultice that will reduce his pain."

Weito seized hold of her arm. "How do you carry so many years? It is not... you did not..."

"Shido," answered Senieta with shame vaster by far than the paltry embarrassment she had once felt when admitting her relation to the river people to this same preacher years past.

Both men were aghast at this, but she ignored them, as a strange feeling came over her.

She had climbed the great stair. Unlike Khajar who had made use of a steed, she had stepped on every step. A sacred feat. Since she had made the last step a change had started upon her.

Her forehead itched and then it burned. Her mind expanded and then her soul followed it.

A new eye burst open on her forehead. New dimensions were stripped bare before her. Curtains that had always secretly limited her senses were torn away. She saw elements of reality, both familiar and not: truer versions of the objects her mortal eyes revealed. She saw the life of Weito like a candle-flame, dying out. She saw Khajar's life like a campfire and her own, a bonfire.

She poured some of her life into Weito. She could not explain how, any more than one can explain how one draws breath or commands one's limbs. With her new senses these things were simple.

The fire of Senieta's life could sustain the wounded holy man against death, but it could not heal his wound. Only time and medicine could do that.

As if by providence, the stair-top garden provided many herbs, which Khajar had the skills to make into strong medicines. He had sworn only to stab Weito's heart, and with that heart stabbed, he was free from his oath and could treat his wounds.

For some weeks they lived together there, the three of them. Senieta sat by Weito, pouring fire into his soul. Khajar fed them both and provided for the restoration of Weito's body.

When at last his healing was completed Weito went to the edge of the garden, and stood near an infinite precipice. He held aloft his glass phial to trap the light of a bright new dawn. Senieta wondered at those precious sunrays, born at the easternmost horizon of the world and gathered here at its western edge. How far they had come.

"I have what I came for. I must now take this to the great pagoda to heal the kingdom," he said, holding the phial of sunlight for them to see.

"I asked you once before to delay your quest for a wedding," said Senieta, taking Khajar by the hand. "Perhaps you can delay for another before *we* set off for this pagoda?"

The pilgrim gladly led the service for a second wedding. This ceremony had no guests, except maybe the doves that lived in that blessed garden.

5
KISS THE FROG
SKY SOMMERS

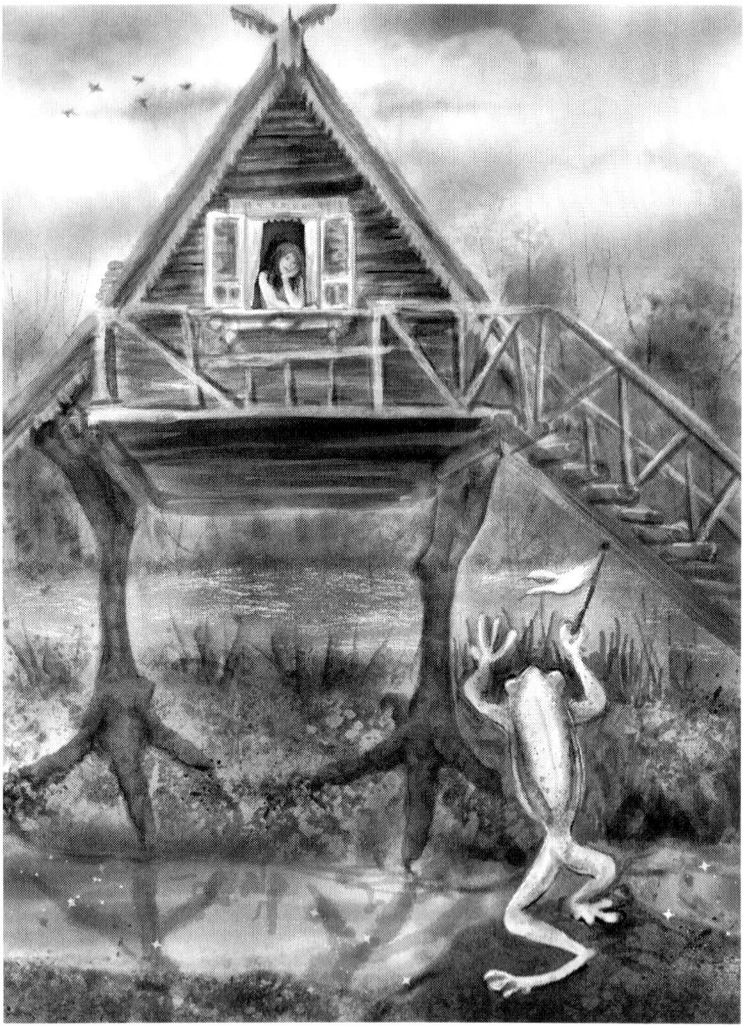

KISS THE FROG

Just as he spied the dilapidated hut, where he hoped someone was waiting for him, the man felt himself shrinking and he gripped his breeches until he was sitting on top of them. The folds of a creamy shirt billowed in their descent and reminded him of the laundry the maids had hung up in the wasteland behind their palace. That had been India, Earth, a thousand years ago and this was now, his present, albeit in a different dimension.

The Magic Kingdom.

A giant rose from the local royal gardens lay on the wet earth next to pine needles half his size. He hadn't thought Beast would miss a single rose from his gardens as his curse had long since been broken.

The man raised his hand. Instead, he saw an elongated green limb with three digits and a membrane nested between them.

He tried shifting to another dimension and ... couldn't. The cocoon of light refused to form. As if his teleporting powers were switched off.

Someone had cursed him to become a frog without an opportunity to leave.

But why?

For daring to take one of Beast's roses for his paramour?

For temporarily ditching said paramour?

Magic Kingdom had been his first stop on the way to freedom from the shackles of running an entire Agency of Guardian Angels across 63 known dimensions and a couple of unknown ones. As luck would have it, he had stumbled upon a rather distressed damsel on his first day in this dimension whom the cruel Goddess of Fate had placed in the Magic Kingdom as per her own silly wish. While a few relaxing drinks had seemed like a good idea at the time, overnight he had gotten something more than he had bargained for.

In the morning, he had remembered he had other worlds to see, other damsels to…ahem…befriend. Magic Kingdom was merely been the first stop of many.

Strangely, though, wherever he went and whoever he met, his thoughts kept straying to the dapper twenty—five-year-old damsel and her ink-black curls and mind-melting curves.

The frog eyed the hut. A woman in a black skirt with bright red poppies appeared and sifted through the herbs in what looked like two dozen planters.

Judging by the appearance of the damsel and her hut, the lady's occupation in this world now appeared to be herbal healer. Which was really a synonym for local witch. Mere months after their impromptu get-together. She was resourceful, he had to give her that.

Surely, she couldn't have learnt magic in a few months?

Or learnt to curse unsuspecting visitors who dared infringe on her solitude? If she cursed everyone who tried to approach her hut, she would have no customers left.

He couldn't have been gone more than a couple of months. Probably. It could have been years. Time was shifty in the

Magic Kingdom, on account of fairy-tales being read and re-read, new ones made and old ones remade.

Whoever had deigned to curse him was in for a nasty surprise. Because he would find out. He had his ways. Or rather, the Agency had. But before he asked them for help, he would make his own investigation, yes siree.

Since his paramour was closer than the royal palace he decided to start his interrogations with the woman about her suddenly acquired craft rather than question the Beast about the consequences of taking one of his roses.

The frog took one look at the red rose and then at the hut across the meadow. He would have to brave the trek in the open.

In broad daylight. In frog form.

He could almost taste the adrenalin.

Ah, to feel alive again!

Coming back to this dimension had been an excellent idea.

It took a while for him to amble from the edge of the meadow to the hut.

Half a day later, the frog climbed onto the windowsill. The window was open. He was winded from his long trek, he had scrapes all over from climbing the rough logs and was oozing with regret over ever stepping into a dimension where he could be cursed so lightly.

The fact that all of his calls for help aimed at the Agency had fallen on deaf ears didn't help his foul mood. That and the fact that he had caved and reached out to the Agency before he had even gotten to the witch.

Someone would have to answer for daring to turn him into an amphibian! And for not returning his pleas for help.

The witch better know how to turn him back or else...

Inside, the woman headed straight for him and for the open window.

He forgot his anger for a second and just admired the view.

There she was, coming at him, with her waist-length black curls, gorgeous body of a twenty-something-year-old, long legs, flowing poppy skirt, eyes half across her face, just the way he liked them. Although she had looked much more pleased to see him last time.

Before he could croak a greeting the woman flicked her finger at his forehead and sent him flying backwards.

A few hours later, when he had managed to climb up to the window again, it was closed.

Cursing under his breath, the frog ambled down and started towards the door. Not that it was open. But maybe someone would come visit the woman and he could gain entrance.

Nobody came.

He guessed the witch wasn't that popular. Yet.

His night was spent shivering, huddled next to the door, under the bottom-most log. He couldn't hazard hopping back to the forest for food or shelter. There were owls about.

In the morning, he once again started his arduous ascent to the window.

He coughed to get the woman's attention. 'Marina, darling, a bit of help, please? It seems that I'm enchanted and...'

That was what he heard inside his head.

What came out of his mouth was 'Croak, croak, croak, crrrrrroak, croak, croak...' and then some.

Before he could say anything else, she said, 'You again! Buzz off.' Then she slammed the window shut, making him lose his balance and topple back onto the porch. Hours of work wasted.

With a heavy heart, sweating and swearing, the frog reached the windowsill before high noon. He had to mime his needs, because his telepathy wasn't working and she didn't understand frog-speak.

'Oh, no. Not you again. Stop with the funny dance. Go find a frog to romance. I'm sick and tired of you and your theatrics.

Shoo! Get out! Or do you want me to try some French cuisine tonight? Fried frog legs, yum!' This time, she flicked the kitchen towel at him, which sent him flying again.

The frog croaked and scampered off.

So much for help from his paramour.

Correction, his former paramour.

He doubted he would be able to bed her in his present form. Not until he turned back into a human. Maybe not even then.

With one last long look, the frog hopped to the safety of the forest. Traveling under the leafy ferns should keep him out of the purview of the crows during the day and owls come nighttime.

Where could he go? Where could he figure things out in peace?

On his way to the hut, he had spotted marshlands to the East. Frogs and marshes. That seemed appropriate.

Two years later

Appropriate accommodation did not equate to popular lodgings. So far, the frog hadn't seen a single human soul in the marsh wetlands during the entire duration of this stay.

One day the frog spotted a huge toad hopping about as if searching for something.

'Baby? Can you hear me? Where are you?' The toad croaked and bumped into a tree root. And then into a rock. And then slipped on a tuft of grass.

A female toad with eyesight problems, looking for her offspring.

Now there was his chance.

'Mama?' The frog croaked, hoping his croaks were understandable and that a toad mother's relief over finding her son would make her ignore the fact that the son she had found was entirely the wrong species. Might just work on a half-blind female.

'Baby? Is that you?' The toad ambled closer.

'Yes, mama. I'm so glad you found me. I need a bride.'

'A bride? Why, but you're only a baby.' The toad squinted at him. 'You've lost weight, baby. Oh, no, have you been going hungry while mama was away?'

The frog thought about it. 'I was so sick with worry while you were gone. But the good news is, I matured real quick. And I noticed that the world is made of couples.'

His adoptive mother opened and closed her mouth for a while. 'We'll have to go back to...'

'No.' The frog was resolute. 'I've seen the world and its beauty. I want a beautiful bride. Different from us.'

'What kind of different?'

'Fairy kind of different, mama.'

'Where would I find a fairy for you, son?'

The Boss remembered how, why and when he had enlisted Loretta, his fairy-turned-pixie to be a Watcher at the Agency of Guardian Angels. She had mentioned something about having been abducted from a house where she had lived with an old human woman. The woman had to be a witch. Luckily, Time was relative in this dimension. The past could be the present and the future in the making as the fairy-tales were told and retold over and over again. Now, if he could tap Loretta just before she was abducted, maybe he could get the Hel out of here.

'Someone told me that somewhere around here, but I don't know where precisely, there lives a childless woman who keeps one tiny fairy as a prisoner. Maybe we can help set the fairy free and she'll be so grateful that she'll... *tell someone about seeing me here when she gets to the Agency half a year later*' he thought, but out loud he said, 'Kiss me...and then marry me.'

He didn't need fairy magic to disenchant him. All the fairy needed to do was send up a prayer for help and the Agency would have to respond. If Loretta - or still Etta at this point in her story - refused to help him, he could make her pray for help. Hands around her neck, if he had to. Any means to an end. But he had to find her first.

The toad mama nodded her slow assent. 'Well, if it's rescuing a fair maiden, that would be a noble thing, I guess.'

The frog hopped closer to her and leaned into the bulbous mass, 'Yes, mama. Yes, it would.'

Another two years later

Well, that endeavour had been a let-down. It had taken his adoptive mother a year to find Loretta. She even managed to abduct her, but her grave mistake had been to hop to her adopted son to tell him the good news instead of bringing the girl to him at once. By the time they reached the lily pond where she had left the girl, someone had already stolen the fairy from under their noses. Worse, the witch who had housed the fairy was also gone. And his periodic pleas to the Agency still went into a black hole.

He needed to come up with another plan.

'Heeeeelp!'

A lone female cry echoed across the marshlands.

She hadn't said the magic word though.

His angels wouldn't come running.

He hopped closer to the mud pit that he was sure the woman had taken for safe grassy land. Swamps were sneaky that way. If you didn't know it wasn't grass, you had no hope in

Hel. The woman had unwittingly stumbled into the oldest, boggiest part of the wetlands, taking a shortcut through the marshes.

A wicker basket lay on its side, having expunged a freshly-baked loaf of bread and a pungent wheel of cheese.

The frog hopped closer to the basket and looked at its owner.

The woman stared right at him.

'Help…' she whispered, despair oozing off her in tangible vibes as she kept struggling. 'Please.'

She had to stop struggling.

The frog rose up on his hind webbed feet, did a rigid military salute and froze in place.

From sheer surprise the woman stilled and spread her hands, the mud pit squelching up air bubbles at her waist.

When she noticed her sinking had slowed down, the woman's eyes darted around, looking for things to grab.

The frog brought his front webbed foot to his eyes, the motion making her look at him. He then pointed at her eyes that were still wide as saucers, then motioned back at his.

The woman kept her eyes trained on the frog and gave one quick nod.

As there was no point in talking to her, he croaked and hopped to point out the safe tufts that she could grab.

She seemed to understand as he beckoned her to follow.

The woman grabbed the tuft of grass he was pointing at. Then she pulled and lifted herself half an inch from the pit.

He hopped onto another tuft that was within her reach.

She grabbed for that one with her other hand and pulled, flinging herself onto her stomach over the rim of the deceitful pit.

Slowly, but surely, he helped the woman crawl out of the mud and onto the grass.

When she was safe, sitting on dry land, her skirts muddy

and one shoe missing, she turned to him and said, 'Thank you, little frog! I owe you my life. Is there anything I can do for you?'

Rapt attention from the first human he had seen in years sent the cogs in the frog's head spinning.

If he remembered the Earthen fairy-tales correctly, a kiss had been a standard remedy in quite a few instances. Kiss the girl, she wakes up. Kiss the girl and stumble while carrying her casket and she has the good luck to dislodge the poisonous apple stuck in her throat. Kiss the girl and she'll keep her human legs forever.

If for all practical purposes he was mute, he had to use pictorial language.

The frog hopped to a wooden peg he saw sticking out from the grass, smoothed the mud on the rim of the bog and started drawing.

Half an hour of hopping and dragging later, the frog stood next to something that looked like himself with a crown, something akin to a girl's face and a pair of lips.

This was as pictorial as it got.

Get a girl to kiss me and I'll become a prince.

Well, he had been a prince once. The son of a Maharaja in India a thousand Earth years ago. He had been revered as a God for another thousand years after that. He was royalty and any maiden should be so lucky as to get a kiss from him.

This woman was no maiden, but he wasn't picky. He would settle for any half-ass kiss.

She eyed his scribbles and didn't seem to be getting it.

The frog motioned for her to keep eye contact and puckered up.

'Eeew!' The utterance escaped from the woman's lips before she clamped her hand over her mouth. 'Oh, I'm sorry, I didn't mean to...'

Yes she did. And he didn't care.

'Are you enchanted?' she asked.

He nodded.

'Is there a way out of the enchantment?'

What was she, daft? The frog glanced at the mud that was now baking and caking. How much plainer did he have to make it?

'I'm married, already, little frog, I can't be going around kissing other men...frogs...males. But don't you fret. If you show me a safe way out of the marshes, I will come back and find you and together we can figure this out, ok?'

The frog frowned. She seemed sincere. A normal response after escaping the clutches of death. She might even mean her promises right now.

But it didn't mean she would come back after he had guided her out of the danger.

The frog sighed. Once a guardian, always a guardian. He simply could not leave her be. He had to help her.

Even if it meant she would forget him as soon as she was out of dire straits.

And another two years later

Where was the woman?

At first, she promised to come by once a week.

And she did, true to her word.

With her, she had brought all sorts of children's books and stories. These were usually half-baked, focusing on the reasons why someone would be turned into a frog.

Either the stories were just starting to develop in the Magic Kingdom or the woman didn't have access to a decent library.

There were very few tales about frogs. Hardly any. What fairy-tales the woman found, all had similar morals to the story of their ruling monarchs - Belle and Beast. At least that story was helpful in terms of helping the woman to believe in enchantments and curses. The royal family's story seemed to be told and retold, instilling into their young the cautionary point of the tale: be nice and polite to strangers.

Briefly, he wondered what Earthlings would say to this heresy, but unlike Earth, Magic Kingdom was not fraught with kidnappings and murderous predators.

The fairy-tales about frogs she read him were suggesting rather unsuitable ways to disenchant someone. He was already past the moral of 'don't cross the witch or you'll be cursed'. The other story the woman had read ended with the princess throwing her frog husband against the wall and breaking the spell. No, no, no. Two things did not sit well with him. The obvious one of being thrown by someone who did not wish to break the spell but kill him. He was no longer the Boss of the Agency. Immortality was no longer a given. He wasn't going to risk it. But what worried him even more was having to marry the damsel.

Marriage? Him? Never!

For that reason alone, he wasn't quite willing to try that option to break his curse. Or then he would have to be a cad and not uphold his end of the bargain about the marriage part. Because most of the stories she had read him, the maiden was rescued by a prince and marriage inevitably ensued. Brrr.

Another story suggested that the frog should spend a night on a princess' pillow, but alas, the kingdom had no princess, only a prince. He had tried spending the night on his witch's pillow without her noticing and that hadn't worked.

He saw that each time something hadn't worked, the woman seemed more reluctant to come again.

At some point, she started coming by once a month.

Did he grumble?

No.

But her visit was due and he had prepared accordingly.

He had made the same drawing as the day he had saved the woman. In the same place he had saved her.

He hadn't figured out how to convey to her that the girl who had to kiss him had to be a maiden.

Get a maiden to kiss me and I'll become a prince.

If he could get that across, he was sure damsels would be lining up to claim their prince.

Now, if the damsels' overactive imaginations should whisper that he would marry one of them later as per the story books, that was purely their own misunderstanding.

The Magic Kingdom was not a Victorian aristocratic society. Kissing wasn't anything dishonourable. At least where the village and farm girls were concerned.

The aristocrats would certainly expect him to pop the question.

As long as he avoided those, his conscience would be clear.

The woman could help him lure a maiden to his rescue. He would make sure that she did.

One maiden. One kiss. All he needed was one.

But if it didn't work with one, he would keep trying until it did work.

Now where was she?

Thirty years later

The frog sighed, picking away at a tuft of grass. The sun was shining mercilessly, drying out the marshes. His home of more than thirty years was shrinking. Not that Time was important. He had lived for millennia, he had been bored for the last century, but why, oh why, did he have to come to this blasted Magic Kingdom dimension!

He sighed again and poked the mud with a peg. If it hadn't

been for the rain last night, he wouldn't have been able to replicate his pictorial call to action.

The frog spotted a girl traipsing along the rather well-worn, but overgrown path toward his abode and perked up.

After he had tried to convey his needs to the woman all those years ago, she left and never came back. She had sent a maiden to help him, though. And then another came. And another. Although his fame had spread by word of mouth, the maidens had been few and far in between over the past thirty years. And so far, none of their kisses had worked. But he was still hopeful.

Maybe the one to disenchant him hadn't been born yet?

Be that as it may, here was a fair maiden to brighten his day!

A kiss was a kiss was a kiss.

He puffed out his chest and tried to look regal. As regal as it was possible to look with webbed feet.

'Pucker up, you ugly toad!' Goldilocks said, grabbing him and smooching him before he could make any sound of indignation.

'Croak! You think that's what you should say to an enchanted prince to get him to like you?' The frog mumbled.

The damsel squealed, 'It speaks!' and dropped the amphibian who looked equally surprised.

'You...you can understand me?' The frog croaked.

'Of course, I can understand you when you speak human.' The maiden huffed. 'You gave me quite a fright, you know.'

The frog blinked. Somehow, in the last thirty-six years, he had regained his ability to speak. Was magic increasing in this Magic Kingdom of theirs? Or could it be that all the damsels could have understood him all along, if only he had deigned to speak to them?

But then why had his paramour of old, his favourite damsel in distress heard him croak?

Could it be that the only person who couldn't understand him was the one who had cursed him?

Or worse, had she understood every word and simply ignored him?

Should he have kept trying to talk to her?

Could he have saved himself thirty plus years of silence?

The frog slapped his forehead.

Countless girls had kissed him and nothing.

Zero. Zip. Nada.

The frog sighed and concentrated on the conversation. 'By the way, I'm a he, not an it. Or else you wouldn't have kissed me.'

'About that. When are you going to turn into a prince?' The girl asked, wiping her mouth.

'You should probably wipe a bit harder. Toads have warts and all. You might get herpes or something.' He was a frog, a different thing entirely, but she clearly couldn't tell these two species apart. She had called him an ugly toad.

The girl scooped some water from a nearby pond and scrubbed her mouth raw.

'That's filthier than me, darling.'

'You didn't answer my question.'

'If it hasn't happened by now, it's not going to happen. Sorry to disappoint.' The frog croaked.

'You don't sound sorry. I'm the one who's sorry. Sorry I believed that stupid story.' The girl pouted and straightened her skirts.

'Oh, that. Yes, it was quite clever of me.' The frog puffed out his chest.

'You? You spread the stories? But how?' The girl's eyes goggled.

'I know someone who knows someone.' The frog winked.

'No. Seriously. How could you have persuaded a human to tell all those lies about a frog prince living in the marshes,

Enchanted Waters

waiting for a girl to come and find him and turn him back with a daring kiss?' The girl sidled up to the frog on a neighbouring tuft of dried grass.

The frog chuckled. 'I saved a woman in these marshes once. Since she owed me her life, she has been doing...she promised she would find maidens to come to the marshes. I left the how up to her.'

'Couldn't she have disenchanted you?'

'Married.'

'And you need...'

'A maiden.'

The girl coloured to her roots. 'Ah.'

'Ah-hah. But if you're not, why did you come here?'

'I thought if it's just a kiss, maybe I could help you out and you'd be grateful and instead of marrying me, I could persuade you to give me a hefty dowry,' the girl said, the pink reaching her nose and ears.

It was the frog's turn to goggle at her. 'You're rather honest. And stupid.'

'So are you. Luring the maidens to come to the marshes, when everyone knows that a True Love's Kiss is pretty much the only remedy that works when nothing else does,' the girl said. 'None of the girls you have lured here knew you, how could we love you? The only person who could possibly love you is someone who knew you before you were turned.' She gave him a once over as if doubting anyone could ever love him at all.

The frog blinked.

A True Love's Kiss.

It seemed that the Magic Kingdom had evolved as far as magic and stories were concerned. He just hadn't taken an interest or seen a story book in years.

'True Love's Kiss, True Love's Kiss,' the frog mumbled.

Was it too much to hope that SHE would hear about him,

and knowing her charming personality, storm here, give him a talking-to and disenchant him?

No, it had to be a True Love's Kiss.

His fairy-tale had just got complicated beyond belief. It was his own fault for not taking notice in thirty years. Of course things had changed.

But a True Love's Kiss?

Where would he get one?

Heck, he'd settle for Half-Assed Kiss at the moment.

From she who had cast the curse.

Even if it was one-sided.

Or if one of them was unconscious. Erm...asleep.

Who knew, maybe all he needed to do was lock lips with her and he'd be human again? No True Love's Kiss and everything that came with it, required.

Another arduous trek to the witch's hut suddenly seemed worth it. It would take him at least a week to get to her hut.

Yes, he could hop over there, slither into the hut while she was asleep and...

If her magic had turned him, she could live with being woken by a kiss from an amphibian.

Sleeping Beauty hadn't minded being woken by a stranger smooching her.

Yes, that's what he would do.

Next week.

Out loud the frog said. 'Alas! You were not my true love. Better luck next time. Spread the word!'

'How old are you anyway?' The girl asked.

'Why do you want to know?' The frog retorted.

'Well, I'm sixteen. If I decide to tell my brave friends and they happen to disenchant you, maybe you'll be too old for them?' The girl said. 'To marry.'

'Who said anything about marrying?' The frog asked, squinting his eyes against the morning sun.

'What? You want a girl, your true love, to come find you and kiss you and you're not even going to marry her? Why, you... you...are the most despicable, dishonest, slimy...'

'Frog.' The frog added helpfully.

'That I have ever known!' The girl finished.

'Met many talking frogs in your life, have you?' The frog asked.

'No.' The girl huffed.

'Why do you even assume that I will turn back into a human? Maybe I'll turn into an even more horrible beast than I am now?' He suggested. 'Maybe the girl will turn into a frog instead?'

The girl blanched and bit her lip. 'I doubt there is anyone more horrible than you.' The girl huffed. 'Inside and out.'

'Watch it!'

'You watch it! Why are you being nasty to me? I only wanted to help!'

'But you didn't.'

'But I still can, if I tell my friends. Well, I was going to tell Betty, but now, after your rudeness...'

'Honesty.'

'Rudeness. I'm not inclined to tell anyone. Betty has an aristo on a leash, who might marry her if she...never you mind.'

'Oh, I wouldn't mind. Not at all. But you and...Betty, was it?...are both severely mistaken, if you think someone will marry you after a bit of a roll in the hay.'

'Men! You're all alike!' Spat the girl and got up.

'So, what are you still doing here?' The enchanted being of the male disposition asked the angry female.

'I'm leaving!' She stomped off, careful to retrace her steps.

'About time!' The frog yelled after her. 'Finally, some peace and quiet.'

Now, if that girl didn't go and complain about his attitude to someone, hopefully the witch who had cursed him, then nobody would. All he had to do was stay put and wait. For a few days anyway.

Part of him knew that on some level he probably deserved the predicament he was in. The other part, the part that had been free to pull all sorts of strings across dimensions couldn't accept that his own wits and guile were not enough to help him break free of the curse. And, unfortunately, that second part was the disgruntled voice in his head.

He knew whom to blame. Two people. Well, not people per se. One was an angel and the other a witch.

If his second-in-command Gabriel hadn't suggested that he go tour some nice dimensions to regain his faith in a lot of things, he wouldn't be here.

Nice dimension indeed.

Where the first fun female he happened upon was initially very welcoming, only to curse him later.

He had never been a praying man. Rather, beings of all shapes and sizes had directed their prayers at him.

Now, thirty-six long years later, he was willing to pray that the offended girl would go straight to the witch to complain about him. Or would tell a friend who would tell a friend who would tell the witch about a nasty rude enchanted frog prince in the marshes.

When the witch finally deigned to come here herself to sort out the offending frog, he would be free.

Else he would have to trek to her and steal that kiss.

He could only hope that she was not the type to hold a grudge this long.

Hmm, then again, from what he remembered of their brief encounter, she had been quite feisty.

The frog prepped and preened and sat himself down on his favourite tuft of grass as if it were a throne and waited.

Nobody came that day.

The next day, she didn't come to find him either.

Nor the day after that.

Three days later

At midday on the third day, two women who didn't look anything like maidens appeared. One of them was wearing men's breeches. If it weren't for her wayward shoulder-length curly hair sticking every which way and for the slight sway of her hips, he would never have figured her for a woman. The other looked as old as sin and he dismissed her at once.

Just as the frog was wondering whether they were the irate kin of the girl he had offended that came to air their grievances and whether now would be a good time to panic or not, the women were upon him.

'Come here, you ugly thing,' the old hag told the frog, who croaked in surprise.

'I think you offended him,' the younger woman offered.

To the frog, she looked slightly familiar.

After being stuck in the Magic Kingdom for what seemed like a lifetime, he was having a hard time remembering where he could have seen her before.

'Shut it,' the crinkled old bat told the younger woman, 'He should be grateful he's getting any help. It didn't go too well with the maidens then, did it?' she asked him.

The frog puffed out his chest. What was the harm in asking a few innocent maidens to help a being in need?

'They all ran screaming, didn't they?' the witch asked.

'Do you have to goad him?' The younger woman defended him.

Such a bleeding heart. As if she were one of his flock.

That's it! That's where he knew her from!

Why, it was Grace! Gabriel's Grace.

The frog smirked.

'Do you think it's ok to get a woman drunk, have your way with her and leave her pregnant to raise the kid by herself?' the old witch asked.

What? The frog felt slightly nauseous. Did the old bat just say that he had procreated with her? HER?

Wait a minute. Was this the witch who had cursed him? She was old and weathered, her flyaway hair was white, but it curled to her waist. If it were ink-black and she had fewer wrinkles...

It could be her.

Marina.

His witch had found him at last.

While still affronted, the frog grinned.

Finally!

'I don't think that's how you tell someone he's a dad,' Grace said.

'Shut it,' Marina said and leaned down, puckering her lips,

'Come here, darling. Kiss me quick and let's be done with it, shall we?'

Kiss those weathered lips? It would be like kissing a crocodile-skin bag! She could have at least used butter or olive oil to moisturise or something. The frog tried to close his eyes to avoid seeing all the wrinkles, but the woman was too quick for him.

As soon as her lips touched his, a blast of light threw them both back a few feet.

For the first time in aeons, the Boss felt like himself. Flying through the air, his appendages turned to limbs, his hair regrew and even the stubble that he had come to miss returned and he felt the world shrink.

Except when he lay on the grass, buck naked, all he could think was *THAT was a True Love's Kiss and this, THIS is my true love?*

He eyed the old woman warily. It could be worse.

The woman eyed him right back. 'Now we know for sure wishes are like curses and kisses can break anything. Even if it isn't a True Love's Kiss.'

Wait…she didn't think it was a True Love's Kiss? Wasn't she in love with him? He certainly didn't fancy her. Well, he might have, if she were still young and beautiful, which she wasn't.

Relieved things had worked out so well, the former frog sighed, stretched on the ground in his birthday suit and said, 'Finally.'

Next thing he knew, Grace started stripping.

Well, well, well, this was promising.

As her breeches fell, the former frog noticed how elongated the woman's limbs had become, with her bones sticking through the skin. Well, that wasn't so sexy. Metamorphosis. She was turning into something…someone…else. Next, a black wolf was barking at him, 'Hel-lo. Boss-man.'

'What do you mean finally?' The witch's hands had gone to

her hips. 'I should have let you rot here some more. You owe me an apology.'

'You owe me one first. Come on. A frog? For thirty-six years? For a brief night of hanky-panky that wasn't even the best I've ever had?' the former frog accused.

'I'll show you not even the best you've ever had...' Marina said, narrowing her eyes at him.

'Put. On.' The wolf nudged the clothes towards the witch who threw them at the man's face in one swift motion.

Deciding to be the bigger person, the former frog turned to the wolf. 'Hello, Grace. I should have known that you, as the protector of magic, would end up in the Magic Kingdom someday. How are you finding it here?'

'Gabe. Turned. Me. Wants. Me. To. Guard. Like. You. Did. My. Kid. Is. Here. Man. Too. So. OK.' Grace barked. 'Why. Not. Ask. For. Help. From. A-gen-cy.'

The man shot the witch he knew as Marina a dirty look and started putting on the clothes. 'I did ask. Fat lot of good it did me. For some strange reason, asking for angelic help fell on deaf ears. I sent up countless prayers for help and...nothing. No response from the Agency. I know for a fact they have one priority screen trained on this dimension at any given time. It must be you,' He pointed his finger at Marina, 'and your magic. You cursed me,'

'I did no such thing!' The old woman huffed and mumbled. 'Not on purpose anyway. Well, not entirely on purpose. I made a wish that if there was an ounce of ick in your soul over what you did, that your body would follow that sentiment. So, I guess you did feel icky.'

'Believe whatever you want to believe. But you do have magic.'

'Yes and you are one of the reasons why I try not to use my powers here,' the witch said.

'Be that as it may, it seems that whomever your magic

touches,' he pointed his finger at himself, 'is prevented from speaking to you. And since you are here only temporarily...'

'If you call almost forty years temporary,' the old woman huffed.

'A mere wrinkle in time,' the former frog waved her off, 'the other wrinkle being that anyone your magic touches seems unable to leave this dimension until you do or until you allow them to leave. I tried to leave, but it didn't work. I asked for help from the Agency, they didn't hear me. Your curse magically blocked me.'

The witch stared at him, 'Sure, blame it all on the woman. Maybe your angels didn't want to rescue you? Ever thought of that?'

He had thought that perhaps someone at the Agency didn't want him back, but the witch's magic barring all contact with the Agency seemed more likely. The Watchers knew better than to leave him, HIM, stranded. He had just...well, more than thirty years...thirty-six, so seventy-two Agency years ago to be precise, given them the perfect gift wrapped with a bow - Gabriel as the head of the Agency for all eternity.

The witch looked cross. If he wanted to find his way out of here, he better be sweet to her.

The man tried to pat his old flame on her rump. She swatted him away. 'Darling, I always knew it had to be you who broke the spell.'

'Yeah? So, why did you lure young virgins into the swamp then?' the witch asked.

'Don't make a mockery out of it. Do you even know what it takes to persuade one human to persuade another human to help a frog? It's hard work, you know.' He tried to look stern but vulnerable, hoping he could make her feel guilty.

'One could hope,' the weathered witch shot back.

Marina had mentioned they had procreated. Perhaps it was wise to find out a little about that.

'So, I have a...son?' He started cautiously.

'A daughter. She glamours people into seeing what she wants them to see.' The witch said.

That startled him. 'She has one of my...angelic abilities?'

Marina smirked, 'I guess, although there is nothing angelic about her. Your granddaughters are a bit better. Ella married into the royal family and Greta is running a restaurant almost by herself at age fifteen. Your grandson, Hans, is hacking at trees and bringing wooden things to life, so I don't know if he'll become a warrior or a warlock, but one does not necessarily preclude the other. And you have a great-grandchild as well,' the woman added viciously.

'Whoa,' was all the former frog could say. 'Never in my travels across all the millennia did I produce offspring and now I'm a granddad?'

The witch spread her arms wide, 'Hello, Magic Kingdom? Anything can happen here.'

The wolf nodded. 'It. Can. And. Of-ten. Does.'

After the wolf left and the two of them frog-marched back to the hut that had sprouted chicken legs since last he saw it. He entered, ducking his head and looked around, trying to sense if the witch lived alone or if there was a man in her life. The innards of the hut looked the same as they had thirty-six years ago. A lone cauldron hung over the fire and a pitcher of water was set in the middle of a long wooden table. Apart from a white cloth hanging in the corner, the room housed one armchair, two long benches that fit under the table and the tiniest of kitchens with a miniature stove. No sight of male over-clothes or boots.

The man smirked and demanded a bath and food. He also

wanted to ask for some shaving equipment, but Marina cut him off with, 'Don't you dare use my razor.'

When he returned after a long hot bath, he found Marina at the table with plates of food that had gone cold.

Seeing something he liked, he grabbed a chicken leg off Marina's plate and bit into it with relish.

'Manners!'

'Hungry!'

'Well, well, well, who do we have here to keep your old bones company?' An apparition in a purple sari said from the doorway.

'Hello, Mellie,' the old woman started pouring tea onto the linen table cloth. Before the first drop hit the cloth, a new cup to match the others materialised out of thin air.

'Melisandra, if you will,' the newcomer huffed.

Hmm, by the looks of the older woman, the younger one who just stepped through the door was a relation. Sister? Granddaughter?

'Are all my granddaughters as sweet as this child?' The man hazarded a guess.

'Granddaughter?' Mellie gaped.

'Daughter,' Marina said. 'Come here, girl. Meet your father.'

Father?

This was his daughter?

The former frog put his chicken leg down, wiped his hands and stood up, intending to offer a formal greeting.

'Father? What father? Him? No way!' Mellie said, giving the man a once-over from head to toe. 'He doesn't look anything like me.'

'Charming. Yes, I dare say you are more like your mother. No filter between her brain and her mouth either.' The former frog countered.

'You're the rogue who abandoned her after a night of fun, aren't you?' The woman fixed her brown eyes on him.

'I tried to come back,' the man said.

'Doubtless hoping for another booty call,' the witch mumbled.

Why did that woman paint him so black? Sure, he wasn't without blemishes, but nobody was perfect. Maybe the woman's anger had something to do with their argument? The same argument that had sparked a fight that had ignited something else entirely.

'I wanted to apologise. You did tell me how you had been... betrayed and I later found myself regretting being so...callous in my judgment that what had befallen you was proportionate to the magnitude of your wish,' the man said, sitting back down onto the wooden bench.

'Is that an apology?' Mellie gaped. 'Coz you suck at them.'

He couldn't help it, she made him laugh. He liked the mouth on that one.

'Great! Now I have two hellions to tame,' he stage-whispered to the witch and got a death stare back.

'Care to go back to where I found you an hour ago?' The witch retorted with a syrupy smile.

'Where DID you find him? Did he just appear out of thin air? Or have you been harbouring him all along, a secret lover that comes and goes as he pleases?'

'Nobody is harbouring me,' the Boss said as Mellie silenced him by putting up her hand.

His daughter thought her mother had kept him a well-guarded secret. Well, in a way she had and in a way she hadn't.

'I never left,' he said, looking at the witch. 'In a misguided attempt at revenge or jealousy, I have trouble determining which, your mother turned me into a frog, and I've lived in the nearby marshes ever since.'

'You turned your one-night-stand lover into a FROG? What's wrong with you? You could have made him marry you, and I could have had a semblance of a family,' Mellie gave her father another once-over, 'or you could have kept him as your love slave, but noooo... you had to go and punish him for something I'm pretty sure you both agreed to at the time!' Mellie threw up her arms.

The former frog's lips drew into a thin line. He was no longer sure that he did like the mouth on that one. She made men sound like...a necessity or worse, a pleasant pastime.

'No wonder my relationship with Oz is not working out. Thanks, mom! Thanks, dad!' Mellie sat down on the bench and crossed her arms, but not before she swiped a cinnamon roll into her mouth.

The man blinked. 'Is she always like this or do I bring out her charming side?' He stage-whispered to the mother.

'She's always like this,' Marina said, making Mellie huff.

Oz? Was that a boyfriend? If he were ever to befriend this offspring, he could try and be the father she so obviously lacked in her life.

'Who's this Oz? Your boyfriend? Do I need to meet him? Kick his ass?' The man asked, leaning in close enough to catch a whiff of Mellie's sweet perfume.

'Oz. Is the love of my life,' Mellie sighed and took another cinnamon roll, 'Not that he cares. He is also the father of all of my children.'

Children? Oh, those were the promised grandchildren Marina had mentioned in the marshes.

'And he keeps coming and going as he pleases without any regard for me. Seems that you have that in common,' Mellie accused, in between mouthfuls.

'How many children do you have?' The man asked the next logical question, taking advantage of information being imparted, trust being built, blah blah and sidled closer to Mellie on the bench.

'Four,' Mellie said.

'I have four grandkids?' As far as frogs went, this was nothing. As far as humans went, that was...a lot.

'I thought you only had Ella and the twins, Hans and Greta?' The older woman asked.

'There is also Ellie. She should be three by now...' Mellie's eyes misted over.

'Oh, I'm so sorry, I didn't know...hadn't realised...' the older woman patted Mellie on her shoulder.

'She's not dead, you daft woman. She's with her father. At least Oz said he was going to take her to the Emerald City and come back for me, but that was three years ago...' Mellie ended in a whisper.

By all accounts, his daughter sounded like she wasn't happy with her lot in life. She had borne the man four children and the man had taken the toddler and disappeared.

'Right. So I should go to this Emerald City and bring him back here to face his obligations,' the former frog said and puffed out his chest.

That was the least he could do, a multi-dimensional being who could travel the worlds. Well, he hoped he could travel, now that he had been disenchanted. He hadn't tried yet.

'Would you?' Mellie looked at him with something close to adoration.

He recognised manipulation when he saw it. His daughter was trying to push the 'be the dutiful parent' button. Then again, why not? He didn't have so many offspring that he could just disregard their wants and wishes. And that Oz should take responsibility for his wife and his children. Before he said any of this aloud though, maybe he should just try...before he issued promises he couldn't keep.

A cocoon of silvery light started forming around him and he disappeared in a gust of wind, looking rather surprised.

'Well, that was...efficient.' Mellie mused.

'Assuming he went to the Emerald City to speak to Oz and did not evaporate just to get out of here.' The old woman said.

'Oh, ye of little faith,' Mellie said, looking considerably happier.

'The books don't mention anyone putting the fear of God... quite literally...into the Wizard of Oz,' Granny muttered.

'Books? What books? There are books about Oz?' Mellie looked like it was the first day of school. 'Show me!'

AUTHOR'S NOTE

If you want to know how Mellie fared with Oz, pick up Book #3 Ash: Crooked Fates.

If you're keen to learn what happened to the fairy whom the toad mama abducted, please read Thumbelina: The Bride Experiment.

6
SEA GHOST OF THE ISLE
N.D.T. CASALE

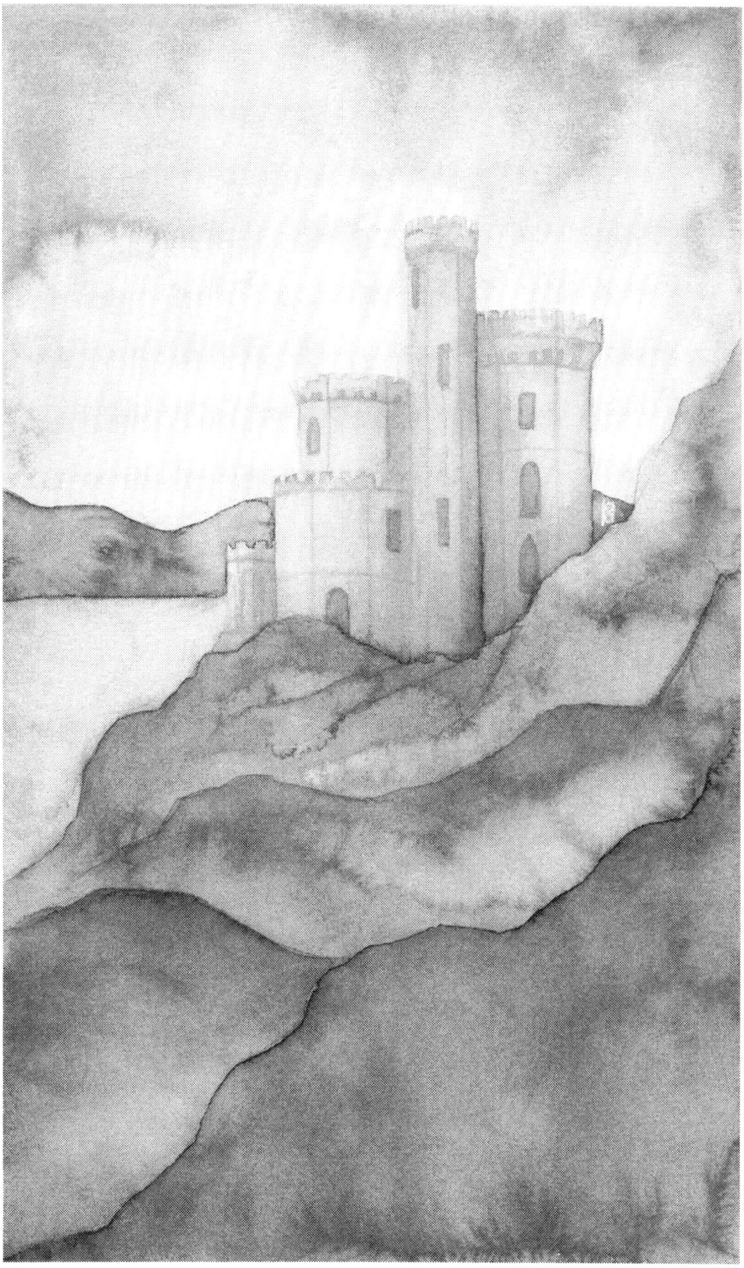

SEA GHOST OF THE ISLE

For centuries Scotland has captivated the world with its beauty and mystery. From the highland peaks down to the isles, secrets roam freely on the tongues of natives to the ears of tourists. One particular mystery is The Sea Ghosts of Eilean Cairistiòna, an uninhabited castle island off the northern coast. According to local villagers, it is a place of history, curses, and treasures. When the stars dance across the night sky, "sea ghosts" or Asrai emerge from the waters to bask in moonlight. They are beautiful translucent creatures who call the sea their home. Sometimes Asrai are friends and other times foes. Some will lure humans to the deepest waters and drown them. Others will help humans rise to their fullest potential. However, the Asrai are given only the dark hours in which to play. When sunlight signals a new day, they must disappear into the water, for exposure to sun will melt them away.

Seventeen-year-old Nessa MacCowen touched the Celtic cross around her neck. It was a gift from her aunt whom she had not seen in ten years.

"Yer not from around 'ere are ye lass?" the cab driver boomed. As he drove the car through the narrow road in the highlands, his voice interrupted her thoughts.

Nessa shook her head, "I'm from New York."

The cabman nodded, "Well by th' looks o' yah, ye wull fit right in."

Nessa smiled. Her long red hair reached her waist and her bright blue eyes hid the anxiety in her heart. She was Scottish on both sides of her family, but had never set foot in the motherland. Her parents had emigrated from Scotland to New York before she was born. All of her life had been spent in the States.

Her intention was to spend the summer with her aunt Countess Aileene-Edith Campbell. Her parents had decided to move back to Scotland because her mother had been appointed CEO of a high-tech company nearby. Her father, an entrepreneur, was spending the summer monitoring a start-up company in Tokyo, Japan. Her mother had gone with him, but her parents felt it was better that Nessa live with her aunt in Scotland before the entire family was reunited in the autumn. Aileene-Edith lived in the countryside beyond a small village called Applecross. It was her parents' plan to reside with Countess Aileene-Edith in her castle until they found a home of their own. Her parents felt it was important for her to reconnect with her Scottish roots and her aunt.

The car rounded a corner and a giant castle with a waterfront view came into focus.

"It's right up 'ere, lass." The driver pointed at the massive edifice that appeared before them.

"A castle?"

"Ye dinnae ken yer aunt was a countess, lass?" inquired the cab driver.

"I did; but I didn't know she lived in a house the size of Buckingham Palace."

The elderly driver chuckled. "If ye look carefully out intae th' water ye can see Eilean Cairistiòna, an auld castle isle that is famous fur th' tales o'..."

"Asrai," finished Nessa. The story her aunt had told her years ago flowed through her brain.

The shiny car pulled up to the front doors of the estate. Nessa was fascinated by the fifteenth-century architecture adorned in a modern flair. Its towers stretched towards the sky. The grand old house had thirty-two bedrooms, and the red sandstone walls gave Nessa Shakespearean vibes. The three hundred acres attached to the estate had been turned into a rescue farm by her aunt who gave dozens of animals a forever home and offered work to many local people.

Nessa felt her heart beat in her ears. She had not seen her aunt since she was seven. In her middle years, Aileene-Edith had fallen ill and had not been able to make the trip to New York. As time passed they had lost touch. Now the young teen was in Scotland by herself. Would her aunt like her? Would she be able to make friends? The questions slowly rose into her conscious mind and consumed her thoughts like quicksand. Her mother had reassured her this change would be an adventure; but instead, Nessa felt anxious and fidgeted with her necklace.

The castle door opened and her aunt ran over to the car.

"Nessa," she called and pulled her into a bear hug as the red-haired girl got out of the backseat. "Aye, lass, ye have grown 'n' yer sae bonnie. It's bin sae lang, mah precious wee bairn. I prayed every night yer family would return tae our heritage home, 'n' thank Providence th' Lord delivers. Now let me have a good look. My! What a beautiful young lass ye have grown tae be."

Countess Aileene-Edith was a slender woman in her late fifties, with vivid blue eyes and blonde hair neatly arranged in a becoming style.

Nessa turned and saw the heads of children in the doorway looking at her.

"Come, wee bairns," Aileene-Edith waved them over. "Come meet yer cousin."

Five children sprinted over and stood next to her aunt.

"I have cousins?" whispered Nessa racking her brain to remember if her aunt ever had children.

"Aye," answered Aileene-Edith. "I know it has bin ower ten years, Nessa, n' this is a bit o' a surprise. Yer uncle passed away lang before ye were born, 'n' I always wanted bairns. This castle can be very lonely, so I have adopted bairns tae call mah own. This is Beatrice. She is ten. William is eight. Agnes is seven. Michael is six. Alice is four." Aileene-Edith pointed out each child and beamed with pride.

"How come ye ne'er cam tae visit us?" asked Agnes. "Why is this th' first time?"

"Is it far from New York tae 'ere?" asked Michael.

"Ye'r bonny," shouted out Alice.

"I thought she would be taller," whispered Beatrice.

"Such bright red hair," added William.

"What is New York like?" asked Beatrice.

"I heard 'tis dirty," chimed in William.

The children surrounded Nessa and fought for her attention the way seagulls fight for bread crumbs.

"Hush, mah sweet bairns!" said Aileene-Edith. "Yer cousin has traveled a lang way. Let her git settled."

Nessa gave the children a wan smile. "It is nice to meet all of you." Although their chatter made her head spin.

Aileene-Edith placed her arm around Nessa's shoulders and gestured towards the people standing in a straight line in front of the carved double doors that opened into the great house. "Ower 'ere we have some o' th' staff who will help ye if ye need anything at all. This is Julia, mah head attendant; Ewan is mah advisor; Lawrence is th' chef…"

The rest of the names were a blur to Nessa as Aileene-Edith guided her into the castle. Clyde the butler took her bags from the cab driver to take to her room.

She stepped across the threshold into the great hall. Her footsteps echoed across the stones as ancient as the mist on the nearby mountains. The reverberations of her shoes were muted by thick rich Persian carpets. A massive fire flickered and sparked from the grate. Secrets lurked, hidden in the rafters and floated lazily in the halls.

"Nessa," her aunt's voice penetrated her wandering thoughts. "Would ye like tae see yer chamber?" She motioned towards the grand staircase.

Nessa nodded, eager to get away from her cousins. She climbed up the stairs and made her way through the massive corridor. This was home. The words had a comforting yet scary resonance to them. This was the first time she had been away from her parents for any considerable length of time. Even though she would see them at the end of the summer, her heart ached for them, and she wished they could be here with her. This was not how she had envisioned this move to be. It was supposed to be just her and her aunt, the way it had been when the countess had visited her family in New York. Now her aunt had children, and her cousins were like a group of chattering birds. She knew her time with her beloved relative would be limited. She felt as if she had ventured into another world, so strange in scope and scale that the enormity of the massive building nearly caused her to feel unwell.

"Nessa, ye seem affy peely-wally," The countess felt her niece's forehead. "I know this is difficult fur ya," Aunt Aileene-Edith continued as they walked up a second set of winding stairs. "Ye hae ne'er bin tae Scotland, 'n' yer parents are away on business. Ye need to be gallus, wee lassie. We love ye sae much, 'n' we are sae happy ye are 'ere. I know it will be an adjustment wi' all the bairns in the house…'n' animals…"

"Animals?" interrupted Nessa,

"Aye, ye haven't had a chance tae explore th' grounds yit, but a portion o' mah land is an animal rescue sanctuary. It provides work fur th' people o' th' village 'n' saves many animals' lives. We keep pets in th' castle, ye might as well ken that now."

At long last, after what seemed an endless journey, the friendly countess reached an intricately-carved oak frame and stopped. She tugged at the latch and pushed the heavy door open.

Nessa stepped into the largest bedroom she had even seen. There was even a fireplace with comfy chairs next to it. On the opposite side of the room was a beautiful canopy bed with lavender curtains. A large mirror was positioned above a table. Silver accents gave the room a homey touch. Nessa stared in awe. She had never seen anything so regal.

A barking sound interrupted the quiet. Nessa looked up to see an Irish wolfhound lumber over from its dog bed by the fireplace. The dog was beige and shaggy. It licked her hand with its warm pink tongue.

"This is Anna. She is a rescue 'n' a gift fur ye," said Aileene-Edith.

Nessa had always wanted a dog; however, Anna was the largest specimen of canine the young teen had ever seen. Her head reached the girl's midsection. Nessa was able to scratch Anna behind the ears without even having to bend down.

"I wull leave ye tae settle yersel'," offered Aunt Aileene-Edith. "Supper is at six."

After enjoying a delicious meal prepared by castle chef Lawrence, the family sat in front of the fireplace in the study. Nessa felt comfortable on the floor with Anna while her cousins played and danced around. Soon the children begged her to join them, but the tired teen shook her head. Jetlag was settling in and she was not in a playful mood.

"Mother, tell Nessa th' story o' th' Asrai," cried Beatrice.

Aileene-Edith smiled. "I used tae tell mah dear niece that story a lang time ago when she wis around yer age."

Nessa gave a knowing smile, "I remember, but it has been a long time since I heard such a tale."

"Very well," replied Aunt Aileene-Edith. She took a deep breath and began. "The isle o' Eilean Cairistiòna wis not always abandoned. In truth, 'twas not always an island. Hundreds o' years ago 'twas ruled by a beautiful queen named Cairistiòna. She wis kind 'n' generous. Th' people loved her. An evil witch named Doileag wis jealous o' her beauty, kind heart, 'n' riches. Doileag formed a plan tae kill Cairistiòna 'n' claim th' castle 'n' fortune fur herself. However, her plan wis overheard by th' birds who warned Cairistiòna tae leave her estate immediately. Cairistiòna buried her riches somewhere on th' land surrounding th' massive pile sae Doileag could ne'er find th' wealth. When Doileag stormed th' battlements, Queen Cairistiòna escaped intae th' night. Doileag became sae filled wi' rage at her inability tae kill th' beautiful queen, she used her magical powers tae break th' lands, hills, valleys, 'n' mountains away from th' mainland, transforming Cairistiòna's realm intae an island in th' Sound of Shiant. Tae secure her magic, th' witch conjured creatures known as Asrai tae populate th' waters surrounding th' ill-gotten treasure until she could locate th' hiding spot o' th' hidden jewels. Asrai are stunning translucent water creatures who look exactly like men and women. Their goal is tae lure humans tae th' waters 'n' drown them. Some storytellers say those drowned humans died; 'n' others believed th' humans became Asrai themselves 'n' joined Doileag's water army. However, th' Asrai only come out at night, fur exposure tae sunlight wull melt them."

"Like a water vampire?" asked William.

"Nae," laughed the Countess. "Doileag inhabited th' castle fur years, but try as she might, she could ne'er find the Queen's hidden treasure. Later she wis killed by a brave maiden named Faye, a cousin of Cairistiòna. Faye's brother had been taken captive by th' Asrai 'n' she wis determined tae git her revenge. While Faye plotted tae avenge th' capture o' her brother, Doileag kept a magical secret unknown tae th' brave maiden. The amulet Doileag wore around her neck held th' key tae reversing th' spell that would free an Asrai. Over time, Faye found th' amulet 'n' won her brother's freedom. She stabbed Doileag in th' heart 'n' hid th' amulet wi' th' treasure somewhere on th' castle grounds. As th' tale unfolds, legend has it that th' amulet is a solid oval ruby encased in gold. On th' back is an engraving of th' triple spiral or triskele. Tae this day no one has ever found th' treasure o' Eilean Cairistiòna. Bairns are warned tae stay away from th' waters at night. The sea ghosts still guard Eilean Cairistiòna under Doileag's wicked spell, 'n' 'tis their purpose tae lure innocent souls tae their demise."

"What happened tae Queen Cairistiòna?" asked Agnes.

"She escaped from th' castle 'n' traveled tae a faraway land. There she settled intae life as a villager. She married, had children, 'n' wis very happy wi' her new identity. She ne'er desired tae go back tae her castle. Her treasure still remains hidden tae this day," replied Aunt Aileene-Edith.

"I thought Asrai could be good?" asked Michael.

"Aye, yes. After Faye killed Doileag, th' Asrai had no leader. They became split intae good 'n' bad. Th' evil Asrai hae no soul 'n' continued tae lure humans tae a watery grave tae prevent them from coming tae Eilean Cairistiòna. However, th' good Asrai, who are believed tae have been humans, chose tae protect people tae save them from th' same fate. Many historians have explored Eilean Cairistiòna tae try tae find th' treasure; however, th' curse o' Doileag seems tae have a hold on th' isle tae this day. Something strange 'n' tragic always happens when humans try tae inhabit th' isle."

"Has anyone ever seen an Asrai?" asked Beatrice.

"There have bin sightings on occasion," noted Aileene-Edith, "but 'tis all speculation. Th' last known encounter I believe wis in 1952. An eighteen-year-old fisherman caught a female Asrai in his net. Asrai can sometimes shift 'n' take oan a different appearance. This Asrai looked like a mermaid. Th' young fisherman wis captivated by th' mermaid Asrai's beauty 'n' wanted tae marry her. He also believed that he would become wealthy if he captured th' other Asrai 'n' showed them off tae the world. Th' captured Asrai told him tae let her go, but he didnae listen 'n' wis determined tae make her his bride. He brought her home 'n' locked her up. In th' morning, the fisherman wis greeted by a puddle o' seawater on th' floor. The Asrai wis gone."

"No one has ever found th' treasure?" asked Beatrice, her eyes wide.

"Maybe one day it wull be found," replied the countess.

"I want tae find th' treasure," said William jumping to his feet. "I wull be rich!"

"This story is always one o' my favorites," giggled Alice. She turned to Nessa and gave her a smile.

Nessa nodded, "Mine, too."

Nessa tossed and turned in her bed. The mattress was comfy but her spirit was restless. The castle was her new home but it felt unfamiliar. Home was where her parents were, and even though she loved her aunt, a part of her felt lost. Her thoughts were interrupted when Anna jumped on the bed and barked.

"What's wrong?" asked Nessa, spitting out dog hair. Anna landed on top of the sleepy girl in a great heaping weight of canine, which felt like having a pony on top of her. It was a surprise Anna did not wake up the whole house. Then again, the castle was so large her family probably wouldn't hear the noise.

Panting in great breaths, the dog lay across the girl's body. Nessa felt suffocated, trapped, riveted by the weight of the Irish Wolfhound. While the creature could take breaths, Nessa could not. Heat from the great wolfhound's body filled her nostrils. Still spitting out dog hair, she pushed at the mountainous animal that covered her. Anna jumped off Nessa and the pretty redhead felt her lungs return to normal. On alert, the hairy watchdog padded over to the door, looked back at Nessa, then scratched at the great wooden barrier.

"I'm coming," replied Nessa, catching her breath. She slid off the bed into her slippers and put her robe over her pajamas. She forgot that having a dog meant it had to be taken outside to relieve itself. She fumbled to clip the dog leash to the hound's collar in the half-dark.

Anna seemed to know the way out as she navigated Nessa through the long hallways and staircases. Finally, they were out in the yard.

"Ok," said Nessa groggily, "do what you have to do,"

Instead of relieving herself, the loyal protector lunged forward ripping the leash out of Nessa's hands. She tore down the hill barking excessively on her way towards the sea.

"Anna!" cried Nessa bolting after the Irish Wolfhound. The young teen stumbled down the rocky path following her shaggy guardian.

Abruptly Anna stopped and sat panting at the edge of the waves. Her tongue waggled back and forth.

"Anna! What is the matter with you? Crazy dog," gasped Nessa. She bent down to pick up the leash when she saw what Anna was staring at.

The moon was at waxing gibbous in the night sky. The

moonlight illuminated the Sound of Shiant. In the distance Nessa clearly saw the turrets of Eilean Cairistiòna. A cloud of mist appeared above the lapping swells. Nessa saw the transparent image seemed to take on human form as it wavered back and forth across the waves.

Nessa felt confused. *Asrai?* She thought. But that was impossible. It was a Scottish legend. A tale told to children so they would not stray too far into the water.

A snorting sound came from behind her. Nessa whirled around to see a highland bull standing on the sand. The creature was covered in a shaggy coat, and it lowered its long horns. Even though the bull's eyes were covered by its thick hair, the animal pawed the earth as though it was possessed, bucking its head. The shaggy beast seemed tense and angry.

Nessa's heart leaped to her throat and her palms grew sweaty. She looked around for a place to run, but the only escape was into the arms of the sea. Even though she knew how to swim, after the tales her aunt had told that night, she was wary about running into the ocean's depths. Anna on the other hand did not bark or growl. She stood in the same spot staring out at Eilean Cairistiòna.

While the canine kept vigil, the bull bellowed, its feet scattering sand, and, to Nessa's horror, began to charge the frightened teen. Nessa's feet felt glued to the ground and unable to react. She lifted her arms, turned her head and flinched, awaiting the impact of the treacherous horns.

Out of nowhere a figure stepped between her and the raging animal. Instead of harming Nessa, the beast rammed into the figure and bounced back howling. A portion of its fur seemed to have turned to ice. It ran into the water and disappeared.

"That was not real," murmured Nessa. She clasped her hands to her chest in an attempt to calm her rapid heartbeat and heavy breath. She shuddered to think what would have happened if the mysterious silhouette had not come to her rescue.

"O' course, 'twas not real. Bulls would not be oot late at night." The figure turned around to reveal itself to be a handsome man. He was tall and muscular with russet wavy hair and a close-shaven beard. He appeared to be in his late teens to early twenties. "'Twas an Asrai, transformed into a mirage tae chase thee tae thy death."

Warmth rushed up to her cheeks. The mystifying fellow was stunning and beautiful from head to toe. Her heart came alive, leaping in her chest--woken after a long slumber. Her tongue was a useless lump in her mouth, and she struggled to form her thoughts into words.

The man stepped closer to her. His skin shimmered in the moonlight, and his appearance wavered. "Ye need tae git back tae yer home 'n' never set foot near th' water at night time again."

He walked into the sea and melted into the waves.

Nessa awoke hours later with sunlight streaming in her face and Anna sleeping at her feet. She sat up and felt disoriented. Then her thoughts drifted to what had transpired on the edge of the sea and to the comments spoken by the mysterious man. Had last night really happened?

She got up and after breakfast took Anna for a walk along the water. The Scottish coastline was breathtaking. Blue waves lapped at the sand and birds flew overhead. Eilean Cairistiòna glowed in the distance. Further down the coast Nessa ran into a man sitting at the edge of the dock. He was an old Scottish fisherman. He had a grizzled appearance: plump, a graying beard, and an old fisherman's cap. Anna began to bark and dragged Nessa towards the man.

"Well, what a braw beastie ye may be," the man reached over to stroke the wolf-like creature on the head.

"I'm sorry," Nessa cried as she caught her breath.

"Na apologies. It gets quite lonely out on these waters. Ye mist be new. I hae ne'er seen ye 'ere before," the man replied.

"My name is Nessa. I'm living with my aunt at Castle Campbell," Nessa replied.

"Laochailan," the man tipped his hat in a polite manner. "Mah cottage is juist doon th' way. I'm sure ye passed it oan yer travels."

Nessa noticed on Laochailan's right forearm was a tattoo of a mermaid. In his other arm he cradled a jar of what appeared to be saltwater.

"Are you fishing?" asked Nessa.

"I used tae be a fisherman. Noo I juist enjoy th' patience o' th' sea," Laochailan replied. "I sit 'ere, look out tae th' isles, 'n' bask in memories 'n' legends."

"My aunt told me about the legends of the Asrai who guard the waters around Eilean Cairistiòna."

A dark look crossed Laochailan's face. "All that stuff is hogwash 'n' bairn's play. None o' it's real." Then he went silent staring out into the sea.

Nessa nodded and continued on her walk.

It was half-past-one in the morning, and once again Castle Campbell's newest member could not sleep. All she could think about was the man who had melted into the tide. His tall stature, his angular cheekbones carved down toward a chiseled jaw, and his emerald irises beneath thick lashes caused her heart to begin to beat faster. He was the most beautiful man she had ever laid eyes on. What was a man like that doing at the edge of the sea in the middle of the night? She remembered how his athletic physique had walked into the swells and disappeared. Could he be an Asrai? Did they really exist? Had the encounter with the highland bull been a dream? No, it felt too real to be a dream. The questions banged around in her imagination giving her a headache. She kicked back the covers. If the mystery man were an Asrai, then he would be by the edge of the water again tonight. She had to find out for herself if such a striking gentleman were real. She took Anna outside down to the lapping waves where she could gaze at Eilean Cairistiòna. What secrets did the isle have hidden in her mystical mists?

"I told ye not tae come," a familiar voice rang out in the darkness.

Nessa turned to see the male model standing next to her. Green orbs under dark lashes glared disapprovingly at her for intruding.

"I needed to know if it was real or a dream," replied the curious girl.

"Ye should hae settled on a dream," cautioned the attractive stranger. The moonlight highlighted the muscles of his exposed arms.

"You're an Asrai," stated Nessa, noting the man's ghostly glow. "It is true. You are real."

"Real as life 'n' death," he replied. "Noo git tae yer house before ye git intae more trouble. I may not be able tae keep ye from harm a second time."

"You saved my life, and I don't know your name?"

"Cailean," replied the secretive silhouette.

"Why did you save my life? Why didn't you let the Asrai beast lead me to my death?"

"Tis a fankle ye begin wi' asking sae many questions, lass, " answered Cailean irritably. Then he softened his voice. "I dinnae wish anyone tae fall prisoner tae th' same fate as has befallen me."

Nessa looked at him questioningly. Cailean groaned. His plump lips curved downward in annoyance. "That great stone at th' edge o' th' water would seem tae offer comfortable seating fur yer ladyship. We shall sit there together. Methinks ye are not going tae leave until I satisfy yer curiosity."

Nessa sat on the boulder and Anna settled on the ground next to her. It seemed to the teen the Irish Wolfhound found the man of the mist pleasing. Cailean took a deep breath and began.

"Many years ago, I wis as human as ye in th' flesh. I wis Duke Cailean o' Scotland 'n' in th' line o' succession tae th' throne. 'Twas th' night o' April 15th, 1503. I cuid nae sleep. I walked doon tae th' waters tae gaze at th' night sky. I met a beautiful maid who wis mysterious 'n' alluring. She enticed me intae her mischief on a moonlight stroll when she dropped her necklace intae th' water. I offered tae swim after it. Once in th' water, th' necklace kept slipping from mah fingers. It led me farther 'n' farther from th' safety of mah human soul 'n' th' waves consumed me. Tae mah regret, I realized th' maiden wis an Asrai. Her name wis Sìonag, 'n' she wanted me tae be her lover. The myths about Asrai luring humans tae their deaths are true. However, when ye are drowned by an Asrai, 'tis similar tae death, but in truth 'tis not death at all. The victim's soul becomes trapped in limbo, 'n' becomes an Asrai tae serve as part o' Doileag's cursed army. Each imprisoned victim must guard Eilean Cairistiòna forever 'n' continue tae grow th' clan o' sea ghosts. Once ye become an Asrai there is no aging. I look th' same as I did 518 years ago. I am unchanged."

"I thought Doileag was killed by Faye?" asked Nessa.

"She was. However, Faye's destiny wis fur her brother, 'n' she had no sympathy fur th' other sea ghosts who were captive. She wis selfish. She freed her brother but took no risk at breaking th' curse. She left th' amulet somewhere in th' castle. She left us Asrai tae suffer between life 'n' death, tae guard a treasure that may ne'er be found. Alas 'ere I am neither dead nor alive tae wander through th' night until dawn. If I walk upon th' sandy coast past th' time th' sun rises, I wull melt intae nothing. Once an Asrai melts that is th' end of existence wi' no chance o' th' afterlife."

"What happened to Sìonag?" asked Nessa. "Did she expect you to become her lover?"

"She did 'n' I told her nay." A smirk crossed Cailean's lips. "I jooked her lik' th' plague, but she harassed me fur centuries. Finally, I wis put out o' mah misery whin her hobby o' luring men tae thair death backfired. A fisherman caught her in his net 'n' decided tae take her home wi' him 'n' make her his wife. Yit whin th' sun made contact wi' her th' next day, she melted intae a puddle."

"Wait a minute. That's the story my aunt told me. The last sighting of the Asrai was in 1952."

"August 4. What a glorious day. Justice wis served. However, I wis still cursed as an Asrai. Instead o' wallowing in pity, I took it upon masell tae begin tae defend other folk from huvin th' same fate as I suffer."

"Can the curse be ended?" asked Nessa.

"Only if ye kin find Doileag's amulet 'n' break it. Then th' curse wull be goosed, 'n' th' souls that hae bin held captive as Asrai wull be set free," replied Cailean.

"Free as in going to the afterlife? Or free as in becoming human again?"

Cailean scratched his head. "I dinnae ken; th' curse is bound by magic. I may become human, I may join mah family in th' afterlife. We dinnae ken 'til th' amulet is broken."

"If you become human will you be the same age you were when you died, or older?"

"Ye ask tae mony questions. Maidens in mah years wid hae ne'er bin sae bold," scowled Cailean turning away from her, his broad shoulders parallel to the ocean. Nessa sat in awe drinking in his beauty with her eyes as he stood before her.

"Enough blether. Tak' yourself back tae where ye came from before ye git hurt. I git enough innocent folk tae protect wi'oot having tae deal wi' a curious lassie, too." The gravely calm yet toneless voice told her the discussion was over.

The fondness Nessa felt for Cailean hardened. *Curious lassie.* Her face flushed. She grabbed Anna's leash. Her new home was full of chattering cousins, and now the sea did not want her company, either. There seemed no place where she was accepted. The red-haired girl placed one foot on the bottom stone of the steps that joined the castle to the sea, when a gust blew her red curls across her face. She batted them away and paused. She stopped in her tracks and turned to look at the young duke. Cailean stood so close to her in the moonlight, his muscular back facing her. He seemed so strong, yet so lonely. The rejection and embarrassment she had felt a few moments ago melted into pity.

"I can help you," said Nessa. "I can help you find the amulet and break the curse."

"Yer going tae help me 'n' I dinnae ken yer name," replied Cailean slowly turning to face her. His eyes narrowed under thick eyebrows.

"My name is Nessa, and I moved to Scotland from America. I am living with my aunt at Castle Campbell."

"Aye, Castle Campbell," Cailean stroked his beard. "I ken it well."

Nessa grew quiet.

"Ah dinnae need yer help. Th' curse wull ne'er be broken. This is mah fate 'n' ah have tae live wi' it forever. What yi"ll need tae dae is head back tae th' castle 'n' ne'er come 'ere again," said Cailean. He walked into the sea; the waves parted taking him prisoner, then swallowing him. Nessa was left alone with her thoughts.

The next morning Nessa had her aunt's chauffeur Harold take her into town. She wanted to research the history of Castle Cairistiòna.

The red-haired teen had spent a sleepless night thinking about Cailean's fate. Cailean's life had been cut short by a selfish evil spirit full of lust for his beauty. He had died a senseless death and was now doomed to roam the waters guarding a curse. He spent his days battling the vile Asrai to make sure innocent folk were not dragged into the waves where their breaths would be stolen and their hearts ceased to beat. Nessa shuddered to think what Cailean's emotions had been through as he faced this turmoil and the bitterness he must have felt. He had not been able to say goodbye to his family, and his loved ones had never known what had become of him. Cailean had been forced to imagine everyone he loved grow old from his deep shadows of the sea. He had never been able to marry and produce children of his own. The young lord had sensed that all his relations had passed onto the afterlife while he suffered in misery. Nessa's thoughts shifted to the other good Asrai who were Cailean's prison mates. What were their stories? What misfortune had befallen them to be forced to wander aimlessly throughout the night? No one deserved such torment. No one deserved to have their souls held captive in the grips of eternity forever. Nessa understood what it felt like to be surrounded by others yet still feel alone, not to understand where one belonged. She looked at her reflection in her cell phone case; her sapphire eyes showed her decision. Even though Cailean had told her to stay away, she could not. She had to help him and the other Asrai out of limbo and into the afterlife. She had to break the curse.

Harold dropped her off at Lochorn Library in downtown Applecross. Nessa walked in and was greeted by a plump gray-haired librarian.

"How can I help ye, lass?" The librarian flashed her a smile.

"I am looking for some information on Castle Cairistiòna. Floor plans, architecture, anything about the layout of the castle and the legend," replied Nessa.

"I suppose yer one o' those treasure hunters." The woman peered closer at the redhead. "Na, hauld yer horses, ah ken ye. Yer Aileene-Edith's niece, come tae live wi' her."

"Yes I am."

"Yer aunt brags about ye all th' time. She is sae happy ye 'n' yer parents are comin' tae live wi' her forever."

Nessa nodded. The townsfolk knew her; yet she did not know them. She missed her friends back in New York City; she missed the bustling of day-to-day traffic, the skyscrapers, and the diverse aromas that filled the streets. She cleared her throat. "Where would the information on Castle Cairistiòna be?"

"Right this way, lass," the librarian motioned her to a desk at the back of the library. "Juist a moment." Then she disappeared into a nearby room labeled "Archives." She returned with a huge antique book. It was worn around the edges and caked in dust.

"I'm afraid nae mony folk come 'ere asking fur th' history o' ancient castles." The librarian placed the book on the table and a cloud of dust rose into the air. Nessa coughed.

"Noo this is a very auld non-circulating book. In ither words, it cannae leave th' library at all," the librarian advised.

Nessa nodded.

The librarian had given her a pair of gloves to handle the ancient tome. She began to peruse each yellowed page with the utmost care. Nessa realized the book had been written to detail every castle in Scotland. She looked through several pages until she reached the entry about Castle Cairistiòna.

There were drawings of the exterior as well as the floorplan for the two-hundred rooms spread over multiple levels. According to the diagrams, beneath the living quarters of the castle was a dungeon. Historians noted in their searches they had never been able to locate the crypt. However, a notation suggested the entrance to the burial site might reveal itself under a full moon once a month.

"That sounds like a good place to store a treasure and an amulet," the teen mused.

In the silence of the library a sudden noise caught her attention. She turned to see Laochailan standing behind her. The fisherman's nose was buried in a book, and he held the jar of saltwater in the crook of his arm.

"Laochailan?" she asked.

"Young lassie," the fisherman seemed to be in a brighter mood than when she had last seen him. "Fancy running in tae ya 'ere."

Nessa nodded. "That appears to be an interesting book."

Laochailan smiled. "Ya know an old man like me ain't got

nothing else tae do except read by th' water 'n' feel nostalgic. Whit are ye researching? Castles?"

"Just doing some research to get more familiar with my new home," replied Nessa.

"Smart lassie. Weel, ah best be getting alang. Nice tae see ye again." Laochailan disappeared between the shelves but not before Nessa noticed the title of the book he had been reading revolved around mermaids, castles, and Scottish mythology.

"Nessa, how many times have I told ye tae stop comin' 'ere," Cailean's voice was a mixture of amusement and irritation. "I am not going tae help ye if ye keep insisting on comin' 'ere knowing an Asrai might drown ye."

"Last I checked, you don't own the coast," sassed Nessa.

Cailean muttered, "Stubborn lassie."

"I decided I am going to help you," replied Nessa.

"Help me?"

"I am going to break the curse to set you and the other Asrai free."

"Yer aff yer heid!" Cailean's eyes held Nessa in its smoldering gaze. Nessa could see though the shinning pools that Cailean believed she had gone insane. "I dinnae need yer help. Th' curse is 'ere forever. Nessa, I drowned five hundred 'n' eighteen years ago. Mah body is an Asrai. Na langer human but not a spirit either, juist a translucent ghost set tae roam th' waters at nighttime 'til th' sun calls me intae hiding."

"Cailean, stop! It doesn't have to be that way. Stop thinking only about yourself; there are many other good Asrai who have suffered the same fate as you. They deserve freedom as much as you do. You said so yourself, that if we can find Doileag's amulet, we can break the spell that holds everyone captive."

"That is impossible. Historians have scoured that isle fur

centuries 'n' have failed in thair explorations. Even if ye did fin' th' amulet 'n' break it, there is no guarantee I wull magically become human again. I might juist cross the realms 'n' disappear altogether." Cailean paced back and forth.

"It doesn't matter to me if you become human or cross over. Your soul deserves to be free, and you deserve to be reunited with your family again. I'm sure you miss them."

Cailean lowered his eyes, his sculpted jaw tensed. "Ah, family. Mah beloved mither ne'er understood what happened tae me, how I could juist disappear wi'oot a word. Mah family wur broken 'n' spend thair lives in sorrow. In thay hearts thay knew I wis dead even though thay ne'er found mah body. Family is important; ye dinnae realize this 'til yer locked in limbo. That is why ye shuid be spending time wi' yer aunt 'n' cousins instead o' trying tae help a woebegone misfit lik' me."

Nessa looked at him curiously.

"I ken everything that goes on throughout th' coast," continued Cailean. "Whin th' sun comes I hide in th' shadows o' th' waves. In that dark place, I watch bairns play in th' light 'n' people go about their day. Castle Campbell is in direct view o' where I lay 'n' wait for night. I ken yer family lik' they're mah family. I hear their joy, sadness, 'n' wishes on th' winds."

Nessa looked down at her hands. "I feel as if I don't fit in with them," she murmured.

Cailean looked at her inquisitively.

Nessa sighed. "I haven't seen my aunt in ten years. She used to come visit me when I lived in New York, but then she fell ill, and we lost touch. Now in my current residence I have made a discovery. She has five adopted children who demand her attention all the time. I feel left out. I try to have conversations with her, but my cousins are always interrupting. If we want to go somewhere, my cousins have to come. My aunt and I can never be alone the way it used to be. My parents keep making decisions for me without asking how I feel. They decided to move here permanently when my mother was assigned to a very high position in a large business enterprise. They made up their minds that I am going to move here first while they go to Japan for the summer. My dad is monitoring a start-up company there. I just feel like everything is moving way too fast, and I have no control over my life."

Cailean nodded. "I have felt th' same way fur centuries. Mah parents ne'er inquired about mah feelings on mah future. I wis close tae th' eldest. 'Twas mah duty tae marry well. I wis ne'er asked how I felt about it. I ne'er had a choice even in a wife."

"Did you not want to marry?" asked Nessa.

"Aye 'n' nae. I am a descendant o' Th' House O' Stewart. As a duke I wis destined tae bring wealth 'n' glory tae th' family. But whin I died, all those dreams died wi' me. My great great great grandniece wis th' last Scottish monarch. Sometimes I feel guilty. If I had not died, maybe mah children or masell cuid hae done something tae stop th' Scottish crown from being combined wi' Britain's crown. I often wonder what kind o' monarch mah son wuld have bin. What kind o' leader I wuld have bin. I liked th' idea o' making a change tae th' kingdom 'n' helping citizens; but there were other rules which I felt took mah freedoms 'n' mah ability tae choose away. Sometimes I think drowning by Sìonag stopped me from having tae make a choice at all, but often I have regrets."

Nessa looked at Cailean. He was dressed in a white tunic and white breeches. His feet were bare and his whole body sparkled in a way that pleased the eye. A change of clothes and he could fit in with any of the young men here in town. Nessa smirked. Even though he had been alive centuries ago, it seemed not much had changed with parents making decisions for their children without asking them what they wanted.

"Are you happy being an Asrai?" she asked.

"Are ye daft, woman?" replied Cailean. "'Tis worse than

bein' married tae someone ye dinnae love. An Asrai cannae venture past th' boundaries o' th' water; cannae stay out past daylight. I am not alive 'n' I am not dead. I am juist an unworthy creature bound tae a curse. Thare is no chance o' freedom."

Cailean's face fell and he looked down at the sand beneath his feet. Nessa felt sorry for him. He was so much more than an unworthy creature. He could have spent his days drowning in bitterness, praying on the souls of the townspeople to grow the Asrai army; but instead, he chose to protect humans from the evil Asrai. He was a pure soul like the other good Asrai who followed his lead. He deserved to be free from the pain he endured. Nessa looked down at his hands resting on his thighs. She felt a strong desire to comfort the saddened sea ghost. Her hand reached forward to grab his hand. No sooner had her fingers become entwined in his when she felt pain shoot up her arm like flames. A cold burning sensation danced in her palm where she had touched his translucent flesh. It felt like little needles were being continuously jammed through her skin. Tiny black spots were beginning to form, and when she rubbed her fingertips together, she felt nothing.

"Ouch!" Nessa howled.

"Are ye all right? asked Cailean.

"What happened?

"I forgot tae tell ye. Ye cannae touch an Asrai. We are cursed. If ye touch an Asrai, th' skin on ye palm n' fingers wull become cold 'n' lifeless like us. This means that where ye have touched us wull lose feeling 'n' begin tae die." He pointed at her fingertips. "Ye barely touched me, sae most likely ye wull lose a wee bit o' feeling in yer fingertips. If ye had grabbed ontae me 'n' held on fur a lang time, th' skin on yer hand would hae turned black 'n' started tae rot."

"Why didn't you tell me that?" cried Nessa. She shuddered at the thought of a dead hand.

"I didnae think ye were going tae try tae hold mah hand," replied Cailean nonchalantly.

"I-I.." Nessa stumbled over her words feeling the heat of embarrassment creep across her face.

"Sae, this research ye did," interrupted Cailean, "where dae ye think this amulet cuid be hidden?"

Nessa was relieved to have a distraction. On her phone she pulled up pictures of the floor plans of Castle Cairistiòna. While the librarian had been busy attending to other patrons, Nessa snapped photos of the pages with her phone.

"Whit's that?" asked Cailean.

"A phone."

"A what?"

"A phone. You don't know what a phone is? Oh wait, they didn't have those in your time. Well, it's a place where you can look up things, send messages to people, take pictures, and talk to people that are far away."

"How intriguing. Such a magical device."

"Yes. Anyway, according to what I researched in the library; it appears that there is a secret crypt hidden underneath the castle. Historians wrote about it, but it was never marked on the maps because no one knows where the entrance is. I believe that is where we will find the amulet and the treasure. The book I studied noted that once a month on the full moon the entrance to the crypt will reveal itself. Tomorrow night is the full moon. My aunt has a boat in her boathouse right over there. I was thinking tomorrow night we could go to the castle and explore."

"I dinnae ken, Nessa. Ye heard th' tales aboot Eilean Cairistiòna. Bad things happen whin humans go thare."

"Do you want to be an Asrai forever or do you want to be free? This is not only about you. Remember, there are many good Asrai who long for the taste of freedom."

"I see ye wull not take nae fur an answer."

"Then I will see you tomorrow night," replied Nessa as she began to climb the stone steps that led up to the castle.

"Nessa?" called Cailean.

Nessa turned around and looked at him silhouetted in moonlight.

"I would have liked tae have held yer hand as well." Then he disappeared into the water.

Nessa felt her breath quickening as warmth filled her heart, and her stomach fluttered. Since the day Cailean had saved her life, she had been awestruck by his looks, but now that she had gotten to know him, he had proven to be much more. He was honest, honorable, and selfless. A true gentlemen. Cailean was different from the boys back in New York. He had a unique sense of wit and charm. She liked spending time with him, and maybe his coy response meant he liked her back.

It was around eleven the next night. The moon was a mysterious white circle beaming in the dark sky. It outshone the sprinkle of stars pouring their lights onto the water. Nessa had spent the whole day being pestered by her cousins. They always wanted to do something with her: playing, drawing, going into town. She never had a moment to herself, and whenever she tried to speak to her aunt or anyone else, they were always there interrupting her. She was grateful when her family was finally asleep. At long last she crept down to her aunt's boathouse and removed the cover of the speedboat.

"Nessa," a voice called.

Her heart froze. She looked up to see her aunt standing in the doorway.

"What are ye doing?" Her aunt asked, concern etched on her face.

"I-I'm helping a friend," she stuttered.

"At eleven o' clock at night?" Aunt Aileene-Edith moved closer to her. "What is going on wi' ye? I have bin watching ye leave th' castle every night fur th' past week."

Nessa sighed. "You wouldn't believe me if I told you."

"Why not?"

"Because you and I are not close anymore. When you used to visit me every summer in New York, we always went on adventures. Now ten years have passed, we are finally together again but you have no time for me. You have five children. You are busy with your animal rescue operation..." Her voice trailed off.

"Oh Nessa, ye really think that?" The countess pulled her shawl tighter around her shoulders. "That is not true. Ye are mah one 'n' only niece. No matter how many bairns I have, I would ne'er abandon ye or make ye feel unwanted. I know yer cousins kin be a handful; 'tis juist that they look up tae ye. I am sae sorry ye felt that way. I love ye, 'n' I am always going tae be here fur ye no matter what. Noo tell me whit's going on."

Nessa sighed. "I know you are going to think I am crazy." She poured out the whole story of the Asrai. When she finished, her aunt raised her eyebrows and had a faraway look in her eyes.

"I knew you weren't going to believe me."

"Oh, I believe ye, Nessa. Dae ye know why I always told ye th' story o' th' Asrai? Because I lived it masell."

Nessa was confused.

"Th' 1952 encounter o' th' Asrai wis not th' last sighting. When I wis a young girl around yer age before I met yer uncle. I fell in love wi' an Asrai."

Nessa was shocked.

"'Tis true," continued Aileene-Edith, "mah grandparents owned this castle before I inherited it. One night I wis drawn tae th' shore 'n' almost killed by an Asrai, but a good one named Arran saved me. We became friends 'n' grew close ower th' months. I even went tae Castle Cairistiòna tae locate th' amulet tae free him 'n' th' other Asrai, but 'twas no use. Eventually, we knew our friendship cuid nae become something more, sae we went our separate ways, 'n' I ne'er saw him again. Then later on, I met yer uncle. I loved him dearly, but I always wondered what happened tae Arran."

"That's my exact problem!" cried Nessa. "I like Cailean a lot. He is a good man and deserves to be free along with the other Asrai. But if we do not find the amulet, we are in the same situation as you. What should I do?"

Aileene-Edith nodded towards the boat. "Ye must go tae Castle Cairistiòna 'n' find th' amulet. Th' moon is full 'n' will show ye th' way. Ye have tae try. Ye ken more than I did about where th' crypt is. Ye do not have tae have th' same outcome I did. Set th' Asrai free."

"Do you want to come with us?" asked Nessa.

Her aunt shook her head. "This is yer journey, nae mine. Have ye ever heard th' saying 'don't put all yer eggs in one basket'? Something is telling me we shuid nae all go at once. But I will be waiting 'ere fur yer return."

"Thank you, Auntie. I love you!" Nessa wrapped her aunt in a hug.

"I love ye, too. Noo hurry. Ye dae nae have much time until sunrise. Make sure ye be careful too. If anything happens tae ye, yer mother will have mah hide."

Nessa got into the driver seat and drove the speedboat out onto the water.

As she headed out to sea, Cailean appeared. He stood on top of the water. The mist swirled around him as he spread his arms outward. The waves rippled, and other glowing creatures emerged from the depths of the sea. They encircled the boat.

"These are th' good Asrai who wull help us journey safely across. I wull stand at th' bow 'n' draw th' villainous Asrai away," declared Cailean.

Nessa maneuvered the boat out into the open water. She could make out the turrets of Castle Cairistiòna. Cailean floated at the bow, his feet gliding over the water. Nessa felt him take control of the boat and cast an invisible shield around them. The good Asrai sank under the boat pushing it faster. Nessa glanced over the side of the craft and gasped as thousands and thousands of other Asrai appeared below the surface. Men and women of all shapes and sizes gathered around them. They seemed different from the good Asrai. They had a dull lifeless shimmer and did not shine as brightly. Their bodies twisted and turned in the water as if they were performing a synchronized swimming routine. Their hands reached towards her breaking the surface as if inviting Nessa to come and swim.

"Dae nae look at them," Cailean's voice warned. "They are evil! They trying tae lure ye overboard 'n' drown ye. Look at th' floor o' th' boat or th' sky but dae nae look at th' water!"

Nessa did as she was told and minutes later they were at the Isle of Eilean Cairistiòna.

"We are 'ere," declared Cailean as he watched Nessa step onto the sand and drag her aunt's speedboat higher onto the land.

The curly-haired teen scanned the water, but all she saw was darkness.

"What are ye looking at?" asked Cailean.

"I thought I heard a sound like a boat following us?" murmured Nessa. She hoped it had been her aunt but it was not

"Doubtful," replied Cailean. "No one is going tae come out on a boat at night. 'Twas probably th' devil Asrai making ye think there wis a boat sae they could distract ye 'n' drown ye."

Nessa nodded and turned around to see Castle Cairistiòna come into view. Even though the structure had been abandoned for centuries, its beauty took her breath away. Its gigantic turrets cast long shadows. In the darkness, Nessa could see that the huge stone towers were twice the size of those at Castle Campbell. The medieval architecture seemed to have jumped right out of the pages of a storybook. Windows were aligned in perfect symmetry; turrets appeared to brush the night sky; and the dark bluish stone walls held the secrets of a lurid past.

Nessa began to hike her way up toward the elaborately-carved doors.

"Wait fur me," called Cailean falling in step behind her.

"You can come onto land?" asked Nessa.

"Th' castle is in th' middle o' th' water, sae aye, I can. I shall not permit ye tae go into that castle by yersel'."

Nessa felt grateful. She wanted to help Cailean and the other Asrai, but she was nervous about setting foot in the centuries-old edifice alone.

They approached the large front doors that were covered in cobwebs. Nessa turned the latch and the ancient wooden barrier swung back slowly.

Nessa placed her foot on the stone. The torches and candles immediately lit one by one with glowing flames. Fearlessly, the red-headed teen walked through the doorframe with Cailean. Even though no one had lived in the castle for a long time, the way the light danced on the floor of the hall and upon the furniture seemed to appear as if the rooms had been lived in all this time. Everything was shiny and looked new, not dusty and dingy the way she had thought.

"Why does everything look so new?" she whispered.

"Curses wull do that," hissed back Cailean. "It may look new, but Doileag's dark magic is still alive 'n' well."

Nessa glanced at the layout on her phone. "I believe the entrance to the crypt should be somewhere on the main floor." She left the entranceway and began to walk into the castle.

A crack sounded above her head.

"Nessa, look out!" Nessa felt Cailean's icy fingers grab her arm and pull her back. The chandelier came loose from its bearing and crashed onto the floor where the two adventurers had been standing only seconds before.

Nessa winced and held her arm. The cold touch from Cailean sank deep into her bones and she felt goosebumps breaking out along her skin.

"I am sorry," cried Cailean. "The chandelier wis going tae crush ye. Have ye been hurt?"

With firm resolve, the brave-hearted young woman shook her head. As she released her hand from her arm, she saw a black spot beginning to form. The flesh was dying, and she would no longer have feeling in the spot, just as she had lost feeling in her fingertips.

Cailean's expression turned angry when he saw the mark. "I told ye we shuid nae have come 'ere. I told ye th' isle does nae treat humans kindly. Now ye are going tae have those marks on yer arm forever."

"It is not that bad. It will be worth it if we can set you free. Besides, that is why they make makeup. If we find the amulet, the marks will disappear. I understand the risk, but we have come too far to quit now."

They stepped around the broken chandelier and ventured deeper into the castle. For hours they searched chamber after chamber with no clue as to where the crypt could be found. Nessa felt her chest begin to tighten. According to what she had read at the library, the entrance to the crypt revealed itself once a month on the full moon. They needed to find the amulet and break the spell tonight or risk having to wait another month before returning.

As they turned one last corner, a glint of light shone from outside one of the windows. Stepping out the nearby door, the two allies found themselves in a beautiful garden near the sea.

"Cailean, look at this," she called.

"Aye, yes," replied Cailean. "'Tis Cairistiòna's garden still in bloom tae this very day. 'Tis th' only thing Doileag's spells cuid nae touch. There she is." Cailean nodded toward a beautiful statue that was surrounded by heather and primrose.

The marble sculpture of Queen Cairistiòna stood tall and proud. The image was adorned in blue robes and a beautiful golden crown. The creation's eyes looked out at the sea as if searching for a way to break the curse.

"She is beautiful," whispered Nessa.

As if hearing her compliment, the moonbeams shone down on the statue. Queen Cairistiòna was illuminated in moonlight. Nessa and Cailean slowly approached the figure. A green light glowed at the bottom of the base. Nessa crouched down and peered closer. Written in stone was an inscription that was covered by overgrown weeds. When the moonbeams touched the name plate, the weeds began to move away on their own to reveal an engraving.

Wisdom always escapes the eyes of a fool.

On either side of the message, a triple spiral had been carved, a triskele. Nessa ran her fingers along the words and felt an indentation at the letter 'W.' She pressed down. The marble figure jolted forward and moved back to reveal a door that opened into an entryway.

"Th' crypt entrance!" cried Cailean. "Wisdom always escapes th' eyes o' a fool. 'Ere th' entrance wis right in front o' all these historian's noses 'n' they missed it."

"Because the entrance only reveals itself once a month on the full moon, if they were not searching on a full moon night, they would never have find it," replied the brave teen.

The two descended the long staircase down into the crypt. The torches seemed to have a mind of their own and lit themselves as Nessa and Cailean reached the bottom. The chamber had arches held up by thick columns. Water dripped down from the ceiling staining the floor. Different slabs on the floor were a darker shade then others. Nessa noticed the darker shades created a triple spiral that stretched across several stones. Four coffins rested in a cross pattern in the center of the crypt. At the head of each casket a triskele had been engraved. Situated in the middle of the formation created by the coffins loomed a six-foot Celtic cross.

"Whose coffins are these?" asked Nessa as they walked closer.

"I am nae sure," replied Cailean. "I ken Queen Cairistiòna's family wis buried beneath a church, not thair castle."

The engraving flooded Nessa's mind. *Wisdom always escapes the eyes of a fool.* Four coffins with no engraving and no description of who rested inside, only a triskele for identification. The triskele held the energy of growth and change. Whoever found Queen Cairistiòna's treasure would have found good fortune. The triskele always symbolized female power; Queen Cairistiòna was a powerful woman.

Nessa stood quietly looking at what she and Cailean had found. Stories are not always in books, she realized. Sometimes stories occur in formations. If she were to reason with wisdom, she would begin to realize that the position of the tombs held the secret to the treasure. There was more to this crypt than the warning at the gate. She knew she was no fool.

These beds of eternal rest held something more than bodies. In a moment of pure clarity, Nessa felt the spirit of Queen Cairistiòna speaking to her through the full moon. Before fear overtook her, Nessa reached out to the nearest coffin, undid the latch, and by her own power with Queen Cairistiòna's guidance, she raised the cover.

"Nessa have ye taken leave o' yer senses!" cried Cailean, "Ye cannae disturb th' final resting place o' th'…" his voice trailed off.

Nessa's tongue seemed unable to form the words as she stared inside the casket.

There was not a skeleton resting there. Instead, gold coins, jewels, and other valuable objects glittered in the lights of the flickering torches.

"The treasure of Cairistiòna!" cried Nessa. "It does exist! Come on! The amulet must be here somewhere." The two opened the remaining caskets and were met with the same sight of gold and jewels; however, an amulet of a ruby encrusted in gold was nowhere to be found.

Nessa growled in frustration, then looked at the Celtic cross. *How odd,* she thought. *This cross is raised three inches off the ground leaving a small space for a tiny hand to fit beneath it.*

Nessa squatted down on her knees and delicately slid her fingers under the stone. Her hand closed around something soft, and she pulled it out. It was a silk drawstring bag. Carefully opening the ancient velvet, into her palm fell Doileag's amulet.

"I dinnae believe it! It does exist. Ye did it, Nessa!" cried Cailean. "I would hug ye but I dinnae want tae freeze ye."

"Ah would freeze if ah wur both o' yah," a cold voice sounded behind them. Nessa and Cailean whirled around. A small yelp escaped Nessa's lips. She clutched the amulet to her chest and realized her earlier suspicions were correct. There had been another boat that had followed them in the night. The inhabitant of that old tug was Laochailan. He stood before them with the jar of saltwater in one arm and a gun pointed at both of them.

"Noo hand ower that amulet 'n' na yin gets hurt!" snarled Laochailan. "Ah ken ye have it, give it!"

"What are you doing here?" cried Nessa, her voice soft and shaky.

"I followed yah 'ere o' course."

"Why?"

"Fur th' amulet. Dinnae waste mah time trying tae gimme wee blether, lassie. Th' amulet."

Nessa felt a coldness hit the pit of her stomach creating a heavy feeling that weighed her down. She clutched the amulet tighter. This was not happening. Her skin tingled. They were moments away from breaking the curse, from Cailean and the Asrai being set free. Now Laochailan was going to ruin it all. Nessa looked around for a place to run, but Laochailan blocked the only escape.

"You can't have the amulet!"

"Lassie, ye aff yer heid! Yer giving me that amulet if ah git tae shoot ye tae git it!"

"The Asrai deserve to be set free! They have suffered enough."

"Lassie, I dinnae care aboot a bunch o' stupid ghosts, I care aboot one Asrai, mah bonnie. Fur years I have bin searching fur th' amulet o' Doileag 'n' th' treasure o' Cairistiòna but I cam up hee haw. Then th' day I met ye by th' water wit ye little dog 'n' ye mentioned Asrai it aroused mah suspicions. I followed ye tae th' library 'n' whin I saw ye research, I knew ye ken something I didnae. Sae, I decided tae take a chance on ye wee lassie, ye bonnie foreigner, 'n' ye turned out tae be cleverer than I gave ye credit fur. Noo hand ower that amulet 'n' ye won't get hurt."

Nessa hesitated, her muscles rigid. How could she have been so naïve; she should have known better then to talk to people she did not know. As she looked at the barrel of the gun pointed at her, fear began to bubble up inside of her, but her fingers refused to let go of the amulet.

"Nessa, give him th' amulet," hissed Cailean. "I will nae die, if a'm shot, but ye will."

He gestured toward Laochailan and reluctantly Nessa handed over the amulet. As Laochailan extended his hand to take the jewel, the tattoo of the mermaid on his forearm became visible.

Laochailan snatched the prize, held it up, and looked at it. "At last, noo I shall have mah bride."

Nessa's mind was spinning, then hearing the word "bride" it all made sense. The tattoo that was on Laochailan's arm was not a mermaid. It was an Asrai in mermaid form.

"It was you!" she cried. "You're the fisherman that everyone says saw the last sighting of the Asrai in 1952.

"What?" cried Cailean.

"It's true. It all makes sense now. He was the young fisherman who caught the Asrai who trapped you. Sìonag. That is the tattoo that is on his arm. It is Sìonag when he saw her in mermaid form!"

"Th' lassie speaks correctly," replied Laochailan, the amulet now in his hand. He held up the jar of water. "'Ere lies her remains as we speak. How wis I supposed tae know Asrais cannae be exposed tae sunlight? I have bin searching fur this amulet ever since. Noo that I have it I will resurrect Sìonag 'n' make her mah wife. Then I wull have th' rest o' th' Asrai under mah control, 'n' wit Cairistiòna's treasure I wull be th' most powerful 'n' richest man in all o' Scotland. Noo ye two stand ower there." He motioned to the far corner of the crypt with his gun. Nessa and Cailean obeyed. Then Laochailan tucked the jar of Sìonag's watery remains under his arm and walked up the stairs with his treasure. The door slammed.

"Goon laddie! Fur an old man, he is quite light oan his feet," cried Cailean as the two sprang into action.

They raced up the steps and Nessa pushed at the opening. The door would not budge.

"It's locked!" Nessa looked up and saw streaks of light slithering their way into the crypt through the cracks in the ceiling.

"We have to hurry. It will be sunrise and you will melt!" She wished Aunt Aileene-Edith had come with her, but then, her aunt would be trapped with them. Her phone did not have service since Eilean Cairistiòna was in the middle of nowhere. They were trapped while Laochailan became the master of the Sea Ghosts with Sìonag by his side.

"Step aside," said Cailean. He moved closer to the door and placed both his palms on the wood. The carved oak froze as ice covered the planks from top to bottom. Then with a loud crack, the ice broke and the door melted freeing them into the garden.

Nessa ran through the flowers and out into moonlight. In light of the moon, she felt the source of her power. Cailean was immediately behind her. She rounded the corner and stopped. Laochailan stood on the edge of a rock surrounded by the sea. He held the amulet out so it caught the light from the stars. The jar of Sìonag's contents glimmered with an eerie light of its own. The water at Laochailan's feet began to bubble, and the steam that billowed out began to take the shape of the Asrai mermaid, Sìonag. In the fisherman's hand the central jewel turned a fiery red, and the Asrai began to surface from the depths of the ocean. They began to move towards Laochailan, their new leader.

"That evil Asrai," shuddered Cailean, glaring at the jar. Suddenly the young nobleman jerked forward as if pulled by an invisible rope. "Tis th' curse, it binds me tae th' amulet!" Cailean tried to move backwards but was jolted forward. "I must go tae him. What are we going tae dae? Laochailan is going tae have a huge army o' Asrai at his control."

Nessa did not answer. Without hesitation she ran at Laochailan from behind, her feet slapping the water. The old man was so intent on resurrecting Sìonag, he didn't notice her until it was too late. Nessa jumped on Laochailan and tackled him to the ground. They landed half in the water and half on land. The amulet fell from his hands and bounced into the sand.

"Eejit lassie!' yelled Laochailan. He moved to grasp the jewel, but Nessa was faster. She picked it up and threw it with all of her might at a nearby boulder. In an instant, the gemstone shattered into millions of pieces.

"No!" screamed Laochailan.

A white mist began to rise up from the broken pieces of red glass. The water that bubbled in the jar stopped and the slowly-forming shape of Sìonag evaporated, leaving the jar empty. The thousands of Asrai that stood on the water paused and began to waver in the moonlight. Nessa turned and saw Cailean become encased in the same glimmer. She looked out into the sea as the Asrai became one with the waves. Small individual balls of light began to rise up from the swells to the sky. The souls of the good Asrai were finally free, while the bad Asrai disintegrated into the ocean depths.

"We did it Cailean! We broke the spell!" Nessa turned but Cailean had disappeared. "Cailean?" Her heart leaped into her throat. "Cailean?" No answer. Tears began to prick at her eyes. Cailean was free along with the rest of the Asrai. Deep in her soul she thought he might become human again, but that had been a hollow wish. She was happy Cailean had crossed over into the afterlife, but she still felt sad.

"Eejit girl! I'll gie ye a skelpit lug!" Laochailan wheezed behind her. Nessa looked and saw the old man pointing his gun straight at her. "Ye ruined everything! Ye killed mah beloved 'n' now I will kill ye!"

"Ye wull dae nothing o' th' sort!" yelled a familiar feminine voice.

It was Countess Aileene-Edith. She raced out of the shadows with a rifle and wacked Laochailan on the head. The fisherman fell forward and his gun spun out of his hands. Nessa rushed forward and picked it up. Relief washed over her, and her body began to relax. Her aunt had come to her rescue, after all.

"Dae nae move," barked Aileene-Edith pointing her rifle at Laochailan. "The police are on thair wey. I think I hear thair sirens in th' distance."

Laochailan sat up rubbing his head and grumbling, but when he saw the two women each with a gun, he stayed silent.

A few minutes later two Scottish police arrived at the isle. They handcuffed Laochailan and brought him to their boat. After handing Laochailan's gun to one of the police officers, Nessa ran to her aunt.

"Nessa, yer safe!" Aileene-Edith wrapped her in a deep hug.

"How did you know I was in danger?" asked Nessa.

"Remember when I told ye nae tae put all yer eggs in one basket? I had planned th' whole time tae follow ye tae Eilean Cairistiòna. But after ye left, I saw another boat following ye. I realized I needed stronger backup, sae I called th' police, then followed ye 'ere. This old hunting rifle came in handy, after all," said the countess. "I will always be here fur ye, no matter what."

Nessa smiled and hugged her aunt. In the moment of that hug, Nessa saw the black spot on her skin disappear, and the feeling return to her fingers.

"What happened wit yer Asrai?" whispered her aunt.

"He is gone," replied Nessa, tears streamed freely down her cheeks. "I'm glad he is free, but I miss him." Aileene-Edith drew her close.

A hacking noise sounded from behind them. Nessa pulled herself away from her aunt to see a figure coughing while climbing out of the water.

It was Cailean emerging from the waves.

Nessa's spirits brightened and happiness glowed inside of her. "Cailean!" she called. She raced over to him and pulled him close to her, not caring if he froze her to death. Instead of his ice-cold body, his flesh was warm and full of life. Cailean was no longer translucent but in solid form.

"You're..." she began

"Human," he finished with a sly smile.

"How?" cried Nessa.

"Th' good Asrai received a choice. Fur protecting folk we cuid choose if we wanted tae return tae human form or move on tae th' afterlife. I dinnae want tae cross over. Mah mither always told me if ye love someone ye fight fur them 'n' ye are a stubborn lassie, Nessa, but I love ye."

"I love you, too," she whispered.

Nessa turned to the countess. "Auntie! This is Cailean."

Aileene-Edith stood on the rocks and beamed with pride. "Yer Asrai, noo turned human.

Well, 'tis a pleasure tae meet ye young man..."

Before Aileene-Edith could finish her greeting, another raspy cough caught their attention. Everyone turned to see a second man crawling from the water onto the sand. He looked about the same age as Aileene-Edith. He had dark black hair sprinkled with gray, and his dimples showed as he smiled.

Aileene-Edith froze, and her open palm spread out across her chest. "Arran!"

"Aileene," Arran struggled to his feet. He slowly walked over to her. "Still beautiful efter all these years."

"I dae nae believe it!" cried the countess. She clasped his hands in hers. "How is it possible yer as auld as me! Ye wis a teenager whin ye died."

Arran gave her a wink. "Th' magic o' th' curse. When yer niece broke th' spell, I chose tae become human. Even though we haven't spoken fur years, I've bin watchin' ye from th' sea and protecting ye. I missed ye, 'n' I wanted tae come back tae ye. Noo that I have the chance, I cuid nae come back a teenager, 'n' I feel adulthood suits me. I love you, Aileene, 'n' I hope ye will have me."

Ye know I would!" cried Aileene-Edith giving him a kiss.

Nessa smiled, "Your Asrai now turned human."

Aileene-Edith and Arran headed to the boat docked at the edge of the Isle of Eilean Cairistiòna. Nessa turned to follow, but Cailean pulled her back.

"I have bin waiting forever tae dae this," he said. Then he put his hands on Nessa's face and pulled her into a kiss.

Aileene-Edith gave Cailean a job as a worker on her rescue farm. Cailean loved animals and was happy for the opportunity. She also gave him his own room in the castle. Nessa and Cailean claimed the fortune of Queen Cairistiòna with the help of the Scottish government and made plans of all the things they wanted to do together. Nessa made peace with her cousins, and they became best friends. Finally, she had found a place where she belonged. Countess Aileene-Edith and Arran were wed. Arran's happiness deepened when he became operations-analyst at the rescue farm and found his forever home at Castle Campbell in the arms of his countess.

"Nessa, I am glad yer parents made th' choice tae move 'ere," Cailean whispered in her ear as they walked holding hands along the coastline one summer afternoon, their bare feet covered by the waves lapping the sand.

Joy engulfed Nessa. "I'm glad they did, too."

With her hand gently clasped in the warmth of Cailean's love, Nessa had found her destiny. She remembered the words etched onto the statue of Queen Cairistiòna, that knowledge goes to those who have wisdom and not to those who are fools.

Scotland once seemed distant and cold, but now felt close and warm. Here she was loved, truly loved by Cailean, by her parents, by her aunt, and by her cousins. What began as the telling of an ancient legend had transformed the young teen into a woman fully grown. Nessa was ready to take on the responsibilities of adulthood and become a powerful feminine spirit.

AUTHOR'S NOTE

*To Mom, Dad, and Ashley. Thank you for everything. I love you –
Nicole*

To Edith. This story was written to honor you and your maternal Scottish roots. Thank you for your support. I love you. – Nicole

Follow more of N.D.T. Casale's storytelling adventures on Instagram @ndtcasale (https://www.instagram.com/ndtcasale/)

7
THE NAIAD'S CURSE
ASTRID V.J.

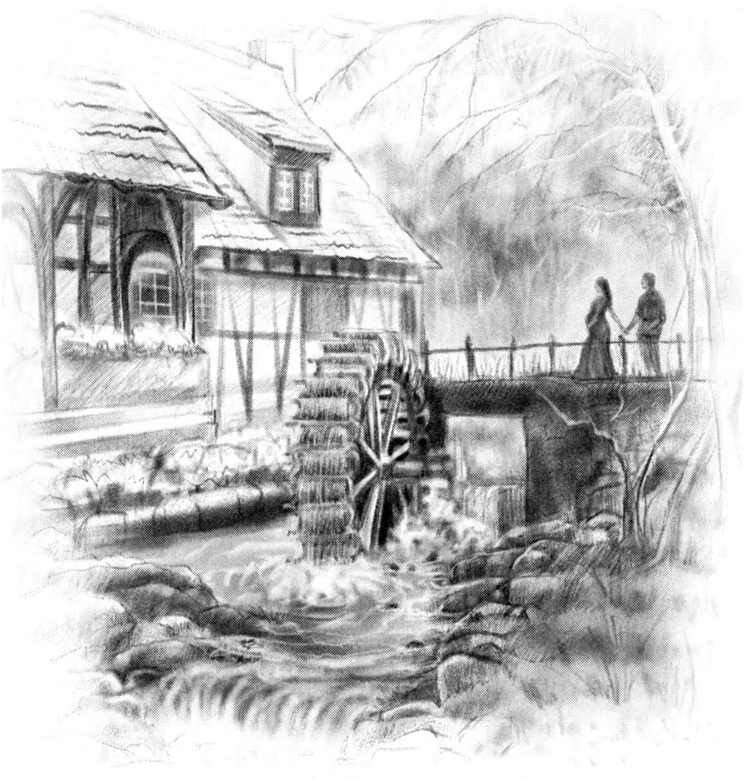

THE NAIAD'S CURSE

Nate watched his wife walking beside the mill pond, its knee-high stone wall running along the south-eastern bank and keeping her skirts from view. Hilda's ebony hair played about her shoulders and her voice drifted to him. She was singing a lullaby, stroking the round protrusion of her belly. She looked up and her chocolate gaze met his. He noticed how her cinnamon skin glowed in the sunlight. Everything about her resonated happiness.

The realisation squeezed his chest. Worry pulled around him, drew him in and threatened to pull him down into a well of mist. He looked away, avoiding the satisfied smile playing on her lips and found his gaze glancing at the still wheel beside his mill.

How could he care for his growing family and keep that serenity in her gaze when he couldn't make ends meet? She deserved this new start, especially after everything that had happened, but he was certain he would bring her nothing but distress and sleepless nights spent worrying. Since that confounded Peter set up a windmill on the other side of town, everyone, even the baker, had moved their business there, leaving his watermill silent—practically deserted. In the past few weeks, Nate's last customers had all but dwindled away, leaving him with nothing.

What could he do? What did a miller without grain to grind do?

Hilda approached him, holding out her hands to him and Nate made an effort to smooth the lines of concern etched into his face. He took her hands, trying to keep anxiety from showing in his eyes. "My darling." He managed a quick smile. "You look radiant."

"Oh, Nate! It's wonderful to be expecting again. I've missed this tranquil season. This baby will be a blessing to our family, I can just feel it!" Her melodious voice trembled with her passion and excitement and her eyes sparkled although he noted the undercurrent of past grief. *She's putting on a brave face. My dearest Hilda, always so strong for others.*

Nate felt his lips twitching heavenward in a response honed by years of practise. Where she was the pillar holding up everyone around her, supporting through grief and strife and difficulties, Nate knew he had to be her strength lest she wear herself out on behalf of others. He needed to lighten her burdens.

"I'll go up now and rest my legs. Mandy said she had some clothes I could look through and I need to see Jeoff about the cradle. Isn't it exciting? In just a few weeks we'll be three." Her hand stroked over her belly as she spoke.

"Rest, dear," he said, cupping her shoulder with his hand while his heart raced off with the speed of fear at the mention of the cradle. Didn't they have a cradle from the last baby? No, he remembered now, she'd given it away years ago to soothe the pain of their loss. He brushed a hand over his brow. How was he going to pay for a new cradle?

"You know," he called from the doorway after her retreating form, "you rest and take it easy. I'll go and speak to Jeoff. I haven't seen him in a while. It would be good to catch up. Maybe Mandy can come visit you here? It makes me worry when you're out on your own."

"Oh, Nate!" she turned back to him, waving her hand to dismiss his fears. "I'm still weeks away from birthing. You are too easily distressed. Women have been doing this since time began."

"I know, I know," he grumbled, showing an uncharacteristic interest in the flagstones at the threshold and noting how worn his boots were. "Please just humour me," he added, capturing her eyes.

"As you wish, my love," she laughed and climbed the stairs to their room above.

Nate turned and walked the half mile into the village. The small stone houses with their thatched roofs came into view beyond the forest. Children scampered through the dusty streets, laughing. The adults went about their business, dedicating themselves to their crafts. This was Kvarn, his home since childhood. Nate smiled at the tailor and waved at the wainwright. His ears picked out dull thuds coming from the smithy and he breathed in a series of nostalgic scents: the perfume of summer flowers, the acidic tang from the tanner's shop and the smell of fresh bread. He decided to take a detour and avoid the bakery, wanting to avert a confrontation with Bertrand for his recent betrayal. How could one of his oldest friends, who should have been his best customer, leave him in the lurch and take his business to the windmill—to the competition?

Nate passed the church, a simple whitewashed building with a single bell-tower. A picket fence bordered the building and its garden which was awash with spring flowers. The heavy wooden door stood open and welcoming, but Nate walked by. He couldn't bear the thought of confessing his failures.

As Nate approached the carpenter's home, he became aware of a creaking sound that emitted at regular intervals. Looking up, his gaze fell on the windmill—the agent of all his suffering. He cursed Peter under his breath. Who did the man think he was? Coming into town a year and a half ago, setting himself up with his family in the old Norton farm house at the edge of town, and then investing in and building a windmill, when there was already a perfectly functional watermill in Kvarn.

Nate ground his teeth together when he remembered Peter's reasoning. *It's too far away to come all the way to you, Nate. It's nothing personal, just business.* The man was detestable.

Stepping into the cool of the carpenter's shop, Nate knocked on the wooden door frame. "Hello, hello," he called.

"Come in. Come in," came the reply.

His eyes accustomed to the gloom and Nate made out the hunched figure of his friend, Jeoff, leaning over a worktable by the window. He was at the opposite end of the single room that took up the full length of the building's ground floor. Jeoff's dark curly hair obscured most of his face as he chipped away at the piece of wood under his fingers. Then he blew off the dust and put down the chisel with a soft thunk.

"Nate!" he exclaimed with his arms flung wide, crossing the space cluttered with chairs, tables and other furniture. "It is good to see you, my friend. You haven't been over in a while; I wondered where you'd gotten to."

"Things have been busy," Nate explained, trying to keep the weight out of his voice.

"Yes, yes. I can imagine. The harvest was good last year. Everyone rejoiced. You must have much to do at the mill, especially in preparation for the coming season."

Jeoff stopped, his expression changing. It was as though his brain finally caught up with his words. "Oh, Nate. I wasn't thinking. I'm sorry, I forgot about your troubles with Peter."

Guilt settled into the set of Jeoff's shoulders while Nate tried to hold back the biting comment wanting to spill from him. With a calming breath, he focused on the purpose of his visit. Hilda. The baby. That was all that mattered in this moment.

"I came to see you about a cradle. Do you have an old one? Or know anyone who might? I'm afraid I can't afford to commission one from you."

Jeoff nodded and Nate watched his friend's mind spark into action. The carpenter spun around and walked through the clutter of his shop, waving his hands in the air and muttering under his breath. He rooted around, pulling some pieces of wood from under his work table. After another moment, he clapped his hands together and smiled.

"You go on home, Nate. I'll take care of this and don't you worry. I'll get it done free of charge. You get yourself back to your missus and take care of her."

Their eyes met and relief poured through Nate at the expression of goodwill in his friend's eyes. "Thank you."

A few days later, Nate took a walk into the forest beyond the mill-pond. He needed to clear his head and find a way around his financial troubles. He couldn't keep accepting things on credit. Earlier that morning, he'd checked his books as he'd done several times a day over the past weeks. The dwindling stack of coins in his cash drawer was like a fist around his heart, squeezing until pain blazed through his being. His nerves were soothed by walking in the fresh air and listening to the birds twittering in the spring day.

He noticed a bright yellow flower sprouting from the grass at his feet. Stooping, he plucked it, twirling the saffron bloom between his fingers, admiring the changing intensity of the colour, greener at the stem, lemon yellow at the tips. *All things are transitory*, he thought. His gaze wandered from the bloom to the verdant trees around him. Then his thoughts floated beyond that to days gone by when he took his wealth and esteem for granted. In his mind's eye, he called forth his children and how they'd been snatched from him. The whirlwind of grief was brief now—many years later—but he recalled Hilda's frame, bowed under the burden of their loss, in the months following their personal tragedy. Three children, the epitome of health, snuffed out by pestilence in the space of a few weeks. As time passed, even that became lighter, somehow. *Every experience, whether good or bad, is a passing thing. It may leave scars, but they are the proof of life after healing.*

Holding onto this revelation, Nate turned his feet homeward. His wife needed him. She was right. Somehow they would work it all out and he agreed with her premonition that the baby was a sign of change for the good. He could trust in that. Hope filled him, lifting his spirits and letting him join the birds winging through the sky above him. However, his lightness of being didn't last long.

By the time the thatch roof of his home, which was windswept and sorely in need of re-thatching, peeked through the leafy branches, his mind had taken a nose-dive again. He paused beside the pond, once a symbol of his success but now a sore reminder of money spent unwisely. He'd put so much into building the pond to help keep his mill running through the months when the stream ran dry, but now he didn't have enough customers to warrant the mill functioning all year round. In years past, his business had grown steadily and he'd made the investment in anticipation of an even better future. Instead, life handed him poverty and want in exchange for the unlimited supply of water.

Nate gazed at the glassy surface that reflected the sky and the trees around him. It was a rippling mirror showing up the distortions of life: from a distance it looked like perfection but up close it became teased and tugged into a meaningless muddle. The disjointed imagery on the water's surface brought further fractures to his mind. There was nothing he could do to right the hopelessness of his situation. He was stuck and knew, with absolute certainty, that only a miracle could rescue him from destitution.

Hilda— and the baby. His ribs turned into iron bands, constricting his chest. He imagined his wife's beautiful eyes looking up at him, blazing with disappointment and ridicule. *I've brought this on my family.* In hindsight he knew he hadn't done enough to avert this outcome. He'd been complacent, ignored the signs, hoped for a change in the winds, but now, here he was—doomed.

Shame swamped him, dousing him with thoughts of the scorn he'd receive from his acquaintances and friends in the town. He remembered the look of pity Jeoff bestowed on him and in a heartbeat his mind transformed it into the disappointment he expected to see from Hilda. There was no way she would forgive this. *What was I thinking? She won't be able to see past this.* His wife's probable disenchantment bored into his soul, crushing any remnant of hope he'd harboured.

Nate's eyes fell upon the reflective surface of the water lapping softly at his feet. The stillness and soft promise of rest was inviting. He leaned forward, contemplating the possibility of release. To lay down his burdens and allow the anxiety to slip away—*that* would be bliss. He hesitated a moment, thoughts racing through his mind in an overwhelming string. He pushed back, yearning for freedom from it all. The water sparkled in the sun's light.

My honour would be forfeit, but Hilda could start anew. She'd be able to sell what's worthwhile in this place, move back to her parents and find a new life with another, better capable of taking care of her. What point is there in having an heir with no legacy to leave him, other than debt and poverty?

His decision made, Nate glanced one last time at the house, nestled in a clearing with trees growing all around it, except for a meadow for his sheep and a vegetable garden. The patch was barren this season because Hilda hadn't been able to plant anything in her condition. The water wheel, beside the wall of the building stood still and silent: yet another rebuke to his misjudgements and the final seal on this resolution and the action he was about to take.

The water at his feet sparkled. Ripples formed, lapping against the stone wall, as he stepped onto its top. He cast about him for something heavy to help weigh him down. He needed something to make at least this final, macabre decision a success so he could be free and Hilda also. A splash sounded a few yards away and Nate looked up in surprise.

A pillar of water, solidified by some unknown art, rose above the pond's roiling surface and upon it sat the most beautiful creature Nate had ever seen. Raven hair spilled over creamy shoulders and a pair of sea-green eyes gleamed from under thick midnight lashes. Rose lips parted to reveal razor-sharp teeth and Nate took a step back, floundering down from the low wall and knocking his knee against the stone. Pain struck down to his toes, briefly numbing his left leg.

It took a moment for the discomfort to pass and then his mind snapped back to the vision he'd seen. He looked up again. It was no figment of his imagination. The creature perched on her column of water and wore a shimmering gown of grey-green liquid that left her shoulders and throat bare. *Nix*, his mind latched onto the term his people gave to the magical creatures of the water. Before he could think of any stories about these beings, she opened her mouth again, showing off those pointed teeth.

"Why so sad, Miller?" Her voice sang to his being, pouring soothing balm into his aching heart and unbolting the worries he'd kept tightly locked inside. He told her everything; shared even details he'd never revealed to his wife.

When he fell silent at last, the water spirit tilted her head in thought. At length, she said, "And you wished to end your life by throwing your lot in with me?" Her melodious song left him breathless and gaping—a fish out of water. She laughed, the tinkling of water spilling over a rock wall. "Although it is lonely down here in my home, you cannot offer the company I seek. What would you give me if I helped you overcome these troubles?"

"Anything!" he blurted out, nervous tension contracting his tone.

She smiled again, pleased with his reply. Her attention drifted towards the house, her eyes shimmering dark like wet algae in the sunlight. She paused. Snapping her attention back to Nate, she said, "I will make a deal with you, Miller. Your troubles will be gone and within a month your business will resurge. Your fame and renown as the best miller in the region will grow and people will send their grain to you from far afield. In exchange, you will gift me the newborn creature whose cry you will hear as you cross the threshold into your home."

What might that be? Nate wondered whether the cat might have had her litter, or perhaps the ewe dropped her lamb. *Well, no point in dragging this out. I don't care what she wants the animal for, this is probably the only opportunity I'll get and it's certainly the best option I have right now.* He raised his head, looking straight into the nix's eyes, which were now a rippling shade of turquoise. "I'll gladly give you the first newborn whose cry reaches me after setting foot in my house, for the financial stability you promise."

Her sharp teeth glittered like moonstones. "It is done!" she exclaimed, clapping her hands in glee.

The black mane of her hair billowed about her as she turned away from him. With a resounding splash, the column disintegrated and the magical manifestation of water returned to her home in the pond, spraying Nate with searing droplets of chill.

She was gone. Several rings surged from the place where the spirit creature disappeared, lapping small waves against the wall where Nate stood. It was curious he'd come across the nix in that moment of need. Perhaps the Great Dragon in the Sky really was watching and had found a way to lighten his burden. Shrugging, he turned towards his house, lighter of heart than he'd been in many, many months.

A note crossed his lips and he whistled a brisk ditty as he walked towards the building. He checked on the ewe, left in a separate enclosure beside the house. She was still fat as ever, munching on what little grass was left in her pen. With a shrug of his shoulders, he hopped onto the large stone step leading into his home, still whistling and searching for the cat.

Upstairs, he heard a commotion. Someone was rushing about on the top floor, then his wife screamed and he bounded up the stairs calling to her. Another voice shouted something Nate couldn't make out but it sounded triumphant and this was followed by a baby's high pitched wail.

Nate's heart stopped. He stood, suspended on the third-last step as the sound washed over him. Agony, unlike any he'd experienced before, shot from his heart to his fingertips and down to his knees. He faltered, slipping, aware of the motion as it filtered to him through the fog in his mind. The cry was cut short and time sped up again, leaving Nate in a crumpled heap two stairs lower than he'd been. His heartbeat started up erratically and his extremities throbbed. A dull pain in his hip cleared his mind, helping him focus on the tumble he'd taken and how lucky he was he hadn't fallen down the whole flight.

Muffled voices filtered through the closed door of the upstairs room and Nate pulled himself to his feet. The baby came early. His whole body trembled as the nix's words slashed through his being: *you will gift me the newborn creature whose cry you will hear as you cross the threshold into your home.*

"What have I done?" The stormy seas of his despair threatened to drown him. How could he go on? How could he ever face Hilda? This was so much worse.

Hesitating on the staircase, Nate contemplated rushing out and never returning. He could fling himself as an offering to the nix and break the curse he'd brought upon his family, his own blood—his only child. Shock held him captive and he remained on the stairs, petrified.

The door to the room creaked and a figure came into view. The person was practically rectangular, boasting a vertical line from shoulders to hips with no indentation for a waist. The corpulent woman strode out carrying an armload of bloodied sheets and Nate recognised Olaya, his in-law's retainer. Nate swallowed hard and stood pressed against the railing to let the woman pass.

"Oh, Master Nate! You must be so pleased! 'Tis a boy, to be sure. Such a blessing!" She skipped passed him, her age obscured by her elation and delight.

His feet were lead. Each motion was lethargic and clumsy. He needed to focus on the whole process of walking, making sure he raised his feet enough to clear the step in front of him.

He held onto the bannister for support while his heart sputtered and his lungs wheezed. Beyond keeping his attention on getting up the stairs, Nate's mind was a swirling fog. He didn't know what to think or what he could say.

With an inordinate effort, he made it to the landing and stretched a trembling hand towards the door, pushing it open with numb fingers. His vision tunnelled onto his wife. Hilda's dark hair was in disarray, strands plastered to her oval face and her dark skin glowed with life. She looked tired. In her arms, she cradled a bundle pressed to the round protrusion of her exposed breast. She cooed softly, murmuring sweet nothings, while her baby sucked and gurgled.

Beautiful. A vision of peace. A pang in Nate's heart reminded him of the news he owed his wife. What could he tell her? His memory of the deal with the water sprite plunged another agonizing dagger into his chest.

Hilda looked up. Her chocolate eyes overflowed with love. "Oh Nate," she whispered. "He is splendid. Perfectly healthy, if a little early." She stopped, her eyes hardening into jewels as a cloud of worry passed over her visage. "Whatever is the matter?"

She shifted, trying to scoot to the edge of the bed so she could stand. Another figure bustled into sight beside her. "Not now, Hilda. You must rest. All is well, but your body is not young anymore, you must give it time after the birthing." The woman whose hair was mostly grey turned her wrinkled face to Nate and he recognized Tandra, the village wise woman and midwife. Tandra shifted her attention to Hilda and pushed Nate's wife back against the pillows, settling her into a good position with the feeding child.

Something tickled on Nate's cheek and he wiped his hand over it to find tears coursing in rivulets. He was so distraught he hadn't even realised it. The streams on his cheeks and the reason for them stirred a dark smear of horror through the blissful image of his wife and child. Living such contrast was torture. Nate wanted to bury his face in his hands and wail but he sensed his wife's eyes upon him. He knew what he had to do —what he owed her—but his whole being quailed at the thought of destroying her peace.

She'll never forgive me if I don't tell her immediately. He sighed, admitting to himself, *She's never going to forgive this—ever. No matter what.* He turned, wanting to leave, to handle the confrontation at another time, without the witnesses. A creak on the stairs indicated Olaya's return.

Just before he slipped away, his gaze caught Hilda's. Her eyes were hard, her face solemn. "What is it, Nate?" Her voice gave him no doubt, he couldn't escape this now. "Why won't you look at your son?" There was accusation there; and resentment.

Nate took a faltering step towards her. The multitude of words wanting to come out blocked at the back of his throat, strangling him. How could he tell her? What could he possibly say? He knew he couldn't get out of it but, still, the blockage remained and nothing but garbled sounds pushed forth from him. He exerted himself, trying to make his words intelligible but it was in vain and then his trembling knees gave way.

Strong arms caught him from behind. Olaya murmured soothingly, rubbing his back with one hand while supporting him with the other. Tandra joined them, touching his forehead and looking into his eyes. Hers narrowed. She brushed a finger on the side of his neck, then looked down at his hands, examining them. Dark splotches bloomed on his hands and arms. He'd never seen the like before.

"What is this?" Nate's voice trembled.

The ancient woman looked into his eyes. Her voice filled with compassion "You've been touched, Nate."

Hilda and Olaya gasped, their faces etched in horror while his mind grasped the word. *Touched*. He was bound to a magical creature. His memory played over the encounter with the spirit being and latched onto the moment she'd sealed the deal, spraying him with water and leaving him with these magical marks that bound him to his agreement. *Touched.*

"Tell me what happened." Tandra stepped to his right side, gesturing towards a wicker chair.

Nate slumped into it and recounted what happened with the nix in the mill

pond. When he came to the terms of the accord, guilt, horror and shame clawed their way around his voice box, cutting off his account.

"She wants my baby?" The ferocious growl emanating from the bed sounded more like an angry bear than Hilda.

Nate looked up, meeting her gaze, acknowledging with his eyes what his treacherous voice couldn't admit.

"And you agreed?" The pitch in her voice rose, splitting Nate to the core.

"I didn't know that's what she meant. She tricked me; said a newborn creature. I thought it could be the ewe or maybe the cat had her litter. You weren't due for at least another week and I didn't know you'd gone into labour while I was out—" A wail burst from his lips, cutting off the torrent of his explanation as he buried his face in his hands. Determination and action took hold of him. Nate jumped to his feet, "I'll go back and make this right. I will do what I must to see you and the little one safe."

A wrinkled hand settled onto his chest and gestured for him to stay put. Light flamed in Tandra's eyes and there was strength in her arm when she shoved him back in the chair. "Taking your own life won't save either of them from this curse," she said, her voice laced with kindness. "I don't know how powerful this creature is, nor how the magic intertwines with your lives, but there are ways to bind it. You stay here, Nate, and take care of your wife and child. They are still your responsibility and you will care for them. I will go and speak with the priest. Together we may be able to avert this tragedy."

After swallowing, Nate opened his mouth to speak. No sound came forth. He tried again but everything had knotted up inside him once more, the emotions and words keeping each other locked in an impossible battle over his vocal chords.

Tandra laid a hand on his shoulder. "I understand, son. We will all do our best." She straightened but kept her eye on him as she continued, "You stay here with your wife. I won't pass on the extent of the bargain. You have enough trouble on your hands as it is. It is best people know only of the nix's wish for the child, nothing more."

Nate nodded and glanced over at Hilda who glared at him. She was a mother wolf, all teeth and bristles, staring at him with unblinking eyes. He shrank back into his chair, lowering his gaze in deference to her. Silence stifled the room, growing thicker as time passed, suffocating Nate in its blanket.

He rose, needing to get away, but a growl from the bed made him fall back into his seat. His wife's cold eyes glared at him and he swallowed, remembering the midwife's insistence he stay put. Nate's gaze fell on the marks on his hands and arms. He traced patterns with the splotches on his skin, waiting for release from his wife's disapproving muteness. Nate knew he was stuck: stuck in this impossible situation with his wife, trapped in between the *nix* and Hilda; held hostage by the probable loss of his son, his fourth child but the only living one.

What father was he? What kind of husband? He wasn't even worthy of calling himself a man.

The baby woke and began to whimper. Hilda and Olaya turned their attention to him and set about changing his soiled nappy. Nate was relieved by the shift in attention and observed the interaction between the two women and the infant while trying to remain as unobtrusive as possible. A softer, more comfortable silence blanketed the room when the child drifted back to sleep and Nate noticed Hilda dozing as well.

A creak emanated below, announcing Tandra's return. Moments later, the midwife shuffled into view and cleared her throat. "The priest will arrive just before sunset and he'll perform a binding, calling upon the High Lord Dragon to protect you and keep the child safe."

Hilda nodded, shooting a piercing glare at Nate who kept his head bowed while coming to his feet. He thanked Tandra on his way out and headed into the kitchen below, hoping to keep himself occupied while he waited.

That evening, the priest arrived, his flowing yellow robes of office billowing out behind him as he strode to the pond. He marched right past the mill, all his attention on the task at hand and the fiend that needed to be fettered. Nate watched as the robust man raised his hands above his head and recited some incantation. The older man glanced over the still water but nothing happened. Nate wondered whether the binding had worked.

After a few minutes, the priest spun around and marched back the way he'd come, stopping at the doorway to the mill. His salt and pepper hair was windswept from his sojourn at the water's edge and the hem of his robe was damp. Nate looked up into the man's bearded face and felt his heart plummet in response to the defeat he saw in those brown eyes.

"I cannot seem to affect the creature in the water," he said, shaking his head. "It appears to be a powerful curse you landed yourself with, Nate my boy. I wonder if a cleansing could work." His eyes shifted, looking through Nate, off into some unseen distance.

Nate allowed his thoughts to turn inwards, swirling around his guilt at bringing this situation upon his family because he didn't heed the warnings about making deals with magical creatures. There was always a catch, everyone knew that. Why had he been so easily swayed by the dazzling nix with her terrifying teeth?

With a rustle of his sunlight robes, the priest shifted, shaking his head. "Yes," he said, blinking while refocusing on Nate. "A cleansing could do the trick. We'll prepare and do it the way it should be. I'll call in some help from the surrounding towns and villages. The Dragon on High will not let your child be taken in this way. I get the impression this is a warning to you, Nathaniel. You need to return to the Dragon's Way and doing so will avert this calamity."

"Yes, Paderi. Tell me what I must do to make this right."

It was a moonless night. Stars brightened the sky with their incandescent pinpricks. Nate looked up at the twinkling spots on the dark canvas and contemplated the legend of the Great Dragon in the Sky whose shed scales shone in the night to guide travellers on their way. A commotion drew Nate's attention away from the spectacle above and brought him into the midst of preparations for a grand ceremony. People, many he didn't know, milled about between his home and the pond where his nemesis reigned: the beautiful and terrifying creature that had turned his world into a pit of despair.

Men strode about, calling to each other in gruff voices while the ceremonial garb they wore clinked as they walked. They were covered from shoulders to shins in what appeared to be scales. Leather, dyed varying shades of blue, interspersed with gleaming mother-of-pearl half-moons. Many carried carved and painted masks, readying themselves for their dance.

"Out the way," someone grumbled, shoving Nate towards the house.

Nate slunk away, his heart in his stomach. These men were here to save him and his family. They were performing the ritual on his behalf because he could not. Being touched meant he was cursed by the Great Dragon and had to have others intercede for him. He leaned against the wall of his home, hoping to stay out of the way but still witness what the men gathered there would do.

"'Tis strange, to be sure," a woman's voice drifted to him, muffled by the bricks separating them.

"I know," another replied. "Not a sign of damage here. It's as though the wind never happened."

"Not like in Kvarn," the first speaker dropped her voice. "The windmill and the bakery—in a shambles. Never seen or heard of wind like that 'afore."

"'Tis mighty curious, that's what I say. As if this curse business weren't enough."

Nate wondered if they would put two and two together. He remembered the gale, which had torn through this part of the valley a fortnight ago. It had been frightful, although the dell where his mill was, remained protected. If these women made the connection, his life would be forfeit. The townspeople would not tolerate one who made a deal with a spirit. It was only those lured into a magical trap who could be forgiven their transgression. If they knew he stood to benefit from the bargain he made with the nix, his life would be over. He'd be dragged to the stockade and the mob let loose on him. Trembling, he stood, straining his ears to hear their conversation, but it shifted abruptly when someone else stepped into the kitchen demanding more tea for the men.

The sound of rumbling voices drew Nate's attention towards the pond. The water was obscured by the men who'd formed a half-circle around it, walling off the open space beside the pool on the side where trees didn't grow. They had donned their masks and began chanting, stamping their feet in a rhythm that vibrated to Nate's core. Bells chimed in time to the dancers' movements.

Voices rose into the darkness, banishing the minion of water dragons to her liquid home, and beseeching the Great Dragon in the Sky to break the curse or, at the very least, to protect the babe. Drums sounded, adding their pounding vibrations to the mix.

Nate looked up at the sky. It was a cloudless night and he thought about the moon, the eye of the Great Dragon Lord, damaged by the incessant attacks from the water dragons who coveted the sky domain. It was on these nights, when the Sky Dragon's power was at its weakest, that humans could aide his cause and offer strength by keeping the water dragons and their minions at bay. Legend told that as the moon returned in strength, so too did the Great Dragon's powers. A binding performed on this night would become more and more powerful as it set during the coming fortnight and then it would become permanent.

When the moon was full and the Great Dragon on High watched over his creation with both eyes, one for the day and one for the night, it would be Nate's turn to perform his penitence and ask for forgiveness for his transgressions. As he watched the men dancing, calling upon the creative powers of the Great Dragon, he contemplated what he might say to atone for what he'd done.

The night wore on and one group of chanters broke away, seeking a brief respite to refresh themselves. They filed into the miller's home in silence, accepting a drink before returning to their posts at the water's edge. When they were done, the other half did the same. At some point, Nate drifted to sleep, still standing with his back to the wall.

He woke with a start in the chill pre-dawn. Silence blanketed the dell where he lived. Mist swirled about his feet, obscuring his view of the pond and what took place there. A shadow loomed out of the silver mist and Nate cringed while his mind struggled to discern what he saw. More figures came into view. They were large and some made eerie sounds. The chime of a bell drew Nate's attention into the distance and then he gasped. Right before him, a human figure stepped out of the fog. The bulky shape was made more so by the outfit of fake scales and the mask the man grasped in one hand.

Nate nodded to the man, acknowledging his participation. All he received in return was a grunt.

More men appeared out of the mist and made their way up the wagon tracks leading back to Kvarn. Some of the women who'd stayed the night to observe the ritual joined their husbands and disappeared back into the fog that lay thick over the forest.

Seeing a flash of yellow, Nate turned his attention on the last figure to emerge from the cloud. "Thank you, Paderi," he murmured.

The man nodded; the bags under his eyes were darkened from fatigue. "It is the first step. We shall continue our intercession at the church until your appeasement in a fortnight. All we can do is ask the Great Dragon in the Sky to support our cause and bind the creature's powers in the water, cleansing any magic that lingers beyond her domain."

Nate thanked him again and bid the priest farewell. He turned to go into the house, which was still now and he wondered how Hilda and the babe had fared on this night. As he crossed the threshold, a woman's voice made him turn back towards the mist.

"Just a minute, Nate, my boy."

He squinted into the formless substance from which the voice had emanated. A moment later, Tandra's wiry figure and wizened face melted into view. She took his hand, slipping a glittering stone into his palm.

"Take this," she said, her voice strong and brooking no contradiction. "See that your son wears it. It will help to protect him from the wiles of the nix." She glanced about and dropped her voice conspiratorially. "I've also done my part." She winked, her face crinkling into an infinite number of folds. "I targeted the second part of your bargain so the water sprite can't continue to wreak havoc such as the blast of wind that swept through Kvarn two weeks ago. I have told no one of that part and now, any success you experience will be of your own doing, not hers."

Nate's vision blurred as he stammered his thanks. The old woman patted his shoulder, her grip firm and her sharp gaze met his tearful eyes. "You are welcome, my boy. I know you let your worry wear you down and that gave the nix her window of opportunity. I also know you won't make such a mistake again."

Burying his face in both hands, Nate wiped the tears from his cheeks and nodded, words failing him. Relief stole his voice completely and she patted him on the back, sending him off to bed and warning him to seek rest and stay clear of the pond for the next while. Acquiescing, Nate stumbled inside, closing the door behind him and collapsed in a basket chair in his work area where sleep overwhelmed him while he clasped the protective stone for his son, pressing his hand against his heart.

Years passed. Nate was lulled into complacency with each passing day that his son, Phillip, remained safe. The rumours dissipated after a while and peace returned to Kvarn and the outlying dell where the water mill stood. Business returned to Nate's mill and he prospered as never before.

Although he didn't like to dwell on it, the thought did cross his mind that all the nix had promised him came to pass. He kept reminding himself of Tandra's words, that his success was his own but as time drew by, he began to doubt. He hid the knowledge that the nix's prophecy came true, burying it deep where it weighed on his conscience while his wife rejected him, only keeping up the bare bones of a façade when others were around. While his business prospered and his son grew, his marriage crumbled to dust. He tried to salvage what he could, but Hilda refused him at every turn. She spoke to him only when she had to. She made him sleep in a separate bed and as the years passed, she forced him into a room of his own.

Nate understood her though. The loss of their three children had been Fate. Her hand had snatched them away when the sickness swept through Kvarn, taking many little ones with it. This was different. He, Nate, was to blame for this woe upon his family and the threat to their Phillip. This was his fault and Nate could not deny it. He should have asked the nix for specifics.

The feeling of entrapment held Nate fast, keeping him bound and unable to move forward. Hilda wouldn't forgive, even though Phillip grew bigger and stronger day by day. Their fear of the nix and the threat of their unfulfilled part of the bargain hung over Nate, crushing him. On occasion, Phillip would be lured towards the water by some magical means and Hilda's over-protectiveness worsened, building a wall between Nate and his family.

Any sign of wealth enraged Hilda and after the first few years of their prosperity, Nate began to hoard his takings, unable to share his successes with his wife for fear of unleashing her anger and resentment. The very things he'd feared that spring morning, manifested and his wife was his judge. She spent all her energy keeping their son safe and away from the water's edge. With a heavy heart, Nate watched his once-smiling wife turn in on herself and become bitter and anxious. The woman he loved, who'd barely been touched by age in the first three decades of her life, aged thirty years in the space of ten.

By the time their son reached his maturity, Nate was an outcast in his own home and Hilda's energy was spent. A wisp of possibility sent its tendrils to Nate's heart when Phillip walked into their home with Amina on his arm. After Phillip refused Anabelle, Nate had thought everything really would crumble to dust because of the nix's curse, but Phillip's marriage to Amina squeezed Nate's heart, bringing both joy and immeasurable sadness. While his only surviving child took his vows, the old miller watched his beloved wife, the woman he'd shared so many unbearable hardships with, give in to the weight of her burdens. He sensed her giving up when she'd seen their only living son safely to adulthood. Once Phillip left their home to start his own life, all reason for Hilda's existence ceased. Every breath she'd taken for the past twenty years was to keep him alive and away from the nix. Once that was achieved, all strength left her, dissolving in the waters of her relief. Nate's heart ached as she continued to refuse his company and he watched her waste away within the space of a few weeks.

All alone, Nate gave in to the ruthlessness of life. Despondency took him to the depths of his being where darkness and hopelessness reigned supreme. With his wife departed into the realm beyond and son living in the town, there was no purpose left for him. Nate's wealth was ashes to him, something to spread to the four winds and hope it would serve other, more fertile soil. Going back wasn't possible. Moving forward was out of the question. Nate remained stuck in the web of the nix's curse, trapped by the promise of his worries being taken away, when his wish transformed itself into the shackles that bound him ever more tightly to his moment of misjudgement.

One afternoon, Nate rose from a stupor, kicked away the empty bottles lying at his feet and squinted against the pain throbbing in his head. He stumbled forward and came face to face with his own reflection. He hadn't looked at himself for a long time and the face staring back at him gave him pause. Bloodshot, watery eyes gazed out from underneath sagging eyelids. His beard was mostly white now, a thin and scraggly growth protruding from his jaw.

He stared long at the broken creature in the mirror. It appeared less than human and he cursed himself for a fool. Dropping his eyes, his attention was drawn to his wizened hands, knotted veins and sinew, marred by gouged holes weeping a pink-tinged liquid. For years he'd kept the proof of his bargain out of view but in recent months it had become difficult to dissimulate the wounds inflicted on him by the nix's magic. With each passing year, the marks her spell had left on his hands and neck had grown more pronounced. They were a reminder of his failure to keep his end of the bargain.

Shuddering at the realisation he'd become a lowly beast and would soon openly be rejected, Nate stumbled into the kitchen in search of more drink to drown out the remnants of his sharp mind, which continued to rebuke him.

The sun was low in the sky and Nate was on his second bottle of the foul-smelling brew he favoured for its strength, when an anguished cry tore through the tranquil evening. The sound pierced Nate to the core. There was something so deeply tormented in the reverberation, he came to his feet with his mind almost clear.

Stepping out into the fresh air, he became aware of the acrid stench he'd been subjecting himself to. He took several faltering steps outside, gulping the sweet forest air into his stale lungs. A long wail reached his ears and Nate turned his bleary eyes towards the sound. It came from somewhere beyond the nix's infernal pond and he shuffled towards the cry.

"Give him back!" a high-pitched voice screamed, followed by heaving sobs.

Nate adjusted his direction, coming upon a plump young woman kneeling in the grass beside the pond. Her dark, waist-long braids lay crumpled on either side of her head which rested upon the soft loam. She jerked her torso upright again, her jowls wobbling from the motion, braids snapping through the air as she screamed something unintelligible. Raising a fist, she shook it at the crystalline waters of the mill pond.

Nate approached and he thought he recognised her. Through the fog of his inebriated brain, he saw the image of this same woman dressed in bridal blue with joy sparkling in her dark brown eyes. His heart cramped, sending numbing lightning strikes through his legs and arms. He stumbled.

The woman's round face snapped onto him and a renewed bout of heart-rending sobs tore through her. Reaching her, Nate tried to fold his arms around her large body.

"What is it, Amina?"

She wailed louder. Through a series of hiccups and sobs, Nate made out some words.

"Phillip— missing. Hunting. Shoulda— back— hours ago." Amina held up a large, flat object that flapped and shook it in Nate's face. "—found this— 'ere."

Nate grabbed her hand, stilling it so he could see what she held. It was a leather satchel, smooth and worn with use. Recognition slammed through him and he gasped as he took the pouch from her. "This is Phillip's?"

"Yeeees," Amina howled.

Nate crumpled to the soft ground and gazed over the still pool. There was no sign of any living thing but in his heart he knew what Amina indicated. Sadness attached weights to his being. What was the point in fighting? Everything he'd done to avert this precise outcome had proven futile. All they'd done was draw out the inevitable. Looking at his distraught daughter-in-law, Nate felt calm take hold of him for the first time in years.

"Oh, Amina," he murmured, gathering her into his arms. "It was inevitable. We duped ourselves into believing we could keep the nix's curse at bay, but we never stood any chance against her magic. She was always going to get her way, all we did was drag it out." He paused, collecting his thoughts while the storm of her emotions calmed. "We were gifted with the beauty of time. We had these moments with him and we cannot ask for more."

Amina pushed away from him, her brow furrowing and her eyes flashing. "No," she spat. "I will not give in. I will not let her win. He is mine, bound to me before the Great Dragon in the Sky and I will not let him go. I will not let our child grow up without his father." Her hand came to rest on her middle and Nate gasped.

"You are with child?"

She nodded, gazing over the smooth pond before snapping her eyes back to his. "We were going to share the news soon." Her attention shifted to the water lapping against the stone wall in front of her. "I can sense him. He's alive." A shudder tore through her.

"How can you know?"

"I don't know how— I just know. It's a strong feeling, right here," she patted her chest. "I can sense him and he is fighting. He wants to come back to me. I can't leave him to that beast." Her gaze drifted to the pouch, lying between her and Nate. Determination glinted in her eyes and set in her jaw. "I will rescue Phillip. For his sake, for mine and especially for this child's," her hand brushed her stomach again,

"I'll do what it takes to get him back. He doesn't deserve to waste away down there." Her gaze seemed to pierce through the green waters before her, seeing into the depths where she sensed her husband. "I don't know how I'll do it," she went on. "All I know is *I* must."

In the three months that followed, Nate sensed a shift. Something released in him with every full moon. He didn't understand why he sensed a growing lightness around his chest, allowing his breaths to flow more freely. He stopped drinking, cleared away the bottles and cleaned the house. Something drove him to replace broken boards and worn railings, and with each small improvement, Nate felt like he renewed himself. He spent hours on his knees scrubbing the floor, as if washing it could remove the stain that had been left on his soul. To the miller's amazement, the weeping wounds on his hands and neck closed.

With a start, Nate woke in the middle of the night. The light of the full moon streamed in through the window of his room. In an instant he realised it was the third one since Phillip's disappearance and Amina's decision to find a way to release him. The air hummed with energy, drawing Nate outside. He needed to be out there, to see what was happening. Hope blossomed in his heart. He couldn't understand why. What was he hopeful for?

Nate's feet found their way past Hilda's empty room and his heart twinged at the memory of all the wasted time and how much she'd suffered because of him. His legs moved of their own accord, brushing away the sadness with their purposeful movement. He strode down the stairs and pushed the door open.

Frigid air hit him square in the chest and Nate grabbed his coat from a hook beside the door. He shrugged his way into it while he absorbed the scene unfolding before him. At the edge of the pond, a few steps away from him, sat a thin woman he didn't know. A golden spinning wheel hummed as it turned and a silver thread filled the bobbin. The moon slipped behind the trees beyond the mill pond, and the whirring wheel stilled.

The woman unclasped the bobbin from its place on the spinning wheel and turned her attention to the pond. Nate observed the short cut of her hair and her narrow waist, obscured a little by a dress too large for her. Although his eyes couldn't place her, Nate's heart told him he knew this woman.

She placed the shimmering bobbin onto the wall bordering the pond and looked out over the still waters. Struggling to place her, Nate took a step forward, trying to get a better look at her face. The sound of rushing water drew his attention away from the svelte figure by the banks. The liquid in the pond parted, leaving a path through the muddy pond floor.

A shadow moved in the distance. It was a rake thin figure, more shade than man, who shuffled forward, a heart-rending cry bursting from his lips. *Amina.* The name echoed in Nate's mind and he knew it truly was her, standing there by the banks of the nix's pond, releasing Phillip from that watery prison. She looked nothing like her former, overweight self. Her short-cropped hair and hour-glass figure hinted at changes far greater than anything Nate had ever considered possible—not in the short span of three months, at least.

Nate's vision blurred in the instant he saw his son wrap his arms around his wife. In the same instant, something snapped inside Nate. It was as though a reptilian claw released its grip on him, the pressure that had trapped his diaphragm, lungs and heart in its clutches for decades, melting away as the first pale light of pre-dawn found its way into his awareness. He was free. The magic was gone and Nate was himself again.

Blinking away the tears obscuring his sight, Nate felt a veil lift from his eyes and he experienced a presence prickling across his skin. It was beyond his scope for understanding, greater than anything he could describe. The being he could sense but not see was infinitely kind, bathing Nate in unconditional love. His whole life rippled into a coherent entity he could understand. His memory picked out that moment twenty years before when he'd plucked the flower and grasped the transitory nature of life. Moments later, he'd been tested. The nix offered him what seemed an easy solution to his transitory problems, and instead of standing firm in his new understanding, he'd caved in to his fears and clutched at straws.

Renewed tears coursed down Nate's cheeks. There was so much kindness and love in the revelation. He was overwhelmed. Nate had spent an inordinate amount of time clinging to his self-hatred and guilt. Experiencing it disappear in the gentlest breath of air was a release of such compassion, his heart filled with gratitude and a promise: he would make up for lost time. All the goodness he'd missed out with Hilda and Phillip could be atoned for. He needed only rise to the fullness of his capability, achieve the wholeness he'd always known, and he would find the solace he sought.

The presence withdrew. Nate was left blinking, his mind still coming to terms with the revelation while energies swirled around him, leaving him at the eye of a storm. He realised only a heartbeat or two had passed since Phillip emerged from the waters and flung his arms around Amina, but Nate saw the triumph was not to be.

A wall of water obscured the forest. It gathered like a rabid beast ready to pounce and foaming at the mouth. Glancing about for the cause of this new calamity, Nate's eyes fell on the nix, her raven hair billowing about her face and her hands held up behind her, as though she were controlling the wave with her power.

Nate ran forward, screaming at her to stop, to let Phillip go, but before he could take more than two steps towards the couple cowering beneath the cusp of the wave, they both vanished with an audible *pop*. Something grabbed Nate and pulled him backward. As his body was shoved towards the house, Nate saw two things. First, the nix's face was drawn and she looked as if she were fighting something monstrously big. In a flash, Nate understood she was holding the wave back, giving Amina and Phillip whatever time she could to get them to safety.

Yellow robes floated in his peripheral vision and Nate realised he was being pulled towards the house by the village priest. If the priest was leaving things be, there had to be an explanation for it all. *This, too, is part of the greater workings. It is meant to be.*

Nate breathed.

The priest shut the door behind them both, blotting out the scene unfolding by the mill pond, and began reciting an incantation. He invoked the Great Dragon on High, praying for a reprieve and for the safety of Kvarn.

A rumble shook the foundations of the house and something crashed into the wall with great force, but the bricks held, as did the wood of the door. The priest slumped into the chair beside Nate.

"What is going on?" Nate ventured.

The priest took several deep breaths while his eyes examined Nate in the dimness. At length, he said, "Amina succeeded in freeing Phillip with the nix's help. I know we thought the water sprite was to blame, but it seems the whole fiasco was based on a misunderstanding. The nix knew of your prior losses and wished to save Phillip from you and Hilda whom she'd deemed incompetent parents. If she'd known your other children had passed from illness and it wasn't your fault, she would never have made that bargain with you. As it is, she never called in the bargain. It was the power of the magic itself that required fulfilment, but because Hilda constantly worked against that call from the pond's magic and because I bound the nix, containing her powers in the pond, the magic went on a limb. It created a vortex which was on the verge of destabilising. That wave was all that remained of the magic that's been growing and festering over the past twenty years, gaining a life of its own. The nix helped Amina and Phillip escape, and I think she managed to slow the force of the blast to protect Kvarn."

The old man with his snowy beard pushed himself to his feet. The movements were slow. Lethargy turned him into a tortoise. Nate stepped forward and helped him up. "We must head to the village and find out what the damage is. That wave was headed straight for Kvarn."

Nate supported the older man as they stepped out into a transformed world. The mill wheel to the left of the building was a shredded mess. The layer of dirt on the wall had been sheared off by the force of the blast. All plants in the wave's direct path had been wiped out of existence, leaving a brown streak cutting a straight line away from the pond towards the village.

Where the pond had once been, now only a muddy, plant-strewn hole remained. Some water trickled in from the stream, but it would take time to fill up. In the mud, Nate made out a figure fading in and out of view. He pointed and the priest stopped. Together, they watched the nix as she drew on what little liquid remained around her to maintain her humanoid form.

She lay on the pond floor, mud coating her as she flickered. With great effort, she lifted her head and locked eyes with Nate. *I'm sorry*, her words reverberated in his mind. *I did my best. They will survive the wave, and perhaps they will find happiness. As for the town, it did not reach that far. The tannery may have a little damage, but all else is contained.* The blue-green of her eyes blazed and then the creature of magic and water snuffed out.

Even as Nate lamented the loss of Phillip and Amina, along with the knowledge his grandchild was beyond his reach, the presence from earlier impressed itself upon his mind for a second time. *This, too, shall pass. Amina and Phillip are facing their own test, and shall overcome their fears when they are ready to be reunited.*

Air filled Nate's lungs. Never had it tasted so sweet before.

With tingles prickling over his skin, the miller felt life coursing through him. He was alive. And he was able to rejoice.

Taking the priest by the arm, Nate headed towards Kvarn for the first time in months. Frost lined the parts of the road that remained undisturbed by the magical upheaval that had coursed through the countryside at dawn. The sun sent its soft wintry light out between the sentinels of leafless trees. A laugh bubbled up inside Nate, and he gave joy full rein.

"I am back!" he exclaimed and the priest nodded, weariness tugging at his eyes and mouth. "I am back!" Nate reiterated, letting go of the older man's arm and turning full circle, his arms held up to the glory of the morning.

"Yes," the priest replied. "And I'm sorry I didn't realise how trapped you were in all of it. If I'd noticed the jumbled ball of magic gathering there sooner, I might have been able to help you."

Regret unloaded its weight on the priests shoulders, but Nate slipped in beside the old man once more, offering him a hand. With a smile, Nate said, "It has all been as it needed to be. I would like to look forward, and what I wish to do, in Hilda's memory, is set up a children's home at the mill. It is what feels right."

AUTHOR'S NOTE

If you would like to explore the nix's version of events and join Amina and Phillip on their continued adventure, you can pre-order Naiya's Wish, which is due to release 5th November.

8
THE ARCTIC MERMAID
N.D.T. CASALE

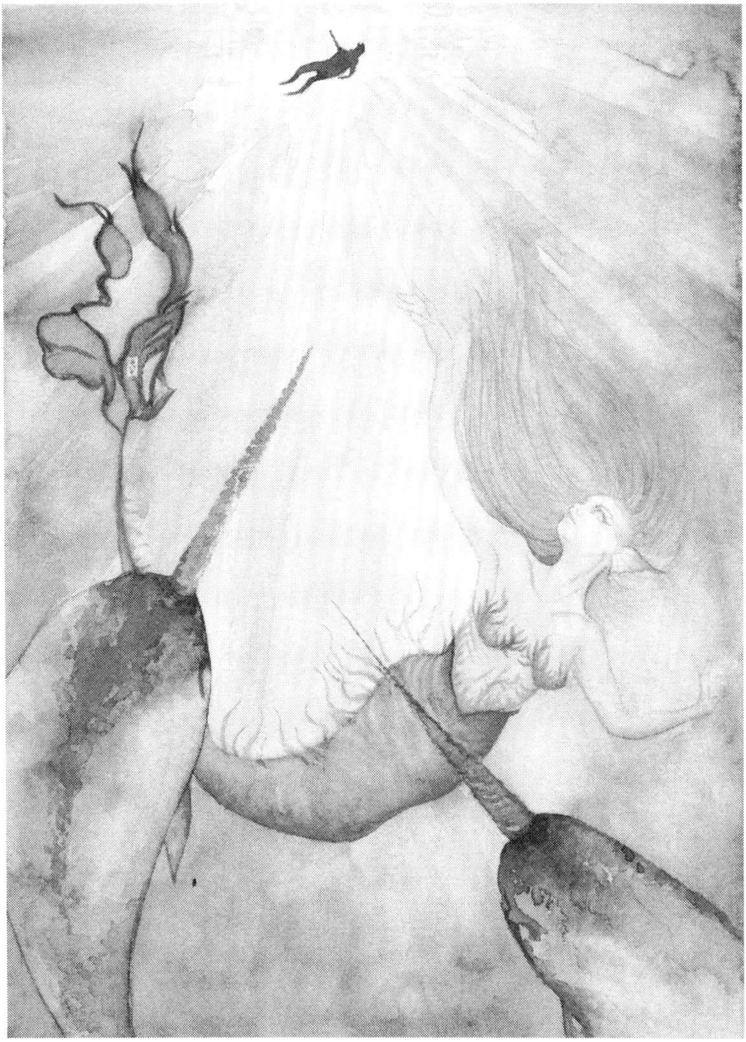

THE ARCTIC MERMAID

"What do you mean you can't save him!" Aerwyna shrieked. Her hands clenched into fists that turned her knuckles white.

"Shush, Aerwyna," Maj the Sea Witch grabbed the mermaid's arm and hustled her outside into the hall of mermaiden's family home. "Your father is trying to rest."

"My father is dying!" cried Aerwyna. She shook her head and attempted to remove the image of the sick merman lying in his bed. His body and tail were covered with stone-size hives, his skin was light blue, and his breath had become shallow.

"As I told you, he is having an allergic reaction from his attack," hissed Maj. "The poison has seeped into the cuts and mixed with his bloodstream."

Aerwyna's eyes burned with oncoming tears. Her father, Namazzi, had been ambushed by a squad of jellyfish in the shallow waters near Lowvainia. The stings from the poisonous tentacles had released toxins that had made her father very ill. Each day his condition grew worse, and Maj informed her that without enchanted medicine, he would die.

"There is nothing you can do to save him?" whispered Aerwyna.

As one of the most powerful creatures in the depths of the ocean, Maj had the magical abilities to heal innocent beings in ways that ventured beyond common understanding.

With kindness in her eyes, the sea witch looked at the purple-haired mermaid who floated before her. "He needs an antidote to save his life. There is a remedy, but I do not want to raise false hope. What is required is a lock of freely-given human hair."

Aerwyna wiped her tears. "A lock of freely-given human hair!"

"Yes, Aerwyna," replied Maj. "You had better hope that in the human world there is need for mermaid enchantment. When you grant a wish, you will receive what you desire."

Aerwyna's desperation for a human wish would soon come true, for in the kingdom of Lowvainia, Prince Neifion had gone missing.

It was the night after the prince turned seven months old. A veil of darkness swooped into the royal nursery like a gust of spite and swallowed him at just past midnight. When beams of sun streamed into the room the following morning, they revealed a barren cradle. His mother Callopey's cries of anguish woke the whole castle. In her grief, she failed to see the hexagram etched into the blue satin pillow. However, King Aalton's eyes did not miss the meaning behind the emblem. He remained silent. The symbol of witchcraft was burned into the back of his eyeballs; his stomach twisted into knots, and his heart tightened in his chest. His soul held secrets he would never reveal. He knew who was behind the symbol: Nerissa the Enchantress of the North. Aalton knew the Enchantress was far more powerful than any force in the human realm. The only power open to him for help would have to come from a mythological source.

He knew he needed the Arctic mermaids.

For centuries the wondrous tales of the Arctic mermaids flowed from the lips of Nordic storytellers. These magical beings lived deep beneath the waters of the Arctic Sea and had the power to grant wishes in return for a favor. All a person had to do was write the heart's desire on parchment, put it in a bottle, and throw it deep into the sea for the Arctic mermaids to find.

His Royal Highness's misfortune was the solution to Aerwyna's dilemma. Thousands of feet below the ocean, her father's condition worsened as the toxins took their toll on his body.

Aerwyna was the only daughter of Namazzi and his wife Odina. Recently the young mermaid had turned twenty-one years old. Instead of joy on her birthday, she was plagued by sleepless nights and headaches as the need for an antidote weighed heavily on her mind.

"I must find a way to get a lock of human hair. Whatever it takes," whispered the young sea maiden. Aerwyna was an attractive creature with long purplish-blue hair and a shiny lavender tail. She craved adventure; but now her father's predicament was the greatest challenge of her life.

Consumed with apprehension, Aerwyna sat on the shallow ocean floor with her friends, twin narwhals Koral and Kaia. They sought a way to do the impossible. Sunlight streamed down from the water's surface, drawing their attention to a shiny object half-buried in the nearby sand. A glass bottle with papyrus inside glittered in the beams of the sun.

According to Nordic lore, wishes written with heart-felt emotion upon a sheet of papyrus, placed into a bottle sealed with hope and love, would find its way to the magical Arctic mermaids. Living safely beneath the turbulence of the frigid Arctic Sea, the mermaids took delight in welcoming such a bottle with its contents rich in human emotion.

Aerwyna pulled out a note. Her heart pounded, her breathing quickened, her hand tightened around the neck of the glass. Could this be the answer to her prayer?

> *O' powerful mermaids of the Arctic North grant me my only wish. My son has been taken from me by the Enchantress of the North. Return him unharmed, and I shall grant you a favor, whatever your heart desires. I wish no harm to come to the beautiful Nerissa. She lives in a castle of ice, deep in the Northern Mountains where snow falls ceaselessly. You are my only hope.*
>
> -King Aalton of Lowvainia

"It is from the King of Lowvainia," cried Aerwyna,

"Lowvainia?" inquired Kaia. "Don't they hate all things magic?"

"His mother did, the former queen. She and her husband are the ones who created the ban," replied Aerwyna. Her face fell. "It says here that King Aalton's son has been taken." She showed the message to her friends.

Kaia nodded, "I heard the dolphins gossiping about it yesterday. Prince Neifion has gone missing, and no one in the kingdom knows who the kidnapper is. However, according to the walruses, it seems the king is holding his tongue with secret knowledge."

"Enchantress of the North?" asked Koral. "The sea speaks of her. She is a very powerful spell charmer who lives far away in the Northern Mountains. Her name is Nerissa."

"This is the answer to our prayers," stated Aerwyna. "If we

rescue Prince Neifion from the Enchantress, we can have a lock of the king's hair and save my father!"

"Aerwyna, do you know how risky this is? The Enchantress of the North is dangerous. Anyone who gets in her way mysteriously disappears. The waters around the Northern Mountains are unpredictable," added Kaia. "Nerissa lives in a castle in the mountains. How will you save the baby when you have no legs?"

Aerwyna paused. "I don't know." Anxiety gripped her heart and would not release. She needed to rescue that baby. "We must swim to Maj. She is the only one who can help us."

Aerwyna flowed in butterfly motions to the sea witch's cave in the eastern waters. Maj was a healer, a wish granter, and a strong asset to the ocean community. No one knew much about her past, but they knew if they needed a potion for whatever they desired, Maj had the magic.

It took only a few minutes to navigate through the chilly waters.

Maj invited the mermaid into her cave, and Aerwyna explained her situation.

"Did you tell your father about this?" asked Maj, her voice sleek and icy.

Aerwyna shook her head. She knew her father would try to stop her. He would never allow his only daughter to place herself in harm's way for his benefit.

"Aerwyna, you are going to need a limbo potion. It will give you the ability to morph between mermaid and human," declared Maj as she twirled her long red hair entwined with shells and starfish. Banging her silver tail against a nearby shelf, and an emerald bottle fell into her hands. Her expression was grave. "You know this spell is permanent. It will toy with your soul. You will no longer be pure mermaid; you will forever be an embodiment of mortal and mermaid. You must realize this potion has not been tested. Not many sea maids request to become two halves of different entities."

Aerwyna swallowed and nodded. "I understand the risks, but I need to save my father." She sighed. "Why would a powerful enchantress steal a baby anyway?"

"Oh, my dear," replied Maj, "this is about more than stealing a baby. This is about a woman seeking revenge for a broken heart."

Aerwyna cocked her head.

"No one is ever born evil, Aerwyna. Evil emerges when the soul has lost hope and when the spirit is broken. Every villain was once a good person who gave too much, cared too much, and was betrayed to the point the heart turned to ice. A long time ago Nerissa was a young woman in love with a man who became King Aalton of Lowvainia."

Aerwyna's eyes widened, "The king and the Enchantress of the North were in love?"

Maj smirked, "The deepest pain comes from the stories that are never told. My dear Aerwyna, in order to heal the wounds, you must understand how this all began. Only then can forgiveness reach the soul."

Maj waved her hand. A large silver cauldron appeared in the center of the watery cave. The sea witch swam around tossing various ingredients: eel's eye; squid ink; Johnson's seagrass; mangroves and fragrant herbs that tickled Aerwyna's nose.

The sea witch's magic allowed the potion to begin to bubble and gurgle even though they were underwater. Aerwyna was fascinated at how the elixir boiled without fire. Time seemed to pass slowly as the contents in the cauldron emitted fumes and changed colors into spirals resembling a whirlpool. After what seemed like hours, Maj looked up at Aerwyna. The purple-haired mermaid watched as the potion turned a deadly shade of magenta and black.

The sea witch dipped her finger into the cauldron. "Still not ready," she mused. "That should give me plenty of time to tell the tale." She took a deep breath and the story flowed in the music of the ocean.

"When King Aalton was young, he loved to explore in the mountains north of the kingdom of Lowvainia. His mother begged him to stay out of the frigid peaks.

'The winds of the cliff sides carry distractions and temptations that a man finds hard to resist,' she whispered. 'Your loyalty must always be to your kingdom.'

"A long time ago, Aalton's parents, King Merv and Queen Aegelmaer, of Lowvainia, passed a law that all mythical creatures were barred from inhabiting the kingdom, and all magic was banned. They believed a realm should run on normalcy. Magic would cause distractions. The Northern Mountains were home to everything the king and queen feared most. Enchantment existed from the peaks to the oceans. The queen would not allow her only son to associate with the beings who inhabited those frosty forbidden spires.

"However, Aalton did not listen. He continued to explore the caves and the waters that ran through those lofty towers. One day while climbing the icy cliffs, he slipped. His head hit a boulder, and he fell fifteen feet into the freezing ocean. Aalton would have drowned if it had not been for Nerissa, a young and beautiful enchantress who called the mountains her home. Using her magic, she was able to rescue Aalton from the depths of a watery grave. She healed him by means of her secret and powerful spells. When fourteen-year-old Aalton opened his eyes, his heart beat with love for the sorceress who had saved his life. Succumbing to magical beauty, he began a passionate relationship with the Enchantress.

"As time passed, Aalton's love for Nerissa deepened. When the young prince turned twenty-one, misfortune gripped Lowvainia. King Merv died unexpectedly from a sudden illness. By royal law, Aalton's duty was now to become king.

"This meant as king, he would take a bride and produce an heir. In Aalton's mind, his bride would be Nerissa. However, when he spoke of this to his mother, she reminded him that a romance between a king and an enchantress was forbidden. The monarchy's ban on magic still tainted decision making in its iron fist.

'Lowvainia does not allow magic here,' warned the queen. 'We are people of sensibility and you are a man of importance. Your father and I created this ban to keep you and the people safe from magic. How would it look to your subjects if you fell under the spell of a woman of the dark arts?' hissed Queen Aegelmaer. 'My own son married to a witch! You cannot take that woman for your bride. Your father would have never allowed it and neither do I!'

'But Nerissa is good, Mother!' retorted Aalton. 'She saved my life.'

'She would not have had to save your life if you had listened to me in the first place. Lowvainia is an exemplary kingdom, and we will not have interlopers of magical tendencies in positions of power. If I ever see you with that witch again, I will have her captured and killed.'

"Aalton was distraught. When he became king, his every move would be watched by his mother, advisors, and the guards. This would not allow him the freedom to explore the Northern Mountains, nor the time for him to spend with Nerissa. He wished not to put the young Enchantress in danger. If it came to light the monarch was having romantic relations with an enchantress, the army would wage war against her.

"Nerissa had turned twenty-one. Her powers were now unbeatable. She was dangerous. The young king knew it was best not to upset her. The Enchantress would vanquish the soldiers without a thought, if they came too close, which would weaken Lowvainia and bring shame to the crown.

"Aalton realized he could not let his father down. The monarchy must come first; but maybe after time, he could persuade his mother and the people to be more open minded. He ventured into the mountains to seek an audience with Nerissa for the last time. In their awkward conversation, the unwitting future king told her he had to attend to his royal duties, and he promised her he would never love nor marry another maiden no matter how beautiful or accomplished she might be. Nerissa would forever have his heart.

"Once his coronation as King of Lowvainia came to pass, the monarch planned to change the laws forbidding magic. In Aalton's mind he truly believed he could reverse the regulations to allow him and Nerissa to be together. The current decrees were old and outdated. Once the guidelines were more compassionate, magical beings and humans could inhabit the realm together. Under the new enlightened rule, he would return for the Enchantress, and they would marry.

"However, once Aalton was crowned, he realized his attempts to change the mandates were rejected by his mother, the dowager queen. After multiple failed attempts to vouch for his true love, the king unwillingly succumbed to the wishes of the steadfast matriarch and allowed her willpower to manipulate his decisions. He became the dowager queen's puppet, and his frustrations mounted as he was unable to lead as he pleased.

"Meanwhile Nerissa waited for Aalton's return. Days turned into years and years turned into decades. Eventually Nerissa realized she had been disappointed by the one she trusted most. Aalton was not coming back. Instead of sending word to her, he had made her wait around like a fool. Aalton's abandonment caused a break in the heart of the Enchantress that never healed. The break festered like an ugly sore that oozed bitterness, pain, and jealousy. She retreated deep into the mountains to tend to her heartbreak. The abundance of emotions wrapped around her heart like thorny vines transforming the Enchantress into a cold evil being. She was thirsty for revenge against the man who had broken her heart.

'Aalton will pay for this.' She whispered the promise to the ocean waters."

Maj paused and dipped her finger into her potion.
"What happened next?" cried Aerwyna.
"I will leave that for you to find out."
Aerwyna felt her lungs tighten. Nerissa's revenge was exquisite. "She took what mattered most to King Aalton -his son," finished Aerwyna.
Maj nodded. "It seems extreme, but heartbreak can make a kind person lose all sense of self, and pain can transform a loving heart into a vengeful one."
"We have a note left in a bottle written in the king's own hand. He still has feelings for Nerissa. In the note he wrote he wishes no harm to come to her. There is a reason he is not telling his household who has taken his child. But the winds always carry their secret wisdom wherever they go, even reaching the depths of the ocean."
Maj turned to Aerwyna. "Are you ready to undertake this quest to return the child to the king?"
The lavender-tailed mermaid nodded.
Maj smiled. "Much magic has occurred here today. If you agree to the bond with this magic, Aerwyna, your life as a mermaid will be changed forever."
A silence fell between them. The sea maiden looked at the witch and nodded.
In one swift motion, the spell-binder grabbed the purple-haired adventuress and threw her into the bubbling cauldron.

Aerwyna thought the potion would burn her; but instead, the liquid felt like a velvet curtain. Gold dots began to form on her skin until her whole body was outlined in a white halo which quickly disappeared. Fumes seeped into her lungs as she clung for dear life onto the enchantment and pulled herself up.

"The spell is complete," said Maj as she helped Aerwyna out of the bubbling elixir. Dizzy and somewhat outside of herself, the new species of sea creature flopped onto the ocean floor. A soreness began to encase her beautiful body.

"You are no longer a pure mermaid nor are you a human," continued Maj. "You are a hybrid of both. When your tail touches land, you will appear human, and when your toes touch water, you will return to your mermaid form. As you begin your quest to save your father, I have gifted you something far more precious than a potion. I have given you Knowledge, and with that Wisdom you will be able to heal instead of harm,."

Not sure exactly what Maj meant, Aerwyna took the sea witch's words to heart. She looked down at herself. She was still a mermaid; but something felt different, as if her body had been split in two. She felt new, almost reborn. A smile crossed her face. The first step of her mission to save her father was complete.

"You're no longer a mermaid?" asked Kaia as they left the sea witch's cave.

"Yes, I am. I am just half mermaid now," replied Aerwyna.

Koral leaned closer and sniffed her, "You still smell like a mermaid."

"I am a mermaid, just half," repeated Aerwyna.

"Have you tested to see if the potion is true?" asked Kaia.

Aerwyna shook her head. How would it feel to be human?

What would it be like? She twirled her hair around her finger and felt compelled to experiment

A shadow loomed above them at the ocean's surface.

"What is that?" asked Koral as they swam into open waters.

Aerwyna looked up to see a figure floating among the waves. The sun rays beat on the water and created bright sparkles around the shadow. Aerwyna realized it was a human.

She swam to the surface with the narwhals. As she came closer, the shadow revealed a man. He appeared to be in his early twenties and was facing down, unconscious in the water.

"Is he dead?" asked Kaia.

Aerwyna did not reply. She was too busy turning the human over so that his face caught the sun. She began to pull him to shore.

A few moments later, Aerwyna pushed hard enough until the majority of the man's body was on the beach. She lay him on his back.

The lapping waves came up to his knees. Sunshine illuminated the beads of water on his thin beard and sandy brown hair.

Aerwyna noted how his face was different from the faces of the mermen in the ocean. He had high cheekbones and a strong jawline that drew her attention. The Arctic mermaid also observed the mysterious man had long gashes on his arms and chest. It appeared he had been attacked by someone or something. She placed her fingers under his nose. He wasn't breathing. She took her heavy purple tail and whacked the man on the chest three times. His eyelids flew open to reveal hazel irises. Lurching forward he began to cough. After a wheezing spasm, he leaned to the side and began to spit out the salty ocean water.

"Aerwyna!" Koral's voice rode on the breeze to her eardrums. "Get back into deeper water. What if he sees you?"

Aerwyna spun around to dive beneath the waves when

something held her back. This young man might be able to help her save the prince. Normally humans were not supposed to see mermaids, but she was no longer a pure specimen of her kind.

Half in the water and half on the sand, the convulsing adolescent turned to look at her, and his eyes widened as he saw Aerwyna lying in the shallow water on her stomach, her hands under her chin, and her tail swishing back and forth.

"Hello," she said.

Eyes wide open, he gaped at her. "Puffer fish and seaweed! You are stunning! Am I dead?"

Aerwyna chuckled at the sailor's compliment. "You could have been if I hadn't saved you."

"You're a mermaid?"

"Half mermaid," answered the mischievous Aerwyna. She scooted forward so her entire body was no longer submerged. As soon as the water was gone, Aerwyna felt a tingling sensation throughout her flesh. Her tail split in two, and she experienced her body with two legs for the very first time.

"Half human," she finished. "I am Aerwyna."

Stunned by her beauty, the young seaman stared at her.

"Aloysius," he coughed as he cleared his throat. "My friends call me Aloy. Thank you for saving my life."

Aerwyna stood before him in her human form. Under the spell of the sea witch's magic, she was dressed in a beautiful diaphanous gown of royal purple embellished with a golden sash that accented her hourglass waist. The dress was dotted with sparkles like diamonds that glittered in the sun.

She studied him. "What were you doing in the water?" she asked.

"I was out fishing on my grandfather's boat. I felt a tug on my line. I thought it was a huge fish at the other end. I tried to reel it in. I struggled for about five minutes before it pulled me overboard. When I fell into the water, I was attacked." He looked down at the gashes on his arms. "I don't remember much. I know its eyes were red. I tried to fight back, then everything went dark. When I woke up, I saw you."

Aerwyna turned her head and felt the sun warm her cheeks. An idea formed in her mind. Aloy was a human with hair...

"Are you a sorceress? If you are, please allow me to thank you. Now I must go find my grandfather and explain to him how I lost his boat." Aloy stood up to leave.

"Wait, you can't leave," cried Aerwyna. She moved to go after him; but since it was her first-time walking, she had no idea how to use her human legs. She wobbled like a toddler and fell into Aloy's arms.

"I thought you said you were half human?" asked Aloy.

"I am. Today is my first day."

Aloy looked at her as if she had three heads.

Aerwyna continued. "You cannot leave. I saved your life. Now you owe me a favor."

"A favor?"

"Yes. Whenever a mermaid saves the life of a human, there must be an equal exchange."

"Aye, aye, Miss Aerwyna. What can I do for you? Although I doubt I can be helpful to a mermaid sorceress."

Aerwyna opened her mouth to request his hair, but the words would not come out.

No, her father's voice came to her mind. *By removing the message from the bottle, you agreed to fulfill the king's wish. If you take this fisherman's hair for my benefit, the baby you seek will die. I will not permit you to sacrifice an innocent infant for my health.*

Guilt swept over Aerwyna's body and she knew the truth.

Aerwyna, Maj's voice called to her on the sea breeze, *you still have time.*

The Arctic Mermaid found her own voice, "You are a

human, and I need you to take me to the castle of the Enchantress of the North."

"The Enchantress of the North? Do you have any idea how dangerous she is?"

"Only because she suffers from a broken heart," replied Aerwyna.

Aloy looked at her in confusion but continued. "To get to her icy oasis, you have to chart the northern waters, then climb a treacherous path that is almost impossible to get through."

"You are forgetting you are speaking to a mermaid," replied Aerwyna, "and you owe me a favor."

Aloy threw up his hands. "It is true. The lore speaks of it. You win, mermaid. I will see you in this place tomorrow at dawn."

The young man headed off down the shoreline.

Aerwyna turned and saw Kaia and Koral poke their heads up from the water. She gave them a thumbs up. "It worked!" She moved too quickly and teetered on her new legs. Belly-flopping into the water, her legs reformed into a tail.

At sunrise the next morning, Aerwyna found Aloy in a boat near the shore. She poked her head out of the water and called his name.

"I was wondering when you were going to get here," sighed Aloy as he helped her into the boat. Aerwyna's tail flopped around until it realized there was no water and split into legs.

"You really need to learn how to walk," replied Aloy.

"I have been practicing," huffed Aerwyna. She had spent all last night trying to walk on the rocky coast while Kaia and Koral shouted instructions. "I see you found your boat."

"Yes, it turned up on shore late afternoon," Aloy looked at

the pretty mermaid who smirked at him. "Did you have something to do with that?" asked the young sailor.

Aerwyna chuckled. The Arctic mermaid and the narwhal twins had found the abandoned boat during a late-night swim after a long evening of learning to walk. "Let's just say you owe me two favors now," smiled the young adventuress.

Aloy groaned. "Thank you. My grandfather is a fisherman and he was very upset I lost his boat. He and my grandmother raised me in childhood after my parents died." With an admiring glance, the young man looked at her lavender dress that appeared whenever she transformed from mermaid to human. "You are going to need warmer clothes than that, especially if we have to hike up a frozen mountain." He reached into his knapsack and pulled out a sweater, jacket, boots, and pants. "I took these from my sister. You seem to be about the same size."

"Thank you," murmured Aerwyna as she awkwardly put the clothes on over her dress. This was what it felt like to wear human clothes.

"You never mentioned to me why it is so important for you to go to the castle of the Enchantress," stated Aloy. "If I owe you a favor that puts my life at risk, I would like to know the reason."

"I need to rescue Prince Neifion from the Enchantress of the North," began Aerwyna.

"Prince Neifion? I heard about his disappearance. The Enchantress took him?"

Aerwyna poured out the whole story to him as the sailboat drifted farther into the Arctic waters. Fog settled above the icy surface making it difficult to see.

"I understand and respect what you are doing for your father," replied Aloy as he piloted the fishing boat. "If my father were alive I would do the same thing."

"Do you know where you are going?" She asked.

"Yes. My grandfather and I run a similar route on our fishing charts. This area has some of the best fish, and it makes for a better profit."

Aerwyna was about to reply when a scream sounded through the fog.

"What was that?" she asked

"I didn't hear anything," replied Aloy.

"It sounded like a scream; do you ever hear noises when you go out here?"

"I have never been out this far before. According to my navigations, we are about a sea mile away from the enchanted mountains."

The purple-haired mermaid turned towards the back of the sailboat and saw a long tentacle snake up from the water.

"Aloy," she hissed, "look!"

Aloy turned to see the tentacle slide back into the water. "It cannot be," he muttered.

"Aerwyna!" Someone screamed her name as a giant octopus emerged from the depths of the murky waters.

"It's a kraken!" yelled Aloy. He raced to the pilot wheel and jerked it sharply to avoid colliding with the face of the beast.

About twenty-five feet high with giant immobile eyes that gazed lifelessly at the two young people in the sailboat, the monster looked terrifying. It wasn't the eyes that caused Aerwyna's heart to freeze in fear but the fact that in two of his eight tentacles he held her friends Kaia and Koral.

That was the scream she had heard earlier. Her narwhal friends must have been following her.

The mermaiden fell forward onto her stomach as the boat came to an abrupt halt. The kraken had reached out and encircled the prow of the tiny craft in two of its tentacles. A sound of wood snapping resonated against her eardrums. In all her life of swimming in the frozen waters, she had never encountered such a creature. She looked up and saw Aloy throw an ax at another tentacle that was trying to grab him. However, the limb batted the ax away like an annoying fly.

Next the tentacle proceeded to wrap around Aloy's waist pulling him into the air.

Aerwyna felt paralyzed where she had been knocked to the deck by the rocking of the craft. She watched as Koral, Kaia, and Aloy twisted around in the air, waiting for when the kraken decided to consume them. In a rage the great beast continued to break apart the little boat with its five free tentacles. Droplets of water began to force their way up through the cracks in the floorboards as the little boat began to sink.

Broken boards knocked over the box on the table above her. A sea chest fell open to reveal a shiny sword. Aerwyna crawled to her knees and picked up the weapon. An idea began to form in her mind. A high-pitched wail caused her to look up. A bird had come out of nowhere and was pecking at one of the kraken's eyes. The action distracted the sea creature, who began to use its remaining tentacles to try to whack the bird, but the attacking wings were too fast.

The distraction allowed Aerwyna to jump off the battered boat into the ocean. She returned to mermaid form. She swam under the enraged cephalopod and behind it. Stabbing the back of the beast caused his giant head to jerk in her direction. The sea maiden jumped onto the head and stabbed the eight-limbed villain in each of its three hearts. Releasing her three friends from its tentacles, the attacker disappeared into the ocean taking the precious gift Aloy's grandfather had loaned him.

Aerwyna believed the danger was gone until the dying kraken wrapped one of its tentacles around her waist and began to pull her down into the trenches, too.

Arctic mermaid, your attempt to rescue the child from the Enchantress is worthless.

Even the ocean waters carried rumors to beasts as well as to allies. Apparently the kraken knew the purpose of her journey.

Aerwyna struggled to free herself. She felt his Kraken's words rattle through her mind and realized he was speaking to her with his mind and his dying breath.

She will never forgive him. He betrayed her.

"What are you talking about? Let me go!" She shouted to the giant octopus.

I heard the sea witch begin to tell you the story through the currents of the ocean waves; however, she did not tell you the whole tale. The Enchantress will never forgive King Aalton because he took a wife.

"A wife?" Aerwyna responded with surprise.

Listen closely, Arctic Mermaid, for I will continue the saga of woe.

Aalton was at last crowned King of the Realm. Over time he realized his mother would not allow him to marry his true love. He remembered his promise in the audience with the Enchantress. On many occasions he tried to return to the Northern Mountains. The young king wanted to explain the truth to Nerissa and set her free. However, the dowager queen had the guards follow the newly-coronated monarch, and they caught him before he could reach the peaks. Every time he tried to leave the castle, he was seized by the guards. After repeated attempts, Queen Aegelmaer stationed soldiers at the foot of the mountains making the pathway to Nerissa impossible to traverse. At long last, Aalton gave up.

Decades passed and the king ruled with his heart endlessly broken. When the dowager queen died and he was finally free from his mother's grasp, too much time had passed. Aalton was surprised Nerissa had not leveled the kingdom in her impatience. The King of Lowvainia knew if he tried to contact the Enchantress, she would not believe his failed attempts to return to her. Nerissa was stubborn. To make matters worse, each time the year completed another trajectory around the sun, the pressure mounted on him to produce an heir.

"You must take a wife," his advisor Jakob hissed. Having interests of his own, Jakob had replaced the deceased queen as the dominant voice of reason to the throne. This powerful advisor meant well but did not understand the king's broken heart. "You will not live forever. The people of Lowvainia grow uneasy knowing their future is in jeopardy. They need a reason to celebrate the throne and the king as their ruler. They desire a royal wedding, and they long for a royal heir."

Aalton delayed surrendering to his advisor's warning regarding marriage; but there seemed no escape from the inevitability of duty. The monarch knew Nerissa hated him after all the long years, but he had to speak with her nonetheless and explain his absence. When darkness came, Aalton was able to bypass the guards and enter the Northern Mountains; however, he could go no further. On multiple nights, he tried to climb the peaks, but he failed. He realized his mother and Jakob had paid a sorcerer to cast a curse as another barrier to make sure he never set foot in the mountains again. The dark spell fulfilled the dowager queen's dying wish.

Jakob continually urged the king to choose a royal princess from a nearby land and take her as his wife. The advisor's choice of queen became Aalton's betrothed. Her name was Callopey.

"Callopey's bloodline is pure and she will make an excellent queen," urged the well-intentioned confidante.

Once again, Aalton succumbed to the wishes of everyone else and met Callopey. She was a pretty maiden but not his soulmate. Callopey revealed to him that, like him, she was also pressured to marry. This gave Aalton an idea that would suit them both. They would enter into a marriage, and in so doing, they would produce an heir; but they would live secret separate lives within the castle walls. Kind and beautiful, Callopey agreed to this arrangement.

The night before his wedding, Aalton tried one last time to return to the Northern Mountain. His attempt was met with failure, for he could not bypass the curse.

The marriage was broadcast throughout Lowvainia, a gesture

that satisfied the people. After the passage of one year of marriage, King Aalton and Queen Callopey welcomed into the world a son they named Neifion. Everyone throughout the kingdom rejoiced. The subjects' cheers and happiness carried on the winds of spite to the betrayed Enchantress nestled deep among the canyons and valleys of the frozen mountains. The realization that the king had continued to live his life without her caused her thirst for revenge to become a throbbing ache that tormented her day and night.

The isolation of being on the outside, being forbidden to enter the kingdom just because she practiced magic haunted her. With a twist of her hand, she could make the Kingdom of Lowvainia a barren wasteland, full of skeleton houses, and a castle turned to dust. As a consequence of such dark magic, the monarchy would learn to respect sorcery instead of banning it. However, the thought of King Aalton with his wife and son brought tears to Nerissa's eyes. Did he not know how much she wanted to marry him and have a family with him? How dare he enjoy happiness while she suffered misery? No, an elimination of a realm was far too easy; she wanted him to know the depth of the sadness she had endured over the years of his reign. The Enchantress felt she would never know peace until Aalton felt her pain.

Nerissa formulated a plan. To fulfill her thirst for revenge, she would take away his precious child. Leaving the safety of her frozen home and by means of her enchantments, the sorceress found her way to the newborn prince's cradle. He was beautiful in his slumber. Her heart wept deeply. She was not sure why. She lifted the child and held him close. With a wave of her hand, she transformed into a veil of darkness clutching the infant against her heart as she flew over the waves to her mountain peaks of ice.

"What are you trying to say?" gasped Aerwyna as the weight of the kraken's tentacle around her waist hindered the flow of words from her captive breath.

I'm saying no matter what you do, the Enchantress will never give you the child. Her heartbreak runs too deep. All the ocean crea-

tures in the Arctic waters know this to be true, for they heard her speak it to the icy waves. She will never forgive King Aalton even though he tried to return to her. The Enchantress is headstrong and will not find peace until the king is as grief-stricken as she is. You will never get your lock of human hair, Arctic Mermaid. You should have let me eat you and your friends. What the Enchantress will do to you will be much worse. Your father will have died in vain."

With its dying breath, the kraken finally released Aerwyna and descended to a watery grave.

With a sense of urgency, the courageous mermaid swam to the ocean surface and burst out of the water.

"Aerwyna!" Aloy's voice called to her. The Arctic mermaid turned to see the young man clinging to a remaining plank from his destroyed boat. He paddled over to her.

"Thank the sea gods, you are all right; you were underwater for a long time. I thought something happened to you. I mean I know you are a mermaid and can breathe underwater, but I thought you were wounded."

Before the mermaiden could reply, she heard her narwhal friends calling to her.

"Kaia! Koral! Why are you here?" yelled Aerwyna as she pulled herself through the waves to her friends.

"We wanted to make sure you were unharmed, but the kraken surprised us," answered Koral.

"You can talk?" shouted Aloy as he drew closer to them.

"All animals can talk if you take the time to listen," replied Aerwyna.

"That was so brave of you stabbing the kraken in the hearts," praised Kaia.

"I would not have been able to overcome the beast if it had not been for our new friend," Aerwyna nodded to the bird who had pecked out one of the eyes of the misbegotten creature.

Swooping down in an elegant glide, the beautiful bird hovered above them.

"Thank you," Aerwyna said looking up with a smile.

"It is a good thing I came when I did. I normally do not fly this way. But I am glad I was able to help."

"What is your name?" asked Koral.

"Kawai," replied their new friend. He was a small, short-tailed bird with a long bill. The upper part of his body was blue gray, while the underbelly was orange. He also had black eye stripes that gave him an air of mystery. "I am a wood nuthatch," he said proudly. "Now what are you doing way out here in the Arctic so far from land?"

"We are going to see the Enchantress of the North. Do you know the way to her castle?" asked Aerwyna.

"Yes, I fly past her castle all the time. Why, the other day I was daydreaming and almost flew into one of her turrets. Why would you want to go see her?" asked Kawai. "One trespasses into her domain in peril."

"I will answer your questions as you guide us along the way," replied Aerwyna.

"So be it, then. Follow me."

Sometime later, the companions reached the dock of the Enchantress of the North. Aerwyna pulled herself onto the wooden structure. She dragged her heavy tail across the boards until she felt her human legs return. Aloy offered his hand and helped the mermaid to her feet.

"Kaia and Koral, you need to go back home," said Aerwyna. "This is not your fight."

"Have you decided how to complete your quest when you have reached Nerissa?" asked Kaia.

Aerwyna shook her head. "Not yet; but I will know what to do when the need arises. Go back home where it is safe."

Reluctantly her narwhal friends set off. There was nothing they could do when the castle was on land.

Kawai flew onto Aerwyna's shoulder. "I will help, too. I must know how this story ends."

Aerwyna turned to Aloy. "Are you ready?"

"I am always ready for a good fight," he replied. "However, I am going to have to explain to my grandfather again how I lost his boat, and this time it will not return to shore."

Aerwyna looked down and realized she was still holding Aloy's hand from when he had helped her up. Her delicate hand felt warm in his calloused palm. Her eyes met Aloy's, and she took her hand back.

"What is taking you so long?" interrupted Kawai, swooping down. "I never knew humans were this slow."

From the dock there was an icy pathway that led up into the trees towards Nerissa's castle. The two trudged along and Aerwyna was grateful for the warmth of her human clothes. She was learning how to use her legs and becoming more stable. A few times she stumbled and fell into Aloy, but the young sailor never complained. Kawai flew on ahead and kept yelling to them how it was not much farther.

After what felt like forever, they reached the last step up the mountainside, and the Enchantress of the North's home emerged before them. Aerwyna's jaw dropped as she took in the immaculate castle surrounded by snow-covered pine trees nestled against the side of the magical mountains.

The massive edifice was encased in ice. The reflection of sun on its turrets made the structure shimmer in an eerie white light. Icicles grew like daggers under the windowsills. Overall, the estate was breathtaking and appeared to be a beautiful place to live. No one would ever suspect a vengeful sorceress had taken an infant prisoner behind the intricately carved doors.

"She lives here by herself?" she whispered.

"I guess that is what happens when the heart is broken," replied Aloy. "So, what is your plan? Are you going to walk up to the Enchantress and be bold enough to ask her to give you the young prince?"

"I have not thought that far ahead," she replied.

Kawai swooped down. "I saw through the nursery windows a bassinet. I believe the monarch's heir is in that crib. I assume he is unharmed."

"I guess the Enchantress decided not to kill the infant after all," replied Aloy.

"It was never her intention to kill…" Aerwyna's words were cut off as a creature jumped out in front of their path. It was a large wolf-like animal with pointy icicles along its back and tail. The dog-like creature blocked their entrance to the castle. It scratched the ground and snarled at them. Its yellow eyes revealed that it was ready to slash them to pieces.

Aerwyna turned around to see another wolf-like creature leap out from behind the snowy bushes. More and more followed, and in a few seconds they were surrounded.

"It seems the Enchantress guards her castle with powerful magic," said Kawai, landing on Aerwyna's shoulder. "There are too many eyes here to try to peck out."

"Stand down!" yelled a voice. An elf appeared at the entrance to the castle. The wolves paused and looked at the elf for their next set of instructions.

"Who dares disturb the Enchantress?" bellowed the elf. "You are trespassing and you better have a good reason before I let her army devour you."

"How rude," murmured Kawai.

"We wish to speak with Nerissa, the Enchantress of the North," replied Aerwyna.

"The Enchantress does not wish to speak with anyone," replied the elf.

"It is of utmost importance," cried Aerwyna. "We deliver a message from the king that I am sure she will want to receive."

The elf scratched his beard then shrugged. "I suppose. Follow me."

Aerwyna and Aloy followed the elf through long passages until they reached the throne room.

Icicles began to form on Kawai's shiny feathers. "This place is really cold as ice," hissed the brave nuthatch. Aerwyna looked at the dark palace. It was apparent the owner had been suffering for a long time.

The Enchantress sat on a throne of ice. Even though decades had passed, they had not robbed her of her beauty. She had long wavy blonde hair that fell to her waist. She was clothed in a navy-blue gown that had pearls in the stitching. A headpiece with drop crystals illuminated the sadness in her eyes. She picked up her head and glared at the three intruders.

"What do you want?" asked Nerissa. "How did you even get all the way up here? No one has ever gotten this far…only…" her voice trailed off.

"Only King Aalton," blurted out Aerwyna.

Nerissa's eyes flashed. She waved her hand and a magical current came forth pulling the mermaid closer to her. "What do you know about that, girl?"

Feeling a lump grow in her throat that prevented the words from flowing, deep within her mind Aerwyna remembered the words Maj had told her. *I have given you Knowledge. With that Knowledge you will be able to heal instead of harm.*

Inhaling deeply, the mermaid took a deep breath. "I know that you have stolen King Aalton's son Prince Neifion."

If looks could kill, Aerwyna would be dead from the way Nerissa looked at her. The eyes of the Enchantress sent out invisible daggers straight at the young adventuress's heart. The Enchantress's pupils burned with hatred at the mention of King Aalton's name. "How dare you come to me in this manner and accuse me in my own castle?" She gestured to the elf who stood close by. "Tyrion! Feed them to the wolves!"

"I do not come to level blame for your actions," countered Aerwyna.

The sorceress's eyes narrowed. "Yes, I took King Aalton's child just as he took years of my life. I stopped everything to wait for him to convince a kingdom to accept me. After the passage of years, the North Winds informed me that he continued to live his life while I stayed here in isolation. He disappointed me and he deserves to have his son taken from him." She pointed a long blue fingernail at Aerwyna. "Who are you, anyway? I suppose he sent you three here to convince me to return the missing boy? Your effort is futile. He can suffer just as I have suffered. If any of you try to touch that child, I will turn you all into ice!"

"My name is Aerwyna and I am one of the Arctic mermaids of the ocean."

"You are a mermaid? Where is your tail? What kind of trick are you trying to employ?"

"I am half mermaid now."

The Enchantress snarled and got up from her throne. She raised her palm and an invisible force pushed the Arctic mermaid into the wall. Nerissa walked to the window and stared out at the wintry landscape. Far away in the distance were the turrets of King Aalton's towers in Lowvainia.

"You lie," she hissed, "just as Aalton lied to me."

Aerwyna cleared her throat, "I was told of the great love you shared with the King of Lowvainia. He promised you his heart forever then left you alone. He took to him a wife and they begat a child. Such news must have caused you great pain."

"He betrayed me. After I saved his life, after years of our love. He left me to partake in the glory of royal duties. He had no choice, he said. He had to honor his father. A king who would never approve of me, to govern a kingdom that would never approve of me. Then he had the nerve to tell me he would never love another; never marry; and what did he do? He became king! Never came to see me again. He married a woman of royal blood for her title. Do you think she would have risked her life in the icy waters to save him, then bring him back from death's doorstep? I think not! Then he has a child with her. A child!" The Enchantress stopped, and Aerwyna saw the tears that the sorceress attempted to blink away.

"Your heart never healed from the betrayal," pressed the sea maid, "so you took his heir for revenge to hurt him as he had hurt you."

"How else was I going to lure him to come back to me?" snapped Nerissa. "We had an audience together, he owes me an explanation for betraying me, and when I hear it, I plan to turn his heart to stone and his body to ice as he has done to me."

She walked in circles on the carpet before her throne. She rubbed her hands together and fought back tears.

"I have waited a lifetime but he has never come. He does not care about his son just as he did not care about me! Not only did I take his precious beloved, but I placed a curse of infertility on him and his queen. That will teach him to play with my emotions!"

She stopped in her tracks. Her icy eyes stared at Aerwyna.

"Have you ever been in love, mermaid? Do you know what it is like to watch the man you love give his heart to another woman, to watch them interact with their son as a beautiful family while I sit here on the mountains childless, and sad?!"

Nerissa paused, "The ice tells me you have a reason of your own for coming here to see me. It is an intention that benefits you."

The Arctic mermaid nodded, "I came here to bring the prince back to his father so that the king would grant me a lock of his hair for the potion needed to save my father's life. My father is dying. I took a draught to make me half mermaid, half human. But I realize now it was wrong of me to try to take the baby from you."

"What?" yelled Aloy, "You mean we almost died for nothing!"

Aerwyna ignored him. "You need to return Prince Neifion to the king. You loved King Aalton and he broke your heart. There is good in you, Enchantress. You have permitted your heartbreak to consume you. However, stealing an innocent child is wrong."

"He stole my youth!"

"She is an ice queen, she does not age," whispered Aloy.

Aerwyna glared at him.

"Your anger prohibits you from thinking rationally, Nerissa. Prince Neifion did nothing to you. Your quarrel is with King Aalton. You need to resolve your feelings with him, not take them out on an innocent child."

Nerissa's eyes glared in anger. "I suppose..." She let out a cry of fury. "Your words, mermaid, have the ring of truth in them. It is wrong to steal an innocent baby." She turned again on the carpet. "When I stole Prince Neifion, I tried to hate him; but he is a likeable infant. The whole time we flew to my palace, he never cried once. Everything I tried to make him miserable entertained him. Over time, I found him charming. I have felt so alone all these years, it brought me comfort to have a friend. You are correct, mermaid. I feel goodness in you, as well. It has stirred warmth in me. You may return the child to his royal highness." Nerissa's heart turned frosty at the mention of the child's father. "I will conjure another way for Aalton to pay for breaking his promises to me."

"King Aalton still loves you!" yelled Aerwyna.

Nerissa stopped as if she had seen a ghost. "What did you say, mermaid?"

"He loves you. He wrote this note to the Arctic Mermaids

asking for the return of his son," said Aerwyna. "Aalton knows you took Neifion, and he wishes no harm to come to you. That is why he has not come here. If his subjects discovered that you had taken the prince, they would come to kill you."

A shadow crossed the ice queen's face. "They would waste their time; a flick of my fingers and they would become faceless statues in my frozen garden."

Pushing back a wave of fear, the Arctic mermaid crossed the room to stand before the Enchantress. "The king is trying to keep you safe because he still loves you! You must end your grief. You are permitting your broken heart to turn you into someone you are not, Nerissa." Aerwyna took a step closer to the sorceress. She looked her in the eye. Her fear strengthened under the gaze of the ice queen, but she spoke nevertheless. "There is goodness within you. It lives deep in your heart. You yourself must take the child back to his cradle and talk to Aalton once again."

Nerissa clasped one hand to her heart. "No, mermaid. He has a wife, and he is king to a kingdom who hates magic."

"Yes, he is the monarch of the people, but as a leader, he can break his marriage vow and end his union to the queen. People can change. If Lowvainia knew that you were the one who saved Prince Neifion and returned him home safely, the citizens would accept you as a protector of their realm." Aerwyna felt Maj's Knowledge pulse through her veins.

She handed Nerissa the message the king had written to the mermaids. "It says right there; he wishes no harm to come to his son or you. Your name is written right there. He is trying to keep you safe, Nerissa, because he loves you." Knowledge burned with a warmth of wisdom through her entire body.

Aerwyna saw a flicker in the sorceress's eyes as she read the note. After decades of sorrow and sadness, a glimmer of hope appeared behind the ice. An aura enveloped the enchantress, and she seemed brighter.

"I-I...it is worth a chance," she whispered.

"You have to give hope a chance," replied Aerwyna. "No matter the distance, no matter the situation, love can conquer all, but you need to try."

"Love! You speak of love, mermaid! There is no love here!"

Aerwyna's heart filled with sadness as she watched the light of hope in the ice queen's eyes slip away.

"No! I cannot! I cannot forgive him for what he did. The pain I suffer is endless." Nerissa crumpled the note and threw it into the nearby fire. "He had his chance to see me, but he chose not to. He chose to be a cowardly sloth, a mime to his mother!"

"Nerissa, you don't understand. Aalton tried to see you, but guards and dark magic got in his way."

A look of disgust crossed the Enchantress's face. "Oh, please mermaid, you believe such a weak excuse. If Aalton wanted to come talk to me he would have found a way. He spent years watching me perform magic here in my castle; he himself could have made a potion to return; he could have outwitted his guards at night; he could have even sent a message with a homing pigeon! He chose to do nothing; his lack of interest told me I mean nothing to him!"

Tears began to brim in the corners of her eyes, and she brushed them away. "As I said, you may return the child. No reason for him to suffer; my pain is not his fault. My feud with Aalton does not end here." Her frigid gaze turned dark and forbidding. "I will recompense Aalton another way."

Aerwyna felt defeated and stepped back.

"Come, I will take you to the baby's room," commanded Nerissa. "He has been a great companion for me these last few days."

They followed the Enchantress out of the throne room and down the grand hallway.

"When did you become so wise?" Aloy whispered.

"When she was facing death," hissed Kawai.

"Stop it! I told you she was not evil," answered Aerwyna.

"Not evil to us; but she did say that she is still going to make the King of Lowvainia suffer for what he did," added Aloy.

"She is heartbroken. Pain will turn any heart to revenge. It takes hope to heal the wounds."

"Aerwyna, there is no hope. The King of Lowvainia might as well write what he wants written on his tombstone, because when that Enchantress gets him..."

"Aloy, how can you say such a thing?"

Aerwyna was cut off as Nerissa screamed. "No!"

They rushed into the castle nursery to find Nerissa standing in front of an empty cradle. Nearby was an open window.

"The prince was here a few moments ago when I looked in," cried Kawai.

"Did you actually see the prince?" urged Aerwyna.

"I saw a pile of blankets and I assumed the prince was wrapped in them."

"What happened?" asked Aloy.

Nerissa reached into the blankets and pulled out a slimy piece of scaly skin. It was not human skin.

Aerwyna gasped and covered her mouth. The scabby skin meant they had bigger problems to deal with than a broken-hearted Enchantress. Prince Neifion had been stolen once again only this time; it was by Loquoqui.

"Loquoqui!" The mermaiden gasped.

"This is all my fault," wailed Nerissa.

"Who is Loquoqui?" asked Aloy.

"Loquoqui is an evil mermaid," explained Aerwyna. "People think she is a legend, but she is real. She leaves behind a piece of scaly skin to prove she exists. She is part fish, part mermaid, part human, and all monster. She eats humans, mermaids, children, sea creatures, and anything that satisfies her wicked cravings. She is known for her red eyes."

"If she can only survive in the water, how can she possibly climb a mountain to steal a baby?" asked Kawai.

"She has an army of evil birds that work for her. Vogelles. They are similar to pelicans only they have a wider pouch. They prey on innocent babies. They scoop them up in their gaping maws and bring them to Loquoqui to feast," said Aerwyna. She turned to Nerissa. "How is this your fault?"

Nerissa buried her face in her hands. "Loquoqui took the baby because I told her to. Before my heart felt tenderness toward the child, I wanted the King of Lowvainia to suffer. The day before I kidnapped Neifion, I sold his flesh to Loquoqui. I sought to pierce Aalton's heart. However, after the baby won my affection, I knew I could not let the evil mermaid have him, so I betrayed a dangerous monster. I knew Loquoqui could be vengeful, but I thought I had placed the proper spells around the castle. I forgot about her magical Vogelle army." Nerissa growled. "I am such a fool! I should have sold Aalton's flesh to Loquoqui. It is the betrayer who needs to suffer, not the child."

"Nerissa! You cannot mean this," said Aerwyna. "We must go after Loquoqui."

Aloy had remained quiet, lost in thought. "You said red eyes, right?"

Aerwyna nodded.

"I think that is what tried to attack me when I fell off the boat and almost drowned. I remember being in the water and these webbed hands with claws were trying to slash my chest. I looked up and saw red eyes, then I passed out. I thought I imagined them at first."

"This is all my fault," murmured Nerissa. "If I had not been so enraged with jealousy, that baby would be safe and not in the hands of such a rapacious beast. I must save Aalton's child. I shall make a spell that will break his heart as he has broken mine."

"Nerissa! He truly does love you," cried Aerwyna.

"If he loved me, he would never have married and had a child!" snarled Nerissa.

"How about we forget about King Aalton and focus on Prince Neifion. How are we going to save him?" asked Kawai, "and how do we know Loquoqui has not already consumed her delicate meal?"

"Loquoqui only feeds at night, and it is still daytime. I will go to the cave of the Loquoqui further north."

"We will go with you," added Aerwyna. "You cannot undertake a quest this dangerous alone."

"You want to help me after I almost killed you?" asked Nerissa.

"Everyone deserves a second chance," added Aerwyna.

"Besides, the only person you are going to kill is King Aalton, not us," chimed in Aloy.

Aerwyna elbowed him in the ribs.

The Enchantress smiled for the first time. She waved her hands and they were transported to the dock. The foggy ocean reminded them of their recent encounter with the kraken.

"We will take my ship." Nerissa waved her hand, and the side of the mountain opened, and a huge caravel ship emerged.

The group sailed north towards the cave of the Loquoqui. Aerwyna summoned Kaia and Koral through vibrations on the waves. Moments later, her narwhal companions swam alongside the ship while Kawai flew ahead to try to detect any dangers. However, Nerissa assured them there were no monsters living in this quadrant of the ocean, and if there were, her magic would vanquish them.

Aerwyna gripped the railing of the ship and looked out into the ocean. She tried to use the Knowledge Maj had given her, but she still could not convince Nerissa to relinquish her thirst for revenge against her former lover. She was grateful the

Enchantress had realized Prince Neifion was not at fault. Yet, she could not understand how to stop the sorceress from seeking revenge.

"Aerwyna," whispered Aloy. "What's wrong? You should be happy we are going to return Prince Neifion."

Aerwyna rubbed her arms. "It's not only that. I cannot find a way to convince Nerissa to forgive the king. She is only hurting herself the longer she holds a grudge. I know the king loves her. I do not know how to make her see that."

"Sometimes things just can't be fixed," replied Aloy. "The pain becomes such a part of life the heart cannot change."

"We have to fix this," hissed Aerwyna.

"Are you forgetting the king has a wife? It is only a matter of time before Nerissa finds him and kills him."

"Aloy, stop it. I know she is not going to kill the king; she loves him!"

"Let's just focus on rescuing the baby before we try to play matchmaker," Aloy stated with a shrug.

After what seemed like hours, the fog parted and the sea caves where Loquoqui lived came into view. Nerissa anchored the large vessel outside one of the caves. The entrance consisted of bones and fish scales that formed a half circle. The ocean flowed through the mouth of the cavern into the dark unknown. The depth swallowed up the rays of setting sunlight that struggled to illuminate the entrance to the monster's grotto. Goosebumps formed along Aerwyna's skin. What were the stories behind those bones? Who had Loquoqui destroyed with her cannibalistic essence?

"We must switch vessels," declared Nerissa. She waved her hand and a smaller lifeboat appeared next to the ship. Aerwyna, Aloy, and Nerissa descended into the little boat.

"It's getting late," replied Aloy, nodding toward the setting sun.

"There is nothing we can do; we cannot turn back; and we

cannot rest," stated the powerful sorceress, "Loquoqui is active at night and darkness is her feeding time. At any moment the monster could devour that child, and it will be all my fault," whispered Nerissa.

"Aerwyna," said Aloy, " are you staying aboard or switching to mermaid form?"

"Mermaid," replied Aerwyna. "We have the best option of success if we cover all angles. Kawai will fly high, Koral, Kaia, and I will go low, then you two can aim straight." Aerwyna dove off the boat into the ocean.

"Whatever your highness wishes, is my command," replied Kawai.

The group entered the cave. Once inside, the cavern held a beauty of its own. The walls shimmered in amethyst. The purple mineral glowed, illuminating the sea cave in an eerie light. Stalactites hung down from the ceiling like icicles. Aerwyna looked out to see the moon beginning to appear through a hole that opened high above their heads.

Nerissa waved her hands and a ball of light appeared in between them. She threw the ball into the air and it hovered. "This magic will guide us to the prince."

The pulsing light slowly began to move down the center tunnel. Aerwyna's heart hammered in her chest, and anxiety reverberated along every nerve. Would they make it in time to save the baby?

They traveled deeper into the grotto until they reached a section that opened into three canals. The ball of light evaporated as Loquoqui's evil magic took it hostage.

"Which way do we go?" asked Kaia.

"Shush," hushed Kawai. "Do you hear that?"

Everyone became quiet and listened. The faint sounds of a baby's cry echoed off the cavern walls.

"The prince is still alive. We must hurry," cried Nerissa, relief in her voice. "We should split up. Aerwyna, Kaia, Koral, and Kawai can take the tunnel on the right. Aloy, you take the rowboat and go straight. I will enter the water and take the tunnel on the left. With the blessing of the sea gods the different tunnels will lead us to the same place." Nerissa dove off the rowboat transforming into a mermaid herself. With a flip of her navy-blue tail, she disappeared under the water.

"Let's get a move on," yelled Kawai, "the last thing we want is this journey to end in tragedy."

"Be careful, Aerwyna," murmured Aloy.

Aerwyna turned and their eyes met. "I will. Are you going to be safe by yourself?"

Aloy grinned, "An experienced sailor like me should know what to do if any trouble arises."

With a wan smile, the intrepid mermaid entered into the dark tunnel

"These caves are very complex," whispered Koral.

They rounded a corner and into an opening. Aerwyna retrenched into the shadows. She peeked around the corner.

Inside the cavern, the water became shallow and kissed a sandy shore. There were apertures in the ceiling that allowed the moonlight to shine on the tips of the ocean waves. Prince Neifion rested in a cage filled with leaves and straw. The makeshift prison had been placed on a wooden table. A large cauldron bubbled next to him. A grunting noise caught their attention. The gruesome creature crawled onto the ledge from out of the depths on the opposite side of the rocky shelf. It was Loquoqui.

Aerwyna gasped and covered her mouth. She had never seen Loquoqui in person, and it was the most horrifying vision she had ever witnessed. The evil mermaid was about six feet tall with a skeletal frame. A sickly sallow skin covered the bones with barely any muscle. Stringy dark hair hung lifeless to her hips. Loquoqui's eyes were red like scorching embers that burned into the deep parts of the soul. Her hands and feet were webbed, and her mouth was that of a fish with what looked like stitches on the side.

The villainous monster stood upright and slithered toward the baby. Babbling and sucking his fist, completely oblivious to the danger that threatened him, the infant was unaware of the shiny butcher knife that was next to him.

"She is going to kill the baby and cook it!" hissed Aerwyna. She looked around to the opening where the Loquoqui had emerged from the water. Nerissa and Aloy were nowhere to be found, and the stalwart companions could really use Nerissa's magic right about now.

"We must distract this beast," hissed Kawai. "The twins and I will make an interference and you grab the baby."

Before Aerwyna could reply, Kawai flew overhead squawking loudly. Loquoqui's grip on the ladle in her cauldron loosened, and she looked up at the small bird making a ruckus. Koral and Kaia moved into action. They began to whistle and make noises that sounded like a buzzsaw.

Loquoqui grunted and approached the water. She looked down with her beady eyes. Kawai swooped and began pecking her head. The female monster swatted him away and then jumped into the icy waves.

Aerwyna swam quickly to the edge of the shelf and crawled on the sand. Her tail transformed into two long legs. She pushed herself to her feet with the Knowledge given to her by the sea witch. Her legs were stronger and she felt as if she had lived with them her whole life. She ran over to the baby; she opened the cage; and picked up the child. She cradled him in her arms and looked down at the small face. Chubby cheeks and big gray eyes smiled at her.

"Let's get you home," muttered the sea maiden in a maternal whisper. She turned to hop back into the water when she paused.

"*Prince Neifion is not a mermaid; he will not be able to breathe underwater,*" she thought. She needed a boat to transport the little one safely. Nerissa and Aloy were still nowhere to be found.

"Aerwyna, look out!" shrieked Kawai.

Having spent too much time pondering, the pretty rescuer did not see Loquoqui slime out of the water. Before she could react, an eerie scream sounded, and the skeletal creature attacked her.

"How dare you take my dinner!" snarled the monster.

"You cannot eat the prince!" cried the valiant female warrior.

"Why not? The Enchantress of the North sold his flesh and soul to me!"

The red-eyed beast dug its nails into the back of her arms and threw her onto the sandy ground. The force ripped Prince Neifion from the mermaid's arms, and he fell onto the nearby rocky surface of the cave. Startled by pain, the infant began to wail. Aerwyna landed with a thud and a mouthful of water. Blood dripped from her arms and fell at her feet. She looked up to see Loquoqui pick up the butcher knife and swing it high to bring down onto the baby's chest.

"No!" screamed the sea maiden. She launched forward and grabbed the flesh-eater's arm. The motion stopped the blade from reaching its target. Lunging forward at the rabid attacker with a hard twist of her wrist caused the knife to drop into the water. The evil villain hissed and her red pupils flared like flames.

"You are right, mermaid, who needs to eat the prince when I can eat you! You will make a better meal than a small infant!" The corrupt creature jerked her claws towards Aerwyna's throat.

The Arctic mermaid and the villainous Loquoqui became engaged in a ferocious battle.

Webbed hands grabbed purple hair. The mermaiden

reached up, grabbed the soulless creature's face, and smashed it into her knee. The flesh-eater stumbled backwards dazed. Then the skeletal creature howled and slashed Aerwyna with her claws. Gripped together in a battle to the death, the monster and mermaid fell into the shallow water. Human legs became a tail. Fire-red eyes glowed, and mermaid memory had a flashback to when Aloy mentioned he had been attacked by a creature with crimson eyes.

In the water, the two combatants felt at home. Purple tail smashed against red head, but somehow the hungry attacker never ran out of energy. Mermaid muscles grew tired, which allowed the beast to strike harder blows upon her.

Pulling her into the shallow portion of the water and wrapping her arms around purple hair, shimmering shells, and glittering starfish, claws and teeth clung tightly making escape impossible.

"Ah, an Arctic Mermaid will be a tasty meal after I've devoured the prince as an appetizer," snarled Loquoqui. "You should have known better than to fight me, Mermaid."

Just when the beautiful sea maid was about to lose consciousness, the soul snatcher released her hold and let out a shriek. The monster slumped to the side, and Aerwyna looked up to see Nerissa with a bloody butcher knife in her hand. She had stabbed Loquoqui!

The mermaiden gasped and wheezed. Dark spots formed in front of her eyes. Strong hands pulled her onto the rocky shelf so she became human. She looked up to see Aloy.

"Aerwyna, you're alive!" The young sailor wrapped her in his arms and Aerwyna rested her head on his chest. "I entered the cavern, and when I saw Loquoqui strangling you... I – I feared I would lose you. Thank the sea gods for Nerissa." Aerwyna could not reply; her body could not move; every muscle was spent, and pain consumed her body as if she were an all-consumed aching mass. Kaia and Koral resurfaced and came as close as they would dare to look at her.

"Aerwyna, are you badly hurt? We believe we have found a way out of here," added Kaia.

Kawai fluttered down and hopped across the cave floor. "You are hurt," he observed, "but you fought well, mermaid."

Aerwyna could feel the gashes all over her arms and legs. She opened her eyes a crack as a dark shadow caught her attention.

"Nerissa! The baby!" she screamed. Everyone turned around to see the hideous Loquoqui crawling towards the prince. The infant would be a tasty meal after all, and the beast's claws were ready to rip the child to pieces.

"Stop!" Nerissa held out her hand. A magic force grabbed Loquoqui and threw her up against the rocks.

"Why should I stop, Enchantress," sneered Loquoqui. "After all, are you not the one who promised me the child?"

"You hideous creature," snarled Nerissa, "you played on my emotions to secure yourself dinner."

"My appearance is a reflection of your own ugly soul, Nerissa. What kind of person sells the flesh of an innocent infant to a monster like me! Who places a curse of infertility on another!

But I have to say, Enchantress, I like this evil side of you. Stop this heroic effort and join me. I'll share the prince with you; together we can feast on Aalton next. You are a villain, Nerissa. There is no goodness left in you. Embrace your transformation."

The sorceress paused and looked into skeletal features.

"Don't listen to her, Nerissa!" Aerwyna struggled to get the words out, but her pain consumed her.

"Hush, dear," whispered Aloy, "the Enchantress faces herself now. There is nothing we can do but wait for her decision."

"Come, precious," hissed Loquoqui to Nerissa. "Come to me, and I will show you how to make Aalton suffer in agony beyond your wildest dreams! You want your former lover to pay? We will make certain of it!"

A turbulence of air descended into the cave, and Maj's voice rode along with it. *No one is ever born evil. Evil emerges when the soul has lost hope and when the spirit is broken. Every villain was once a good person who gave too much, cared too much, and was betrayed to the point the heart turned to ice. Nerissa, you must melt the ice that has taken your heart captive. Knowledge brings healing, and in order to heal, I will show you the truth...*

Another voice broke forth through Maj's power. It was the voice of King Aalton...

What have I done? The monarch's voice echoed off the walls. *She doesn't know the truth; she believes this all to be real. If only I could have returned to the mountains. If only the guards had not caught me. If only dark magic had not cursed me. I tried and tried to escape to return to her, to tell her the truth of my unwilling marriage. If only my mother had not broken me. Now my son is gone, and I have hurt the only person who matters to me.*

Maj's voice returned. *The morning when the golden sun rose above the horizon and King Aalton and Queen Callopey discovered the empty cradle, in their grief they were devastated. No one could pinpoint what happened to the little boy nor who had taken him.*

However, the king knew you were the kidnapper, Nerissa, but he stayed silent. He could not send an army into the mountain. You would kill all of them. The king knew he had to form a plan to see you, to tell you the truth, and rescue his son. However, his advisor Jakob had made good on the dowager queen's dying wish that Aalton would never return to the Northern Mountains. Guards stood at the foot of the peaks day and night. When Aalton was able to bypass them and climb the alps, little did he know the former monarchy had paid a sorcerer to put another curse on the mountains. Nerissa, you could have broken the evil spell if you had known it existed. The dark magic made all of Aalton's attempts end in failure. After spraining his wrist, the king knew in order to get around the curse, he needed a magical intervention of his own. That is why he turned to the Arctic Mermaids.

An image of Aalton appeared on the grim walls of the Loquoqui's grotto. The King of Lowvainia's voice spoke on the North Wind.

O' powerful mermaids of the Arctic North grant me my only wish. My son has been taken from me by the Enchantress of the North. Return him unharmed, and I shall grant you a favor, whatever your heart desires. I wish no harm to come to the beautiful Nerissa. She lives in a castle of ice, deep in the Northern Mountains where snow falls ceaselessly. You are my only hope.

The reflection of the stalactites showed the king raise his arm with a prayer on his lips and hope in his heart. He hurled the bottle with all his strength deep into the tumultuous waves. With the motion of his arm, the image in the wall disappeared.

In order to heal we must forgive ourselves first. Aalton holds a secret of his own he wishes to share with you if you would take the time to listen...

The powerful ice queen looked down at her reflection in the water. Her image rippled and wavered next to Loquoqui's grotesque form.

"No," whispered Nerissa, "this is not who I am." A cracking echoed in the cave as the Enchantress of the North's icy heart melted, and was set free from the prison of bitterness, pain, and jealousy."

Loquoqui let out a deafening scream drowning Maj's words and sending her voice away. "Do not listen to the words of a sea witch. She will never understand your pain, Nerissa.

Come to me and you will be rewarded with the revenge you crave."

"This is not who I am," repeated the sorceress, "I am not you!"

Nerissa closed her outward palms into fists. Then moved her hands upward as a purple light swirled around the Loquoqui.

"Snuff this evil from within and light a seed of hope. From now on you do no harm, only silence and peace to all!" yelled Nerissa.

The Enchantress's spell destroyed the Loquoqui and the monster was gone. In its place was a magnificent example of crystalized amethyst geode. Nerissa walked over and picked it up. "This will look good by my bedside," she mused as her eyes twinkled with victory.

Cries sounded behind her. The beautiful Enchantress turned to see the baby Prince Neifion rolling around on the slippery rocks. The sorceress walked to the child and hesitantly picked him up.

"This is for you." She held up the geode to show to the prince. "I am so sorry for allowing my pain to put you in harm's way. I pray when you become a man, you will look at this miracle of nature and see it for what it is: magic that saved your life."

The baby cooed and reached for the purple sparkle.

"I think that is a yes," called Aloy.

Nerissa snapped back to reality. "Aloy, can you hold the prince so I can heal Aerwyna?"

Aloy took the baby from the blonde spell-charmer. Aerwyna silently wanted Aloy to continue to sit next to her. Through her quest, her heart had warmed with affection for the brave young sailor.

Nerissa knelt down next to her. The Enchantress rubbed her palms together and warm yellow light began to illuminate from her skin. She ran her hands along each of Aerwyna's wounds. Slowly each gash closed as if sewn by an invisible needle. Her energy returned, and she felt better than she had in years. She relayed her thanks to the Enchantress of the North.

"You are a healer, too?" asked Kawai.

"I have always been a healer," sighed Nerissa. "After all, I did save King Aalton from death. That is how I have always used my powers before I became consumed with my heartache." She looked away and muttered to herself, "I should have turned Aalton into a geode!"

"Nerissa. You don't mean it." replied Aerwyna. "You cannot continue to be consumed with bitterness. You are only hurting yourself."

Nerissa hesitated and looked at the ground. "You call my bluff, mermaid, I do not wish to be full of ugliness anymore. I forgive myself for what I have done, but I do not know if I am ready to forgive Aalton."

"Nerissa, I know you hate King Aalton for what he did to you. I understand how you feel. Please come with us. I am sure there is much you wish to say to the king. It has been decades since you two last spoke," begged Aerwyna. "Maj did say the king holds a secret of his own if you take the time to listen."

"Just make sure you talk to him before you try to kill him," added Aloy.

Aerwyna glared at him. She reached over and took the Enchantress's arm.

"Please come with us," she whispered. "I know you want an explanation. This is your chance to get one. If you do not like what you hear, you can do whatever you want."

Nerissa took a deep breath and nodded.

In a powerful gust of wind, the doors to the king's throne room suddenly opened wide. After leaving the sea caves, the group traveled to the castle of Lowvainia. There they spoke with Jakob. They wished to converse with the king on an urgent matter. After consulting with the advisor, they were conducted to the throne room. Aerwyna clutched the blanket that Prince Neifion was wrapped in. The little boy had fallen asleep on their journey. Aloy was on one side of her and Nerissa was on the other. The sorceress kept the hood of her cloak over her head so it masked her face in shadows. Kawai sat on Aerwyna's right shoulder; he wanted to see all the action. Outside in the Arctic waters, Kaia and Koral headed for home.

The king sat alone on his throne. His face was weary, and gray mixed with his blond hair. Slight wrinkles lined what was left of his youth.

"What can I do to help you, young lady?" asked King Aalton. His eyes caught sight of the bundle in Aerwyna's arm. He leaped to his feet.

Aerwyna pulled back the blanket to reveal the sleeping boy.

The king's eyes brimmed with tears and rushed over to take his son from the mermaiden's arms.

"Oh, young lady, you have saved my son! Jakob! Alert Callopey. Neifion has returned. He kissed the boy on top of his head and stroked his hair. "Thank you. Who are you?"

"Your Majesty, my name is Aerwyna. I am an Arctic mermaid. I found your wish in the bottle," began Aerwyna.

The king's blue eyes widened with hope. "You are an Arctic mermaid?"

"Yes. Once. I am now half mermaid, half human."

"Why?"

"I had to undertake this transformation in hopes of saving your son and my father. In your note you wished your only heir to be returned home, and your wish has now been granted."

"Thank you, Arctic mermaid."

"In truth, I did not save your son," admitted Aerwyna. "She did."

Aerwyna nodded to Nerissa who stepped forward and pulled back her hood.

Aalton froze as if he were seeing a ghost. "Nerissa," he murmured.

"Hello, Aalton," replied the Enchantress, her voice cold like a frosty winter wind.

The two stared at each other unsure of what to say. Aerwyna prayed Nerissa would not lash out and turn Aalton into an ice statue, or worse, kill him.

"It turns out Loquoqui took Prince Neifion, and Nerissa helped us find her and save the prince," continued Aerwyna.

"Nerissa," the king walked over to the Enchantress.

Nerissa looked down at her hands and sighed, "Aerwyna is too kind. I was the one who took your son and sold him to Loquoqui. I was so angry with you. You left me and broke your promise. You never told me why. You did not come back to me. You abandoned me, and I-I allowed my pain to turn me into something evil; but I am not evil. Aerwyna and her friends helped me realize I should not permit an innocent child to suffer. But I am still angry with you, Aalton. I-I loved you so much. When you left me, it broke my heart. To see you with a wife and a child while I remained all alone. The pain has been too much. But this is not who I am. I no longer seek revenge; I am so sorry." She was about to continue when the king grabbed the sorceress's face and kissed her.

Aerwyna's eyes widened, and she looked at Aloy who murmured, "I guess you were right. He still loves her."

King Aalton pulled a stunned Nerissa close to him. He stroked her golden hair. "I am the one who should be sorry, Nerissa." He pulled back and looked into her eyes. "I should have never left you. I was a coward. I should not have permitted the monarchy to break my vow. In truth, I really believed I could change my mother's mind; alas, I could not. Still, it is not an excuse. I tried to return to you multiple times, but my mother placed a curse on the mountains to forbid my return. I should have tried harder; I should have found a way. It does not matter to me if you are an Enchantress. You are a good person and a talented healer. You will be an asset to this kingdom, and I want you to share this realm with me."

Nerissa was stunned. "But do you not have a wife? The whole kingdom celebrated your union. I heard it on the wind."

"In a way, yes; however, what the winds never revealed to you was Callopey and I do not love each other. Our marriage was arranged against our will for the sole purpose of producing an heir. The winds also did not tell you that the night before our wedding, Callopey and I went to see a sorcerer. Although the sorcerer could not break the curses of the mountains, he bound our souls in a contract. The contract stated that if both Callopey and I were reunited with our true loves, our marriage would be dissolved."

"I do not understand," said Nerissa.

"It means the marriage is over," a voice called out. The voice belonged to Callopey,

She raced over and took the baby from Aerwyna's arms. "My son! You have returned." She wiped a tear from her eye and continued. "I overheard your conversation. It is true. My people were forcing me to settle in marriage. Aalton and I forged a Document of Troth through a sorcerer in which marriage would occur as the two kingdoms had agreed. Once an heir to the throne was born, should the occasion arise, that either of us should find true love with another, our marriage would be dissolved. For it was written in the ancient tomes, before all magic had been banned from the kingdom, that the truest magic of all is the magic of love. And the truest pathway to love is the magic of forgiveness." Callopey stepped closer to Nerissa and smiled.

"Aalton has been heartbroken since the day he left you. He did keep his promise to you, Nerissa. You are the only woman he has ever loved. Aalton has been a good friend to me, but I have my own true love, a lord at the court of my father and mother."

Callopey nodded towards the door as a knight stepped into the room. He was handsome, strong, and amicable in spirit. "This is Lord Erik, First Knight, and My One True Love." She cradled her son in her arms. "I will leave you two to talk." Callopey, with Prince Neifion, and Lord Erik at her side left the room to retire to their own happiness.

Nerissa turned to Aalton. "Your marriage can be dissolved?"

"Yes. I did learn a thing or two being with you all those years. Nerissa, I know that I am unworthy of your forgiveness. I only hope in time you can love me the way you used to. When I saw your symbol on the crib and realized you had been here, it brought me back to life. For so long I was doing what I thought the kingdom wanted, what I thought my father wanted, instead of what I felt in my heart. I understand why you did what you did. I would have felt the same way if you had taken a husband."

The king took the sorceress's hand and continued, "Nerissa, you are the only person I have ever loved. I do not want to lose you again. I will inform the citizens of Lowvainia that beings of all walks of life are welcome here. All magic is welcome here. Enchantment will be used to help the people. This shall be the new rule in Lowvainia."

Aerwyna and Aloy looked deeply into each other's eyes as they watched Forgiveness take place and Healing begin.

The King of Lowvainia took the Enchantress of the North's hand. "Now there is something I have been wanting to ask you since the day you saved me from death's door."

Aalton knelt on one knee in front of the sorceress. "Nerissa,

Enchantress of the North, will you marry me and be my queen?"

Tears streamed down Nerissa's face. "Yes, I will marry you." The king kissed her.

"Jakob," Aalton called to his advisor. "Inform the kingdom there will be a series of changes. The marriage between Callopey and myself is dissolved through the magical agreement. I am revoking the ban on all mythical creatures and magic my parents created long ago. Everyone will be treated equally in Lowvainia from this day forward. I will address the people this afternoon and tell them there will be a royal wedding in the coming months. A real wedding."

Joy spread across Nerissa's face as her soul finally felt happiness after being drowned in pain for so long.

"Thank you for showing me what a fool I have been all these years," she spoke with humility to the brave mermaiden.

Aerwyna smiled.

King Aalton turned to the purple-haired sea maid. "Mermaid," he said, "a deal is a deal. You have returned my son safely to me. You have reunited me with the love of my life. I cannot thank you enough. Name me your desire and you shall have it."

The Arctic mermaid smiled, "I wish for a lock of your hair."

The king pulled a knife from his belt and cut off a lock of his hair and gave it to her. "Here, Aerwyna, and if there is anything you and your friends need, you are always welcome here."

Hurry, Aerwyna, a voice called in the wind. It was Maj. *Your father does not have much time.*

"Thank you," replied Aerwyna, "I must go now." With her human legs she dashed out of the castle and ran toward the Arctic coast. As she was about to leap off the dock into the water, she heard a voice calling behind her. She turned and saw Aloy.

"You were just going to leave without saying goodbye?" asked Aloy.

"Aloy, I have to go," cried the mermaiden, "my father is dying."

"Will I see you again?" inquired the sailor with affection in his eyes.

"I don't know. Perhaps," replied Aerwyna.

"What do you mean, perhaps? Do you not feel your heart reaching out to mine and mine in return to yours?"

"Yes, Aloy. But you must understand, I am not entirely human. I am not entirely mermaid. Now that I have what I need to save my father, I must come to the realization that I have to live with being half and half forever. I do not even know who I am anymore."

"I don't care who you are," cried Aloy, "I don't care if you are half mermaid, half human. I love you!"

Aerwyna froze.

"When you saved me that day I almost drowned, you were the most beautiful creature I had ever laid my eyes on. At first I thought you were crazy for dragging me off to the Northern Mountains, but now I see what a kind and generous spirit you are." Aloy took Aerwyna's hand. "You sacrificed your life to save your father. It does not matter what or who you are. King Aalton just decreed that everyone is welcome in Lowvainia." The young sailor looked the mermaiden in the eye. "Saving me is akin to what Nerissa did for Aalton. Now they are together. I want you to be with me, Aerwyna. The magic of the enchanted mountains brought us together and you have the power to transform into a human." A smile crossed Aloy's lips. "The day you saved me from dying, I knew we were meant to be together."

Aerwyna was stunned.

Hurry, called Maj.

"I have to go. I am sorry." With sadness in her heart, the

young spirited adventuress threw herself off the dock into the ocean returning to mermaid form once again.

Aerwyna swam as fast as she could to her home. Maj had the potion bubbling in her cauldron. Aerwyna added the lock of hair. As the spell was mixed, the mermaiden's thoughts were restless. All she could think of was Aloy. The Arctic Mermaid chided herself. The powerful Maj ladled the elixir into a syringe. The merwoman swam to where Namazzi lay in his bed. His eyes were closed and his breath was shallow. With tenderness the sea witch injected the antidote into him.

Aerwyna clasped her mother's hands and prayed they had reached her father in time to save his life. After a few minutes, the color began to return to Namazzi's cheeks. His eyes opened and he smiled at all of them.

"The antidote worked," cried Maj. "He is himself again."

Aerwyna threw her arms around her father and hugged him.

Out of respect, the sea witch quietly left the room leaving Aerwyna alone with her mother and father.

"My beautiful daughter, you saved my life," whispered Namazzi, "thank you. You are the cleverest mermaid ever."

Aerwyna took a deep breath, "I am afraid I am no longer pure mermaid, Father." She explained the whole story to her parents.

"You battled the Loquoqui, Aerwyna! Thank God you have survived," cried her mother.

"Honey, you are a brave young mermaid. Insofar as to the question of who you are as a mermaid, it does not matter if you are half sea creature, half human. What matters is what is on the inside. Your soul is good, and everyone loves you regardless," replied her father. "What is on the inside will always prevail."

Once again, Aerwyna's thoughts drifted to Aloy, the young sailor who had been by her side the whole journey.

"You are in love," noted her father.

Aerwyna nodded.

With kindness, the elder merman took her hands in his, "You must go to him, my child. True love is the rarest and purest form of magic there is. Once you find it, never let it go."

Aerwyna kissed her father's cheek. "I will be back," she whispered and plunged off into the sea.

On the day following the return of Prince Neifion, Aloy stood on the edge of the Nordic waters readying his boat for a day of fishing.

"Hey, fisherman," a voice called. The sailor looked up to find Aerwyna in human form standing before him on the sandy beach.

"Aerwyna," cried Aloy, "is your father well again?"

Aerwyna ran to him and kissed him.

"Yes, his good health is restored," she blurted out. "And I love you, too. I am sorry I had to rush off yesterday."

Aloy smiled. "I understand."

Aerwyna smirked. "Do you need some company on that boat of yours?" She nodded in the direction of the sail ruffling in the breeze. "Or someone to save you from danger? I happen to know a sea maiden who is very good at both those endeavors."

Aloy kissed her in answer.

The marriage between King Aalton and Queen Callopey was dissolved according to the magical axiom. The two agreed their son would spend equal time with each parent. Callopey headed back to her kingdom and reclaimed her right to the throne with Lord Erik by her side. The two wed and lived in the comfort of their love.

King Aalton introduced Lowvainia to Nerissa. He created rules that allowed humans and creatures of every walk of life to exist peacefully in his domain. No longer would anyone be judged, and anyone would be free to love whomever they desired. The Enchantress broke all the curses surrounding the Northern Mountains, and Jakob was retired as advisor to the throne. Kawai was knighted as the new chief advisor and preened his feathers with pride.

In very little time the realm fell in love with Nerissa. She became a prominent healer in the kingdom. Not long after all these momentous events, the wedding of the new queen and King Aalton was celebrated. The ceremony was held at the edge of the Arctic waters so that Koral, Kaia, and all sea creatures could be in attendance. Aloy and Aerwyna in her human form stood beside the king and queen as they exchanged their vows.

"What do you think our next adventure will be?" whispered Aloy as Aalton and Nerissa sealed their union with a kiss.

"I have no idea," replied Aerwyna, "but so long as the wind is strong, the sea is blue, and air is pure we shall always be together."

AUTHOR'S NOTE

To Mom, Dad, Ashley, and Edith. Thank you for everything. I love you – Nicole

Follow more of N.D.T. Casale's storytelling adventures on Instagram @ndtcasale (https://www.instagram.com/ndtcasale/)

9
HEARTLESS MELODY
ALICE IVINYA

Enchanted Waters

HEARTLESS MELODY

I fell in love with Natalia when I was four years old.

The memory was faded, and probably riddled with the moth-holes of untruth that fray recollections over the years, but one part was clear: the tingling rush of wonder shooting down my spine when I saw her. She was five and dressed in a scarlet dress with a blossom crown nestled amongst raven hair. I thought she was perfect and told my mama I was going to marry her. She laughed and picked me up to nestle me on her hip. She said I was too young for such things, and that I would forget I'd said it by winter.

But I didn't forget. Or any winter after.

Natalia was the daughter of the goldsmith. He was so talented that people came from all over Avia to bring him custom. When I was ten, he even worked metal for the King and Queen. The finished product had been transported from our village in chests surrounded by colourful soldiers on gleaming horses. I had climbed onto the roof of our barn and gripped onto the string tying the thatch together so I could watch the sun gleam off their armour and the wind play with the bright plumes in their helms. Flags had snapped on their spears and the horses had towered above the onlookers.

The soldiers had looked magnificent, but Natalia was beside the road and stole all my attention. She stared at those men in open admiration and whispered to Lila beside her, her cheeks colouring slightly. With a giggle she ran up to one and offered her handkerchief. The man, three times her age, had taken it solemnly and saluted her, before tucking it into the top of his breastplate.

Jealousy stirred in my stomach, and I had gripped the thatch until my hands ached. One day, it would be me she looked at like that. Her eyes would be wide with admiration, and her cheeks would flush when I looked at her. I decided then and there that I would be a soldier for the King and Queen.

But, I had a long way to go, being the youngest son of a rat catcher.

Natalia loved music, and she was happiest when dancing, so I saved up for years for a pipe. When I was fourteen, my da finally gave one to me for my birthday. It was plain and unpainted, but it worked well enough. I practised every morning before work, and every evening before bed until my fingers cramped. Sometimes I imagined she could hear the music drifting through the village and kept her window open to listen, cradling her delicate chin in her long fingers and dreaming about who might be playing it. She would perch on her window sill, entranced, wondering at the source, slowly falling in love.

The law in Avia stated that nobody could be recruited as a soldier until they turned sixteen. Candidates presented themselves to the garrison in Fairhold, the capital city, and if they were approved, they would be given a real gold coin. However to get to Fairhold I needed my own supplies, and that cost money. And to make money I had to catch a lot of rats.

There were three types of rat in the land around our village of Heathmire. The common brown, the stub-tailed and the grey. The common brown were easy to catch in store houses, but any cat or trap could stop those. The mayor paid a penny for ten, and nobody could get to Fairhold on pennies. The stub-tailed were secretive and harmless, but their pelts were soft and the tanner would pay five pennies a head. But it was the greys I concentrated on hunting. For a single grey, you would be given a crown by the mayor, and then a further half-crown by the apothecary for the body.

Grey rats spread disease, nibbled children's toes while they slept, and killed the town dogs and cats. Three foot in length, they were much harder to kill, and were far craftier than their little cousins. They mostly lived in the forests and mountains, but were never beyond stealing from towns and villages, and now and then a bold one would make its home under a barn or house and terrorize the neighbourhood.

The winter before my sixteenth birthday, heavy snow brought a grey rat infestation to several villages around ours, particularly affecting the houses of the less sanitary goblins. The timing couldn't have been better. This was my chance to earn enough money to leave this village. I would no longer be a rat catcher, but could return on a tall horse in armour and whisk Natalia away to Fairhold. We would get married in the mountains on the way, in one of the groves filled with the music of dancing sprites, and once we made the capital, I would use my gold coin to buy us a house with all the furnishings she wanted.

Of course it would be hard every time I had to leave her to go on an assignment as a soldier, but I couldn't imagine I would be gone for more than a few days. Avia had not been to war for hundreds of years, and its inhabitants were peaceful now the land was rid of trolls. Hopefully, I could be a guard in the castle and come home to my Natalia every evening. I could tell her about the lords and ladies that lived there, maybe the King and Queen themselves. She would listen with her dark eyes wide, and laugh at how strange their customs were. Every evening I would play my pipe so she could dance by the firelight, her skin glowing like dark amber. She would smile at me and...

A boot kicked me in the side and I groaned.

"Get up, boy. Those rats aren't going to walk into that bag of yours." I blinked into the dusty light as I felt Da's boots shake the floorboards as he strode away. I sat up, pushed my blanket off the pallet and stretched. The cold air hit my bare skin where my shirt sleeves had rolled up, and I hurried to pull them down again.

Jack and Thomas were still asleep, snoring softly on their pallets, heaped with blankets. They both worked as dexters in the dye-works, since our village made the best dyes in all of Avia. Normally I thumped my boots louder than necessary out of jealousy that their jobs didn't require them to rise early, but this morning there was a purpose to rising at dawn. The more hours I had to catch rats, the quicker I would be on the road to Fairhold with new clothes, and a pouch of coins jingling merrily on my hip.

Heathmire was surrounded by fields of flowers used for dyes, or blue fields of flax for linen. The people who lived here were just as colourful, dressing in the brightest of shades to advertise our skill. Master Graff, the imp who controlled the canal, operating the gates to irrigate different fields, or flood the pits where dyes were mixed, was my first call today. His urgently scrawled note said he was overrun with greys. Perfect.

Imps were more terrified of the rats than humans or goblins due to their small stature and delicate wings. I'd even heard of imps rendered flightless by a night of nibbling by the intruders. Hopefully Master Graff would give me a tip.

I spent the morning trapping and baiting and jumping over

vats of indigo and crimson. Occasionally, I had to fish a dead rat out of the dye before Master Graff or one of the dexters noticed. I'm sure a dead rat wouldn't affect the colour that much. One grey rat even fell into the canal when I hit it square on the head with a stone from my slingshot. Without thought, I leapt in after it to recover the body. No body, no proof, no money. The water was acidic, stinging my eyes and leaving a metallic taste in my mouth. But it would all be worth it for my Natalia.

After lunch, I continued onto the village of Hillfield and helped a goblin housewife get rid of the rats in her well and parlour. When I had raided every nest and blocked every hole, I trudged back to Heathmire, holding a sack of conquests. My clothes were still wet and plastered to my body, and specks of dye stained my skin and clothes. However, all I could think about was that maybe today I had earned enough to leave.

Like a dream, Natalia glided down the path towards me. Behind her, the flowers of the flax fields brought out blue tints in her black hair and made her dark eyes glow. It was as if nature itself conspired to show how beautiful she was. Her hair was braided with blue and yellow ribbons down her back, but gentle curls fell beside her cheeks. A chain of buttercups shone around her neck and coiled around the handle of her basket.

She was here, about to pass me on the same road, just as I had caught my last rat. It had to be fate. My brain startled and stumbled over a rehearsal of what to say. I realised I had stopped walking, which had caught her attention, and I opened and closed my mouth as she approached. What should I say? How could I put into words how beautiful, how perfect I thought she was?

She reached my side and gave me a quizzical look through dark lashes. "Good afternoon." She gave a little nod, a small smile, and started to walk past me.

My heart rate rose in panic. No. I needed to speak with her, explain. I needed her to wait for me. "I'm leaving," I yelled.

She turned with raised eyebrows, taken aback by the loudness of my voice. My heart thudded in my ears, and my stomach coiled around itself so tightly, I felt sick and lightheaded. I cleared my throat, hoping I looked more composed than I felt. I softened my voice. "I wanted to let you know that I'm leaving for Fairhold. I'm going to become a knight. Or at least a soldier."

She blinked in surprise and clasped her hands across her front, her basket sliding down her arm. "Oh. Good luck."

"I was... eh... wondering if you would wait for me?" I swallowed down the building sense of nausea and attempted a smile.

She frowned, and my stomach dropped. "Wait for you?"

I shifted my weight. "You know, I eh... I wish to ask for your hand in marriage when I get back."

Her eyes widened, and her mouth formed a perfect 'o'. I felt heat rush up my neck to my cheeks. "I didn't realise..."

I held up my hands, one still holding the bag. "I'm not proposing now. I want to court you later. You know, when I'm a knight so I can treat you properly. And I'll have the gold coin then. I could buy us a house."

She took a step back. "Em, that's very sweet, eh, Peter?"

I realised with horror that she wasn't even sure of my name. I firmed my lips. No, that was a good thing. It was better for her not to know me as a rat catcher, but only as a knight. I would make a better impression that way. She just needed to wait for me.

I flourished a small bow. "I just request you don't accept an offer until I'm ready to present mine. I should be back in a year or two."

I realised I didn't actually know how long it took to train to be a soldier or make it to knighthood. Natalia's eyes fell to my bag and her shoulders relaxed a little. "What are you carrying?"

A dozen answers flitted through my head. Should I lie?

Exaggerate? Distract? But my lips answered with a will of their own. "Dead rats."

Her eyes widened and she took another step back. No, no, no... I needed to leave her with a good impression. "I was in Hillfield today. They had a rat problem, and I thought I could help them, since they were struggling. You know, it seemed like the right thing to do. Especially the imps, so they don't get their wings chewed off." I forced a grin.

She chewed her bottom lip, her eyes still on the bag. "Where are you taking them, now?"

I held myself tall. "Well these are not ordinary rats. These are greys. You know, the really big, dangerous ones? It's why the people in Hillfield were struggling. Not just anyone can catch and kill a grey." Her look was sceptical so I reached inside the sack and pulled out the largest grey by a paw. Its head lolled to one side where its neck was snapped. Blue dye made its fur stick out in tufts but didn't disguise the horror of the beast.

Natalia put both her hands over her mouth.

I grinned. "You see? They're terrifying creatures. Not every man would face them." She looked a little pale, so I put the rat back in the sack before it could scare her further. "Some of their body parts can be used in tonics, so I'm taking it to the apothecary so they can be used for good. I like helping people. They may even save some lives. I can't imagine tonics made of that taste any good, though." I barked a laugh.

Natalia shook her head. Her lips parted but no words came out, her eyes fixed on the sack as if in disbelief. Well, I was pretty impressed by that one myself.

"I play the pipe, as well. I know you like music and dancing. There is nobody else in the village as beautiful as you when they dance. Or as beautiful as you doing anything, for that matter." I paused as her face went blank, and she didn't react to my words at all. I wondered if I'd accidentally insulted her. "Or anyone more beautiful than you from any other village as well," I added quickly. "I understand Heathmire is not very big."

She twitched a nod and seemed to come alive again, lowering her gaze and tucking a stray curl of shining hair behind her ear. "Well, it was nice to see you, Peter. I wish you luck in Fairhold."

I took a step towards her, and she stumbled back so fast she almost lost her footing. "Sorry, I didn't mean to startle you. I just... will you wait for me?"

She gave me a quick nod and hurried away down the road, pulling up her scarlet skirt to reveal pretty white and yellow petticoats. My heart didn't slow as I watched her speed away. I should have asked to walk her home, but she'd clearly been quite overcome by our conversation.

I grinned. She'd said yes! That meant she would wait for me, and next time I would be wearing armour and a sword. I would be looking down from a towering horse, framed by colourful banners. Next time I wouldn't stink of rat or be dirty from a day's work. I'd been waiting for her my whole life. Just a year or two more and she would be mine.

Three years later...

I took a last look around my plain room in the barracks, to make sure I hadn't missed anything. Our new house was bought, and the barracks boy was taking the last of my belongings there in his cart. It lay right on the edge of Fairhold with a view over the wall and you could see straight to the perfect turquoise of the lake, nestled between the shadow-draped mountains. From the other side you could see the pale marble and sandstone towers of the palace. Fairhold was the most beautiful place in any world, and Natalia was going to love it.

I just had to ride home and win her heart. I'd saved for over a year and bought the prettiest necklace I could find made of rose gold that would make her skin glow. I'd practised every line that I would say and even requested a poet write me a sonnet. I wasn't willing to leave anything to chance.

I pulled on my riding gloves and hurried to the stables, feeling energy rush down my legs with every step. Today was the day. Would she remember me? I almost hoped she wouldn't. I had changed a lot in three years. I was at least a foot taller, broader, and my whiskers were less patchy. I still might have not have reached the position of knight, but hopefully, I was enough for her. I would give her everything I could.

I opened the stall and heard a sharp voice behind me. "Captain Peter."

I turned to see the head of the Royal Guard striding towards me. He was dressed in a heavy travel cloak and practical riding boots. I bowed, then realised my error and changed to a salute. I didn't think Lord Jason had ever spoken to me before. I was honoured he knew my name.

"Captain Peter, I need you to replace one of my men in the Royal Guard who has fallen sick."

I glanced at my horse. "I'm afraid, my lord, that I've just started my leave, I was about to..."

Lord Jason's face grew red, and he straightened. "Captain Peter." He bit off each syllable. "The Queen herself needs you. Being in her Guard is the utmost honour. You may never have this chance again. Now get your horse to the golden courtyard. On the double, Captain."

My heart sank but then a shiver of excitement rippled up my spine. If I had a chance to impress the Queen herself and got a place on the Guard, I would be able to offer Natalia so much more. I would be a knight, my pay would be better, and I would be able to link her to royalty. We would be invited to some of the castle events, and she could dance in a glittering ball gown on velvet shod feet.

What was another week or two?

The weather had been a miserable drizzle for the whole three days on horseback, keeping people's eyes down and cloaks wrapped tight. Only Queen Oda still rode with her back straight, her large blue cloak shedding raindrops in rivulets. Captain John whispered that it was woven with nixie hair so its wearer could never get wet. The more I looked at the queen's perfect gold hair, coiled into a crown, and her pristine dark makeup, the more I believed him. She would belong in a palace as easily as on the road right now. I never looked at her for long, though, scared that she would notice and turn those dark, fathomless eyes on me. She unnerved me, but what did I expect? I'd never been around royalty before, let alone the Queen of all Avia. Her skin was pale, unlike the King, which was rare in Avia, and even more so in the villages around Heathmire. She reminded me of a marble statue, another creature entirely, mysterious, graceful and dangerous. I had no idea how to act around her, so I kept away. Doing so wasn't very hard. Her two bodyguards were so enormous, everyone gave them a wide berth. From their grey-toned skin and square jaws, I guessed they were both part troll. With them at her side, I wasn't sure why she needed the rest of us. Maybe we were a sign of importance with our limp but colourful banners and well bred horses. Or maybe whatever was out here to the east was very dangerous.

We passed few signs of habitation, the land closely grazed by rabbits and pockmarked with bogs. The odd tree broke through the ground, stunted and nibbled free of leaves, despite the long thorns that stuck in every direction. The creatures here were hungry, and I wondered why I rarely saw them grazing in the open by day. Wolves broke the quiet of every night with their howls.

Ahead the land swelled into hills that bowed before a huge mountain. Its top was snow-capped but the rock was a faded black, rather than the light blue-grey of the mountains around Fairhold. We never wavered from our path towards that peak, and soon it wasn't just the rain making me wrap my cloak tighter. Nobody seemed to know what our mission was apart from the Queen and Lord Jason, and wilder and wilder ideas ran through my mind. I held my tongue, however. Best not to voice such things out loud.

Every night I played my pipe around the fire, and the men sang along or listened, staring into the flames. The constant damp had made the pipe warp out of tune, but the guards didn't care. Soon my real name was forgotten, and they just called me Piper, clapping me on the back when the evening was done. I felt included, welcomed into the Royal Guard. I had found my place. Natalia was sure to be impressed.

On our fifth day east, we reached the hills, and the presence of the black mountain weighed me down. It blocked the sun for a third of the day, and we picked our way across goat trails in a constant gloom. The Queen was alert now, giving orders to her most trusted men and studying the landscape around her. Soldiers rode out to scout, and frequently I saw them on the top of the hills we curved around, spy glasses glinting in the fragile light.

At last one of the guards returned with an eager expression and had a quick conversation with the Queen. She called a trot and I did my best to keep up, my muscles aching and sore, my clothes sticking with rain and sweat. I was not as used to the saddle as these men were, or as fit.

We rounded a curve in the hill into a shadowed valley. The rough path was lined with an avenue of strange trees. Their branches were twisted, every tree pointing in a different direction, as if each had been shaped by a different wind. Their leaves were maroon, and no animal had nibbled these, despite every other plant being stripped barè. The Queen didn't hesitate but led us down the living hallway. I studied the trees as we passed, and I was sure they studied me back. Here and there the bark looked unnatural. There was a curve that could almost be a mouth, a branch that bent like an elbow, two slits that looked like eyes with heavy lids. They blinked.

I jumped and looked at the other men, but none of them reacted. Maybe I had imagined it. I kicked my horse faster and rode abreast of another guard. He raised his eyebrows and grinned at me, making my cheeks heat, but I didn't fall back in behind him.

The path ended on the shores of a lake. The water was a light blue, despite the poor light, and looked out of place in this barren wilderness. Indeed, I could see none of the signs of life I would normally expect around so much water. Maybe it was salty? But no, that wouldn't be possible so far inland.

The Queen called for us to dismount and make camp. "We're a day early," she announced, not moving her gaze from the pale water and the black mountain behind. "But tomorrow night, we shall achieve what we are here for. Rest."

That night as I got out my pipe, the Queen loomed over my shoulder. "Not tonight, Piper. This place is for others' music."

I replaced the pipe with shaking hands and nodded. I had hoped to play some jolly pieces to soothe my nerves. However, as night fell the most beautiful music rose from the lake. Thin, pure notes that sliced straight to the heart. Tunes of longing so strong it ached. Hope tangled in hopelessness. Music of desire yet despair. It made me feel like something wonderful was before me, but I would never touch it, never have it. I could sense it, but never know its name. I fell asleep with my cheeks wet with tears.

The next day passed slowly, with nothing to do except watch the strange patterns of light on the water or frown at the eerie trees behind us. I was half certain they had moved in the night, but nobody commented, so I tried to ignore them.

As the sun disappeared behind the mountain, and we were thrown into an early dusk, the Queen ordered us to pack our weapons, and hide any iron or charms. We were to wear only our shirts, breeches and boots. I stared at her as if she had gone mad, but the other guards didn't hesitate to obey. Most of them had been with her for years and they trusted her. I hurried to strip down, wondering if we were about to swim in that strange water. The thought sent shivers up my spine.

A strange cool light bathed the campsite, and I turned to see the moon rise. It was larger than I had ever seen before and was oddly rimmed with a halo of gold. It seemed to tug at me, making my heart pound. As it rose into a star-speckled sky, music filled the air. So much music I didn't know which tune to focus on. There were joyous melodies and dirges of despair that almost screamed. Loud flutings and soft strummings like a harp. Yet the cacophony fitted together in a way I couldn't explain.

"The Gilded Moon," Captain John whispered beside me. "Never did I think it would be so beautiful, or that I would live to see it. I hope it looks just as beautiful for my family in Fairhold"

"What's that music?" I asked.

He gave me an excited, eager smile. "This land is full of magic, and things that have slept for a thousand years will be woken tonight by that moon."

My breath caught, and I looked around at a world turned blue, silver and subtle gold by the moon's light. A world completely alien. "What do I do?"

Captain John shrugged. "Whatever you want. Our job was to guard the Queen on her journey here and afterwards return her safely. Tonight, we cannot help her. Me? I'm going to dance."

I raised my eyebrows. "Dance?" I looked around again. Shadows were detaching themselves from the hills, the trees... no the trees themselves were moving, starting a juddering dance. "Is it safe?" My voice was a higher pitch than I'd expected.

Captain John coughed a laugh. "Safe? Of course not, boy. But few of the best things in life are safe." He turned to the lake and pointed. "Look."

The moonlight rippled on the water, dazzling. Then the light seemed to join, flicker, brighten, move on its own.

Captain John had a silly grin plastered on his face. "Water nymphs. My missus is never going to believe me." He turned back to me. "Sit and watch, if you wish, Piper, but I'm going to dance. Did you know water nymphs can grant you your heart's desire? Their magic is stronger than fate."

I opened my mouth to ask what that meant when the Queen moved to the shoreline. She had changed into a gown of glistening silver, and her pale hair was loose down her back. She looked like she belonged here on the lake, like a nymph made of silvery light. Elegantly she stepped into the water, but she didn't sink. I gasped. A fine mist appeared around her feet, and she walked across the surface of the lake towards the dancing lights that were looking more and more human.

I jumped as Captain John clapped me on the back, then ran onto the water himself with none of Queen Oda's elegance. Other Royal Guards sped after him and ran across the water, leaping and spinning. The music swelled and, from behind me, drums echoed from the hills. Deep, pounding beats that seemed to replace the beat of my heart and move my blood in a new rhythm. A beat that was impossible not to respond to.

I spun around and saw the trees had turned into dark-skinned maidens, holding hands and whirling in a frenzied dance. Their maroon hair seemed weightless, fluttering around their inhuman heads. Some still had branches and leaves, and some had bark instead of faces.

I turned back to the water and realised I was on my own. The Guard had dispersed, some going to the tree nymphs, if that was what they were, some leaping across the water. The beat continued, pounding inside my chest, making me want to leap and whoop and dance until my feet bled. Above it all the gilded moon tugged my heart and tricked my eyes.

Water nymphs can grant your heart's desire... Did that mean they could make me good enough to win Natalia's heart? Make me desirable, lovable? I wanted her more than anything. I always had.

I stepped out onto the lake, letting my terror add to my exhilaration. I could feel the water swell and ripple beneath my boots, but I didn't sink. The sickening rush of adrenaline spurred my feet as they gave into the dance. Everything became a blur as the light reflecting off the water dazzled my eyes. Maidens made of pale water and silver light laughed before me, then vanished. Mist ebbed and flowed around my feet, and the only constant thing was the music spurring me to dance on and on, tearing wild laughter from my lips.

A nymph appeared before me, her hair floating around her as if she were still underwater. Her face was exquisite, dainty, and not quite human. She held out a hand to me and grinned with sharp teeth like a pike. I took her hand, and her skin felt like water, cool and malleable. She whirled me around and lightning shot up my arms. My heart beat so fast, my whole chest ached. Then she held me still, leant forward, and kissed me on the forehead.

She vanished, and I plunged down into the lake. Cold engulfed me, and I kicked my legs in panic. Water filled my ears, and I could no longer hear the music. My lungs burned, already trying to gasp from the dancing. I kicked towards the silver light and broke the surface of the water. I dragged in deep breaths and shook water from my eyes. Silence. The music was gone and all I could see was mist. I swam a few strokes, disorientated.

"Hello?" I shouted. Cold seeped into my limbs and my boots weighed down my feet. My muscles ached, and I felt so weary. "Hello?" I could hear the panic in my voice, however much I fought for calm.

A shadow loomed through the mist and strong arms grabbed me. They pulled me forward and I didn't know whether to fight or aid them. Then there were pebbles rattling beneath my feet and the arm let me go. I staggered out of the water and fell onto the beach, shivering furiously and gasping.

"So you were granted a wish too." A cool voice made me look up. Queen Oda sat on the pebbles beside me. She too was drenched, and her silver gown clung to her body. A cloak made of fur and owl feathers was wrapped around her arms. One of the grey-skinned guards took a step back, dripping with water, and I realised he had swum out to rescue me.

"Where are the others?" I rubbed my freezing arms and staggered to my belongings to find my cloak.

Queen Oda stared out at the mist-clothed lake. "They still hear the music. They still dance." She turned to me and smiled, but her eyes were angry. "But we are the fortunate ones who have been given our heart's desire." She looked to my side, and I followed her gaze.

Strapped to my waist was a pipe. It was long and silver and engraved with ivy. I traced it with my fingers and decided it was the most beautiful thing I had ever seen. Attached to it was a note that was dry despite the water.

'Whoever hears my song will be placed under my master's spell and do as he wishes. I am his and no others.'

I cried out as the pipe was torn from my hands by the bodyguard and handed to the Queen. She studied it and frowned, long fingers tapping her pale lips in thought.

I looked at the pipe in her hands in growing horror. No, this wasn't my heart's desire. I didn't want to enchant Natalia. I wanted her to fall in love of her own accord. Did this mean there was no hope unless I enchanted her? Was I never going to be good enough as I was?

The Queen stood and loomed over me. In one hand she held my pipe, in the other were two wooden boxes. From the lower box dangled another message, and I couldn't help but read it.

'Heartwood. Whoever's heart resides within will no longer feel, whether grief or love, until their heart is returned. No one will enchant them.'

The Queen's face was cold and calculating. Not at all the expression of one who had gained her deepest wish.

"I don't understand," she said at length. "I wanted a child, that is my desire." She looked at me as if this were a riddle I knew the answer to. I stared at her helplessly. I could only think this was a cruel joke.

One of the bodyguards scratched his thin black hair. "Maybe one box is meant for you, the other for your husband, your Majesty? So you no longer feel the pain of childlessness."

Her face contorted into rage. "Silence," she snapped. She closed her eyes and smoothed her features as if desperate to remain calm. The bodyguard bowed and took a step back.

The Queen placed the boxes down and focused on my gift, turning it around in her fingers. "Maybe the gifts are the wrong way around? Maybe your pipe is meant to bring me my child." She focused on me with the cold eyes of a predator.

My stomach twisted ,and I stumbled to my feet. "It said I was the only one who could play it, your Majesty." She couldn't be right, because how would the box help me? Removing my heart would hardly mean I won somebody else's. Unless Natalia was already wed and removing my heart was the only way I could stop the agony of it breaking?

The Queen studied me, her lips pursed, her eyes dark. Her expression terrified me more than anything else I had seen tonight. I took a step back and looked around, wishing the rest of the Guard was here. Wishing I hadn't danced with the water nymphs and been given this twisted gift.

Queen Oda dropped her gaze and knelt down. I took a deep breath as she placed the pipe and two boxes on a flat rock. Reverently, she opened one box and gazed at it with her head cocked. Then she pushed the open side of the box against her chest. I watched with sickened fascination as what little colour she possessed, drained from the Queen's face. She closed her eyes and let out a gasp and a moan, then pulled the box away from her. With shaking hands she snapped the lid shut. Her eyes met mine and they were strangely empty. Hollow. I gaped at her. She really had just removed her own heart, and now her eyes flickered to my chest. She reached for the second box.

Cold fear spiked my stomach, and I turned to run, but huge hands clamped over my arms. Panic bubbled up to my chest and squeezed the air from my lungs, making it hard to breathe. I threw myself to either side, but their grip didn't loosen. One twisted my arm behind my back, and they forced me to my knees in front of the Queen. I panted, looking down at her boots splattered in mud, and the sodden hem of her dress.

The Queen opened the second heartwood box and stepped forward. I struggled, but the guard tightened my arm, and I screamed as the tendons tore. Quick as a snake, she pressed the gaping box to my chest. I gasped as the wooden sides touched me. Agony flooded from my centre, darting down my limbs, cold and hot all at once. It pulsed in my head, lights flashing behind my eyes.

Then it was gone and there was calm. No pain. No fear. No panic. Just... dullness. Apathy. Everything that had just happened, had happened to somebody else. Somebody distant from me. I looked down and saw the Queen withdraw the box from my chest. Inside was my trembling heart. It beat fast as if in terror and glowed softly, red and gold.

The Queen snapped the box shut, and the light was closed off. I heard a click as the box locked. I stood and met her eyes, feeling nothing but exhaustion deep in my limbs and the throbbing in my shoulder. I had to admit, it was nice to no longer be afraid.

"I will keep your heart safe, Piper. You can have your heart back when you give me one simple thing." She raised a finger. "Two children for my own. A suitable boy and a girl. Enchant a selection and bring them to the castle so I may choose. Then we will have no use for these boxes."

I looked at her and looked at the box. I felt no surprise, no dread, nothing. I needed my heart back. Needed it so I could love my Natalia. But it was hard to remember that. Hard to remember Natalia at all.

I shrugged. "I will bring you your children."

The Queen gave me an empty smile and handed me the pipe.

...to be continued in Silent Melody.
Available on amazon.

10
THE WISHING WELL
ELENA SHELEST

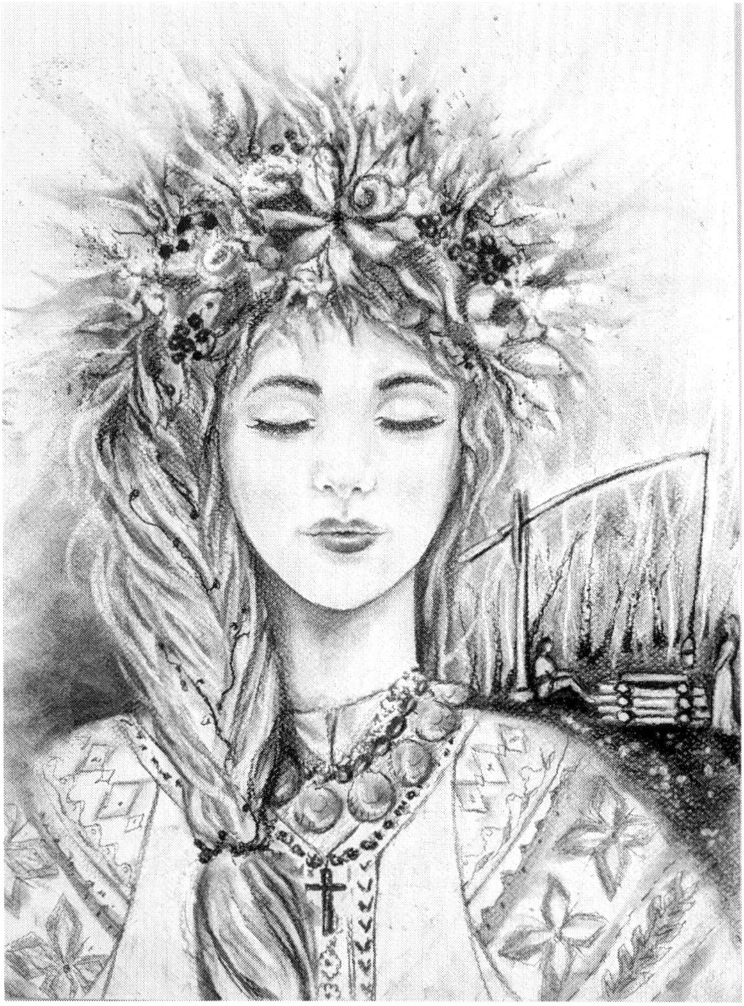

THE WISHING WELL

"Mighty Dnipro, the father of all rivers, the bloodline of the nations. It spreads over the wide steppe of Cossacks and flows through the heart of Kiev. Willful and proud, with peaceful lagoons and untamed rapids, it gives life and shelter to wild creatures and men alike. But on the midsummer day of Ivana Kupala when the sun reaches the highest point in the sky and stays still, peril awaits by its banks and trouble is stirred in its blue depths. The water spirits come out to play and entice careless passersby."

"Which ones come out?" Savko, a boy of about nine, asked.

He leaned over the wooden table, trying to get closer to the older man who sat on the other side. The boy's face, even if not thoroughly washed or plump, was still what one would call endearing. Entranced by the speaker's rehearsed tale, Savko's dark eyes shone brightly underneath the overgrown heap of brownish hair, urging the story to go on.

Kyrylo, seemingly dazed by the interruption, scratched his balding head. "Well, all of 'em could stir trouble tonight, I reckon. That's why no one goes swimming 'til morrow. Even *mavki*, who usually appear in spring, gather on the shore to sing and dance. They comb their long hair to lure unsuspecting young men."

The child's eyes widened. "Have you seen one? What do they look like?"

"God forbid that I do." The older man crossed himself hastily then lowered his voice. "The lucky ones who escaped say they look like beautiful maidens. Some believe these are the souls of girls who died by drowning. You can tell a *mavka* apart as she does not cast a shadow nor does she reflect in the water."

"What do they do... with them men?" The boy whispered back.

"Eh, they take revenge for their untimely demise by tickling them, sometimes to death. You might get away by giving one of them a comb or by warding yourself with garlic and valerian root."

"Tickling?" The boy leaned back and laughed heartily. "What if I ain't ticklish?"

"You're also not a man yet." Kyrylo chuckled and tousled Savko's already messy hair when the youngster opened his mouth to protest. "But, of course, there are more dangerous creatures like *vodyanoy*. He can pull you into the water and keep you slaving away in his domain."

They were sitting in the middle of a large entry room of the main *hata* with hand-painted walls, newly scrubbed floors, and a clay stove to keep the house warm during winter months. But it was the middle of June, and the sun glared through the open windows, the morning air fresh from a gentle breeze sneaking through the white curtains. Engrossed in conversation, Kyrylo and Savko did not notice the young woman who walked in from the adjoining kitchen. She was tall and regal like a swan, with bright blue eyes and a thick blonde braid that snaked past her slender waist. Even a simple house kaftan suited her. At seventeen, Luyba's beauty was already the talk of the locals, spreading all the way down to the barracks of Zaporozhian Sich and beyond.

When she saw Savko, her rosy lips gathered into a pout. How dare the boy disappear for so long without a word while she worried herself sick? The young woman marched over and slammed the jug she was carrying on the table, hard enough for the milk to splosh and spill.

"Scratching your tongue all morning again, Kyrylo?" she said, then turned to the startled boy, hands on her hips. "Don't you worry about *vodyanoy*. I'll dip you in the river myself for avoiding this place! Both you and your good-for-naught brother. Looks like you can use some washing too."

"*Eh-ge-ge*, such a sour mood so early in the morning and on the holiday too," Kyrylo said softly, gathering wrinkles around his pale eyes. "Save the scolding for next time, Luybashka. Better send the lad over to see the new foal. I came by to tell you the good news."

He picked up his wool hat, winked at the boy, and stepped out the doors. Savko scampered after the herdsman, but Luyba grabbed the collar of his shirt, which was a bit too big for his size, and pulled him back down on the bench.

"Where do you think you're going?" Her icy gaze warmed a bit. "Did you eat breakfast yet?"

The child nodded, his ears turning red.

"Stay. I know you're always hungry."

Still frowning, Luyba poured steaming milk into a tall mug, then went back to the kitchen and returned with a generous piece of warm bread.

The boy swallowed both faster than she could blink.

"So, why are you here now, Savko? I haven't seen you for weeks. And where's your brother?" she asked, annoyance slipping through her words again. "Does he not know we need plenty of hands here to take care of the cattle and horses? How can he leave us like that?"

How could he leave *me* like that Luyba almost said, but pride wouldn't let her. Nor did it allow her to take back the harsh words spoken to Danylo at their last meeting or ride over to his house to ask why he hasn't shown up since. Not that her mother would let her make the trip.

The boy stared at his bare toes, wiggling them as he spoke. "He ain't gonna be a farm hand no more."

"Oh, too high and mighty for us now! How is he to provide for you, your siblings and your mother then?"

Savko lifted a cautious gaze at Luyba. "I ain't supposed to tell ya."

The young woman reached for his ear, but the boy jumped off the bench like a cat, evading her grasp, and yanked a piece of paper from his pocket.

"Maybe he tells you himself in the letter."

"Give it to me!"

Luyba grabbed it like a thirsty person reaching for a cup of cold water and turned away from the boy to hide her flushed face. For once, she was glad she taught Danylo how to write but not Savko how to read yet. The boy was always handy for carrying notes between them.

Luyba, I hope this letter finds you well...

"I'll show you how well I am," she hissed.

I couldn't leave without saying goodbye, especially after the argument we had. Staying away from you was the hardest thing I've ever done in my life, but there was something I had to do. This decision has been on my heart for a while. What you've said only gave me strength to take the right step.

"Where is he going?" She swirled around to stare at Savko, who just shrugged his shoulders. The young woman decided to tease it out of him later.

I hope to see you at the dance tonight if only from a distance. All I am asking for is one glance to let me know you are ready to talk things over. I would do anything to see a smile on your face again.

Please send regards to your dear mother and thank her for everything she has done for our family.

Always your humble servant and hopefully still your friend,
Danylo.

The letter was too smooth. Luyba wondered if Danylo asked for someone's help in putting it together. Her brother was high on the list of suspects. Pavlo had given her the same deflecting shoulder shrug as Savko when she asked if he knew anything. Why would they keep things from her?

Out of the corner of her eye, Luyba noticed the boy inching his way to the door and ran to block it.

"I'll give you a silver coin if you tell me where your brother is going," she said quickly. "Just think of how much candy you can buy at the fair today."

The boy hesitated then stretched out his hand, baring his teeth in the most innocent grin. "Pay me first."

Luyba clicked her tongue, mumbling something about Savko getting too smart for his age, but went to her room and returned with the promised coin. "Spill it out now."

"He went over to the Sich and joined the Cossacks," the child said, puffing out his chest. "Came back last night to bring some money to Ma. But she cried a whole lot. He bought me a new shirt. All of us. You like it? And got Ma *hystka*. Are you gonna cry too?"

All color drained from Luyba's face. She grabbed the boy's arm. "No! And you can go tell your brother that if I ever see him, I'm going to rip his foolish head off before any Tatar would!"

"But your brother is a Cossack too," the boy protested, "and he helped him sign up."

Luyba's nostrils flared. "Oh, did he?"

She released Savko and ran outside.

The sun, or maybe the tears she tried to hold back, blinded Luyba as she marched across the lawn, past workers' dwellings, the sheep pen, and the cattle enclosure, until finally spotting her brother inside the stables. Wearing a simple linen shirt with a leather belt, Pavlo was at least a head taller and broader in the shoulders than everyone around him. The man's sleeves and baggy pants were rolled up, his powerful muscles tightening as he shoed one of the horses. He straightened for a moment and moved the long chestnut *chub* off his forehead with the back of his hand, just in time to see Luyba charging at him.

"Why are you sending Danylo to his death? What did he ever do to you?"

Pavlo wrapped Luyba in his arms while she pounded on his chest and signaled for everyone to get out. Once they were alone, he lifted her chin and smiled into her frown.

"If you're talking about his enlistment, he came to ask for my help himself."

Luyba groaned. "Then you should have talked him out of it! You were trained to hold a sabre since you were Savko's age, and Danylo hasn't swung more than a scythe. Saints, I am a hundred times better with a rifle than he is! He won't make it through the first campaign. Why would he ever do such a thing?"

She could no longer hold her frustrated tears inside, and they ran down her cheeks. Her brother wiped them off with his rough fingers then cupped her face.

"You silly goose. Don't you know why? He's doing it for you. The man knows he doesn't stand a chance as a poor farm help. Mother won't allow it. Not when we have Polish nobles asking for your hand."

"Oh, but she'd rather I marry a Cossack to be left a young widow like herself?" Luyba said bitterly.

Pavlo's countenance fell. "I promise…"

But he couldn't promise to keep anyone safe, could he? Not when he had returned from the campaign without their father years ago. Luyba read the truth in her big brother's eyes and pulled away from his embrace. She would have to do something herself.

"Tell Danylo there is no need for such ridiculous ideas. He is no more than a friend to me. I'll marry *pan* Nowak this year," she gritted out. "Will go give Mother the good news."

The young woman ran outside, ignoring her brother's calls, the curious glances of workers, and the searing ache in her chest. To think that her careless actions and hasty words might lead to Danylo's demise sent shudders through her body. She remembered their silly argument about wealth, who she should marry and why. How tense Danylo's jaw was, how pleading his gaze, as she tried to pull the truth from his lips. He walked away without uttering a single word of what her heart already knew. She could never have imagined what he decided to do instead. It would have been better if they had never met, if he had never come as a shy ragged boy to their *hutor* in search of work, winning everyone over with his diligence and agreeable nature. Danylo was a year older than Luyba, and they'd become quick friends, growing into something more over the years. He was too kind, too amiable, always eager to cover for her mischief when it was Luyba who needed to protect him. And it looked like she had to protect him from herself.

On the way back to the house, she caught up with Savko, who was trekking through the grass field, heading toward the road that led outside of their property and toward the village. She shoved Danylo's note into his hand.

"Tell your brother that I have no desire to see him and hope our paths never cross again. Tell him I'm getting married soon, but he won't be invited."

Then she turned and walked away, keeping her head high. When Luyba was halfway back home, wayward streams rolled down her cheeks again. She slowed her steps, smoothed her hair, and wiped her face before walking back into the house.

Inside, two servant women placed the bundles of nettle and sagebrush on the window seals, filling the room with the sharp odor of the grasses.

Luyba wrinkled her nose, concealing the inner turmoil behind annoyance. "Ugh, you couldn't wait to do this in the evening?"

"It's never too early to ward off the house, God save us from all evil. Especially today." Her mother walked into the room with a smile, graceful and stately like her two children, her beauty evident despite the dark clothing and simple tight head-dress to hide her ash-blonde hair. She placed a candle by the cross in the corner of the room, saying a quick prayer for the day, then turned to the women. "We'll gather more herbs later in the day. Now, take the *kasha* and milk to the men in the fields. The rest we'll bring with us to the village to feed the poor."

After they walked out, Luyba took a big breath to tell her mother of the decision she made, but the words wouldn't come out. Instead, she grabbed the wooden bucket by the door. "I'll go get some water."

Luyba ran past the wicker fence to the well that her father built on their property. The structure above it was named after the bird. It had a simple construction that looked like a giant crane standing on two legs, raising and lowering its head to take a drink. The wooden lever had a counterweight on one side and a bucket attached by a chain on the other. She could pull the water out with as much effort as opening and closing the gate.

"To build a well is to do a good deed," her father used to say. "The underground springs are God's treasures and a source of life. When you discover one, you open it for many to partake in. Be respectful, keep it clean, and you'll be blessed in return."

Luyba greeted the crane-well with a bow. "How was your

day? Lonely? Mine too." She swallowed the knot in her throat. "We might have to get used to it. Our Danylko is not coming."

Luyba opened the lid, filled the bucket, then sat on the logs that were stacked around the shaft. Thinking about her father made her heart ache even more. With a sigh, she remembered the stories of how he found the spot by stumbling upon the field of marsh marigolds. These yellow flowers still sprinkled the area between the birch trees.

"*Tato*, why did you leave us," she whispered. "Is it not enough that I worry about Pavlo every time he leaves? Now Danylko too... But I won't let him."

She splashed the refreshing water onto her face and drank some to cool off the fire inside her. It tasted sweet to the bitterness in her mouth. The place always brought peace to her heart. Luyba came here to think and to meet with Danylo in the mornings. He caught her by the well on his way to the fields, a familiar bright smile on his handsome bronzed face, his dark eyes soaking in the sight of her as if he could never get enough. She would steal his hat and tousle his curly brown hair, teasing as he carried the heavy buckets back home for her. In return, he would try to get her wet or chase her through the gardens, water spilling and the two of them laughing, scrambling back to the well to refill them lest her mother ventured out to inquire what took Luyba so long.

"If you were a wishing well, I would wish for Danylko to be safe," she whispered. "I would do anything to keep him from harm, even marry the man I don't love."

Then he wouldn't have to join the Cossacks. He could stay home and do any work his heart desires. Any girl in the village would be more than happy to have him. She knew how they all looked at him, whispering among themselves that the man was hardworking, kind, and pleasing to the eye. *Her* Danylko. No, she would make things right, even if it meant tearing a piece of her soul away.

"Stay home and find yourself a good-natured girl to make you happy. I am nothing but trouble for you."

A gentle huff of the wind rippled the water in her bucket and whispered in the well. Luyba wiped her eyes and reached into her pocket, digging out another silver coin she had saved in case Savko needed more bribing. She kissed it and threw it into the dark, cool depth of the well, listening for the splash. It never came. The young woman stood up and leaned over the edge to take a look. The bright blue sky was still reflected in the smooth surface of the water inside. Some people thought it was a window to heaven or a passage to another world, and she felt a pull toward its depths as if the well enticed her to jump in. Luyba jerked back, her heart beating out of her chest. She grabbed her bucket and hurried back home where her mother was already setting a hearty breakfast on the table.

"Eat and go out today," she said. "You've been staying at home too much lately and seem to be in low spirits. It's not like you, Luyban'ka. Is this because of Danylo? You haven't been the same since the boy disappeared."

"*Mamo*, I've told you already that we're just friends. Of course, I miss him." Luyba sat at the table and busied herself with food, putting jam on the crepes to avoid looking into her mother's keen eyes.

"I hope you're telling the truth because anything else will only lead to heartache. Maybe it's for the better that he left. You've been spending way too much time together. The boy is not your equal, and he knows it well. Even if he didn't, I made it quite clear."

Luyba shot to her feet, her eyes flashing. "What did you tell him?"

"Nothing that he didn't agree with."

Luyba dropped the knife on the plate with a clank. "I've suddenly lost my appetite, but I think I *will* go out."

She walked past her mother, who grasped her arm. "Don't

do something you will regret later, *don'ka*." Her voice was gentle but firm. "Leave Danylo alone, don't keep him tied up to yourself. It will be better for both of you. Have pity on the boy or do you think he's impermeable to your charm?"

Luyba met her mother's gaze with her chin high. "I think he deserves much better because apparently I am only interested in rich men who are full of themselves. So I will go to the festival and see if I can find myself a few more. The richer the better!"

"Luyba…"

She pulled herself free and walked past the kitchen to her room and dropped onto the bed. Soon someone knocked gently on the door and, despite her angry request for the intruder to leave, a group of young women barged in. Her mother must have sent them to help her get ready. Begrudgingly, Luyba sat up and allowed her hair to be brushed out and braided, then her clothing to be changed while the servants laughed and chatted about the upcoming festivities. They adorned her in a richly embroidered white blouse and a wraparound skirt with red and black ornamental motifs. It went down to her shins, showing off the red boots. Her neck and chest were decorated with Venetian glass and coral beaded necklaces, silver coins, and a jeweled brass cross to ward off evil.

"If I fall in the water with all of this weight on, I'll surely drown," Luyba said bitterly, pulling a few layers of jewelry off.

"God forbid you say such things, Mistress," one of the girls gasped.

"We won't let you get near the water today," another one chimed.

"Only to send the wreath on the river to see how soon you are to marry," the third one jumped in, making the others giggle.

"I can marry as soon as I want to," Luyba announced,

standing up, her face as pale as her blouse. "To the richest man in this region, if I so desire, but where's the amusement in that? I will lose my freedom. It's better to have them all pine for my attention and hang on my every word."

"Can you get anyone to propose to you?"

"Say tonight?"

"Someone you have never met?"

"Let's pick the best looking man at the festival!"

"No, the most important one."

"Make him jump through the fire with you."

The young women joined in enthusiastically. Luyba's eyes gleamed darkly, their words ringing hollow inside her. She felt as if she was throwing herself into the abyss when she spoke again.

"Anyone of your choosing will be begging to do my bidding all evening. I'll bet my pearl necklace on it if you don't believe me."

She would lose herself in this new dare to shut away the ache in her heart. If anything, she'd prove to Danylo how shallow and unworthy of his love she was. She would make him change his mind about risking his life for her sake.

The willow dipped its long branches over the steep bank of Dnipro River like a maiden stooping to wash her hair. Bright yellow orioles sought shelter from the summer heat among its leaves, filling the still air with refreshing melodies. Thankful for the shade, Luyba hitched up her skirts and submerged her bare feet in the cool waters, which bubbled happily over the rocks below. The deep blue surface in front of her rippled from a flock of geese gliding to the other side, and Luyba wished she had a rifle to hunt them instead of gathering silly flowers all day. Fishing with Danylo was even better, but that was not something she wanted to think about.

"Luyba, stop daydreaming and come over here," a young woman called from higher up the hill. She waved so vigorously that flowers came out of her messy dark braid. "We're almost done with the wreaths, and you haven't even started."

"In the name of all saints, leave me alone for once," Luyba mumbled.

Laughter rang through the air when a group of about twenty young women ran closer to the shoreline, skipping, dancing, and pushing each other. Like a flock of colorful birds, they descended on the hill, carrying heaps of flowers in the folds of their skirts and as many in their hair. They piled the fragrant assortments of blooms and herbs on the grass and sat next to them to finish their work. Luyba bit her lip, resentful of their merriment and easy chatter. Why couldn't she forget everything and enjoy the day?

"Come, Luyba, you need to make the prettiest wreath. Or did you forget about our bet?" A robust young woman said as she wiggled her light eyebrows, her round freckled cheeks already flushed bright red from the sun.

"What bet?" several girls echoed.

Soon the news of Luyba's boasting flew through the crowd, not everyone taking a fancy to it.

"You better not set your sights on my Ivanko," one girl said, standing up with a hand on her hip.

"She thinks too much of herself," another one whispered to her friend, close enough for Luyba to overhear.

"As prideful as her mother. The woman never married again because no one was good enough for her. Imagine that!"

"I heard Kosh Ataman himself wanted to marry her."

Luyba ignored them all. She was used to envy. It didn't bother her. Let them gossip. Not one of them would dare to challenge her openly. She had enough physical strength and smarts to overcome anyone who was foolish enough to stand in her way. But most of them wished to catch her brother's eye and tried to butter her up to get closer to him. Luyba didn't take their enmity nor their friendship seriously. And what would all of these girls say if they knew she loved a poor worker with nothing but the shirt on his back and a dozen hungry mouths to feed at home? Her heart would be broken and empty no matter how good of a match her family made. On the outside she'd be the luckiest girl in the region, the prettiest bride, but dying on the inside. Well, she'd never let them see that and gloat.

"You're just jealous because I can get any man I want," Luyba said to the young women around her as she strung bright blue forget-me-nots together to start the wreath. "If you want my pearl necklace, just point someone out for me to charm and see what happens."

"That's not fair. You can't be adding more people to the game," the red-cheeked girl complained.

"What kind of game is that?" someone scoffed.

"If it's a game, we need to set specific rules," another girl, who also worked at Luyba's house, insisted. "So that it's fair."

The chatter, arguments, and laughter started anew and even Luyba joined in the fun while weaving together violet periwinkles and white yarrow to finish the circle. She added a few blue and yellow ribbons in the back and placed the wreath over her hair.

"What if I tell you to make the Underwater Tsar fall in love with you," one of the young women teased, sticking bright red poppies into her chestnut braid.

Luyba cocked her head to the side. "Sure. If you see him in person at our festival, feel free to make your request."

"Look at her. Show-off. Ain't afraid of nothing!" someone shouted from the crowd.

"What is there to be afraid of?" Luyba quipped, stretching her long legs lazily over the grassy hill.

"Last year on Ivana Kupala, Anka dared her to swim to the other side of the river, and she did," one of the young women said.

"Honest truth," another confirmed.

"Maybe, the so-called Underwater Tsar favors me." Luyba lifted her chin and closed her eyes, letting the sun warm her face. Her mother would have had a fit if she ruined her milky skin and got all freckled, but the young woman was in a mood to do contrary things.

"*Ai*, do you imagine yourself Sadko?" someone yelled out.

"She's surely as haughty!"

"The man didn't even pay proper respect to the Underwater Tsar after catching the golden fish and getting all rich."

"And that's why he got in trouble."

"But he had a good heart. He let himself be thrown into the ocean to save his sinking ship."

"And whose fault was it that the ship was sinking in the first place, eh? The Tsar made a storm on the sea because of him."

"Well, Sadko paid his penitence by slaving away at the bottom of the sea and playing the *gusli* for the Tsar."

"If it wasn't for the blessed Saint Nicholas, he would still be there, stuck with the slippery sea maiden for a wife."

The girls giggled again. They were easy to entertain. Luyba only smirked as she listened to the chatter and arguments about the old *bylina* tale.

"But he tricked the tsar," she finally added, biting into a juicy wild strawberry someone picked for the headdress, "and got away."

Luyba was tired of the sun again. The day was getting hotter by the minute, and the desire to take a quick dip in the cool waters of the river became almost overwhelming. She wished to be dared again just to have an excuse for a forbidden swim.

But that part of the Dnipro was treacherous, with hidden undercurrents and rapids coming around the bend. As proof, the wind blew over the hill they were sitting on and rippled the previously smooth surface of the water, stirring small waves.

"Look, look," one of the girls shouted. "The Underwater Tsar is getting ready to come out."

"Oh, he already did!" A rough voice shouted from above them.

The girls yelped and looked up as a group of young men descended on them like a pack of wolves, holding wooden buckets and throwing water in their direction. Chaos ensued as the young women scampered away, squealing at the top of their lungs. The rascals tried to catch a few who were not quick enough to get away, planting a kiss or two, preferably without getting slapped too hard in return. Luyba jumped to her feet, broke off a thick branch from a nearby tree, and stood next to their wreath-making supplies. She balanced the makeshift weapon in her hand, daring anyone to come closer. Luyba had sparred enough with her brother to take a few men out. Several girls got the idea and hid behind her.

"What a fearsome beauty," one of the young men she hadn't seen before taunted.

He was twice her size, but Luyba had a few tricks up her sleeve.

"The bigger they are, the harder they fall," she retorted with a smirk.

"This is Pavlo's sister. Better not mess with her unless you want your neck wrung," someone said behind him.

"I can stand up for myself, Mykola," she bit back.

The brash young man, who must have come from the neighborhood village, bared his teeth. "I'll gladly fight you for a kiss."

"That one," a few girls murmured behind her. "Make him fall for you."

Luyba grimaced. But a bet was a bet. She gave the stranger a syrupy smile. "If you're so sure of yourself, come to the festival tonight and see if you can beat my brother in the arm wrestle. Then I will gladly kiss you."

The men whistled and hooted around them. Some expressed their regrets at not suggesting as much themselves. Others recalled that no one ever won the contest if Pavlo participated. Only one person stood in silence away from the crowd, a dark cloud over his face. He was tall and well-built from days of manual labor. A new embroidered shirt sat smartly on his wide shoulders with a silky red belt encircling his waist. Even hidden under the shade of a tree, he drew a few coy glances from the group of women.

Luyba was too busy to notice.

Danylo had no plans to participate in the festivities. After receiving Luyba's reply from his younger brother, he intended to sit in his room and brood until the world ended, but his friends forced him outdoors. He felt foolish now for buying himself new clothes and hoped to trade them in later for something more useful. It didn't matter what he wore. Nothing mattered. The young man no longer saw a purpose in life.

Joining the Cossacks lost its meaning too, even though Pavlo, the person he highly respected, agreed to stay by his side and help with his training. The idea seemed as futile now as his new outfit. War and riches had no appeal to him, but it was his only chance to make a living worthy of Luyba. Danylo would have never enlisted otherwise, knowing full well that he could die and deprive his younger siblings of their only breadwinner. If not for his family, he would have welcomed a stab in his chest to end the misery; the quicker the better.

Alas, the one person he was willing to risk everything for did not want the sacrifice. The girl who captured his heart from the first moment he looked into her mesmerizing eyes had no interest. She stood on that hill like Lada, the goddess of love and beauty, laughing and daring men for a kiss. Did she not care that his heart now lay broken and bleeding at her feet? Yet he longed to be near her. Even her outward indifference couldn't stop him.

Did all the times they spent together mean nothing to her? When she smiled at him, when her eyes got lost for a moment in his, when they sat side by side talking about their hopes and dreams or listening to the sounds of birds in the fields, he felt as if their two souls were being knitted into one. Even now, when she turned in his direction and froze, a smile slipping off her face, he could feel their connection. The undeniable pull of attraction between them was like an invisible thread stitching them together and making their hearts beat in unison.

A gust of wind ripped through the hill again, billowing her bright skirt and knocking the simple wreath of white and blue flowers off her head. It rolled over the grass and fell from the small cliff into the wavy waters below them. The group let out a collective gasp as the flowers floated from the shore toward the middle of the river.

"I will kiss whoever gets the wreath out for me without damaging it," Luyba announced, her voice chilly.

While the young men murmured between themselves, the current picked up the dainty crown and carried it slowly down the stream. Some might have been wary of the tricky layout of the river. Others preferred not to tempt fate on the day when most didn't dare dip their toes even in smaller bodies of water. The stories of drowning on the day of Ivana Kupala circled every year around the fire, enough to instill caution into the bravest of hearts. But Danylo didn't think twice.

Uneasiness settled over the previously jovial group. Someone said that losing the wreath was a bad omen. Silence was broken by Luyba's laughter.

"Where's all your bravery?"

She stopped abruptly, catching sight of Danylo treading the waters.

"What are you doing? I said it in jest!" she yelled after him. "Come out right now."

He didn't care. Danylo continued until he was deep enough to feel the pull and push of the water weakening his footing. The flowers kept floating further as if teasing him to follow. No longer able to stand, he swam toward the wreath that seemed to pick up speed the further it went. A few people were now shouting from the shore, urging him to return.

Soon their voices were drowned by the constant roaring of the waters around him, but Danylo kept his focus on the white and blue spot of flowers in front of him. A few more strokes and he would reach them. It must have been his wishful thinking, his desire to prove something to Luyba that kept him going when a reasonable person would have given up the ordeal and swam for the shore instead.

The water was now in full control, hitting him against the rocks and threatening to pull him under. As if by a miracle, the small heap of flowers still floated in front of him. Fatigue settled into his body, but he propelled himself forward, reaching for it in one desperate attempt. Something caught his leg. He struggled to free himself only to be yanked down and submerged, taking a last hasty gasp of air.

In the murky waters, Danylo pulled a knife from his belt and turned to see what held him in place. The current swirled and bubbled, blurring his view. Was he imagining it or were a pair of curious eyes watching him through the haze of sand? Another from the cover of algae? He must have lost his mind from the lack of oxygen as he glimpsed pale female faces around him. A bare shoulder here, a slender arm there, moving too fast for his cloudy vision to capture. Danylo struggled to pull himself free, bending to feel his foot that was stuck, wrapped by something that looked like seaweed. The more he slashed at it with the blade, the tighter and higher another strand circled his leg.

It would be a pathetic way to die, he thought, at the hands of *rysalki*. Would Luyba cry? No, he couldn't leave his mother like this. Who would take care of his younger brothers and sisters? He pulled again with all his strength, the last few bubbles of air escaping his lips. Pressure built inside his head. His chest was on fire. The water went up his nose and darkness settled in. Something nibbled his shirt and snaked around his body as if a fish was swimming by, but he could no longer see or care.

Silence set in. All sensations ceased to exist.

In complete darkness, he envisioned Luyba sitting by the well. The carefree, happy times they'd spent there together flashed before his unseeing eyes. Her laughter, her curiosity about the world, the fullness of life that seemed to burst out of her. His brave and fiery Luyba, his bright sun and his starry sky.

How he longed to hold her in his arms one more time, even if for a brief moment and purely by accident. He wanted her to unintentionally lean on his shoulder or touch his hand. He wished for her to fall asleep in the grass next to him and watch her breathe softly, a smile tugging on her lips as she dreamed. Every moment they had shared was seared in his memory. He could not die and leave her.

"If you were a wishing well, I would wish for Danylko to be safe," she whispered in his mind. *"I would do anything to keep him from harm."*

Bright light burst all around Danylo, and a wild shriek rang in his ears, cutting through the silence. A jolt struck him, and his body was pushed forward. The next moment he sat up on the sandy shore, coughing up water. Midday sun blinded his vision. He laughed in disbelief at the sensation of warmth from its rays and the sounds of birds chirping all around him.

"Thank God! I am alive."

Shouts echoed from the grove behind him. People ran through the trees in his direction. Luyba, ahead of them all, jumped over the knolls and the stumps like a young doe. No one could ever outrun her, even in a skirt. She looked like her heart was in her throat. Tears streaked down her cheeks as she leaped on him, tumbling both of them to the soft ground below.

"Why would you ever do this to me?" She cried, pulling the collar of his wet shirt. "It wasn't enough that you signed up at the Sich?! No, you wanted to die right in front of my eyes! I would kill you myself!"

Luyba's shouts were cut off as Danylo pulled her to his chest and covered her mouth with his, their breath entangling, and their hearts once again beating in rapid unison. He was thirsty for her despite drinking half of the river a minute earlier. She burned for him despite running for what seemed to be forever in the blazing heat. Water and fire, incompatible yet united on that midsummer day, sealed their lips and their hearts.

They did not care about the youths who gathered around them. Some peered in confusion at the unexpected scene they came upon. Others grinned widely. The world disappeared as Luyba wrapped her arms tightly around Danylo's neck. He did not want her to ever let go.

"I'm only taking what you've promised," he whispered into her ear with a smile, then put the wet wreath that washed out on the shore next to him on her head.

The young people around them cheered. Luyba hit him on the chest a few more times for good measure and made him promise not to do such a foolish thing ever again.

"There are other less lethal ways to get kisses, you know," she grumbled, wiping blood off his arm with her handkerchief.

The young people started to disperse, leaving the couple to themselves. Luyba curled up next to the still damp Danylo, who put his arm protectively around her and watched the river float lazily by, his heart full and content. It seemed strange that the Dnipro almost overpowered him just a few yards higher up the stream. Was it a trap? He was still confused about what he saw in the water, trying to decipher whether it was real. Instead, he decided to focus on the girl, who at the moment leaned on his shoulder, warming his side and mending his soul.

"Will you go to the dance with me now?" he asked, gently brushing a lock of hair off Luyba's face.

"Will you give up your idea to join the Cossacks now?" she retorted, pursing her rosy lips.

Danylo had to restrain himself not to kiss her pout away. "I can't. I have to do it for us, for my family. What do I have to offer you? A house that's smaller than your smallest barn?"

Luyba hid her face on the side of his neck, her breath tickling his skin. "There is no need. You can live with us. We have enough space. Pavlo likes you, and mother... she will relent if we persist."

The young man shook his head. "I could not respect myself after that, and you won't either. What kind of husband would I be if I can't provide for my wife with my own hands?"

She sat up, her dark eyebrows creased in a frown that he wished to smooth away. "Is leaving me and dying somewhere in a foreign land a better option? What good was it for my father to acquire all this wealth if my mother couldn't share it with him?"

"I won't die." He smiled, tracing her cheek with his hand. "Your love won't let me. It pulled me out of the river."

Then he drew her close and kissed her thoroughly.

As soon as the sun set below the horizon, the fires were lit in the large field by the river. People gathered from several nearby villages and estates. When this tradition started or why it was called Kupala Night nobody could recall, but who would pass by a chance to eat, drink, and be merry? Farmers brought the first fruit of their harvest. Herdsmen roasted pigs, and sheep. Women made *vareniki* and pastries. No one went home hungry.

Young people sang and danced, joining their hands in *horovod*. Children ran around playing games. Men thought of their own ways to amuse themselves, but mostly to show off their strength and agility. Of course, no one could beat Pavlo in arm wrestling. Those in love and brave enough to test their bond, jumped over the fire holding hands to see if they would stay connected on the other side.

Later in the night all the young women took off their wreaths to send them over the waters. Luyba added flowers to hers to make it bigger and sturdier.

"I want to make sure it makes it down the river," she told

Danylo with a mischievous smile. "You better not make me wait too long."

The young man sneaked in a kiss when no one was looking. "Would you not wait for me, *luyba moya, mila moya, serdtse moye*?"

Her insides melted from the sound of his voice murmuring endearments, his breath warm on her cheek. She touched his face, looking up into his midnight eyes that were so full of adoration for her and felt her throat constrict. "Just come back to me, please."

"*Oi*, stop you two already," one of the girls teased.

"What happened to the crowd you promised to keep by your feet tonight?" another one yelled out, inducing a fit of giggles.

Danylo sent Luyba a questioning look, and she winked at him. "This one man is better than a whole throng of suitors."

"Oooh, aaah," women responded. "Let's see if he's the one. Send down your wreath."

Luyba started to get nervous. What if it hit the shore? How many years would she have to wait until Danylo got enough wealth to satisfy her mother? What if it drowned? No, he would never stop loving her, unless... Her chest constricted. She had already used her one wish to keep him safe. But she did have lots of silver coins to throw in where the first one went. The young woman relaxed and smiled to herself. She walked into the water with the others and set the crown of flowers down, a small candle in its midst. Fire and water united and danced, the current carrying a small light down the stream until it disappeared from her view.

She shivered from the chill in the night air then felt a warm embrace, familiar arms encircling her as Danylo pressed her back to his chest. She wished they could stay like this forever.

"What you told me the last time we spoke," he whispered into her hair. "Did you mean it?"

"You think I would have married that self-important rooster who visited from the neighboring estate? He just wanted to combine our steading with his and add a pretty wife to his list of possessions." She turned around, catching a glimpse of worry in Danylo's eyes. "Did you really think I'd be foolish enough to do something like that? I just wanted to get a reaction out of you, to know what's in your heart. I couldn't imagine you'd just get up and leave. I was so mad. Thought you gave up the fight."

She playfully hit him on the chest. Danylo captured her hands and kissed her fingers, making the young woman shiver.

"I'd never give you up, but I was afraid to be late. That's why I decided to do something right away, to talk to your brother, then go down to the Sich. Didn't want to tell you anything until it was all set and done."

Luyba arched a brow. "So that I wouldn't stop you?"

The young man nodded and smiled, caressing her face. "I couldn't let you know how I felt until I was sure there was a chance for me to ask for your hand, but you pulled it out of me anyway. I am no match for your stubbornness."

She wrapped her arms around his waist and leaned into him, listening to the steady beat of his heart as the laughter and shouts of people further up the shore faded into the background. "You're already worthy of my hand," she whispered.

"That's not what your mother thinks." He chuckled, then tightened his arms around her when she tried to wiggle out. "But she is a good woman and wants the world for you."

"What did she tell you?" Luyba said tersely.

"She talked about how good a match this man or the other was for you and asked me to put some sense into your silly head or, at least, to not interfere. I think she had her suspicions. But she was right, Luybyshka, I have nothing to give you."

"Except for happiness?"

"And you think this poor boy could take on rich farmers and nobles?"

"Yes. If he loves me."

"Does he?"

Luyba looked up into his eyes that shone only for her, the dying fires up the shore dancing gently in them, and nodded with a wide grin.

"And does she love him back?" he asked, a smile teasing up the corners of his lips.

She nodded again, and Danylo swept her away in a fervent kiss while the Dnipro River swirled gently around their feet.

Some people said (and people in that region liked to make up tales, especially old Kyrylo) that the Underwater Tsar visited the villagers on that night. Disguised as a human, he drank wine and ate honey, then promised in his tipsy state to not hide the fish from the locals.

As the celebration died down, those brave enough ventured into the forest to look for the magical fern flower that promised to point the lucky ones to hidden treasures. No one found it that year, but older folks knew of a few in their lifetime who had and discovered that happiness was not in the number of coins they acquired.

In the morning, after everyone went for a swim and remembered John the Baptist, asking for blessings and health, Danylo and Pavlo gathered a few belongings and saddled their horses to return to the Zaporozhian Sich. Luyba stood on the road and waved until they were out of sight, then returned home and went down to the well to quiet her heart. She was worried about Danylo returning home safely and wondered if she would have to fulfill her end of the spoken oath now that his life was spared. Could the well protect him again even from far away? Was she allowed to make more than one wish? Did it only work on the holiday? What would be the price? Or was it all just her overactive imagination and a coincidence?

But if Luyba knew what was to come, she would have tossed a coin for her own safeguard instead.

AUTHOR'S NOTE

If you'd like to find out what awaits Luyba as she faces danger back at home, how Pavlo keeps his life but loses his heart to a healer in Istanbul, and whether Danylo survives his first campaign, sign up at the link below. Also follow Savko and his friends six years later as they search for the elusive fern flower that could either fulfill their most sacred wishes or plunge them into the realm of darkness from where there is no escape (exclusive story coming soon).

Sign up here: https://www.subscribepage.com/slavic_fantasy

ACKNOWLEDGMENTS

We would like to thank Alice for getting us all together. Without you, Alice, Enchanted Waters wouldn't exist and we are deeply grateful for this opportunity to work together. You are an inspiration to us all.

Helena and Elena, thank you so much for your incredible illustrations. They are absolutely breathtaking and we are blown away by your contribution to this anthology. You have truly brought every character to life!

We didn't just want to write and publish our stories, but wanted to also do some good on a larger scale. Since this is an anthology about magical water creatures, we decided to pick an ocean protection charity because all of us working on Enchanted Waters agreed that the state of the planet's oceans is something we are deeply worried about. It did take us a long time to decide on which charity to choose, and because of all the deliberation that went into our choice, we would like to take this opportunity to thank Oceana for everything this organisation does. Defending marine biodiversity and protecting fishing to ensure sustainability are mammoth tasks and Oceana does an incredible job of achieving the goals they've set towards reducing our human impact on the oceans.

Special thanks go to the early birds of our street team. Thank you for being behind us every step of the way! Miriam Løvdahl, Ingunn Helgemo, Sherry Hrozenky, Oksana, Heather Toney, Darrah Steffen, Gladys Gonzales Atewell, Madeleine Booth-Smits, Laura Hernandez, Laura D. Child, Nikki Mitchell, Nicole Hiser, Regina Ann King, Monika Vogel, Linda, Toni McConnell, Piret Bossack, Jennifer Sargent, Brittni, Sudha Kuruganti, Sarah Hill, Amanda Marin, Jasmijn, Lindsey Snyder, Lynda Simmons, Sarah Heath, Johanna Taiger, Meagan Meier, Maris, Deirdre, Tasche Lain, Mirna Gabriel, Janine, Skye Horn, Ginger Li, Thi-Léa Vo, Ciarrah, Hepzibah Becca Jael, Bekah Berge, Karen Skillings, Courtney Woodruff, Kristi Shimada, Joy Sephton, Zoe Collyer, and Stephanie Whitfield. To all the other members of our street team, we would also like to thank you for your support of Enchanted Waters.

We also want to thank Rebecca from Dark Wish Designs for her beautiful cover and all the editors involved! Dr Edith A. Kostka, Carolyn Gent, Shreeya Nanda, Astrid V.J, Alice Ivinya, thank you!

Enchanted Forests

Want more magical stories while supporting worthwhile causes? Why not pre-order our next anthology now on amazon! All proceeds will go to woodland conservation.

https://books2read.com/u/4NwKPz

BIOGRAPHIES

Lyndsey Hall

Lyndsey Hall lives on the edge of Sherwood Forest, one of the most magical places in England's history, and the inspiration for her debut novel, THE FAIR QUEEN. She grew up surrounded by books, and loved to write from a young age.

She loves to travel and try her hand at new things, but is most at home when curled up in a chair with a cup of tea and a good book, usually accompanied by at least one dog. She's fortunate enough to share her home with two cherished humans and two beloved dogs.

Find Lyndsey online here:
https://www.lyndseyhallwrites.com

Find out more about THE FAIR QUEEN here:
https://mybook.to/TheFairQueen

Jennifer Kropf

Jennifer Kropf is the author of *The Winter Souls Series* and was a finalist for the *Indie Fantasy Book of the Year* award with Caffeinated Fantasy in 2020. She lives amidst lush Canadian farmland with her husband and three kids, and writes Christmas themed fantasy stories meant to inspire family traditions in households at Christmas time.

She is the founder of Winter Publishing House, and always loved The Chronicles of Narnia by C. S. Lewis growing up.

Learn more about Jennifer here: https://linktr.ee/JenniferKropf

Alice Ivinya

Alice is a USA Today bestselling author. She is also an award-winning, international, and Barnes and Noble bestseller.

She lives in Bristol, England, with her husband, toddler, and the best dog in the world, Summer. She has loved fantasy all her life and her favourite author is Brandon Sanderson. When she's not off galavanting in other worlds, she loves walking the dog and spending time with her church family. That is, when she's not busy working as a small animal vet for a charity.

https://alicegent.com/

Ben Lang

Ben Lang is a fantasy and myth obsessive who loves monsters, adventures and exotic lands. His stories aim to include an awesome setting, a great monster and an emotive plot. He lives in Nottingham, UK at the sufferance of Megan who tolerates his over-consumption of tea and eternal state of foggy optimism.

Thanks for reading, good luck outwitting any monsters that find you.

Sky Sommers

Sky was born to Estonian-Russian parents and for most of her life has lived and worked in Tallinn, Estonia, with brief escapes to all but the top and bottom continents in search of her muse. Her debut e-book in 2012 was about ancient goddesses running amock, trying to get their wilted powers back. She then proceeded to indie publishing her own books and found her way from Greek and Arthurian myths and legend to fairytales retold for young adult and adult audiences. So far, Thumbelina has been updated for suspicious adults, a more sinister version of Cinderella was released on 21.12.20 and an adult Red Riding Hood retelling released on 21.03.21. A Wizard of Oz retelling and a futuristic speculative fiction book are in the works. All her books are peppered with dry humour, linked by some character or another and she loves making you choose at the end – depending on whether you are an optimist or a pessimist. She lives in a house with a small garden with her husband and mostly one, but on occasion plus four kids. No dog.

The Wizard book can be pre-ordered here: https://amzn.to/3xtC6SC

You can best find & interact with me on Instagram: https://www.instagram.com/sommers_sky/

N.D.T. Casale

N.D.T. Casale is an Italian-American author who lives in the United States. She creates magical realms for others to escape to and enjoy.

When she is not hard at work writing, N.D.T. Casale spends her time riding horses, working out, traveling, snowboarding, and looking for her next adventure. She is fluent in multiple languages and always ends her day with a cup of tea.

Instagram: https://www.instagram.com/ndtcasale/

Astrid V.J

Award-winning and USA Today Bestselling Author, Astrid V.J. was born in South Africa. She is a trained social anthropologist and certified transformational life coach. She currently resides in Sweden with her husband and their two children. In early childhood, she showed an interest in reading and languages-- interests which her family encouraged. Astrid started writing her first novel at age 12 and now writes fantasy in a variety of genres, exploring her passion for cultures and languages. When she isn't writing, Astrid likes to read, take walks in nature, play silly games with her children, do embroidery, and play music.

Astrid writes transformation fiction: incorporating transformation principles in novels, rather than writing another self-help book. She loves exploring the human capacity for transformation and potential to achieve success in the face of adversity. Astrid is interested in minority group questions, considerations on social standards of beauty and the negative consequences these have, and would like to make the fantasy genre accessible to people of non-white, non-Christian backgrounds. Astrid feels the fantasy genre has become too restrictive with limited representations of race, ethnicity and culture. She seeks to explore other paths on this writing journey, incorporating her background in anthropology and psychology to create engaging experiences, which also provide food for thought on the diverse topics she finds most important. These include: racism, minority rights, cultural diversity, culture change, intolerance, humanity's environmental impact, the representation of people on the autism spectrum among the general populace, the human capacity for transformation, and much more.

Links:

Linktree: https://linktr.ee/astrid.v.j_author_official

Elisabeth and Edvard's World series of fairytale retellings: https://www.amazon.com/gp/product/B08LZHNSJW

Elena Shelest

Elena Shelest immigrated to the U.S. from Ukraine at the age of 15. She currently resides in Oregon with her husband, two busy kids, and three pets.

Elena is a full-time nurse, an artist, and an avid reader of fantasy and inspirational books. She is hoping to encourage her readers to be able to look beyond what's possible and believe again that everyday miracles do happen.

Her contemporary fantasy about dreams coming true called The Seven Lives of Grace can be found on Amazon: My Book

Follow Elena's art on insta: www.instagram.com/lena_-fiveminutediscovery

To find out what happens next to Luyba + Danylo, to follow Pavlo on an adventure to Istanbul, and to read more magical short stories about the birthplace of Ukraine, sign up for my monthly newsletter: https://www.subscribepage.com/slavic_fantasy

Helena Satterthwaite

Helena is a Welsh/ Finnish painter born and raised in the south west of England. She works predominantly in watercolour and ink and is inspired by everything around her; music, sunrises, misty mornings and night skies, forests and light on water. She is mesmerised by the ethereal beauty of galaxies and oceans and the raw wild power of the animal kingdom.

Her work has an element of dream-like fantasy to it that sometimes verges on the surreal, inspired by the fairytales, myths and legends she grew up with. Having studied languages at university, she particularly enjoys exploring cultures different to her own, and is always on the hunt for new elements she can weave into her art.

Working on Enchanted Waters has been an absolute childhood dream come true, and she is eternally grateful to Alice and the team for entrusting me with their wonderful stories and being a joy to work with throughout.

Follow her art on insta www.instagram.com/cerulean_ink

You can purchase some of the illustrations in Enchanted Waters here: Cerulean-Ink.redbubble.com

Printed in Great Britain
by Amazon